ERLING THE BOLD

A Tale of the Norse Sea Kings

R.M. BALLANTYNE

Frontispiece by John Betancourt. Based on a painting.

ERLING THE BOLD

A Tale of the Norse Sea Kings

R.M. Ballantyne

WILDSIDE PRESS

ERLING THE BOLD

A Tale of the Norse Sea Kings

INTRODUCTION

Robert Michael Ballantyne (1825–1894) was a Scottish author who published more than 100 books. He was also an accomplished artist and exhibited some of his water-colours at the Royal Scottish Academy.

Ballantyne was born in Edinburgh, the ninth of ten children (and the youngest son), to Alexander and Anne Ballantyne. His father was a newspaper editor and printer in the family firm of "Ballantyne & Co" based at Paul's Works on the Canongate. His uncle, James Ballantyne, was the printer for Scottish author Sir Walter Scott. A banking crisis in 1825 resulted in the collapse of the Ballantyne printing business the following year with debts of £130,000,which led to a decline in the family's fortunes.

Robert Ballantyne went to Canada at the age of 16 and spent five years working for the Hudson's Bay Company. He traded with the local Native Americans for furs, which required him to travel by canoe and sleigh to the areas occupied by the modern-day provinces of Manitoba, Ontario, and Quebec—experiences that formed the basis of his novel *Snowflakes and Sunbeams* (1856). His longing for family and home during that period impressed him to start writing letters to his mother. Ballantyne recalled in his autobiographical *Personal Reminiscences in Book Making* (1893) that "To this long-letter writing I attribute whatever small amount of facility in composition I may have acquired."

In 1847 Ballantyne returned to Scotland to discover that his father had died. He published his first book the following year, *Hudson's Bay: or, Life in the Wilds of North America*, and for some time was employed by the publishers Messrs Constable. In 1856 he gave up business to focus on his literary career and began the series of adventure stories for the young with which his name is popularly associated.

The Young Fur-Traders (1856), *The Coral Island* (1857), *The World of Ice* (1859), *Ungava: a Tale of Eskimo Land* (1857), *The Dog*

Crusoe (1860), *The Lighthouse* (1865), *Fighting the Whales* (1866), *Deep Down* (1868), *The Pirate City* (1874), *Erling the Bold* (1869), *The Settler and the Savage* (1877), and more than 100 other books followed in regular succession, his rule being to write as far as possible from personal knowledge of the scenes he described. *The Gorilla Hunters: A tale of the wilds of Africa* (1861) shares three characters with The Coral Island: Jack Martin, Ralph Rover and Peterkin Gay. Here Ballantyne relied factually on Paul du Chaillu's Exploration in Equatorial Guinea, which had appeared early in the same year.

The Coral Island remains the most popular of the Ballantyne novels still read and remembered today, but because of a mistake he made in that book—he gave an incorrect thickness of coconut shells—he prioritized research on his subjects for later books. For instance, he spent time living with the lighthouse keepers at the Bell Rock before writing *The Lighthouse*, and he spent time with the tin miners of Cornwall while researching *Deep Down*.

In 1866 he married Jane Grant, with whom he had three sons and three daughters. He spent his later years in Harrow, London, before moving to Italy for the sake of his health, possibly suffering from undiagnosed Ménière's disease. He died in Rome in 1894 and was buried in the Protestant Cemetery there.

One of the young men influenced by Ballantyne's novels was Robert Louis Stevenson (1850–94). Stevenson was so impressed with the story of *The Coral Island* (1857) that he based portions of his most famous book, *Treasure Island* (1881), on themes found in Ballantyne's classic novel.

—Karl Wurf
Rockville, Maryland

CHAPTER I.

In Which the Tale Begins Somewhat Furiously.

By the early light of a bright summer morning, long, long ago, two small boats were seen to issue from one of the fiords or firths on the west coast of Norway, and row towards the skerries or low rocky islets that lay about a mile distant from the mainland.

Although the morning was young, the sun was already high in the heavens, and brought out in glowing colours the varied characteristics of a mountain scene of unrivalled grandeur.

The two shallops moved swiftly towards the islands, their oars shivering the liquid mirror of the sea, and producing almost the only sound that disturbed the universal stillness, for at that early hour Nature herself seemed buried in deep repose. A silvery mist hung over the water, through which the innumerable rocks and islands assumed fantastic shapes, and the more distant among them appeared as though they floated in air. A few seagulls rose startled from their nests, and sailed upwards with plaintive cries, as the keels of the boats grated on the rocks, and the men stepped out and hauled them up on the beach of one of the islets.

A wild uncouth crew were those Norsemen of old! All were armed, for in their days the power and the means of self-defence were absolutely necessary to self-preservation.

Most of them wore portions of scale armour, or shirts of ring mail, and headpieces of steel, though a few among them appeared to have confidence in the protection afforded by the thick hide of the wolf, which, converted into rude, yet not ungraceful, garments, covered their broad shoulders. All, without exception, carried sword or battle-axe and shield. They were goodly stalwart men every one, but silent and stern.

It might have been observed that the two boats, although bound for the same islet, did not row in company. They were beached as far from each other as the little bay into which they ran would admit of, and the crews stood aloof in two distinct groups.

In the centre of each group stood a man who, from his aspect and bearing, appeared to be superior to his fellows. One was in the prime of life, dark and grave; the other in the first flush of manhood, full grown, though beardless, fair, and ruddy. Both were taller and stouter than their comrades.

The two men had met there to fight, and the cause of their feud was — Love!

Both loved a fair Norse maiden in Horlingdal. The father of the maid favoured the elder warrior; the maid herself preferred the younger.

In those days, barbarous though they undoubtedly were, law and justice were more respected and more frequently appealed to in Norway than in almost any other country. Liberty, crushed elsewhere under the deadweight of feudalism, found a home in the bleak North, and a rough but loving welcome from the piratical, sea-roving! She did not, indeed, dwell altogether scathless among her demi-savage guardians, who, if their perceptions of right and wrong were somewhat confused, might have urged in excuse that their light was small. She received many shocks and frequent insults from individuals, but liberty was sincerely loved and fondly cherished by the body of the Norwegian people, through all the period of those dark ages during which other nations scarce dared to mention her name.

Nevertheless, it was sometimes deemed more convenient to settle disputes by the summary method of an appeal to arms than to await the issue of a tedious and uncertain lawsuit such an appeal being perfectly competent to those who preferred it, and the belief being strong among the fiery spirits of the age that Odin, the god of war, would assuredly give victory to the right.

In the present instance it was not considered any infringement of the law of liberty that the issue of the combat would be the disposal of a fair woman's hand, with or without her heart. Then, as now, women were often forced to marry against their will.

Having gone to that island to fight — an island being a naturally circumscribed battlefield whose limits could not conveniently be transgressed — the two champions set to work at once with the cool businesslike promptitude of men sprung from a warlike race, and nurtured from their birth in the midst of war's alarms.

Together, and without speaking, they ascended the rock, which was low and almost barren, with a small extent of turf in the centre, level, and admirably suited to their purpose. Here they faced each other; the one drew his sword, the other raised his battle-axe.

There was no sentiment in that combat. The times and the men were extremely matter-of-fact. The act of slaying gracefully had not yet been acquired; yet there was much of manly grace displayed as each threw himself into the position that nature and experience had taught him was best suited to the wielding of his peculiar weapon.

For one instant each gazed intently into the face of the other, as if to read there his premeditated plan of attack. At that moment the clear blue eye of the younger man dilated, and, as his courage rose, the colour mounted to his cheek. The swart brow of the other darkened as he marked the change; then, with sudden spring and shout, the two fell upon each other and dealt their blows with incredible vigour and rapidity.

They were a well-matched pair. For nearly two hours did they toil and moil over the narrow limits of that sea-girt rock — yet victory leaned to neither side. Now the furious blows rained incessant on the sounding shields; anon the din of strife ceased, while the combatants moved round each other, shifting their position with elastic step, as, with wary motion and eagle glances, each sought to catch the other off his guard, and the clash of steel, as the weapons met in sudden onset, was mingled with the shout of anger or defiance. The sun glanced on whirling blade and axe, and sparkled on their coats of mail as if the lightning flash were playing round them; while screaming seamews flew and circled overhead, as though they regarded with intelligent interest and terror the mortal strife that was going on below.

Blood ere long began to flow freely on both sides; the vigour of the blows began to abate, the steps to falter. The youthful cheek grew pale; the dark warrior's brow grew darker, while heaving chests, labouring breath, and an occasional gasp, betokened the approaching termination of the struggle. Suddenly the youth, as if under the influence of a new impulse, dropped his shield, sprang forward, raised himself to his full height, grasped his axe with both hands, and, throwing it aloft (thus recklessly exposing his person), brought it down with terrific violence on the shield of his adversary.

The action was so sudden that the other, already much exhausted, was for the moment paralysed, and failed to take advantage of his opportunity. He met but failed to arrest the blow with his shield. It was crushed down upon his head, and in another moment the swarthy warrior lay stretched upon the turf.

Sternly the men conveyed their fallen chief to his boat, and rowed him to the mainland, and many a week passed by ere he recovered from the effects of the blow that felled him. His conqueror returned to have his wounds dressed by the bride for whom he had fought so long and so valiantly on that bright summer morning.

Thus it was that King Haldor of Horlingdal, surnamed the Fierce, conquered King Ulf of Romsdal, acquired his distinctive appellation, and won Herfrida the Soft-eyed for his bride.

It must not be supposed that these warriors were kings in the ordinary acceptation of that term. They belonged to the class of "small" or petty kings, of whom there were great numbers in Norway in those days, and were merely rich and powerful free-landholders or udallers.

Haldor the Fierce had a large family of sons and daughters. They were all fair, strong, and extremely handsome, like himself.

Ulf of Romsdal did not die of his wounds, neither did he die of love. Disappointed love was then, as now, a terrible disease, but not necessarily fatal. Northmen were very sturdy in the olden time. They almost always recovered from that disease sooner or later. When his wounds were healed, Ulf married a fair girl of the Horlingdal district, and went to reside there, but his change of abode did not alter his title. He was always spoken of as Ulf of Romsdal. He and his old enemy Haldor the Fierce speedily became fast friends; and so was it with their wives, Astrid and Herfrida, who also took mightily to each other. They span, and carded wool, and sewed together oftentimes, and discussed the affairs of Horlingdal, no doubt with mutual advantage and satisfaction.

Twenty years passed away, and Haldor's eldest son, Erling, grew to be a man. He was very like his father — almost a giant in size; fair, very strong, and remarkably handsome. His silken yellow hair fell in heavy curls on a pair of the broadest shoulders in the dale. Although so young, he already had a thick short beard, which was very soft and curly. His limbs were massive, but they were so well proportioned, and his movements so lithe, that his great size and strength were not fully appreciated until one stood close by his side or fell into his powerful grasp.

Erling was lion-like, yet he was by nature gentle and retiring. He had a kindly smile, a hearty laugh, and bright blue eyes. Had he lived in modern days he would undoubtedly have been a man of peace. But he lived "long long ago" — therefore he was a man of war. Being unusually fearless, his companions of the valley called him Erling the Bold. He was, moreover, extremely fond of the sea, and often went on viking cruises in his own ships, whence he was also styled Erling the Sea-king, although he did not at that time possess a foot of land over which to exercise kingly authority.

Now, it must be explained here that the words Sea-king and Viking do not denote the same thing. One is apt to be misled by the termination of the latter word, which has no reference whatever to the royal title king. A viking was merely a piratical rover on the sea, the sea-warrior of the period, but a Sea-king was a leader and commander of vikings. Every Sea-king was a viking, but every viking was not a Sea-king; just as every Admiral is a sailor, but every sailor is not an Admiral. When it is said that Erling was a Sea-king, it is much as if we had said he was an admiral in a small way.

CHAPTER II.

Introduces, among others, the Hero and Heroine,
and opens up a View of Norse Life in the Olden Time.

Ulf of Romsdal had a daughter named Hilda. She was fair, and extremely pretty.

The young men said that her brow was the habitation of the lily, her eye the mirror of the heavens, her cheek the dwelling-place of the rose. True, in the ardour of their feelings and strength of their imaginations they used strong language; nevertheless it was impossible to overpraise the Norse maiden. Her nut-brown hair fell in luxuriant masses over her shapely shoulders, reaching far below the waist; her skin was fair, and her manners engaging. Hilda was undoubtedly blue-eyed and beautiful. She was just seventeen at this time. Those who loved her (and there were few who did not) styled her the sunbeam.

Erling and Hilda had dwelt near each other from infancy. They had been playmates, and for many years were as brother and sister to each other. Erling's affection had gradually grown into a stronger passion, but he never mentioned the fact to anyone, being exceedingly shamefaced and shy in regard to love. He would have given his ears to have known that his love was returned, but he dared not to ask. He was very stupid on this point. In regard to other things he was sharp-witted above his fellows. None knew better than he how to guide the "warship" through the intricate mazes of the island-studded coast of Norway; none equalled him in deeds of arms; no one excelled him in speed of foot, in scaling the fells, or in tracking the wolf and bear to their dens; but all beat him in love-making! He was wondrously slow and obtuse at that, and could by no means discover whether or not Hilda regarded him as a lover or a brother. As uncertainty on this point continued, Erling became jealous of all the young men who approached her, and in proportion as this feeling increased his natural disposition changed, and his chafing spirit struggled fiercely within him. But his native good sense and modesty enabled him pretty well to conceal his feelings. As for Hilda, no one knew the state of her mind. It is probable that at this time she herself had not a very distinct idea on the point.

Hilda had a foster-sister named Ada, who was also very beautiful. She was unusually dark for a Norse maiden. Her akin indeed was fair, but her hair and eyes were black like the raven's wing. Her father was King Hakon of Drontheim.

It was the custom in those warlike days for parents to send out some of their children to be fostered by others — in order, no doubt, to render next to impossible the total extirpation of their families at a time when sudden descents upon households were common. By thus scattering their children the chances of family annihilation were lessened, and the probability that some members might be left alive to take revenge was greatly increased.

Hilda and Ada were warmly attached. Having been brought up together, they loved each other as sisters — all the more, perhaps, that in character they were somewhat opposed. Hilda was grave, thoughtful, almost pensive. Ada was full of vivacity and mirth, fond of fun, and by no means averse to a little of what she styled harmless mischief.

Now there was a man in Horlingdal called Glumm, surnamed the Gruff, who loved Ada fervently. He was a stout, handsome man, of ruddy complexion, and second only to Erling in personal strength and prowess. But by nature he was morose and gloomy. Nothing worse, however, could be said of him. In other respects he was esteemed a brave, excellent man. Glumm was too proud to show his love to Ada very plainly; but she had wit enough to discover it, though no one else did, and she resolved to punish him for his pride by keeping him in suspense.

Horlingdal, where Ulf and Haldor and their families dwelt was, like nearly all the vales on the west of Norway, hemmed in by steep mountains of great height, which were covered with dark pines and birch trees. To the level pastures high up on mountain tops the inhabitants were wont to send their cattle to feed in summer — the small crops of hay in the valleys being carefully gathered and housed for winter use.

Every morning, before the birds began to twitter, Hilda set out, with her pail and her wooden box, to climb the mountain to the upland dairy or "saeter", and fetch the milk and butter required by the family during the day. Although the maid was of noble birth — Ulf claiming descent from one of those who are said to have come over with Odin and his twelve godars or priests from Asia — this was not deemed an inappropriate occupation. Among the Norsemen labour was the lot of high and low. He was esteemed the best man who could fight most valiantly in battle and labour most actively in the field or with the tools of the smith and carpenter. Ulf of Romsdal, although styled king in virtue of his descent, was not too proud, in the busy summertime, to throw off his coat and toss the hay in his own fields in the midst of his thralls[1] and house-carles. Neither he, nor Haldor, nor any of the small kings, although they were the chief men of the districts in which they resided, thought it beneath their dignity to forge their own spearheads and anchors, or to mend their own doors. As it was with the men, so was it with the women. Hilda the Sunbeam was not despised because she climbed the mountainside to fetch milk and butter for the family.

One morning, in returning from the fell, Hilda heard the loud clatter of the anvil at Haldorstede. Having learned that morning that Danish vikings had been seen prowling among the islands near the fiord, she turned aside to enquire the news.

Haldorstede lay about a mile up the valley, and Hilda passed it every morning on her way to and from the saeter. Ulfstede lay near the shore of the fiord. Turning into the smithy, she found Erling busily engaged in hammering a huge mass of stubborn red-hot metal. So intent was the young man on his occu-

---

1   Slaves taken in war.

pation that he failed to observe the entrance of his fair visitor, who set down her milk pail, and stood for a few minutes with her hands folded and her eyes fixed demurely on her lover.

Erling had thrown off his jerkin and rolled up the sleeves of his shirt of coarse homespun fabric, in order to give his thick muscular arms unimpeded play in wielding the hammer and turning the mass of glowing metal on the anvil. He wore woollen breeches and hose, both of which had been fashioned by the fingers of his buxom mother, Herfrida. A pair of neatly formed shoes of untanned hide — his own workmanship — protected his feet, and his waist was encircled by a broad leathern girdle, from one side of which depended a short hunting-knife, and from the other a flap, with a slit in it, to support his sword. The latter weapon — a heavy double-edged blade — stood leaning against the forge chimney, along with a huge battle-axe, within reach of his hand. The collar of his shirt was thrown well back, exposing to view a neck and chest whose muscles denoted extraordinary power, and the whiteness of which contrasted strikingly with the ruddy hue of his deeply bronzed countenance.

The young giant appeared to take pleasure in the exercise of his superabundant strength, for, instead of using the ordinary single-hand hammer with which other men were wont to bend the glowing metal to their will, he wielded the great forehammer, and did it as easily, too, with his right arm as if it had been but a wooden mallet. The mass of metal at which he wrought was thick and unyielding, but under his heavy blows it began to assume the form of an axe — a fact which Hilda noticed with a somewhat saddened brow. Erling's long hair, rolling as it did down his shoulders, frequently straggled over his face and interfered slightly with his vision, whereupon he shook it back with an impatient toss, as a lion might shake his mane, while he toiled with violent energy at his work. To look at him, one might suppose that Vulcan himself had condescended to visit the abodes of men, and work in a terrestrial smithy!

During one of the tosses with which he threw back his hair, Erling chanced to raise his eyes, which instantly fell upon Hilda. A glad smile beamed on his flushed face, and he let the hammer fall with a ringing clatter on the anvil, exclaiming:

"Ha! good morrow to thee, Hilda! Thou comest with stealthy tread, like the midnight marauder. What news? Does all go well at Ulfstede? But why so sad, Hilda? Thy countenance is not wont to quarrel with the mountain air."

"Truly, no!" replied the girl, smiling, "mountain air likes me well. If my looks are sadder than usual, it is because of the form of the weapon thou art fashioning."

"The weapon!" exclaimed Erling, as he raised the handle of the hammer, and, resting his arms on it, gazed at his visitor in some surprise. "It is but an axe — a simple axe, perchance a trifle heavier than other axes because it suits my arm better, and I have a weakness that way. What ails thee at a battle-axe, Hilda?"

"I quarrel not with the axe, Erling, but it reminds me of thy love of fighting, and I grieve for that. Why art thou so fond of war?"

"Fond of war!" echoed the youth. "Now, out upon thee, Hilda! what were a man fit for if he could not fight?"

"Nay, I question not thine ability to fight, but I grieve to see thy love for fighting."

"Truly there seems to me a close relationship between the love of war and the ability to fight," returned the youth. "But to be plain with thee: I *do not* love war so much as ye think. Yet I utter this in thine ear, for I would not that the blades of the valley knew it, lest they might presume upon it, and I should have to prove my ability – despite my want of love – upon some of their carcasses."

"I wish there were no such thing as war," said Hilda with a sigh.

Erling knitted his brows and gazed into the smithy fire as if he were engaged in pondering some knotty point. "Well, I'm not sure," said he slowly, and descending to a graver tone of address – "I'm not sure that I can go quite so far as that. If we had no war at all, perchance our swords might rust, and our skill, for want of practice, might fail us in the hour of need. Besides, how could men in that case hope to dwell with Odin in Valhalla's bright and merry halls? But I agree with thee in wishing that we had less of war and more of peace *at home*."

"I fear," said Hilda, "we seem likely to have more of war and less of peace than usual, if rumours be true. Have you heard that Danish vikings have been seen among the islands?"

"Aye, truly, I have heard of them, and it is that which has sent me to the smithy this morning to hasten forward my battle-axe; for I love not too light a weapon. You see, Hilda, when it has not weight one must sometimes repeat the blow; especially if the mail be strong. But with a heavy axe and a stout arm there is no need for that. I had begun this weapon," continued the youth, as if he were musing aloud rather than speaking to his companion, "with intent to try its metal on the head of the King; but I fear me it will be necessary to use it in cracking a viking's headpiece before it cleaves a royal crown."

"The King!" exclaimed Hilda, with a look of surprise, not unmingled with terror, "Erling, has ambition led thee to this?"

"Not so; but self-preservation urges me to it."

The maiden paused a few seconds, ere she replied in a meditative voice – "The old man who came among us a year ago, and who calls himself Christian, tells me that his god is not a god of war, like Odin; he says that his god permits no war to men, save that of self-defence; but, Erling, would slaying the King be indeed an act of self-preservation?"

"Aye, in good sooth would it," replied the youth quickly, while a dark frown crossed his brow.

"How can that be?" asked the maiden.

"Hast such small love for gossip, Hilda, that the foul deeds and ambitious projects of Harald Haarfager have not reached thine ear?"

"I have heard," replied Hilda, "that he is fond of war, which, truly, is no news, and that he is just now more busy with his bloody game than usual; but what does that matter to thee?"

"Matter!" cried the youth impatiently, as he seized the lump of metal on which he had been at work, and, thrusting it into the smouldering charcoal, commenced to blow the fire energetically, as if to relieve his feelings. "Know ye not that the King — this Harald Fairhair — is not satisfied with the goodly domains that of right belong to him, and the kingly rule which he holds, according to law, over all Norway, but that he means to subdue the whole land to himself, and trample on our necks as he has already trampled on our laws?"

"I know somewhat of this," said Hilda.

"No one," pursued Erling vehemently, and blowing the fire into a fervent heat — "no one denies to Harald the right to wear the crown of Norway. That was settled at the Ore Thing[2] in Drontheim long ago; but everyone denies his right to interfere with our established laws and privileges. Has he not, by mere might and force of arms, slain many, and enslaved others, of our best and bravest men? And now he proposes to reduce the whole land to slavery, or something like it, and all because of the foolish speech of a proud girl, who says she will not wed him until he shall first subdue to himself the whole of Norway, and rule over it as fully and freely as King Eric rules over Sweden, or King Gorm over Denmark. He has sworn that he will neither clip nor comb his hair, until he has subdued all the land with scatt[3] and duties and domains, or die in the attempt. Trust me! he is like to die in the attempt; and since his Kingship is to be so little occupied with his hair, it would please me well if he would use his time and his shears in clipping the tongue of the wench that set him on so foul an errand. All this thou knowest, Hilda, as well as I; but thou dost not know that men have been at the stede to-day, who tell us that the King is advancing north, and is victorious everywhere. Already King Gandalf and Hako are slain; the two sons of King Eystein have also fallen, and many of the upland kings have been burned, with most of their men, in a house at Ringsager. It is not many days since Harald went up Gudbrandsdal, and north over the Doverfielde, where he ordered all the men to be slain, and everything wide around to be given to the flames. King Gryting of Orkadal and all his people have sworn fidelity to him, and now — worst news of all — it is said he is coming over to pay us a visit in Horlingdal. Is not here cause for fighting in self-defence, or rather for country, and laws and freedom, and wives, and children, and —"

The excited youth stopped abruptly, and, seizing the tongs, whirled the white mass of semi-molten steel upon the anvil, and fell to belabouring it with

2   The great assembly, or parliament, which was considered the only "Thing" which could confer the sovereignty of the whole of Norway, the other Things having no right or powers beyond their circles. It was convened only for the special purpose of examining and proclaiming the right of the aspirant to the crown, but the King had still to repair to each Law Thing or Small Thing to obtain its acknowledgement of his right and the power of a sovereign within its jurisdiction.

3   taxes

such goodwill that a bright shower of sparks drove Hilda precipitately out of the workshop.

The wrongs which roused the young Norseman's indignation to such a pitch are matters of history.

The government of the country at that time involved the democratic element very largely. No act or expedition of any importance could be done or undertaken without the previous deliberation and consent of a "Thing", or assembly of landed proprietors. There were many different Things — such as General Things, District Things, House Things of the King's counsellors, and Herd Things of the Court, &c., and to such of these there was a distinct and well-known trumpet call. There were also four great Things which were legislative, while the small district Things were only administrative. In addition to which there was the Ore Thing of Drontheim, referred to by Erling. At these Things the King himself possessed no greater power than any of the bonders. He was only a "Thing-man" at a Thing.

No wonder, then, that the self-governing and warlike Norsemen could not bring themselves tamely to submit to the tyranny of Harald Haarfager, or Fairhair, King of Norway by hereditary right, when he cast aside all the restraints of ancient custom, and, in his effort to obtain more power, commenced those bloody wars with his subjects, which had the effect of causing many of his chief men to expatriate themselves and seek new homes in the islands of the great western sea, and which ultimately resulted in the subjugation (at least during that reign) of all the petty kings of Norway. These small kings, be it observed, were not at that time exercising any illegal power, or in the occupation of any unwarrantable position, which could be pleaded by King Harald in justification of his violent proceedings against them. The title of king did not imply independent sovereignty. They were merely the hereditary lords of the soil, who exercised independent and rightful authority over their own estates and households, and modified authority over their respective districts, subject, however, to the laws of the land — laws which were recognised and perfectly understood by the people and the king, and which were admitted by people and king alike to have more authority than the royal will itself. By law the small kings were bound to attend the meetings of the Stor Things or Parliaments, at the summons of the sovereign, and to abide by the decisions of those assemblies, where all men met on an equal footing, but where, of course, intellectual power and eloquence led the multitude, for good or for evil, then just as they do now, and will continue to do as long as, and wherever, free discussion shall obtain. To say that the possession of power, wealth, or influence was frequently abused to the overawing and coercing of those assemblies, is simply to state that they were composed of human beings possessed of fallen natures.

So thoroughly did the Northmen appreciate the importance of having a right to raise their voices and to vote in the national parliaments, and so jealously did they assert and maintain their privileges, that the King himself — before he could, on his accession, assume the crown — was obliged to appear at the "Thing", where a freeborn landholder proposed him, and where his title to the crown was investigated and proved in due form. No war expedition on a large scale could be undertaken until a Thing had been converged, and requisition legally made by the King for a supply of men and arms; and, generally, whenever any act affecting national or even district interests was contemplated, it was necessary to assemble a Thing, and consult with the people before anything could be done.

It may be easily understood, then, with what an outburst of indignation a free and warlike race beheld the violent course pursued by Harald Fairhair, who roamed through the country with fire and sword, trampling on their cherished laws and privileges, subduing the petty kings, and placing them, when submissive, as Jarls, i.e. earls or governors over the districts to collect the scatt or taxes, and manage affairs in his name and for his behoof.

It is no wonder that Erling the Bold gathered his brow into an ominous frown, pressed his lips together, tossed his locks impatiently while he thought on these things and battered the iron mass on his anvil with the amount of energy that he would have expended in belabouring the head of King Harald himself, had opportunity offered.

Erling's wrath cooled, however, almost instantly on his observing Hilda's retreat before the fiery shower. He flung down his hammer, seized his battle-axe, and throwing it on his shoulder as he hurried out, speedily overtook her.

"Forgive my rude manners," he said. "My soul was chafed by the thoughts that filled my brain, and I scare knew what I did."

"Truly, thou man of fire," replied the girl, with an offended look, "I am of half a mind not to pardon thee. See, my kirtle is destroyed by the shower thou didst bestow upon me so freely."

"I will repay thee that with such a kirtle as might grace a queen the next time I go on viking cruise."

"Meantime," said Hilda, "I am to go about like a witch plucked somewhat hastily from the fire by a sympathising crone."

"Nay; Herfrida will make thee a new kirtle of the best wool at Haldorstede."

"So thy mother, it seems, is to work and slave in order to undo thy mischief?"

"Then, if nothing else will content thee," said Erling gaily, "I will make thee one myself; but it must be of leather, for I profess not to know how to stitch more delicate substance. But let me carry thy pitcher, Hilda. I will go to Ulfstede to hold converse with thy father on these matters, for it seemed to me that the clouds are gathering somewhat too thickly over the dale for comfort or peace to remain long with us."

As the young man and maiden wended their way down the rocky path that skirted the foaming Horlingdal river, Hilda assumed a more serious tone, and sought to convince her companion of the impropriety of being too fond of fighting, in which attempt, as might be supposed, she was not very successful.

"Why, Hilda," said the youth, at the close of a speech in which his fair companion endeavoured to point out the extreme sinfulness of viking cruises in particular, "it is, as thou sayest, unjust to take from another that which belongs to him if he be our friend; but if he is our enemy, and the enemy of our country, that alters the case. Did not the great Odin himself go on viking cruise and seize what prey he chose?"

Erling said this with the air of a man who deemed his remark unanswerable.

"I know not," rejoined Hilda. "There seems to me much mystery in our thoughts about the gods. I have heard it said that there is no such god as Odin."

The maiden uttered this in a subdued voice, and her cheek paled a little as she glanced up at Erling's countenance. The youth gazed at her with an expression of extreme surprise, and for a few minutes they walked slowly forward without speaking.

There was reason for this silence on both sides. Hilda was naturally of a simple and trustful nature. She had been brought up in the religion of her fathers, and had listened with awe and with deep interest on many a long winter night to the wild legends with which the scalds, or poets of the period, were wont to beguile the evening hours in her father's mansion; but about a year before the time of which we write, an aged stranger had come from the south, and taken up his abode in the valley, in a secluded and dilapidated hut, in which he was suffered to dwell unmolested by its owner, Haldor the Fierce; whose fierceness, by the way, was never exhibited except in time of war and in the heat of battle!

With this hermit Hilda had held frequent converse, and had listened with horror, but with a species of fascination which she could not resist, to his calm and unanswerable reasoning on the fallacy of the religion of Odin, and on the truth of that of Jesus Christ. At first she resolved to fly from the old man, as a dangerous enemy, who sought to seduce her from the paths of rectitude; but when she looked at his grave, sad face, and listened to the gentle and — she knew not why — persuasive tones of his voice, she changed her mind, and resolved to hear what he had to say. Without being convinced of the truth of the new religion — of which she had heard rumours from the roving vikings who frequented Horlingdal — she was much shaken in regard to the truth of her own, and now, for the first time, she had ventured to hint to a human being what was passing in her mind.

At this period Christianity had not penetrated into Norway, but an occasional wanderer or hermit had found his way thither from time to time to surprise the inhabitants with his new doctrines, and then, perchance, to perish as a warlock because of them. Erling had heard of this old man, and regarded him with no favour, for in his sea rovings he had met with so-called Christians, whose conduct had not prepossessed him in their favour. As for their creed, he knew nothing whatever about it.

His mind, however, was of that bold, straightforward, self-reliant, and meditative cast, which happily has existed in all ages and in all climes, and which, in civilised lands, usually brings a man to honour and power, while in barbarous countries and ages, if not associated with extreme caution and reticence, it is apt to bring its possessor into trouble.

It was with astonishment that Erling heard sentiments which had long been harboured in his own mind drop from the lips of one whose natural character he knew to be the reverse of sceptical in matters of faith, or speculative in matters of opinion. Instead of making a direct reply to Hilda's remark, he said, after a pause:

"Hilda, I have my doubts of the old man Christian; men say he is a warlock, and I partly believe them, for it is only such who shun the company of their fellows. I would caution thee against him. He believes not in Odin or Thor, which is matter of consideration mainly to himself, but methinks he holdeth fellowship with Nikke[4], which is matter of consideration for all honest men, aye, and women too, who would live in peace; for if the Evil Spirit exists at all, as I firmly believe he does, in some shape or other, it were well to keep as far from him as we may, and specially to avoid those erring mortals who seem to court his company."

"The old man is misjudged, believe me," replied the girl earnestly; "I have spoken much with him and oft. It may be he is wrong in some things – how can a woman judge of such matters? – but he is gentle, and has a kind heart."

"I like him not," was Erling's curt reply.

The youth and maiden had now reached a part of the valley where a small footpath diverged from the main track which led to Ulf's dwelling. The path ran in the direction of the hayfields that bordered the fiord. Just as they reached it, Hilda observed that her father was labouring there with his thralls.

"See," she exclaimed, stopping abruptly, and taking her pitcher from Erling, "my father is in the hayfield."

The youth was about to remonstrate and insist on being allowed to carry the pitcher to the house before going to the field; but on second thoughts he resigned his slight burden, and, saying "farewell", turned on his heel and descended the path with rapid step and a somewhat burdened heart.

"She loves me not," he muttered to himself, almost sternly. "I am a brother, nothing more."

Indulging in these and kindred gloomy reflections, he advanced towards a rocky defile where the path diverged to the right. Before taking the turn he looked back. Hilda was standing on the spot where they had parted, but her face was not directed towards her late companion. She was looking steadily up the valley. Presently the object which attracted her attention appeared in view, and Erling felt a slight sensation of anger, he scarce knew why, on observing the old man who had been the subject of their recent conversation issue from among the rocks. His first impulse was to turn back, but, checking himself, he wheeled sharply round and hurried away.

Scarcely had he taken three steps, however, when he was arrested by a sound that resembled a crash of thunder. Glancing quickly upwards, he beheld an enor-

4   Satan, or the Evil One.

mous mass of rock, which had become detached from the mountain side, descending in shattered fragments into the valley.

The formation of Horlingdal at that particular point was peculiar. The mountain ranges on either side, which rose to a height of at least four thousand feet, approached each other abruptly, thus forming a dark gloomy defile of a few hundred yards in width, with precipitous cliffs on either side, and the river roaring in the centre of the pass. The water rushed in white-crested billows through its rock-impeded bed, and terminated in a splendid foss, or fall, forty or fifty feet high, which plunged into a seething caldron, whence it issued in a troubled stream to the plain that opened out below. It here found rest in the level fields of Ulfstede, that lay at the head of the fiord. The open amphitheatre above this pass, with its circlet of grand glacier-capped mountains, was the abode of a considerable number of small farmers, in the midst of whose dwellings stood the residence of Haldor, where the meeting in the smithy just described took place.

It was in this narrow defile that the landslip happened, a catastrophe which always has been and still is of frequent occurrence in the mountain regions of Norway.

Hilda and the old man (whom we shall henceforth call Christian) cast their eyes hastily upwards on hearing the sound that had arrested Erling's steps so suddenly. The enormous mass of rock was detached from the hill on the other side of the river, but the defile was so narrow that falling rocks often rebounded quite across it. The slip occurred just opposite the spot on which Hilda and the old man stood, and as the terrible shower came on, tearing down trees and rocks, the heavier masses being dashed and spurned from the hillside in innumerable fragments, it became evident that to escape beyond the range of the chaotic deluge was impossible.

Hilda understood the danger so well that she was panic stricken and rooted to the spot. Erling understood it also, and, with a sudden cry, dashed at full speed to the rescue. His cry was one almost of despair, for the distance between them was so great that he had no chance, he knew, of reaching her in time.

In this extremity the hermit looked round for a crevice or a rock which might afford protection, but no such place of safety was at hand. The side of the pass rose behind them like a wall to a height of several hundred feet. Seeing this at a glance the old man planted himself firmly in front of Hilda. His lips moved, and the single word "Jesus" dropped from them as he looked with a calm steady gaze at the avalanche.

Scarcely had he taken his stand when the first stones leaped across the gorge, and, striking on the wall of rock behind, burst into fragments and fell in a shower around them. Some of the smaller *débris* struck the old man's breast, and the hands which he had raised to protect his face; but he neither blanched nor flinched. In another instant the greater part of the hurling rubbish fell with a terrible crash and tore up the earth in all directions round them. Still they stood unhurt! The height from which the ruin had descended was so great that the masses were scattered, and although they flew around over, and close to them, the great shock passed by and left them unscathed.

But the danger was not yet past. Several of the smaller masses, which had been partially arrested in their progress by bushes, still came thundering down the steep. The quick eye of the hermit observed one of these flying straight towards his head. Its force had been broken by a tree on the opposite hill, but it still retained tremendous impetus. He knew that there was no escape for him. To have moved aside would have exposed Hilda to almost certain destruction. Once again he murmured the Saviour's name, as he stretched out both hands straight before his face. The rock struck full against them, beat them down on his forehead, and next instant old man and maid were hurled to the ground.

Well was it for Erling that all this occurred so quickly that the danger was past before he reached the spot. Part of the road he had to traverse was strewn so thickly with the rocky ruin that his destruction, had he been a few seconds sooner on the ground, would have been inevitable. He reached Hilda just in time to assist her to rise. She was slightly stunned by the shock, but otherwise unhurt.

Not so the hermit. He lay extended where he had fallen; his grey beard and thin scattered locks dabbled with blood that flowed from a gash in his forehead. Hilda kneeled at his side, and, raising his head, she laid it in her lap.

"Now the gods be praised," said Erling, as he knelt beside her, and endeavoured to stanch the flow of blood from the wound; "I had thought thy last hour was come, Hilda; but the poor old man, I fear much he will die."

"Not so; he recovers," said the girl; "fetch me some water from the spring."

Erling ran to a rill that trickled down the face of the rock at his side, dipped his leathern bonnet into it, and, quickly returning, sprinkled a little on the old man's face, and washed the wound.

"It is not deep," he remarked, after having examined the cut. "His hands are indeed badly bruised, but he will live."

"Get thee to the stede, Erling, and fetch aid," said Hilda quickly; "the old man is heavy."

The youth smiled. "Heavy he is, no doubt, but he wears no armour; methinks I can lift him."

So saying Erling raised him in his strong arms and bore him away to Ulfstede, where, under the tender care of Hilda and her foster-sister Ada, he speedily revived.

Erling went out meanwhile to assist in the hayfield.

CHAPTER III.

Shows how Chief Friends may become Foes,
And Cross-Purposes may Produce Cross Consequences,
involving Worry and Confusion.

When Christian had been properly cared for, Hilda sent Ada to the hayfield, saying that she would follow her in a short time. Now it so happened, by one of those curious coincidences which are generally considered unaccountable, that as Ada ascended the track which led to the high field above the foss, Glumm the Gruff descended towards the same point from an opposite direction, so that a meeting between the two, in the secluded dell, where the tracks joined, became inevitable.

Whether or not this meeting was anticipated we cannot tell. If it was, the young man and maiden were inimitable actors by nature, for they appeared to be wholly unconscious of aught save the peculiar formation of the respective footpaths along which they slowly moved. There was, indeed, a twinkle in Ada's eyes; but then Ada's eyes were noted twinklers; besides, a refractory eyelash might account for such an expression.

As for Glumm, he frowned on the path most unamiably while he sauntered along with both hands thrust into the breast of his tunic, and the point of his sword rasping harshly against rocks and bushes. Glumm was peculiar in his weapons. He wore a double-handed and double-edged sword, which was so long that he was obliged to sling it across his back in order to keep it off the ground. The handle projected above his left shoulder, and the blade, lying diagonally across his person, extended beyond his right calf. The young man was remarkably expert in the use of this immense weapon, and was not only a terror to his foes, but, owing to the enormous sweep of its long blade, an object of some anxiety to his friends when they chanced to be fighting alongside of him. He wore a knife or dagger at his girdle on the right side, which was also of unusual size; in all probability it would have been deemed a pretty good sword by the Romans. There were only two men in the dale who could wield Glumm's weapons. These were Erling and his father, Haldor. The latter was as strong a man as Glumm, Erling was even stronger; though, being an amiable man he could not be easily persuaded to prove his strength upon his friends. Glumm wore his hair very short. It was curly, and lay close to his head.

As he sauntered along he kicked the stones out of his way savagely, and appeared to find relief to his feelings in so doing, as well as by allowing his sword to rasp across the rocks and shrubs at his side. It might have been observed, however, that Glumm only kicked the little stones out of his way; he never kicked the big ones. It is interesting to observe how trifling a matter will bring out a trait of human nature! Men will sometimes relieve their angry feelings by storming violently at those of their fellows who cannot hurt them, but, strangely enough, they manage to obtain relief to these same feelings without storming, when they chance to be in the company of stronger men than themselves, thereby proving that they have powers of self-restraint which prudence — not to say fear — can call into exercise! commend this moral reflection particularly to the study of boys.

After Glumm had kicked all the *little* stones out of his way, carefully letting the big ones alone, he came suddenly face to face with Ada, who saluted him with a look of startled surprise, a slight blush, and a burst of hearty laughter.

"Why, Glumm," exclaimed the maiden, with an arch smile, "thou must have risen off thy wrong side this morning. Methinks, now, were I a man, I should have to look to my weapons, for that long blade of thine seems inclined to fight with the rocks and shrubs of its own accord."

Poor Glumm blushed as red as if he had been a young girl, at being thus unexpectedly caught giving vent to his ill-humour; he stammered something about bad dreams and evil spirits, and then, breaking into a good-humoured smile, said:

"Well, Ada, I know not what it is that ails me, but I do feel somewhat cross-grained. Perchance a walk with thee may cure me, I see thou art bound for the hayfield. But hast thou not heard the news? The Danish vikings are off the coast, burning and murdering wherever they go. It is rumoured, too, that their fleet is under that king of scoundrels, Skarpedin the Red. Surely there is reason for my being angry."

"Nay, then, if thou wert a bold man thou wouldst find reason in this for being glad," replied Ada. "Is not the chance of a fight the joy of a true Norseman's heart? Surely a spell must have been laid on thee, if thy brow darkens and thy heart grows heavy on hearing of a stout enemy. It is not thus with Erling the Bold. His brow clears and his eye sparkles when a foe worthy of — But what seest thou, Glumm? Has the Dane appeared in the forest that thy brow becomes so suddenly clouded? I pray thee do not run away and leave me unprotected."

"Doubtless if I did, Erling the Bold would come to thine aid," replied the young man with some asperity.

"Nay, do not be angry with me, Glumm," said the girl, laughing, as they reached the field where Haldor and his stout son were busily at work assisting Ulf, who, with all his thralls and freemen, was engaged in cutting and gathering in his hay.

"Hey! here come cloud and sunshine hand in hand," cried Erling, pausing in his work, as Glumm and his pretty companion approached the scene of labour.

"Get on with thy work, then, and make the hay while I am shining," retorted Ada, bestowing on the youth a bright smile, which he returned cheerfully and with interest.

This was the wicked Ada's finishing touch. Glumm saw the exchange of smiles, and a pang of fierce jealousy shot through his breast.

"The cloud sometimes darts out lightning," he muttered angrily, and, turning on his heel, began to toss the hay with all his might in order to relieve his feelings.

Just then Hilda entered the field, and Glumm, putting strong constraint on himself, accosted her with extreme cheerfulness and respect — resolved in his heart to show Ada that there were other girls in Horlingdal worth courting besides herself. In this game he was by no means successful as regarded Ada, who at once discerned his intention, but the shaft which flew harmlessly past her fixed itself deep in the breast of another victim. Glumm's unusual urbanity took the kind-hearted Hilda so much by surprise, that she was interested, and encouraged him, in what she conceived to be a tendency towards improvement of disposition, by bestowing on him her sweetest smiles during the course of the day, insomuch that Erling the Bold became much surprised, and at last unaccountably cross.

Thus did these two men, who had for many years been fast and loving friends, become desperately jealous, though each sought to conceal the fact from the other. But the green-eyed monster having obtained a lodgment in their bosoms, could not be easily cast out. Yet the good sense of each enabled him to struggle with some success against the passion, for Glumm, although gruff, was by no means a bad man.

The presence of those conflicting feelings did not, however, interrupt or retard the work of the field. It was a truly busy scene. Masters, unfreemen, and thralls, mistresses and maidens, were there, cutting and turning and piling up the precious crop with might and main; for they knew that the weather could not be trusted to, and the very lives of their cattle depended on the successful ingathering of the hay.

As we have here mentioned the three different classes that existed in Norway, it may be well to explain that the masters were peasants or "bonders", but not by any means similar to peasants in other lands; on the contrary, they were the udal-born proprietors of the soil — the peasant-nobility, so to speak, the Udallers, or freeholders, without any superior lord, and were entitled to attend and have a voice in the "Things" or assemblies where the laws were enacted and public affairs regulated. The next class was that of the "unfreemen". These were freed slaves who had wrought out or purchased their freedom, but who, although personally free, and at liberty to go where and serve whom they pleased, were not free to attend the legislative assemblies. They were unfree of the Things, and hence their apparently contradictory designation. They, however, enjoyed the protection and civil rights imparted by the laws, and to their class belonged all the cottars on the land paying a rent in work on the farm of the bonder or udaller, also the house-carles or freeborn indoormen, and the tradesmen, labourers, fishermen, &c., about villages and farms. Thralls were slaves taken in war, over whom the owners had absolute control. They might sell them, kill them, or do with them as they pleased. Thralls were permitted to purchase their freedom — and all the descendants of those freed thralls, or unfreemen, were free.

The clothing of the unfreemen was finer than that of the thralls. The legs and arms of nearly all were bare from the knees and elbows downward, though a few had swathed their limbs in bands of rough woollen cloth, while others used straw for this purpose. Nearly all the men wore shoes of untanned leather, and caps of the same material, or of rough homespun cloth, resembling in form the cap of modern fishermen. The udallers, such as Haldor, Ulf, and their children, were clad in finer garments, which were looped and buttoned with brooches and pendants of gold and silver, the booty gathered on those viking cruises, against which Hilda inveighed so earnestly.

The work went on vigorously until the sun began to sink behind the mountain range that lay to the north-westward of the dale. By this time the hay was all cut, and that portion which was sufficiently dry piled up, so Ulf and Haldor left the work to be finished by the younger hands, and stood together in the centre of the field chatting and looking on.

Little change had taken place in the personal appearance of Ulf of Romsdal since the occasion of that memorable duel related in the first chapter of our story. Some of his elasticity, but none of his strength, was gone. There was perhaps a little more thought in his face, and a few more wrinkles on his swarthy brow, but his hair was still black and his figure straight as the blade of his good sword. His old enemy but now fast friend, Haldor the Fierce, had changed still less. True, his formerly smooth chin and cheeks were now thickly covered with luxuriant fair hair, but his broad forehead was still unwrinkled, and his clear blue eye was as bright as when, twenty years before, it gleamed in youthful fire at Ulf. Many a battle had Haldor fought since then, at home and abroad, and several scars on his countenance and shoulders gave evidence that he had not come out of these altogether scathless; but war had not soured him. His smile was as free, open, and honest, and his laugh as loud and hearty, as in days of yore. Erling was the counterpart of his father, only a trifle taller and stouter. At a short distance they might have been taken for twin brothers, and those who did not know them could scarcely have believed that they were father and son.

Close to the spot where the two friends stood, a sturdy thrall was engaged in piling up hay with an uncommon degree of energy. This man had been taken prisoner on the coast of Ireland by Ulf, during one of his sea-roving expeditions. He had a huge massive frame, with a profusion of red hair on his head and face, and a peculiarly humorous twinkle in his eye. His name was Kettle Flatnose. We have reason to believe that the first part of this name had no connection with that domestic utensil which is intimately associated with tea! It was a mere accidental resemblance of sound no doubt. As to the latter part, that is easily explained. In those days there were no surnames. In order to distinguish men of the same name from each other, it was usual to designate them by their complexions, or by some peculiarity of person or trait of character. A blow from a club in early life had destroyed the shape of Kettle's nose, and had disfigured an otherwise handsome and manly countenance. Hence his name. He was about thirty-five years of age, large-boned, broad-shouldered, and tall, but lean in flesh, and rather ungainly in his motions. Few men cared to grapple with the huge Irish slave, for he possessed a superabundant share of that fire and love of fight which are said to characterise his countrymen even at the present time. He was also gifted with a large share of their characteristic good humour and joviality; which qualities endeared him to many of his companions, especially to the boys of the neighbourhood. In short, there was not a better fellow in the dale than Kettle Flatnose.

"Thy labour is not light, Kettle," observed Ulf to the thrall as he paused for a few moments in the midst of his work to wipe his heated brow.

"Ill would it become me, master," replied the man, "to take my work easy when my freedom is so nearly gained."

"Right, quite right," replied Ulf with an approving nod, as the thrall set to work again with redoubled energy.

"That man," he added, turning to Haldor, "will work himself free in a few weeks hence. He is one of my best thralls. I give my slaves, as thou knowest, leave to work after hours to purchase their freedom, and Kettle labours so hard that he is almost a free man already, though he has been with me little more than two years and a half. I fear the fellow will not remain with me after he is free, for he is an unsettled spirit. He was a chief in his own land, it seems, and left a bride behind him, I am told. If he goes, I lose a man equal to two, he is so strong and willing. — Ho! Kettle," continued Ulf, turning to the man, who had just finished the job on which he had been engaged, "toss me yonder stone and let my friend Haldor see what thou art made of."

Kettle obeyed with alacrity. He seized a round stone as large as his own head, and, with an unwieldy action of his great frame, cast it violently through the air about a dozen yards in advance of him.

"Well cast, well cast!" cried Haldor, while a murmur of applause rose from the throng of labourers who had been instantly attracted to the spot. "Come, I will try my own hand against thee."

Haldor advanced, and, lifting the stone, balanced it for a few moments in his right hand, then, with a graceful motion and an apparently slight effort, hurled it forward. It fell a foot beyond Kettle's mark.

Seeing this the thrall leaped forward, seized the stone, ran back to the line, bent his body almost to the ground, and, exerting himself to the utmost, threw it into the same hollow from which he had lifted it.

"Equal!" cried Ulf. "Come, Haldor, try again."

"Nay, I will not try until he beats me," replied Haldor with a good-natured laugh. "But do thou take a cast, Ulf. Thine arm is powerful, as I can tell from experience."

"Not so," replied Ulf. "It becomes men who are past their prime to reserve their strength for the sword and battle-axe. Try it once more, Kettle. Mayhap thou wilt pass the mark next time."

Kettle tried again and again, but without gaining a hair's-breadth on Haldor's throw. The stalwart thrall had indeed put forth greater force in his efforts than Haldor, but he did not possess his skill.

"Will no young man make trial of his strength and skill?" said Haldor, looking round upon the eager faces of the crowd.

"Glumm is no doubt anxious to try his hand," said Erling, who stood close to the line, with his arms resting on the head of his long-hafted battle-axe. "The shining of the Sunbeam will doubtless warm thy heart and nerve thine arm."

Erling muttered the latter part of his speech in a somewhat bitter tone, alluding to Hilda's smiles; but the jealous and sulky Glumm could appreciate no sunbeams save those that flashed from Ada's dark eyes. He understood the remark as a triumphant and ironical taunt, and, leaping fiercely into the ring formed by the spectators, exclaimed:

"I will cast the stone, but I must have a better man than thou, Kettle, to strive with. If Erling the Bold will throw —"

"I will not balk thee," interrupted the other quickly, as he laid down his axe and stepped up to the line.

Glumm now made a cast. Everyone knew well enough that he was one of the best throwers of the stone in all the dale, and confidently anticipated an easy victory over the thrall. But the unusual tumult of conflicting feelings in the young man's breast rendered him at the time incapable of exerting his powers to the utmost in a feat, to excel in which requires the union of skill with strength. At his first throw the stone fell short about an inch!

At this Ada's face became grave, and her heart began to flutter with anxiety; for although willing enough to torment her lover a little herself, she could not brook the idea of his failing in a feat of strength before his comrades.

Furious with disappointment and jealousy, and attributing Ada's expression to anxiety lest he should succeed, Glumm cast again with passionate energy, and sent the stone just an inch beyond the thrall's mark. There was a dispute on the point, however, which did not tend to soothe the youth's feelings, but it was ultimately decided in his favour.

Erling now stood forth; and as he raised his tall form to its full height, and elevated the stone above his head, he seemed (especially to Hilda) the *beau-idéal* of manly strength and beauty.

He was grieved, however, at Glumm's failure, for he knew him to be capable of doing better than he had done. He remembered their old friendship too, and pity for his friend's loss of credit caused the recently implanted jealousy for a moment to abate. He resolved, therefore, to exert himself just sufficiently to maintain his credit.

But, unhappily for the successful issue of this effort of self-denial, Erling happened to cast his eye towards the spot where Hilda stood. The tender-hearted maiden chanced at that moment to be regarding Glumm with a look of genuine pity. Of course Erling misconstrued the look! Next moment the huge stone went singing through the air, and fell with a crash full two yards beyond Glumm's mark. Happening to alight on a piece of rock, it sprang onward, passed over the edge of the hill or brae on the summit of which the field lay, and gathering additional impetus in its descent, went bounding down the slope, tearing through everything in its way, until it found rest at last on the sea beach below.

A perfect storm of laughter and applause greeted this unexpected feat, but high above the din rose the voice of Glumm, who, now in a towering passion, seized his double-handed sword, and shouting —

"Guard thee, Erling!" made a furious blow at his conqueror's head.

Erling had fortunately picked up his axe after throwing the stone. He immediately whirled the heavy head so violently against the descending sword that the blade broke off close to the hilt, and Glumm stood before him, disarmed and helpless, gazing in speechless astonishment at the hilt which remained in his hands.

"My good sword!" he exclaimed, in a tone of deep despondency.

At this Erling burst into a hearty fit of laughter. "My bad sword, thou must mean," said he. "How often have I told thee, Glumm, that there was a flaw in the metal! I have advised thee more than once to prove the blade, and now that thou hast consented to do so, behold the result! But be not so cast down, man; I have forged another blade specially for thyself, friend Glumm, but did not think to give it thee so soon."

Glumm stood abashed, and had not a word to reply. Fortunately his feelings were relieved by the attention of the whole party being attracted at that moment to the figure of a man on the opposite side of the valley, who ran towards them at full speed, leaping over almost every obstacle that presented itself in his course. In a few minutes he rushed, panting, into the midst of the throng, and presented a baton or short piece of wood to Ulf, at the same time exclaiming: "Haste! King Harald holds a Thing at the Springs. Speed on the token."

The import of this message and signal were well understood by the men of Horlingdal. When an assembly or Thing was to be convened for discussing civil matters a wooden truncheon was sent round from place to place by fleet messengers, each of whom ran a certain distance, and then delivered over his "message-token" to another runner, who carried it forward to a third, and so on. In this manner the whole country could be roused and its chief men assembled in a comparatively short time. When, however, the Thing was to be assembled for the discussion of affairs pertaining to war, an arrow split in four parts was the message-token. When the split arrow passed through the land men were expected to assemble armed to the teeth, but when the baton went round it was intended that they should meet without the full panoply of war.

As soon as the token was presented, Ulf looked about for a fleet man to carry forward the message. Several of the youths at once stepped forward offering their services. Foremost among them was a stout, deep-chested active boy of about twelve years of age, with long flaxen curls, a round sunburnt face, a bold yet not forward look, a merry smile, and a pair of laughing blue eyes. This was Erling's little brother Alric — a lad whose bosom was kept in a perpetual state of stormy agitation by the conflict carried on therein between a powerful tendency to fun and mischief, and a strong sense of the obedience due to parents.

"I will go," said the boy eagerly, holding out his hand for the token.

"Thou, my son?" said Haldor, regarding him with a look of ill-suppressed pride. "Go to thy mother's bower, boy. What if a fox, or mayhap even a wolf, met thee on the fell?"

"Have I not my good bow of elm?" replied Alric, touching the weapon, which, with a quiver full of arrows, was slung across his back.

"Tush! boy; go pop at the squirrels till thou be grown big enough to warrant thy boasting."

"Father," said Alric with a look of glee, "I'm sure I did not boast. I did but point to my poor weapons. Besides, I have good legs. If I cannot fight, methinks I can run."

"Out upon thee —"

"Nay, Haldor," said Ulf, interrupting the discussion, "thou art too hard on the lad. Can he run well?"

"I'll answer for that," said Erling, laying his large hand on his brother's flaxen head. "I doubt if there is a fleeter foot in all the dale."

"Away then," cried Ulf, handing the token to Alric, "and see that ye deserve all this praise. And now, sirs, let us fare to the hall to sup and prepare for our journey to the Springs."

The crowd at once broke up and hurried away to Ulfstede in separate groups, discussing eagerly as they went, and stepping out like men who had some pressing business on hand. Alric had already darted away like a hunted deer.

Erling turned hastily aside and went away alone. As soon as he reached a spot where the rugged nature of the ground concealed him from his late companions, he started up the valley at his utmost speed, directing his course so as to enable him to overshoot and intercept his brother. He passed a gorge ahead of the boy; and then, turning suddenly to the left, bore down upon him. So well did he calculate the distance, that on turning round the edge of a jutting cliff he met him face to face, and the two ran somewhat violently into each other's arms.

On being relieved from this involuntary embrace, Alric stepped back and opened his eyes wide with surprise, while Erling roared with laughter.

"Ye are merry, my brother," said Alric, relaxing into a grin, "but I have seen thee often thus, and may not stop to observe thee now, seeing that it is nothing new."

"Give me an arrow, thou rogue! There," said Erling, splitting the shaft into four parts, handing it back to the boy, and taking the baton from him. "Get thee gone, and use thy legs well. We must not do the King the dishonour to appear before him without our weapons in these unsettled times. Let the token be sent out north, south, east, and west; and, harkee, lad, say nothing to anyone about the object of the assembly."

Alric's countenance became grave, then it again relaxed into a broad grin. Giving his brother an emphatic wink with one of his large blue eyes, he darted past him, and was soon far up the glen, running with the speed of a deer and waving the war-token over his head.

CHAPTER IV.

*Describes Warlike Preparations, and a Norse Hall
in the Olden Time — Tells also of a Surprise.*

Instead of returning to Ulfstede, Erling directed his steps homeward at a brisk pace, and in a short space of time reached the door of his forge. Here he met one of his father's thralls.

"Ho! fellow," said he, "is thy mistress at home?"

"Yes, master, she is in the hall getting supper ready against your father's return."

"Go tell her there will be no men to eat supper in the hall to-night," said Erling, unfastening the door of the forge. "Say that I am in the forge, and will presently be in to speak with her. Go also to Thorer, and tell him to get the house-carles busked for war. When they are ready let him come hither to me; and, harkee, use thine utmost speed; there may be bloody work for us all to do this night before the birds are on the wing. Away!"

The man turned and ran to the house, while Erling blew up the smouldering fire of the forge. Throwing off his jerkin, he rolled up his sleeves, and seizing the axe on which he had been engaged when Hilda interrupted him, he wrought so vigorously at the stubborn metal with the great forehammer that in the course of half an hour it was ready to fit on the haft. There was a bundle of hafts in a corner of the workshop. One of these, a tough thick one without knot or flaw, and about five feet long, he fitted to the iron head with great neatness and skill. The polishing of this formidable weapon he deferred to a period of greater leisure. Having completed this piece of work, Erling next turned to another corner of the forge and took up the huge two-handed sword which he had made for his friend Glumm.

The weapon was beautifully executed, and being highly polished, the blade glittered with a flashing light in the ruddy glare of the forge fire. The young giant sat down on his anvil and put a few finishing touches to the sword, regarding it the while with a grim smile, as if he speculated on the probability of his having formed a weapon wherewith his own skull was destined to be cloven asunder. While he was thus engaged his mother Herfrida entered.

The soft-eyed dame could scarcely be called a matronly personage. Having married when about sixteen, she was now just thirty-eight years of age; and though the bloom of maidenhood was gone, the beauty of a well-favoured and healthy woman still remained. She wore a cloak of rich blue wool, and under it a scarlet kirtle with a silver girdle.

"How now, my son," she said; "why these warlike preparations?"

"Because there is rumour of war; I'm sure that is neither strange nor new to you, mother."

"Truly no; and well do I know that where war is, there my husband and my son will be found."

Herfrida said this with a feeling of pride, for, like most of the women of that time and country, she esteemed most highly the men who were boldest and could use their weapons best.

"'Twere well if we were less noted in that way, and more given to peace," said Erling half-jestingly. "For my own part, I have no liking for war, but you women will be for ever egging us on!"

Herfrida laughed. She was well aware of what she was pleased to term her son's weakness, namely, an idea that he loved peace, while he was constantly proving to the world that he was just cut out for war. Had he ever shown a spark of cowardice she would have regarded those speeches of his with much anxiety, but as it was she only laughed at them.

"Erling, my boy," she said suddenly, as her eye fell on the axe at his side, – "what terrible weapon is this? Surely thou must have purchased Thor's hammer. Can ye wield such a thing?"

"I hope so, mother," said Erling curtly; "if not, I shall soon be in Valhalla's halls."

"What are these rumours of war that are abroad just now?" asked Herfrida.

Erling replied by giving his mother an account of King Harald's recent deeds, and told her of the calling of the Thing, and of the appearance of the Danish vikings off the coast.

"May good spirits attend thee, my son!" she said, kissing the youth's forehead fervently, as a natural gush of tenderness and womanly anxiety filled her breast for a moment. But the feeling passed away as quickly as it came; for women who are born and nurtured in warlike times become accustomed and comparatively indifferent to danger, whether it threatens themselves or those most dear to them.

While mother and son were conversing, Thorer entered the smithy, bearing Erling's armour.

"Are the lads all a-boun[5]?" enquired Erling as he rose.

"Aye, master; and I have brought your war-gear."

The man who thus spoke was Haldor's chief house-carle. He was a very short and extremely powerful man of about forty-five years of age, and so sturdy and muscular as to have acquired the title of Thorer the Thick. He wore a shirt of scale armour, rather rusty, and somewhat the worse of having figured in many a tough battle by land and sea. A triangular shield hung at his back, and his head-piece was a simple peaked helmet of iron, with a prolongation in front that guarded his nose. Thorer's offensive armour consisted of a short straight sword, a javelin and a bow, with a quiver of arrows.

"How many men hast thou assembled, Thorer?" asked Erling as he donned his armour.

"Seventy-five, master; the rest are up on the fells, on what errand I know

5   Armed and ready.

not."

"Seventy-five will do. Haste thee, carle, and lead them to my longship the Swan. Methinks we will skate[6] upon the ocean to-night. I will follow thee. Let every man be at his post, and quit not the shore till I come on board. Now fare away as swiftly as may be, and see that everything be done stealthily; above all, keep well out of sight of Ulfstede."

Thus admonished, Thorer quickly left the forge; and a few seconds later the clanking tread of armed men was heard as Erling's followers took their way to the fiord.

"Now I will to the hall, my son, and pray that thou mayst fare well," said Herfrida, once more kissing the forehead which the youth lowered to receive the parting salute. The mother retired, and left her son standing in the forge gazing pensively at the fire, the dying flames of which shot up fitfully now and then, and gleamed on his shining mail.

If Erling the Bold was a splendid specimen of a man in his ordinary costume, when clad in the full panoply of war he was truly magnificent. The rude but not ungraceful armour of the period was admirably fitted to display to advantage the elegant proportions of his gigantic figure. A shirt or tunic of leather, covered with steel rings, hung loosely – yet, owing to its weight, closely – on his shoulders. This was gathered in at the waist by a broad leathern belt, studded with silver ornaments, from which hung a short dagger. A cross belt of somewhat similar make hung from his right shoulder, and supported a two-edged sword of immense weight, which was quite as strong, though not nearly so long, as that which he had forged for Glumm. It was intended for a single-handed weapon, though men of smaller size might have been constrained, in attempting to wield it, to make use of both hands. The youth's lower limbs were clothed in closely-fitting leather leggings, and a pair of untanned leather shoes, laced with a single thong, protected his feet. On his head he wore a small skull-cap, or helmet, of burnished steel, from the top of which rose a pair of hawk's wings expanded, as if in the act of flight. No gloves or gauntlets covered his hands, but on his left arm hung a large shield, shaped somewhat like an elongated heart, with a sharp point at its lower end. Its top touched his shoulder, and the lower part reached to his knee.

This shield was made of several plies of thick bull-hide, with an outer coat of iron – the whole being riveted firmly together with iron studs. It was painted pure white, without device of any kind, but there was a band of azure blue round it, near the margin – the rim itself being of polished steel. In addition to his enormous axe, sword, and dagger, Erling carried at his back a short bow and a quiver full of arrows.

The whole of this war gear bore evidence of being cherished with the utmost care and solicitude. Every ring on the tunic was polished as highly as the

6   Longships, or war-vessels, were sometimes called ocean-skates.

metal would admit of, so that the light appeared to trickle over it as its wearer moved. The helmet shone like a globe of quicksilver, and lines of light gleamed on the burnished edge of the shield, or sparkled on the ornamental points of the more precious metals with which the various parts of his armour were decorated. Above all hung a loose mantle or cloak of dark-blue cloth, which was fastened on the right shoulder with a large circular brooch of silver.

The weight of this panoply was enormous, but long habit had so inured the young Norseman to the burthen of his armour that he moved under it as lightly as if it had been no heavier than his ordinary habiliments. Indeed, so little did it impede his movements that he could spring over chasms and mountain streams almost as well with as without it; and it was one of the boasts of his admiring friends that "he could leap his own height with all his war gear on!"

We have already referred to Erling's partiality for the axe as an offensive weapon. This preference was in truth — strange though the assertion may appear — owing to the peculiar adaptation of that instrument to the preservation of life as well as the taking of it!

There are exceptions to all rules. The rule among the Northmen in former years was to slay and spare not. Erling's tendency, and occasionally his practice, was to spare and not to slay, if he could do so with propriety. From experience he found that, by a slight motion of his wrist, the edge of his axe could be turned aside, and the blow which was delivered by its flat side was invariably sufficient, without killing, to render the recipient utterly incapable of continuing or renewing the combat — at least for a few days. With the sword this delicate manoeuvre could not be so easily accomplished, for a blow from the flat of a sword was not sufficiently crushing, and if delivered with great force the weapon was apt to break. Besides, Erling was a blunt, downright, straightforward man, and it harmonised more with his feelings, and the energy of his character, to beat down sword and shield and headpiece with one tremendous blow, than to waste time in fencing with a lighter weapon.

Having completed his toilet and concluded his meditations — which latter filled him with much perplexity, if one might judge from the frequency with which he shook his head — Erling the Bold hung Glumm's long sword at his back, laid his huge axe on his shoulder, and, emerging from the smithy, strode rapidly along the bridle path that led to the residence of Ulf of Romsdal.

Suddenly it occurred to him that he had not yet tried the temper of his new weapon, so he stopped abruptly before a small pine tree, about as thick as a man's arm. It stood on the edge of a precipice along the margin of which the track skirted. Swaying the axe once round his head, he brought it forcibly down on the stem, through which it passed as if it had been a willow wand, and the tree went crashing into the ravine below. The youth looked earnestly at his weapon, and nodded his head once or twice as if the result were satisfactory. A benignant smile played on his countenance as he replaced it on his shoulder and continued on his way.

A brisk walk of half an hour brought him to Ulfstede, where he found the men of the family making active preparations for the impending journey to the

Thing. In the great hall of the house, his father held earnest discussion with Ulf. The house-carles busied themselves in burnishing their mail and sharpening their weapons, while Ada and Hilda assisted Dame Astrid, Ulf's wife, to spread the board for the evening meal.

Everything in the hall was suggestive of rude wealth and barbarous warlike times. The hall itself was unusually large — capable of feasting at least two hundred men. At one end a raised hearth sustained a fire of wood that was large enough to have roasted an ox. The smoke from this, in default of a chimney, found an exit through a hole in the roof. The rafters were, of course, smoked to a deep rich coffee colour, and from the same cause the walls also partook not a little of that hue. All round these walls hung, in great profusion, shields, spears, swords, bows, skins, horns, and such like implements and trophies of war and the chase. The centre of the hall was open, but down each side ran two long tables, which were at this time groaning with great haunches of venison, legs of mutton, and trenchers of salmon, interspersed with platters of wild fowl, and flanked by tankards and horns of mead and ale. Most of the drinking cups were of horn, but many of these were edged with a rim of silver, and, opposite the raised seats of honour, in the centre of each table, the tankards were of solid silver, richly though rudely chased — square, sturdy, and massive, like the stout warriors who were wont to quaff their foaming contents.

"I tell thee, Ulf," said Haldor, "thou wilt do wrong to fare to the Thing with men fully armed when the token was one of peace. The King is in no mood just now to brook opposition. If we would save our independence we must speak him smoothly."

"I care not," replied Ulf gruffly; "this is no time to go about unarmed."

"Nay, I did not advise thee to go unarmed, but surely a short sword might suffice, and —"

At this moment Erling entered, and Ulf burst into a loud laugh as he interrupted his friend: "Aye, a short sword — something like that," he said, pointing to the huge hilt which rose over the youth's shoulder.

"Hey! lad," exclaimed his father, "art going to fight with an axe in one hand and a sword in the other?"

"The sword is for Glumm, father. I owe him one after this morning's work. Here, friend Glumm, buckle it on thy shoulder. The best wish that thou and I can exchange is, that thy sword and my axe may never kiss each other."

"Truly, if they ever do, I know which will fare worst," said Haldor, taking the axe and examining it, "Thou art fond of a weary arm, my lad, else ye would not have forged so weighty a weapon. Take my advice and leave it behind thee."

"Come, come," interrupted Ulf; "see, the tables are spread; let us use our jaws on food and drink, and not on words, for we shall need both to fit us for the work before us, and perchance we may have no longer need of either before many days go by. We can talk our fill at the Thing, an it so please us."

"That will depend on the King's pleasure," replied Haldor, laughing.

"So much the more reason for taking our arms with us, in order that we may have the means of talking the King's pleasure," retorted Ulf with a frown;

"but sit ye down at my right hand, Haldor, and Hilda will wait upon thee. Come, my men all — let us fall to."

It is scarcely necessary to say that this invitation was accepted with alacrity. In a few minutes about fifty pairs of jaws were actively employed in the manner which Ulf recommended.

Meanwhile Erling the Bold seated himself at the lower end of one of the tables, in such a position that he could keep his eye on the outer door, and, if need be, steal away unobserved. He calculated that his little brother must soon return from his flying journey, and he expected to hear from him some news of the vikings. In this expectation he was right; but when Alric did come, Erling saw and heard more than he looked for.

The meal was about half concluded, and Ulf was in the act of pledging, not absent, but defunct, friends, when the door opened slowly, and Alric thrust his head cautiously in. His hair, dripping and tangled, bore evidence that his head at least had been recently immersed in water.

He caught sight of Erling, and the head was at once withdrawn. Next moment Erling stood outside of the house.

"How now, Alric, what has befallen thee? Hey! thou art soaking all over!"

"Come here; I'll show you a fellow who will tell you all about it."

In great excitement the boy seized his brother's hand and dragged rather than led him round the end of the house, where the first object that met his view was a man whose face was covered with blood, which oozed from a wound in his forehead, while the heaving of his chest, and an occasional gasp, seemed to indicate that he had run far and swiftly.

CHAPTER V.

*The Viking Raid — Alric's Adventure with the Dane —
Erling's Cutter, and the Battle in the Pass.*

"Whom have we here?" exclaimed Erling, looking close into the face of the wounded man. "What! Swart of the Springs!"

Erling said this sternly, for he had no liking for Swart, who was a notorious character, belonging to one of the neighbouring fiords — a wild reckless fellow, and, if report said truly, a thief.

"That recent mischief has cost thee a cracked crown?" asked Erling, a little more gently, as he observed the exhausted condition of the man.

"Mischief enough," said Swart, rising from the stone on which he had seated himself, and wiping the blood, dust, and sweat from his haggard face, while his eyes gleamed like coals of fire; "Skarpedin the Dane has landed in the fiord, my house is a smoking pile, my children and most of the people in the stede are burned, and the Springs run blood!"

There was something terrible in the hoarse whisper in which this was hissed out between the man's teeth. Erling's tone changed instantly as he laid his hand on Swart's shoulder.

"Can this be true?" he answered anxiously; "are we too late? are *all* gone?"

"*All*," answered Swart, "save the few fighting men that gained the fells." The man then proceeded to give a confused and disjointed account of the raid, of which the following is the substance.

Skarpedin, a Danish viking, noted for his daring, cruelty, and success, had taken it into his head to visit the neighbourhood of Horlingdal, and repay in kind a visit which he had received in Denmark the previous summer from a party of Norsemen, on which occasion his crops had been burned, his cattle slaughtered, and his lands "herried", while he chanced to be absent from home.

It must be observed that this deed of the Northmen was not deemed unusually wicked. It was their custom, and the custom also of their enemies, to go out every summer on viking cruise to plunder and ravage the coasts of Denmark, Sweden, Britain, and France, carrying off all the booty they could lay hold of, and as many prisoners as they wanted or could obtain. Then, returning home, they made slaves or "thralls" of their prisoners, often married the women, and spent the winter in the enjoyment of their plunder.

Among many other simple little habits peculiar to the times was that called "Strandhug". It consisted in a viking, when in want of provisions, landing with his men on any coast — whether that of an enemy or a countryman — and driving as many cattle as he required to the shore, where they were immediately slaughtered and put on board without leave asked or received!

Skarpedin was influenced both by cupidity and revenge. Swart had been one of the chief leaders of the expedition which had done him so much damage. To the Springs therefore he directed his course with six "longships", or ships of war, and about five hundred men.

In the afternoon of a calm day he reached the fiord at the head of which were the Springs and Swart's dwelling. There was a small hamlet at the place, and upon this the vikings descended. So prompt and silent were they, that the men of the place had barely time to seize their arms and defend their homes. They fought like lions, for well they knew that there was no hope of mercy if they should be beaten. But the odds against them were overwhelming. They fell in heaps, with many of their foes underneath them. The few who remained to the last retreated fighting, step by step, each man towards his own dwelling, where he fell dead on its threshold. Swart himself, with a few of the bravest, had driven back that part of the enemy's line which they attacked. Thus they were separated for a time from their less successful comrades, and it was not till the smoke of their burning homesteads rose up in dense clouds that they became aware of the true state of the fight. At once they turned and ran to the rescue of their families, but their retreat was cut off by a party of the enemy, and the roar of the conflagration told them that they were too late. They drew together, therefore, and, making a last desperate onset, hewed their way right through the ranks of their enemies, and made for the mountains. All were more or less wounded in the *mêlée*, and only one or two succeeded in effecting their escape. Swart dashed past his own dwelling in his flight, and found it already down on the ground in a blazing ruin. He killed several of the men who were about it, and then, bounding up the mountain side, sought refuge in a ravine.

Here he lay down to rest a few moments. During the brief period of his stay he saw several of his captured friends have their hands and feet chopped off by the marauders, while a terrible shriek that arose once or twice told him all too plainly that on a few of them had been perpetrated the not uncommon cruelty of putting out the eyes.

Swart did not remain many moments inactive. He descended by a circuitous path to the shore, and, keeping carefully out of sight, set off in the direction of Horlingdal. The distance between the two places was little more than nine or ten miles, but being separated from each other by a ridge of almost inaccessible mountains, that rose to a height of above five thousand feet, neither sight nor sound of the terrible tragedy enacted at the Springs could reach the eyes or ears of the inhabitants of Ulfstede. Swart ran round by the coast, and made such good use of his legs that he reached the valley in little more than an hour. Before arriving at Ulfstede his attention was attracted and his step arrested by the sight of a warship creeping along the fiord close under the shadow of the precipitous cliffs. He at once conjectured that this was one of the Danish vessels which had been dispatched to reconnoitre Horlingdal. He knew by its small size (having only about twenty oars) that it could not be there for the purpose of attack. He crouched, therefore, among the rocks to escape observation.

Now, it happened at this very time that Erling's brother Alric, having executed his commission by handing the war-token to the next messenger, whose duty it was to pass it on, came whistling gaily down a neighbouring gorge, slashing the bushes as he went with a stout stick, which in the lad's eyes represented the broadsword or battle-axe he hoped one day to wield, in similar fashion, on the heads of his foes. Those who knew Erling well could have traced his likeness in every act and gesture of the boy. The vikings happened to observe Alric before he saw them, as was not to be wondered at, considering the noise he made. They therefore rowed close in to the rocks, and their leader, a stout red-haired fellow, leaped on shore, ascended the cliffs by a narrow ledge or natural footpath, and came to a spot which overhung the sea, and round which the boy must needs pass. Here the man paused, and leaning on the haft of his battle-axe, awaited his coming up.

It is no disparagement to Alric to say that, when he found himself suddenly face to face with this man, his mouth opened as wide as did his eyes, that the colour fled from his cheeks, that his heart fluttered like a bird in a cage, and that his lips and tongue became uncommonly dry! Well did the little fellow know that one of the Danish vikings was before him, for many a time had he heard the men in Haldorstede describe their dress and arms minutely; and well did he know also that mercy was only to be purchased at the price of becoming an informer as to the state of affairs in Horlingdal – perhaps a guide to his father's house. Besides this, Alric had never up to that time beheld a *real* foe, even at a distance! He would have been more than mortal, therefore, had he shown no sign of trepidation.

"Thou art light of heart, lad," said the Dane with a grim smile.

Alric would perhaps have replied that his heart was the reverse of light at that moment, but his tongue refused to fulfil its office, so he sighed deeply, and tried to lick his parched lips instead.

"Thou art on thy way to Ulfstede or Haldorstede, I suppose?" said the man.

Alric nodded by way of reply.

"To which?" demanded the Dane sternly.

"T-to – to Ulf –"

"Ha!" interrupted the man. "I see. I am in want of a guide thither. Wilt guide me, lad?"

At this the truant blood rushed back to Alric's cheeks. He attempted to say no, and to shake his head, but the tongue was still rebellious, and the head would not move – at least not in that way – so the poor boy glanced slightly aside, as if meditating flight. The Dane, without altering his position, just moved his foot on the stones, which act had the effect of causing the boy's eyes to turn full on him again with that species of activity which cats are wont to display when expecting an immediate assault.

"Escape is impossible," said the Dane, with another grim smile.

Alric glanced at the precipice on his left, full thirty feet deep, with the sea below; at the precipice on his right, which rose an unknown height above; at the steep rugged path behind, and at the wild rugged man in front, who could have clutched him with one bound; and admitted in his heart that escape *was* impossible.

"Now, lad," continued the viking, "thou wilt go with me and point out the way to Ulfstede and Haldorstede; if not with a good will, torture shall cause thee to do it against thy will; and after we have plundered and burnt both, we will give thee a cruise to Denmark, and teach thee the use of the pitchfork and reaping-hook."

This remark touched a chord in Alric's breast which at once turned his thoughts from himself, and allowed his native courage to rise. During the foregoing dialogue his left hand had been nervously twitching the little elm bow which it carried. It now grasped the bow firmly as he replied:

"Ulfstede and Haldorstede may burn, but thou shalt not live to see it."

With that he plucked an arrow from his quiver, fitted it to the string, and discharged it full at the Dane's throat. Quick as thought the man of war sprang aside, but the shaft had been well and quickly aimed. It passed through his neck between the skin and the flesh.

A cry of anger burst from him as he leaped on the boy and caught him by the throat. He hastily felt for the hilt of his dagger, and in the heat of his rage would assuredly have ended the career of poor Alric then and there; but, missing the hilt at the first grasp, he suddenly changed his mind, lifted the boy as if he had been a little dog, and flung him over the precipice into the sea.

A fall of thirty feet, even though water should be the recipient of the shock, is not a trifle by any means, but Alric was one of those vigorous little fellows — of whom there are fortunately many in this world — who train themselves to feats of strength and daring. Many a time had he, when bathing, leaped off that identical cliff into the sea for his own amusement, and to the admiration and envy of many of his companions, and, now that he felt himself tumbling in the air against his will, the sensation, although modified, was nothing new. He straightened himself out after the manner of a bad child that does not wish to sit on nurse's knee, and went into the blue fiord, head foremost, like a javelin.

He struck the water close to the vessel of his enemies, and on rising to the surface one of them made a plunge at him with an oar, which, had it taken effect, would have killed him on the spot; but he missed his aim, and before he could repeat it, the boy had dived.

The Dane was sensible of his error the instant he had tossed Alric away from him, so he hastened to his boat, leaped into it, and ordered the men to pull to the rocks near to which Alric had dived; but before they could obey the order a loud ringing cheer burst from the cliffs, and in another moment the form of Swart was seen on a ledge, high above, in the act of hurling a huge mass of rock down on the boat. The mass struck the cliff in its descent, burst into fragments, and fell in a shower upon the Danes.

At the same time Swart waved his hand as if to someone behind him, and shouted with stentorian voice:

"This way, men! Come on! Down into the boats and give chase! huzza!"

The enemy did not await the result of the order, but pulled out into the fiord as fast as possible, while Swart ran down to the edge of the water and assisted Alric to land. It was not until they heard both man and boy utter a cheer of defiance, and burst into a fit of laughter, and saw them hastening at full speed towards Horlingdal, that the vikings knew they had been duped. It was too late, however, to remedy the evil. They knew, also, that they might now expect an immediate attack, so, bending to the oars with all their might, they hastened off to warn their comrades at the Springs.

"Now, Swart," said Erling, after hearing this tale to its conclusion, "if ye are not too much exhausted to —"

"Exhausted!" cried Swart, springing up as though he had but risen from a refreshing slumber.

"Well, I see thou art still fit for the fight. Revenge, like love, is a powerful stirrer of the blood. Come along then; I will lead the way, and do thou tread softly and keep silence. Follow us, Alric, I have yet more work for thee, lad."

Taking one of the numerous narrow paths that ran from Ulfstede to the shores of the fiord, Erling led his companions to a grassy mound which crowned the top of a beetling cliff whose base was laved by deep water. Although the night was young — probably two hours short of midnight — the sun was still high in the heavens, for in most parts of Norway that luminary, during the height of summer, sinks but a short way below the horizon — they have daylight all night for some time. In the higher latitudes the sun, for a brief period, shines all the twenty-four hours round. Erling could therefore see far and wide over the fiord, as well as if it were the hour of noon.

"Nothing in sight!" he exclaimed in a tone of chagrin. "I was a fool to let thee talk so long, Swart; but there is still a chance of catching the boat before it rounds the ness. Come along."

Saying this hurriedly, the youth descended into what appeared to be a hole in the ground. A rude zigzag stair cut in the rock conducted them into a subterranean cavern, which at first seemed to be perfectly dark; but in a few seconds their eyes became accustomed to the dim light, and as they advanced rapidly over a bed of pebbles, Swart, who had never been there before, discovered that he was in an ocean-made cave, for the sound of breaking ripples fell softly on his ears. On turning round a corner of rock the opening of the cave towards the sea suddenly appeared with a dazzling light like a great white gem.

But another beautiful sight met his astonished gaze. This was Erling's ship of war, the Swan, which, with its figurehead erect, as though it were a living thing, sat gracefully on the water, above its own reflected image.

"All ready?" asked Erling, as a man stepped up to him.

"All ready," replied Thorer.

"Get on board, Swart," said Erling; "we will teach these Danes a lesson they will not forget as long as the Springs flow. Here, Alric — where are ye, lad?"

Now, unfortunately for himself, as well as for his friend, Alric was almost too self-reliant in his nature. His active mind was too apt to exert itself in independent thought in circumstances where it would have been wiser to listen and obey. Erling had turned with the intention of telling his little brother that he had started thus quietly in order that he might have the pleasure of capturing the scouting boat, and of beginning the fight at the Springs with a small band of tried men, thus keeping the enemy in play until reinforcements should arrive; for he shrewdly suspected that if the whole valley were to go out at once against the vikings, they would decline the combat and make off. He had intended, therefore, to have warned Alric to watch the Swan past a certain point before sounding the alarm at Ulfstede. But Alric had already formed his own opinions on the subject, and resolved to act on them.

He suspected that Erling, in his thirst for glory, meant to have all the fun to himself, and to attack the Danes with his single boat's crew of fifty or sixty men. He knew enough of war to be aware that sixty men against six hundred would have very small chance of success — in fact, that the thing was sheer madness — so he resolved to balk, and by so doing to save, his headstrong brother.

When Erling turned, as we have said, he beheld Alric running into the cave at full speed. Instantly suspecting the truth, he dashed after him, but the boy was fleet, and Erling was heavily armed. The result was, that the former escaped, while the latter returned to the beach and embarked in the Swan in a most unenviable state of mind.

Erling's "longship" was one of the smaller-sized war vessels of the period. It pulled twenty oars — ten on each side — and belonged to the class named Snekiars, or cutters, which usually had from ten to twenty rowers on a side. To each oar three men were apportioned — one to row, one to shield the rower, and one to throw missiles and fight, so that her crew numbered over sixty men. The forecastle and poop were very high, and the appearance of height was still further increased by the figurehead — the neck and head of a swan — and by a tail that rose from the stern-post, over the steersman's head. Both head and tail were richly gilt; indeed, the whole vessel was gaudily painted. All round the gunwales, from stem to stern, hung a row of shining red and white shields, which resembled the scaly sides of some fabulous creature, so that when the oars, which gave it motion, and not inaptly represented legs, were dipped, the vessel glided swiftly out of the cavern, like some antediluvian monster issuing from its den and crawling away over the dark blue sea. A tall heavy mast rose from the centre of the ship. Its top was also gilded, as well as the tips of the heavy yard attached to it. On this they hoisted a huge square sail, which was composed of alternate stripes of red, white, and blue cloth.

It need scarcely be said that Erling's crew pulled with a will, and that the waters of the fiord curled white upon the breast of the Swan that night; but the vikings' boat had got too long a start of them, so that, when they doubled the ness and pulled towards the Springs, they discovered the enemy hurrying into their ships and preparing to push off from the land.

Now, this did not fall in with Erling's purpose at all, for he was well aware that his little Swan could do nothing against such an overwhelming force, so he directed his course towards the mouth of a small stream, beside which there was a spit of sand, and, just behind it, a piece of level land, of a few acres in extent, covered with short grass. The river was deep at its mouth. About a hundred yards upstream it flowed out of a rugged pass in the mountains or cliffs which hemmed in the fiord. Into this dark spot the Northman rowed his vessel and landed with his men.

The vikings were much surprised at this manoeuvre, and seemed at a loss how to act, for they immediately ceased their hurried embarkation and held a consultation.

"Methinks they are mad," said Skarpedin, on witnessing the movements of the Swan. "But we will give them occasion to make use of all the spirit that is in them. I had thought there were more men in the dale, but if they be few they seem to be bold. They have wisely chosen their ground. Rocks, however, will not avail them against a host like ours. Methinks some of us will be in Valhalla tonight."

Saying this Skarpedin drew up his men in order of battle on the little plain before referred to, and advanced to the attack. Erling, on the other hand, posted his men among the rocks in such a way that they could command the approach to the pass, which their leader with a few picked men defended.

On perceiving the intention of the Danes to attack him, Erling's heart was glad, because he now felt sure that to some extent he had them in his power. If they had, on his first appearance, taken to their ships, they might have easily escaped, or some of the smaller vessels might have pulled up the river and attacked his ship, which, in that case, would have had to meet them on unequal terms; but, now that they were about to attack him on land, he knew that he could keep them in play as long as he pleased, and that if they should, on the appearance of reinforcements, again make for their ships, he could effectively harass them, and retard their embarkation.

Meditating on these things the young Norseman stood in front of his men leaning on his battle-axe, and calmly surveying the approaching foe until they were within a few yards of him.

"Thorer," he said at length, raising his weapon slowly to his shoulder, "take thou the man with the black beard, and leave yonder fellow with the red hair to me."

Thorer drew his sword and glanced along its bright blade without replying. Indeed, there was scarce time for reply. Next moment the combatants uttered a loud shout and met with a dire crash. For some time the clash of steel, the yells of maddened men, the shrieks of the wounded, and the wails of the dying, resounded in horrible commotion among the echoing cliffs. The wisdom of Erling's tactics soon became apparent. It was not until the onset was made, and the battle fairly begun, that the men whom he had placed among the rocks above the approach to the pass began to act. These now sent down such a shower of huge stones and masses of rock that many of the foe were killed, and by degrees a gap was made, so that those who were on the plain dared not advance to the succour of those who were fighting in the pass.

Seeing this, Erling uttered his war-cry, and, collecting his men together, acted on the offensive. Wherever his battle-axe swung, or Thorer's sword gleamed, there men fell, and others gave way, till at last they were driven completely out of the pass and partly across the plain. Erling took care, however, not to advance too far, although Skarpedin, by retreating, endeavoured to entice him to do so; but drew off his men by sound of horn, and returned to his old position — one man only having been killed and a few wounded.

Skarpedin now held a council of war with his chiefs, and from the length of time they were about it, Erling was led to suspect that they did not intend to renew the attack at the same point or in the same manner. He therefore sent men to points of vantage on the cliffs to observe the more distant movements of the enemy, while he remained to guard the pass, and often gazed anxiously towards the ness, round which he expected every minute to see sweeping the longships of Ulf and his father.

CHAPTER VI.

Evening in the Hall — The Scald tells of Gundalf's Wooing —
The Feast Interrupted and the War Clouds Thicken.

It is necessary now that we should turn backwards a little in our story, to that point where Erling left the hall at Ulfstede to listen to the sad tale of Swart.

Ulf and his friends, not dreaming of the troubles that were hanging over them, continued to enjoy their evening meal and listen to the songs and stories of the Scald, or to comment upon the doings of King Harald Haarfager, and the prospects of good or evil to Norway that were likely to result therefrom.

At the point where we return to the hall, Ulf wore a very clouded brow as he sat with compressed lips beside his principal guest. He grasped the arm of his rude chair with his left hand, while his right held a large and massive silver tankard. Haldor, on the other hand, was all smiles and good humour. He appeared to have been attempting to soothe the spirit of his fiery neighbour.

"I tell thee, Ulf, that I have as little desire to see King Harald succeed in subduing all Norway as thou hast, but in this world wise men will act not according to what they wish so much, as according to what is best. Already the King has won over or conquered most of the small kings, and it seems to me that the rest will have to follow, whether they like it or no. Common sense teaches submission where conquest cannot be."

"And does not patriotism teach that men may die?" said Ulf sternly.

"Aye, when by warring with that end in view anything is to be gained for one's country; but where the result would be, first, the embroiling of one's district in prolonged bloody and hopeless warfare, and, after that, the depriving one's family of its head and of the King's favour, patriotism says that to die would be folly, not wisdom."

"Tush, man; folk will learn to call thee Haldor the Mild. Surely years are telling on thee. Was there ever anything in this world worth having gained without a struggle?"

"Thou knowest, Ulf, that I am not wont to be far from the front wherever or whenever a struggle is thought needful, but I doubt the propriety of it in the present case. The subject, however, is open to discussion. The question is, whether it would be better for Norway that the kings of Horlingdal should submit to the conqueror for the sake of the general good, or buckle on the sword in the hope of retrieving what is lost. Peace or war — that is the question."

"I say war!" cried Ulf, striking the board so violently with his clenched fist that the tankards and platters leaped and rang again.

At this a murmur of applause ran round the benches of the friends and housemen.

"The young blades are ever ready to huzza over their drink at the thought of fighting; but methinks it will not strengthen thy cause much, friend Ulf, thus to frighten the women and spill the ale."

Ulf turned round with a momentary look of anger at this speech. The man who uttered it was a splendid specimen of a veteran warrior. His forehead was quite bald, but from the sides and back of his head flowed a mass of luxuriant silky hair which was white as the driven snow. His features were eminently firm and masculine, and there was a hearty good-humoured expression about the mouth, and a genial twinkle in his eyes, especially in the wrinkled corners thereof, that rendered the stout old man irresistibly attractive. His voice was particularly rich, deep, and mellow, like that of a youth, and although his bulky frame stooped a little from age, there was enough of his youthful vigour left to render him a formidable foe, as many a poor fellow had learned to his cost even in days but recently gone by. He was an uncle of Ulf, and on a visit to the stede at that time. The frown fled from Ulf's brow as he looked in the old man's ruddy and jovial countenance.

"Thanks, Guttorm," said he, seizing his tankard, "thanks for reminding me that grey hairs are beginning to sprinkle my beard; come, let us drink success to the right, confusion to the wrong! thou canst not refuse that, Haldor."

"Nay," said Haldor, laughing; "nor will I refuse to fight in thy cause and by thy side, be it right or wrong, when the Thing decides for war."

"Well said, friend! but come, drink deeper. Why, I have taken thee down three pegs already!" said Ulf, glancing into Haldor's tankard. "Ho! Hilda; fetch hither more ale, lass, and fill – fill to the brim." The toast was drunk with right good will by all – from Ulf down to the youngest house-carle at the lowest end of the great hall.

"And now, Guttorm," continued Ulf, turning to the bluff old warrior, "since thou hast shown thy readiness to rebuke, let us see thy willingness to entertain. Sing us a stave or tell us a saga, kinsman, as well thou knowest how, being gifted with more than a fair share of the scald's craft."

The applause with which this proposal was received by the guests and house-carles who crowded the hall from end to end proved that they were aware of Guttorm's gifts, and would gladly hear him. Like a sensible man he complied at once, without affecting that air of false diffidence which is so common among modern songsters and story-tellers.

"I will tell you," said the old man – having previously wet his lips at a silver tankard, which was as bluff and genuine as himself – "of King Gundalf's wooing. Many years have gone by since I followed him on viking cruise, and Gundalf himself has long been feasting in Odin's hall. I was a beardless youth when I joined him. King Gundalf of Orkedal was a goodly man, stout and brisk, and very strong. He could leap on his horse without touching stirrup with all his war gear on; he could fight as well with his left hand as with his right, and his battle-axe bit so deep that none who once felt its edge lived to tell of its weight. He might well be called a Sea-king, for he seldom slept under a sooty roof timber. Withal he was very affable to his men, open-hearted, and an extremely handsome man.

"One summer he ordered us to get ready to go on viking cruise. When we were all a-boun we set sail with five longships and about four hundred men, and fared away to Denmark, where we forayed and fought a great battle with the inhabitants. King Gundalf gained the victory, plundered, wasted, and burned far and wide in the land, and made enormous booty. He returned with this to Orkedal. Here he found his wife at the point of death, and soon after she died. Gundalf felt his loss so much that he had no pleasure in Raumsdal after that. He therefore took to his ships and went again a-plundering. We herried first in Friesland, next in Saxland, and then all the way to Flanders; so sings Halfred the scald:

> "'Gundalf's axe of shining steel
> For the sly wolf left many a meal.
> The ill-shaped Saxon corpses lay
> Heap'd up — the witch-wife's horses' prey.
> She rides by night, at pools of blood,
> Where Friesland men in daylight stood,
> Her horses slake their thirst, and fly
> On to the field where Flemings lie.'"

The old warrior half recited half sang these lines in a rich full voice, and then paused a few seconds, while a slight murmur arose from the earnest listeners around him.

"Thereafter," resumed Guttorm, "we sailed to England, and ravaged far and wide in the land. We sailed all the way north to Northumberland, where we plundered, and thence to Scotland, where we marauded far and wide. Then we went to the Hebrides and fought some battles, and after that south to Man, which we herried. We ravaged far around in Ireland, and steered thence to Bretland, which we laid waste with fire and sword — also the district of Cumberland. Then we went to Valland[7], from which we fared away for the south coast of England, but missed it and made the Scilly Isles. After that we went to Ireland again, and came to a harbour, into which we ran — but in a friendly way, for we had as much plunder as our ships could carry.

"Now, while we were there, a summons to a Thing went through the country, and when the Thing was assembled, a queen called Gyda came to it. She was a sister of Olaf Quarram, who was King of Dublin. Gyda was very wealthy, and her husband had died that year. In the territory there was a man called Alfin, who was a great champion and single-combat man. He had paid his addresses to Gyda, but she gave for answer that she would choose a husband for herself; and on that account the Thing was assembled, that she might choose a husband. Alfin came there dressed out in his best clothes, and there were many well-dressed men at the meeting. Gundalf and some of his men had gone there also, out of curiosity, but we had on our bad-weather clothes, and Gundalf wore

7   The west coast of France.

a coarse over-garment. We stood apart from the rest of the crowd, Gyda went round and looked at each, to see if any appeared to her a suitable man. Now when she came to where we were standing, she passed most of us by with a glance; but when she passed me, I noticed that she turned half round and gave me another look, which I have always held was a proof of her good judgment. However, Gyda passed on, and when she came to King Gundalf she stopped, looked at him straight in the face, and asked what sort of a man he was.

"He said, 'I am called Gundalf, and am a stranger here!'

"Gyda replies, 'Wilt thou have me if I choose thee?' He answered, 'I will not say No to that;' then he asked her what her name was, and her family and descent.

"'I am called Gyda,' said she, 'and am daughter of the King of Ireland, and was married in this country to an earl who ruled over this district. Since his death I have ruled over it, and many have courted me, but none to whom I would choose to be married.'

"She was a young and handsome woman. They afterwards talked over the matter together and agreed, and so Gundalf and Gyda were betrothed.

"Alfin was very ill pleased with this. It was the custom there, as it is sometimes here, if two strove for anything, to settle the matter by holm-gang.[8] And now Alfin challenged Gundalf to fight about this business. The time and place of combat were settled, and it was fixed that each should have twelve men. I was one of the twelve on our side. When we met, Gundalf told us to do exactly as we saw him do. He had a large axe, and went in advance of us, and when Alfin made a desperate cut at him with his sword, he hewed away the sword out of his hand, and with the next blow hit Alfin on the crown with the flat of his axe and felled him. We all met next moment, and each man did his best; but it was hard work, for the Irishmen fought well, and two of them cut down two of our men, but one of these I knocked down, and Gundalf felled the other. Then we bound them all fast, and carried them to Gundalf's lodging. But Gundalf did not wish to take Alfin's life. He ordered him to quit the country and never again to appear in it, and he took all his property. In this way Gundalf got Gyda in marriage, and he lived sometimes in England and sometimes in Ireland. Thikskul the scald says in regard to this:

"*King Gundalf woo'd Queen Gyda fair,*
With whom no woman could compare,
And won her, too, with all her lands,
By force of looks and might of hands
From Ireland's green and lovely isle
He carried off the Queen in style.

8   Single combat: so called because the combatants in Norway went to a holm, or uninhabited isle, to fight.

He made proud Alfin's weapon dull,
And flattened down his stupid skull —
This did the bold King Gundalf do
When he went o'er the sea to woo.'"

The wholesale robbery and murder which was thus related by the old Norse viking appeared quite a natural and proper state of things in the eyes of all save two of those assembled in the hall, and the saga was consequently concluded amid resounding applause. It is to be presumed that, never having seen or heard of any other course of life, and having always been taught that such doings were quite in accordance with the laws of the land, the consciences of the Northmen did not trouble them. At all events, while we do not for a moment pretend to justify their doings, we think it right to point out that there must necessarily have been a wide difference between their spirits and feelings, and the spirits and feelings of modern pirates, who know that they are deliberately setting at defiance the laws of both God and man.

It has been said there were two in the hall at Ulfstede who did not sympathise with the tale of the old warrior. The reader will scarce require to be told that one of these was Hilda the Sunbeam. The other was Christian the hermit. The old man, although an occasional visitor at the stede, never made his appearance at meal-times, much less at the nightly revels which were held there; but on that day he had arrived with important news, just as Guttorm began his story, and would have unceremoniously interrupted it had not one of the young house-carles, who did not wish to lose the treat, detained him forcibly at the lower end of the hall until it was ended. The moment he was released the hermit advanced hastily, and told Ulf that from the door of his hut on the cliff he had observed bands of men hastening in all directions down the dale.

"Thy news, old man, is no news," said Ulf; "the token for a Thing has been sent out, and it is natural that the bonders should obey the summons. We expect them. But come, it is not often thou favourest us with thy company. Sit down by me, and take a horn of mead."

The hermit shook his head.

"I never taste strong liquor. Its tendency is to make wise men foolish," he said.

"Nay, then, thou wilt not refuse to eat. Here, Hilda, fetch thy friend a platter."

"I thank thee, but, having already supped, I need no more food. I came but to bring what I deemed news."

"Thou art churlish, old man," exclaimed Ulf angrily; "sit down and drink, else —"

"Come, come," interrupted Haldor, laying his hand on Ulf's arm, "Let the old man be; he seems to think that he has something worth hearing to tell of; let him have his say out in peace."

"Go on," said Ulf gruffly.

"Was the token sent out a baton or a split arrow?" asked the hermit.

"A baton," said Ulf.

"Then why," rejoined the other, "do men come to a peaceful Thing with all their war gear on?"

"What say ye? are they armed?" exclaimed Ulf, starting up. "This must be looked to. Ho! my carles all, to arms —"

At that moment there was a bustle at the lower end of the hall, and Alric was seen forcing his way towards Ulf's high seat.

"Father," he said eagerly, addressing Haldor, "short is the hour for acting, and long the hour for feasting."

Haldor cast his eyes upon his son and said —

"What now is in the way?"

"The Danes," said Alric, "are on the fiord — more than six hundred men. Skarpedin leads them. One of them pitched me into the sea, but I marked his neck to keep myself in his memory! They have plundered and burnt at the Springs, and Erling has gone away to attack them all by himself, with only sixty house-carles. You will have to be quick, father."

"Quick, truly," said Haldor, with a grim smile, as he drew tight the buckle of his sword-belt.

"Aye," said Ulf, "with six hundred Danes on the fiord, and armed men descending the vale, methinks —"

"Oh! I can explain that" cried Alric, with an arch smile; "Erling made me change the baton for the split arrow when I was sent round with the token."

"That is good luck," said Haldor, while Ulf's brow cleared a little as he busked himself for the fight; "we shall need all our force."

"Aye, and all our time too," said Guttorm Stoutheart, as he put on his armour with the cheerful air of a man who dons his wedding dress. "Come, my merry men all. Lucky it is that my longships are at hand just now ready loaded with stones:

> "'O! a gallant sight it is to me,
> The warships darting o'er the sea,
> A pleasant sound it is to hear
> The war trump ringing loud and clear.'"

Ulf and his friends and house-carles were soon ready to embark, for in those days the Norseman kept his weapons ready to his hands, being accustomed to sudden assaults and frequent alarms. They streamed out of the hall, and while some collected stones, to be used as missiles, others ran down to the shore to launch the ships. Meanwhile Ulf, Haldor, Guttorm, and other chief men held a rapid consultation, as they stood and watched the assembling of the men of the district.

It was evident that the split arrow had done its duty. From the grassy mound on which they stood could be seen, on the one hand, the dark recesses of Horlingdal, which were lost in the mists of distance among the glaciers on the fells; and, on the other hand, the blue fiord with branching inlets and numerous holms, while the skerries of the coast filled up the background — looming faint and far off on the distant sea. In whatever direction the eye was turned armed men were seen. From every distant gorge and valley on the fells they issued, singly, or in twos and threes. As they descended the dale they formed into groups and larger bands; and when they gained the more level grounds around Haldorstede, the heavy tread of their hastening footsteps could be distinctly heard, while the sun — for although near midnight now it was still above the horizon — flashed from hundreds of javelins, spears, swords, and bills, glittered on steel headpieces and the rims of shields, or trickled fitfully on suits of scale armour and shirts of ring mail. On the fiord, boats came shooting forth from every inlet or creek, making their appearance from the base of precipitous cliffs or dark-mouthed caves as if the very mountains were bringing forth warriors to aid in repelling the foe. These were more sombre than those on the fells, because the sun had set to them by reason of the towering hills, and the fiord was shrouded in deepest gloom. But all in the approaching host — on water and land — were armed from head to foot, and all converged towards Ulfstede.

When they were all assembled they numbered five hundred fighting men — and a stouter or more valiant band never went forth to war. Six longships were sufficient to embark them. Three of these were of the largest size — having thirty oars on each side, and carrying a hundred men. One of them belonged to Haldor, one to Ulf, and one — besides several smaller ships — to Guttorm, who chanced to be on viking cruise at the time he had turned aside to visit his kinsman. The warlike old man could scarce conceal his satisfaction at his unexpected good fortune in being so opportunely at hand when hard blows were likely to be going! Two of the other ships were cutters, similar to Erling's Swan, and carrying sixty men each, and one was a little larger, holding about eighty men. It belonged to Glumm the Gruff, whose gruffness, however, had abated considerably, now that there was a prospect of what we moderns would call "letting the steam off" in a vigorous manner.

Soon the oars were dipped in the fiord, and the sails were set, for a light favourable wind was blowing. In a short time the fleet rounded the ness, and came in sight of the ground where Erling and Skarpedin were preparing to renew the combat.

CHAPTER VII.

The Tale Returns to the Springs — Describes a Great Land Fight, and Tells of a Peculiar Style of Extending Mercy to the Vanquished.

In a previous chapter we left Skarpedin discussing with his chiefs the best mode of attacking the small band of his opponents in the pass of the Springs. They had just come to a decision, and were about to act on it, when they suddenly beheld six warships sweeping round the ness.

"Now will we have to change our plans," said Skarpedin.

Thorvold agreed with this, and counselled getting on board their ships and meeting the enemy on the water; but the other objected, because he knew that while his men were in the act of embarking, Erling would sally forth and kill many of them before they could get away.

"Methinks," said he, "I will take forty of my best men, and try to entice that fox out of his hole, before he has time to see the ships."

"Grief only will come of that," says Thorvold.

Skarpedin did not reply, but choosing forty of his stoutest carles he went to the pass and defied Erling to come out and fight.

"Now here am I, Erling, with forty men. Wilt thou come forth? or is thy title of Bold ill bestowed, seeing thou hast more men than I?"

"Ill should I deserve the title," replies Erling, "if I were to meet thee with superior force."

With that he chose thirty men, and, running down to the plain, gave the assault so fiercely that men fell fast on every side, and the Danes gave back a little. When they saw this, and that Erling and Thorer hewed men down wherever they went, the Danes made a shield circle round Skarpedin, as was the custom when kings went into battle; because they knew that if he fell there would be no one so worthy to guide them in the fight with the approaching longships. Thus they retreated, fighting. When Erling and his men had gone far enough, they returned to the pass, and cheered loudly as they went, both because of the joy of victory, and because they saw the warships of their friends coming into the bay.

King Haldor and his companions at once ran their ships on the beach near the mouth of the river, and, landing, drew them up, intending to fight on shore. Skarpedin did not try to prevent this, for he was a bold man, and thought that with so large a force he could well manage to beat the Northmen, if they would fight on level ground. He therefore drew up his men in order of battle at one end of the plain, and Haldor the Fierce, to whom was assigned the chief command, drew up the Northmen at the other end. Erling joined them with his band, and then it was seen that the two armies were not equal — that of the Northmen being a little smaller than the other.

Then Haldor said, "Let us draw up in a long line that they may not turn our flanks, as they have most men."

This was done, and Haldor advanced into the plain and set up his banner. The Danes in like manner advanced and planted their banner, and both armies rushed to the attack, which was very sharp and bloody. Wherever the battle raged most fiercely there King Haldor and Erling were seen, for they were taller by half a head than most other men. Being clothed alike in almost every respect, they looked more like brothers than father and son. Each wore a gilt helmet, and carried a long shield, the centre of which was painted white, but round the edge was a rim of burnished steel. Each had a sword by his side, and carried a javelin to throw, but both depended chiefly on their favourite weapon, the battle-axe, for, being unusually strong, they knew that few men could withstand the weight of a blow from that. The defensive armour of father and son was also the same — a shirt of leather, sewed all over with small steel rings. Their legs were clothed in armour of the same kind, and a mantle of cloth hung from the shoulders of each.

Most of the chief men on both sides were armed in a similar way, though not quite so richly, and with various modifications; for instance, the helmet of Thorvold was of plain steel, and for ornament had the tail of the ptarmigan as its crest. Skarpedin's, on the other hand, was quite plain, but partly gilded; his armour was of pieces of steel like fish scales sewed on a leathern shirt, and over his shoulders he wore as a mantle the skin of a wolf. His chief weapon was a bill — a sort of hook or short scythe fixed to a pole, and it was very deadly in his hands. Most of the carles and thralls were content to wear thick shirts of wolf and other skins, which were found to offer good resistance to a sword-cut, and some of them had portions of armour of various kinds. Their arms were spears, bows, arrows with stone heads, javelins, swords, bills, and battle-axes and shields.

When both lines met there was a hard fight. The combatants first threw their spears and javelins, and then drew their swords and went at each other in the greatest fury. In the centre Haldor and Erling went together in advance of their banner, cutting down on both sides of them. Old Guttorm Stoutheart went in advance of the right wing, also hewing down right and left. With him went Kettle Flatnose, for that ambitious thrall could not be made to remember his position, and was always putting himself in front of his betters in war; yet it is due to him to say that he kept modestly in the background in time of peace. To these was opposed Thorvold, with many of the stoutest men among the Danes.

Now, old Guttorm and Kettle pressed on so hard that they were almost separated from their men; and while Guttorm was engaged with a very tall and strong man, whom he had wounded severely more than once, another stout fellow came between him and Kettle, and made a cut at him with his sword. Guttorm did not observe him, and it seemed as if the old Stoutheart should get his death-wound there; but the thrall chanced to see what was going on. He fought with a sort of hook, like a reaping-hook, fixed at the end of a spear handle, with the cutting edge inside. The men of Horlingdal used to laugh at Kettle because of his fondness for this weapon, which was one of his own contriving; but when they did so, he was wont to reply that it was better than most other weapons, because it could not only make his friends laugh, but his enemies cry!

With this hook the thrall made a quick blow at the Dane; the point of it went down through his helmet into his brain, and that was his deathblow.

"Well done, Kettle!" cried old Guttorm, who had just cleft the skull of his opponent with his sword.

At this Thorvold ran forward and said:

"Well done it may be, but well had it been for the doer had it not been done. Come on, thou flatnose!"

"Now, thou must be a remarkably clever man," retorted Kettle, with much of that rich tone of voice which, many centuries later, came to be known as "the Irish brogue", "for it is plain ye know my name without being told it!"

So saying, with a sudden quick movement he got his hook round Thorvold's neck.

"That is an ugly grip," said Thorvold, making a fierce cut at the haft with his sword; but Kettle pulled the hook to him, and with it came the head, and that was Thorvold's end.

While this was going on at the right wing, the left wing was led by Ulf of Romsdal and Glumm the Gruff; but Ulf's men were not so good as Haldor's men, for he was not so wise a man as Haldor, and did not manage his house so well.

It was a common saying among the people of Horlingdal that Haldor had under him the most valiant men in Norway — and as the master was, so were the men. Haldor never went to sea with less than a fully-manned ship of thirty benches of rowers, and had other large vessels and men to man them as well. One of his ships had thirty-two benches of rowers, and could carry at least two hundred men. He had always at home on his farm thirty slaves or thralls, besides other serving people, and about two hundred house-carles. He used to give his thralls a certain day's work; but after it was done he gave them leave and leisure to work in the twilight and at night for themselves. He gave them arable land to sow corn in, and let them apply their crops to their own use. He fixed a certain quantity of work, by the doing of which his slaves might work themselves free; and this put so much heart into them that many of them worked themselves free in one year, and all who had any luck or pluck could work themselves free in three years. Ulf did this too, but he was not so wise nor yet so kind in his way of doing it. With the money thus procured Haldor bought other slaves. Some of his freed people he taught to work in the herring fishery; to others he taught some handicraft; in short, he helped all of them to prosperity; so that many of the best of them remained fast by their old master, although free to take service where they chose. Thus it was that his men were better than those of his neighbour.

Ulf's men were, nevertheless, good stout fellows, and they fought valiantly; but it so happened that the wing of the enemy to which they were opposed was commanded by Skarpedin, of whom it was said that he was equal to any six men. In spite, therefore, of the courage and the strength of Ulf and Glumm, the

Northmen in that part of the field began slowly to give back. Ulf and Glumm were so maddened at this that they called their men cowards, and resolved to go forward till they should fall. Uttering their war-cry, they made a desperate charge, hewing down men like stalks of corn; but although this caused the Danes to give way a little, they could not advance, not being well backed, but stood fighting, and merely kept their ground.

Now it had chanced shortly before this, that Haldor stayed his hand and drew back with Erling. They went out from the front of the fight, and observed the left wing giving way.

"Come, let, us aid them," cried Haldor.

Saying this he ran to the left wing, with Erling by his side. They two uttered a war-cry that rose high above the din of battle like a roar of thunder, and, rushing to the front, fell upon the foe. Their gilt helmets rose above the crowd, and their ponderous axes went swinging round their heads, continually crashing down on the skulls of the Danes. With four such men as Haldor, Erling, Ulf and Glumm in front, the left wing soon regained its lost ground and drove back the Danes. Nothing could withstand the shock. Skarpedin saw what had occurred, and immediately hastened to the spot where Haldor stood, sweeping down all who stood in his way.

"I have been searching for thee, Erling," he cried, going up to Haldor, and launching a javelin.

Haldor caught it on his shield, which it pierced through, but did him no hurt.

"Mistaken thou art, but thou hast found me now," cried Erling, thrusting his father aside and leaping upon the Dane.

Skarpedin changed his bill to his left hand, drew his sword, and made such a blow at his adversary, that the point cut right through his shield. With a quick turn of the shield, Erling broke the sword short off at the hilt. Skarpedin seized his bill and thrust so fiercely that it also went through the shield and stuck fast. Erling forced the lower end or point of his shield down into the earth, and so held it fast, dropped his axe, drew his sword, and made it flash so quick round his head that no one could see the blade. It fell upon Skarpedin's neck and gave him a grievous wound, cutting right through his armour and deep into his shoulder blade.

A great cry arose at this. The Danes made a rush towards their chief, and succeeded in dragging him out of the fight. They put him on his shield and bore him off to his ship, which was launched immediately. This was the turning-point in the day. Everywhere the Danes fled to their ships pursued by the victors. Some managed to launch their vessels, others were not so fortunate, and many fell fighting, while a few were taken prisoners.

Foreseeing that this would be the result, Haldor and Erling called off their men, hastened on board their ships, and gave chase, while the rest of the force looked after the prisoners and the booty, and dressed their own and their comrades' wounds.

"A bloody day this," said Ulf to Guttorm, as the latter came up, wiping the blade of his sword.

"I have seen worse," observed the old warrior, carefully returning his weapon to its scabbard.

"The Danes will long remember it," observed Glumm. "The ravens will have a good feast to-night."

"And Odin's halls a few more tenants," said Guttorm:

> *"The Danes came here all filled with greed,*
> *And left their flesh the crows to feed.*

"But what is to be done with these?" he added, pointing to the prisoners, about twenty of whom were seated on a log with their feet tied together by a long rope, while their hands were loose.

"Kill them, I suppose," said Ulf.

There were thirty men seated there, and although they heard the words, they did not show by a single glance that they feared to meet their doom.

Just then Swart of the Springs came up. He had a great axe in his hands, and was very furious.

"Thou hast killed and burned my wife, children, and homestede," he said fiercely, addressing the prisoner who sat at the end of the log, "but thou shalt never return to Denmark to tell it."

He cut at him with the axe as he spoke, and the man fell dead. One after another Swart killed them. There was one who looked up and said —

"I will stick this fish bone that I have in my hand into the earth, if it be so that I know anything after my head is cut off."

His head was immediately cut off, but the fish bone fell from his hand.

Beside him there sat a very handsome young man with long hair, who twisted his hair over his head, stretched out his neck, and said, "Don't make my hair bloody."

A man took the hair in his hands and held it fast. Then Swart hewed with his axe, but the Dane twitched his head back so strongly, that he who was holding his hair fell forward; the axe cut off both his hands, and stuck fast in the earth.

"Who is that handsome man?" asked Ulf.

The man replied with look of scorn, "I am Einar, the son of King Thorkel of Denmark; and know thou for a certainty that many shall fall to avenge my death."

Ulf said, "Art thou certainly Thorkel's son? Wilt thou now take thy life and peace?"

"That depends," replied the Dane, "upon who it is that offers it."

"He offers who has the power to give it — Ulf of Romsdal."

"I will take it," says he, "from Ulf's hands."

Upon that the rope was loosed from his feet, but Swart, whose vengeance was still unsatisfied, exclaimed —

"Although thou shouldst give all these men life and peace, King Ulf, yet will I not suffer Einar to depart from this place with life."

So saying he ran at him with uplifted axe, but one of the viking prisoners threw himself before Swart's feet, so that he tumbled over him, and the axe fell at the feet of a viking named Gills. Gills caught the axe and gave Swart his death-wound.

Then said Ulf, "Gills, wilt thou accept life?"

"That will I," said he, "if thou wilt give it to all of us."

"Loose them from the rope," said Ulf.

This was done, and the men were set free.

Eighteen of the Danish vikings were killed, and twelve got their lives upon that occasion.

CHAPTER VIII.

Tells of Discussions and Exciting Deeds at Ulfstede.

While the fight at the Springs which we have just described was going on, Christian the hermit sat in the hall at Ulfstede conversing with Hilda and Dame Astrid, and some of the other women. All the fighting men of the place had been taken away — only one or two old men and Alric were left behind — for Ulf, in his impetuosity, had forgotten to leave a guard at home.

"I hope it will fare well with our men at the Springs," said Hilda, looking up with an anxious expression from the mantle with which her nimble fingers were busy.

"I hope so too," said Christian, "though I would rather that there had been no occasion to fight."

"No occasion to fight!" exclaimed Alric, who was dressing the feathers on an arrow which he had made to replace the one he lost in shooting at the Dane, — and the losing of which, by the way, he was particularly careful to bring to remembrance as often as opportunity offered — sometimes whether opportunity offered or not. "No occasion to fight! What would be the use of weapons if there were no fighting! Where should we get our plunder if there were no fighting, and our slaves? why, what would Northmen find to *do* if there were no fighting?"

The hermit almost laughed at the impetuosity of the boy as he replied —

"It would take a wiser head than mine, lad, to answer all these questions, more particularly to answer them to thy satisfaction. Notwithstanding, it remains true that peace is better than war."

"That may be so," said Dame Astrid; "but it seems to me that war is necessary, and what is necessary must be right."

"I agree with that," said Ada, with a toss of her pretty head — for it would seem that that method of expressing contempt for an adversary's opinion was known to womankind at least a thousand years ago, if not longer. "But *thou* dost not fight, Christian: what has war done to thee that thou shouldst object to it so?"

"What has war done for me?" exclaimed the old man, springing up with sudden excitement, and clasping his lean hands tight together; "has it not done all that it could do? Woman, it has robbed me of all that makes life sweet, and left me only what I did not want. It has robbed me of wife and children, and left a burdened life. Yet no — I sin in speaking thus. Life was left because there was something worth living for; something still to be done: the truth of God to be proclaimed; the good of man to be compassed. But sometimes I forget this when the past flashes upon me, and I forget that it is my duty as well as my joy to say, 'The Lord gave, and the Lord hath taken away; blessed be the name of the Lord.'"

The old man sat down again, and leaned his brow on his hand. The women, although sympathetic, were puzzled by some of his remarks, and therefore sat in silence for a little, but presently the volatile Ada looked up and said —

"What thinkest thou, Hilda, in regard to war?"

"I know not what to think," replied Hilda.

"Nay, then, thy spirit must be flying from thee, for thou wert not wont to be without an opinion on most things. Why, even Erling's sister, Ingeborg, has made up her mind about war I doubt not, though she is too modest to express it."

Now this was a sly hit at Ingeborg, who was sitting by, for she was well known to have a shrewish temper, and to be self-willed and opinionated, in so much that most men kept out of her way. She was very unlike Erling, or her father and mother, or her little sisters, in this respect.

"I can express my opinion well enough when I have a mind," said Ingeborg sharply; "and as to war, it stands to reason that a Sea-king's daughter must approve of a Sea-king's business. Why, the beautiful cloths, and gold and jewels, that are so plentiful in the dale, would never have delighted our eyes if our men had not gone on viking cruise, and fallen in with those rich traders from the far south lands. Besides, war makes our men brisk and handsome."

"Aye," exclaimed Alric, laughing, "especially when they get their noses cut off and their cheeks gashed!"

"Sometimes it takes them from us altogether," observed a poor woman of the household, the widow of a man who had been slain on a viking cruise, after having had his eyes put out, and being otherwise cruelly treated.

"That is the other side of the question," said Astrid. "Of course everything has two sides. We cannot change the plans of the gods. Sunshine and rain, heat and cold, come as they are sent. We must accept them as they are sent."

"That is true," said Christian, "and thou sayest wisely that we must accept things as they are sent; but can it be said that war is sent to us when we rush into it of our own accord? Defensive warfare, truly, is right — else would this world be left in the sole possession of the wicked; but aggressive warfare is not right. To go on viking cruise and take by force that which is not our own is sinful. There is a good way to prove the truth of these things. Let me ask the question, Astrid, — How would thy husband like to have thee and all his property taken from him, and Ulfstede burned about his ears?"

"Methinks he would like it ill."

"Then why should he do that to others which he would not like done to himself?"

"These are strange words," said Astrid in surprise; "I know not that I have ever heard the like before."

"Truly no," said Christian, "because the Word of God has not yet been sounded in the dale. Thou saidst just now that we cannot change the plans of the gods; that would be true if ye had said 'the plans of God', for there is but one God, and His ways are unchangeable. But what if God had revealed some of His plans to man, and told him that this revelation was sufficient to guide him in his walk through this life, and to prepare him for the next?"

"Then would I think it man's wisdom to follow that guide carefully," replied Astrid.

"Such plans do exist, such a revelation has been made," said the hermit, "and the name that stands on the forefront of it is Jesus Christ."

As he spoke the hermit drew from his bosom a scroll of parchment, which he unrolled slowly. This, he said, was a copy, made by himself, of part of the Gospel. He had meant, he said, to have copied the whole of it, but war had put an end to his labours at the same time that it deprived him of his earthly joys, and drove him from his native land to be a wanderer on the earth.

"But if," he continued, "the Lord permits me to preach His gospel of truth and love and peace in Norway, I shall count the sufferings of this present time as nothing compared with the glory yet to be revealed."

"Christian," said Astrid, who appeared to have been struck by some reminiscence, "methinks I have heard Ulf talk of a religion which the men of the south profess. He saw something of it when he went on viking cruise to the great fiord that runs far into the land,[9] and if my memory is faithful he said that they called themselves by a name that sounds marvellously like thine own."

"I suppose Ulf must have met with Christians, after whom I call myself, seeing that my own name is of consequence to no one," said the hermit. "What said he about them?"

"That they were a bad set," replied Astrid,- "men who professed love to their fellows, but were guilty of great cruelty to all who did not believe their faith."

"All who call themselves Christians deserve not the name, Astrid; some are hypocrites and deceivers, others are foolish and easily deceived."

"They all make the same profession, I am told," said Dame Astrid.

"The men of Norway are warriors," returned the hermit, "and all profess courage, — nay, when they stand in the ranks and go forth to war, they all show the same stern face and front, so that one could not know but that all were brave; yet are they not all courageous, as thou knowest full well. Some, it may be very few, but some are cowards at heart, and it only requires the test of the fight to prove them. So is it with professing Christians. I would gladly tell the story of Jesus if ye will hear me, Dame Astrid."

The matron's curiosity was excited, so she expressed her willingness to listen; and the hermit, reading passages from his manuscript copy of the New Testament, and commenting thereon, unfolded the "old old story" of God's wonderful love to man in Jesus Christ.

While he was yet in the midst of his discourse the door of the hall was burst violently open, and one of the serving-girls, rushing in, exclaimed that the Danes were approaching from the fiord!

The Danes referred to composed a small party who had been sent off in a cutter by Skarpedin Redbeard to survey the coast beyond Horlingdal fiord, as he

9   The Mediterranean.

had intended, after herrying that district, to plunder still farther north. This party in returning had witnessed, unseen, the departure of the fleet of North-men. Thinking it probable that the place might have been left with few protectors, they waited until they deemed it safe to send out scouts, and, on their report being favourable, they landed to make an attack on the nearest village or farm.

On hearing the news all was uproar in Ulfstede. The women rushed about in a distracted state, imploring the few helpless old men about the place to arm and defend them. To do these veteran warriors justice they did their best. They put the armour that was brought to them on their palsied limbs, but shook their heads sadly, for they felt that although they might die in defence of the household, they could not save it.

Meanwhile Christian and Alric proved themselves equal to the occasion. The former, although advanced in years, retained much of his strength and energy; and the latter, still inflated with the remembrance of the fact that he had actually drawn blood from a full-grown bearded Dane, and deeply impressed with the idea that he was the only able-bodied warrior in Ulfstede at this crisis, resolved to seize the opportunity and prove to the whole world that his boasting was at all events not "empty"!

"The first thing to be done is to bar the doors," he cried, starting up on hearing the serving-girl's report. "Thou knowest how to do it, Christian; run to the south door, I will bar the north."

The hermit smiled at the lad's energy, but he was too well aware of the importance of speed to waste time in talking. He dropped his outer garment and ran to the south door, which was very solid. Closing it, and fastening the ponderous wooden bar which stretched diagonally across it, he turned and ran to the chamber in which the weapons were kept. On the way he was arrested by a cry from Alric —

"Here! here, quick, Christian, else we are lost!"

The hermit sprang to the north door with the agility of a youth. He was just in time. Poor Alric, despite the strength of his bold heart and will, had not strength of muscle enough to close the door, which had somehow got jammed. Through the open doorway Christian could see a band of Danish vikings running towards the house at full speed. He flung the door forward with a crash, and drew the bar across just as the vikings ran against it.

"Open, open without delay!" cried a voice outside, "else will we tear out the heart of every man and child under this roof."

"We will not open; we will defend ourselves to the last; our trust is in God," replied Christian.

"And as to tearing out our hearts," cried Alric, feeling emboldened now that the stout door stood between him and his foes, "if ye do not make off as fast as ye came, we will punch out your eyes and roast your livers."

The reply to this was a shower of blows on the door, so heavy that the whole building shook beneath them, and Alric almost wished that his boastful threat had been left unsaid. He recollected at that moment, however, that there

was a hole under the eaves of the roof just above the door. It had been con-
structed for the purpose of preventing attacks of this kind. The boy seized his
bow and arrows and dashed up the ladder that led to the loft above the hall. On
it he found one of the old retainers of the stede struggling up with a weighty iron
pot, from which issued clouds of steam.

"Let me pass, old Ivor; what hast thou there?"

"Boiling water to warm them," gasped Ivor, "I knew we should want it ere
long. Finn is gone to the loft above the south door with another pot."

Alric did not wait to hear the end of this answer, but pushing past the old
man, hastened to the trap-door under the eaves and opened it. He found, however, that he could not use his bow in the constrained position necessary to
enable him to shoot through the hole. In desperation he seized a barrel that
chanced to be at hand, and overturned its contents on the heads of the foe. It
happened to contain rye-flour, and the result was that two of the assailants were
nearly blinded, while two others who stood beside them burst into a loud laugh,
and, seizing the battle-axes which the others had been using, continued their
efforts to drive in the door. By this time old Ivor had joined Alric. He set down
the pot of boiling water by the side of the hole, and at once emptied its contents
on the heads of the vikings, who uttered a terrific yell and leaped backward as
the scalding water flowed over their heads and shoulders. A similar cry from the
other door of the house told that the defence there had been equally successful.
Almost at the same moment Alric discovered a small slit in the roof through
which he could observe the enemy. He quickly sent through it an arrow, which
fixed itself in the left shoulder of one of the men. This had the effect of inducing
the attacking party to draw off for the purpose of consultation.

The breathing-time thus afforded to the assailed was used in strengthening
their defences and holding a hurried council of war. Piling several heavy pieces
of furniture against the doors, and directing the women to make additions to
these, Christian drew Alric into the hall, where the ancient retainers were already
assembled.

"It will cost them a long time and much labour to drive in the doors,
defended as they are," said the hermit.

"They will not waste time nor labour upon them," said Ivor, shaking his
hoary head. "What think ye, Finn?"

The women, who had crowded round the men, looked anxiously at Finn,
who was a man of immense bulk, and had been noted for strength in his
younger days, but who was now bent almost double with age. "Fire will do the
work quicker than the battle-axe," answered Finn, with grim smile, which did
not improve the expression of a countenance already disfigured by the scars of a
hundred fights, and by the absence of an eye – long ago gouged out and left to
feed the ravens of a foreign shore! "If this had only come to pass a dozen years
ago," he added, while a gleam of light illumined the sound eye, "I might have
gone off to Valhalla with a straight hack and some credit. But mayhap a good
onset will straighten it yet, who knows? – and I do feel as if I had strength left to
send at least *one* foe out of the world before me."

Ivor the Old nodded. "Yes," he said; "I think they will burn us out."

"I had already feared this," said Christian, with a look of perplexity. "What wouldst thou recommend should be done, Ivor?"

"Nothing more can be done than to kill as many as possible before we die."

"I pray the Lord to help us in our extremity," said Christian; "but I believe it to be His will to help those who are willing to help themselves, depending upon Him for strength, courage, and victory. It may be that Ulf and his men will soon return from the Springs, so that if we could only hold out for a short time all might be well. Have ye nothing to suggest?"

"As to Ulf and the men returning from the Springs," said Finn, "there is small chance of that before morning. With regard to holding out, I know of nothing that will cause fire to burn slow once it is well kindled. An hour hence and Ulfstede will be in ashes, as that sound surely tells."

He referred to a crashing blow which occurred just then at the north door. Nearly all present knew full well that it was the first bundle of a pile of faggots with which the assailants meant to set the house on fire.

"Had this arm retained but a little of the strength it once knew," continued Finn bitterly, as he stretched out the huge but withered limb, "things had not come to this pass so quickly. I remember the day, now forty years ago, when on the roof of this very house I stood alone with my bow and kept thirty men at bay for two full hours. But I could not now draw an arrow of Alric's little bow to its head, to save the lives of all present."

"But *I* can do it," cried Alric, starting forward suddenly; "and if thou wilt show me the window in the roof I will —"

"Brave boy," said old Ivor, with a kindly smile, as he laid his hand on Alric's head, "thy heart is large, and it is sad that one so full of promise should come to such an end; but it needs not that ye should fall before thy time. These shafts may do against the crows, but they would avail nothing against men in mail."

"Is there not a warrior's bow in the house?" asked Christian quickly.

"There is," replied Ivor, "but who will use it?"

"I will."

"Thou?" exclaimed Ivor, with a slight touch of contempt in his tone.

"Hold thy peace, Ivor," said Hilda quickly. "This man has saved my life once, as thou knowest, and well assured am I that what he undertakes to do he will accomplish."

"Now thanks to thee, Hilda, for that," said the hermit heartily; "not that I boast of being sure to accomplish what I undertake, yet I never offer to attempt what I have not some reasonable hope of being able to do. But it is not strange that this old warrior should doubt of the courage or capacity of one who preaches the gospel of peace. Nevertheless, when I was a youth I fought in the army of the great Thorfin, and was somewhat expert in the use of the bow. It is possible that some of my ancient skill may remain, and I am willing to use it in a good cause. I pray thee, therefore, let us not waste more time in useless talk, but fetch me a bow and quiver, and show me the window in the roof."

Ivor went at once to the place where the armour was kept, and brought out the desired weapons, which he placed in the hands of the hermit, and watched his mode of handling them with some curiosity. Christian, unconscious of the look, strung the bow and examined one of the arrows with the air of a man who was thoroughly accustomed to such weapons. Ivor regarded him with increased respect as he conducted him to the loft, and opened the window.

The hermit at once stepped out, and was instantly observed by the Danes, who of course seized the opportunity and let fly several arrows at him, which grazed him or stuck quivering in the roof close to the spot where he stood. He was not slow to reply. One of the vikings, who was approaching the house at the moment with a bundle of faggots on his back, received a shaft in his shoulder, which caused him to drop his bundle and fly to the woods, where he took shelter behind a tree. Almost before that shaft had reached its mark another was on the string, and, in another instant, transfixed the biceps muscle of the right arm of one of the vikings who was preparing to discharge an arrow. He also sought shelter behind a tree, and called to a comrade to come and assist him to extract the shaft.

"Mine ancient skill," said the hermit in an undertone, as if the remark were made half to himself and half to Ivor, whose head appeared at the window, and whose old countenance was wrinkled with a grin of delight at this unexpected display of prowess; "mine ancient skill, it would seem, has not deserted me, for which I am thankful, for it is an awful thing, Ivor, more awful than thou thinkest, to send a human being into eternity unforgiven. I am glad, therefore, to be able thus to render our assailants unfit for war without taking away their lives — ha! that was better aimed than usual," he added, as an arrow passed through his jerkin, and stuck deep into the roof. "The man shoots well, he would soon end the fight if I did not — stop — that."

At the second-last word the hermit bent his bow; at the last, which was uttered with emphasis, he let the arrow fly, and sent it through the left hand of his adversary, who instantly dropped his bow. At the same moment it seemed as though the whole band of vikings had become suddenly convinced that they stood exposed to the shafts of a man who could use them with unerring certainty, for they turned with one consent and fled into the woods — each man seeking shelter behind the nearest tree.

Here they called to one another to stand forth and shoot at the hermit.

"Go thou, Arne," cried the leader; "thine aim is true. Surely one old man is not to keep us all at bay. If my left hand were unscathed I would not trouble thee to do it, thou knowest."

"I have no desire to get an arrow in mine eye," cried Arne; "see, I did but show the tip of my right elbow just now, and the skin of it is cut up as though the crows had pecked it."

In the excess of his wrath Arne extended his clenched fist and shook it at the hermit, who instantly transfixed it with an arrow, causing the foolish man to howl with pain and passion.

"I have always held and acted on the opinion," said Christian to Ivor, who was now joined by his comrade Finn, "that whatever is worth doing at all, is worth doing well. Thou seest," he continued, wiping his brow with the sleeve of his coat, "it is only by being expert in the use of this weapon that I have succeeded in driving bark the Danes without the loss of life. There is indeed a passage in the Book of God (which I hope to be spared to tell thee more about in time to come), where this principle of thoroughness in all things is implied, if not absolutely taught — namely, 'Whatever thy hand findeth to do, do it with thy might'."

"A just maxim," said Finn, shading his one eye with his hands and gazing earnestly into the woods, "and if acted upon, makes a man fit for every duty that falls upon him; but it seems to me that while we are talking here, there is some movement going on. See, Christian (since that is thy name), they are retiring in haste, and exposing themselves. Now, I pray thee, as thine eye is so sure, do drop a shaft on the nape of yonder fellow's neck, that we may have something to show of this night's work."

"I told thee, Finn, that my desire is to avoid taking life."

"Humph," said Finn testily, "whatever thy desire may be matters little now, for he is beyond range. Hark! That shout accounts for the flight of the Danes. Ulf must have returned."

As he spoke, a loud cry, as if of men in conflict, arose from the fiord. Immediately after, the vikings who had not already taken to flight left their places of shelter and dashed into the underwood. The hermit let them go without moving a hand; but Alric, who was actuated by no merciful principles, suddenly opened the north door, sprang out, and let fly an arrow with so true an aim that it struck one of the Danes between the shoulders. Fortunately for him, the Dane had, in accordance with the usual custom of the time, hung his shield on his back when he took to flight, so that the shaft rebounded from it and fell harmless to the ground.

By this time the hermit had descended from the roof. Running out he seized Alric, and, dragging him into the house, reclosed the door.

"Ye know not, foolish boy, whether or not this is Ulf whom we hear."

As he spoke, the tramp of approaching footsteps and the voices of excited men were heard outside. The door flew open, and Ulf, Erling, and Haldor, with a number of the house-carles, strode into the hall and flung down their arms.

"Not much too soon, it would seem," said Ulf, with a look of stern joy.

"Thou wouldst have been altogether too late, Ulf," said Astrid, "had not Christian been here to save us."

"How so?" exclaimed Ulf, turning with an enquiring look to the hermit; "hast turned warrior after all thy preaching of peace? But thou art pale. Ho! fetch a horn of ale here; fighting has disagreed with thy stomach, old man."

"I think," said Christian, pressing his hand to his side, "that one of these arrows must have —"

He paused suddenly, and would have fallen to the ground had not Erling caught him. Letting him gently down at full length, our hero raised his head on his knee, while Hilda came forward with a horn of ale. As she kneeled by the old man's side she glanced anxiously at her lover's face, which was covered with blood and dust, and presented anything but an attractive appearance.

"Hast thou been wounded?" whispered Hilda.

"No, not wounded," muttered Erling, "but —"

"Not wounded!" exclaimed Ulf, who overheard the words, but misunderstood their application, "not wounded! Why, Erling, where have thy wits gone? The man is wellnigh dead from loss of blood. See, his jerkin is soaking. Bring hither bandages; come, let me see the wound. If the old man has indeed saved Ulfstede this day, eternal disgrace would be our due did we let his life slip out under our roof-tree for want of proper care. And hark'ee; get ready all the dressings thou hast, for wounded men enough will be here ere long, and let the boards be spread with the best of meat and ale, for we have gone through hard work to-day, and there is harder yet in store for us, I trow."

Thus admonished, the women went to make preparation for the reception of the wounded, and the entertainment of those who had been more fortunate in the recent conflict. Meanwhile the hermit was conveyed to Ulf's own bed, and his wound, which proved to be less serious than had been feared, was carefully dressed by Hilda, to whom Erling, in the most attentive and disinterested manner, acted the part of assistant-surgeon.

CHAPTER IX.

Shows how the Ancient Sea-Kings transacted National Business.

Scant was the time allowed the men of Horlingdal for refreshment and rest after the battle of the Springs, for the assembling of Thingsmen armed to the teeth, as well as the news that King Harald threatened a descent on them, rendered it necessary that a District Thing or Council should be held without delay.

Accordingly, after brief repose, Haldor the Fierce, who had returned with Erling to his own house up the dale, arose and ordered the horn to be sounded for a Thing.

Several hundreds of men had by that time assembled, and when they all came together they formed an imposing band of warriors, whom any wise king would have deemed it advisable to hold converse with, if possible, on friendly terms.

When the Thing was seated Haldor rose, and, amid profound silence, said:

"Men of Horlingdal, King Harald Haarfager has sent round the message-token for a Thing to be held at the Springs. The token sent was one of peace. The token of war was sent round instead, as ye know. Whether this was wise or not does not much concern us now, as ye have seen with your own eyes that there was good fortune in the change; for we knew not, when the token was forwarded, of the urgent need that should arise at the Springs for our weapons. But, now that the Danes have been sent home — excepting that goodly number who have gone to Valhalla's halls to keep company with Odin and departed warriors — it seems to me that we should meet the King in the manner which he desires until he shall give us occasion to assume arms in defence of our laws. And I would here remind you that Harald is our rightful King, udal-born to the Kingdom of Norway, his title having been stated and proved at all the District Things, beginning with the Ore Thing of Drontheim, and having been approved by all the people of Norway. I therefore counsel pacific measures, and that we should go to the Springs unarmed."

When Haldor sat down there was a slight murmur of assent, but most of those present remained silent, wishing to hear more.

Then up started Ulf, and spoke with great heat.

"I agree not with Haldor," he said sternly. "Who does not know that Harald is rightful King of Norway; that he is descended in a direct line from the godars who came over from the east with Odin, and has been fairly elected King of Norway? But who does not know also, that our laws are above our King, that Harald is at this time trampling on these laws, and is everywhere setting at defiance the small kings, who are as truly udal-born to their rights and titles as himself?"

At this point Ulf's indignation became so great that he found he could not talk connectedly, so he concluded by counselling that they should go to the

Springs fully armed, and ready to brave the worst. There was a loud shout of approval, and then Erling started up. His manner and tone were subdued, but his face was flushed; and men could see, as he went on, that he was keeping down his wrath and his energy.

"I like it ill," he said, "to disagree on this point with my father; but Ulf is right. We all know that Harald is King of Norway by *law*, and we do not meet here to dispute his title; but we also know that kings are not gods. Men create a law and place it over their own heads, so that the lawmakers as well as those for whom it is made must bow before it; but when it is found that the law works unfairly, the lawmaker may repeal it, and cast it aside as useless or unworthy. So kings were created for the sole purpose of guiding nations and administering laws, in order that national welfare might be advanced. The moment they cease to act their part, that moment they cease to be worthy kings, and become useless. But if, in addition to this, they dare to ignore and break the laws of the land, then do they become criminal; they deserve not only to be cast aside, but punished. If, in defence of our rights, we find it necessary to dethrone the King, we cannot be charged with disloyalty, because the King has already dethroned himself!"

Erling paused a moment at this point, and a murmur of approval ran through the circle of his auditors.

"When Harald Haarfager's father," he resumed, "Halfdan the Black, ruled over Norway, he made laws which were approved by the people. He obeyed them himself, and obliged others to observe them; and, that violence should not come in the place of the laws, he himself fixed the number of criminal acts in law, and the compensations, mulcts, or penalties, for each case, according to everyone's birth and dignity, from the King downwards; so that when disputes were settled at the Things the utmost fair play prevailed — death for death, wound for wound; or, if the parties chose, matters could be adjusted by payments in money — each injury being valued at a fixed scale; or matters might be settled and put right by single combat. All this, ye know full well, Halfdan the Black compassed and settled in a *legal manner*, and the good that has flowed from his wise and legal measures (for I hold that a king is not entitled to pass even wise laws illegally) has been apparent to us ever since. But now all this is to be overturned — with or without the consent of the Things — because a foolish woman, forsooth, has the power to stir up the vanity of a foolish king! Shall this be so? Is our manhood to be thus riven from us, and shall we stand aloof and see it done, or, worse still, be consenting unto it? Let death be our portion first! It has been rumoured that the people of southern lands have done this — that they have sold themselves to their kings, so that one man's voice is law, and paid troops of military slaves are kept up in order that this one man may have his full swing, while his favourites and his soldier-slaves bask in his sunshine and fatten on the people of the land! It is impossible for us of Norway to understand the feelings or ideas of the men who have thus sold themselves — for we have never known such tyranny — having, as the scalds tell us, enjoyed our privileges, held our Things, and governed ourselves by means of the collective wisdom of the people ever since our forefathers came from the East; but I warn ye that if this man, Harald Haarfager, is allowed to have his will, our institutions shall be swept away, our privileges will depart, our rights will be crushed, and the time will come when it shall be said of Norsemen that they have utterly forgotten that they once were free! Again I ask, shall we tamely stand aside and suffer this to be? Shall our children ever have it in their power to say, 'There was a time when our mean-spirited forefathers might have easily stopped the leak that caused the flood by which we are now borne irresistibly downward'? I repeat, let us rather perish! Let us go armed to the Springs and tell the King that he — equally with ourselves — is subject to the laws of the land!"

Erling delivered the last sentence in a voice of thunder, and with a fierce wave of the hand, that drew forth shouts of enthusiastic applause.

Instantly Glumm started up, forgetful, in the heat of the moment, of the jealousy that had so recently sprung up between him and his friend.

"I am not a speaker," he shouted gruffly, "but poor is the man who cannot back up and egg on his friend. Erling speaks the truth; and all I have to suggest is that he should be sent by us to tell all this to King Harald Haarfager's face!"

Glumm sat down with the prompt decision of a man who has thoroughly delivered himself of all that he intends to say; and many in the assembly testified their approval of his sentiments.

At this point Ivor the Old arose and gave it as his opinion that the sooner the King should be brought off his high horse the better; whereupon Finn the One-eyed suggested, with a laugh, that the old hermit should be sent with his bow and arrow to teach him due submission to the laws. Then there was a good deal of confused, and not a little passionate discussion, which waxed louder and more vehement until Guttorm Stoutheart stood up, and, although not a dalesman, requested the attention of the assembly for a few minutes.

"It is obvious," he said in the hearty tones of a man who knows that he is sure of carrying a large portion of his audience along with him — "it is obvious that you are all pretty much of one mind as to the principle on which we should act at this time; and my good friend Haldor the Fierce (who seems of late to have changed his nature, and should, methinks, in future, be styled Haldor the Mild) is evidently on the losing side. The only thing that concerns us, it seems to me, is the manner in which we shall convey our opinion to the King — how we shall best, as the scald says:

> "'Whisper in the King's unwilling ear
> That which is wholesome but unsweet to hear.'

"Now, to the quick-witted among you various methods will doubtless have already been suggested; and I am perchance only echoing the sentiments of many here, when I say that it would be worthy of the men of Horlingdal that they should fight the King at once, and put a stop to the burnings, hangings, torturings, jarl-makings, and subduings of which he has been so guilty of late, and which I confess is so unlike his free, generous, manly character, that I have found it hard to believe the reports which have reached my ears, and which, after all, can only be accounted for by the fact that he is at present led by the nose by that worst of all creatures, a proud imperious girl, who has the passions of a warrior and the brains of a bairn! Another method, which would signify at least our contempt for Harald's principles, would be the sending of a thrall to him with a reaping-hook, and a request that he would cut off his own head and give it to us in token that, having ceased to be a king, he is resolved no longer to continue to be a dishonoured man! And that reminds me of one of Ulf's thralls named Kettle Flatnose, who could assist Harald nobly in the work of beheading himself, for last night, when he and I fought side by side against the Danes, he used a hook of his own making, with such effect, that I was fain to pause and laugh, while myself in the very act of splitting an iron headpiece. But perchance that is not a suitable method of compassing our ends, besides it would cost the thrall his life, and I should be sorry to aid in bringing about the death of Kettle Flatnose, whose island is a happy one if it counts many such clear-headed and able-bodied warriors.

"But another plan was proposed by Glumm the Gruff, which seemed to me to have the approval of many present, and assuredly it has mine, that we should send King Erling at once to Harald, to tell him our opinions to his face, to sound him as to his intentions, and to bring back the news as fast as possible, so that we may go armed or unarmed to the Springs, as prudence may direct. Moreover, as it would be unfair to send a man alone on such a dangerous errand, I would suggest that he should have a comrade to keep him company and share his fortunes, and that for this end none better could be found than Glumm the Gruff himself."

This speech settled the mind of the meeting. After a little more talk it was finally arranged that Erling and Glumm should go at once to meet King Harald, who could not yet, it was thought, have arrived at the Springs, and endeavour to find out his temper of mind in regard to the men of Horlingdal. After that the Thing broke up, and the members dispersed to partake of "midag-mad", or dinner, in the dwellings of their various friends.

CHAPTER X.

*Proves that the Best of Friends may quarrel about nothing,
and that War has two Aspects.*

"Now, Erling," said Glumm, with a face so cheerful, that had the expression been habitual, he never would have been styled the Gruff, "I will go home with thee and wait until thou art busked, after which we will go together to my house and have a bite and a horn of mead before setting out on this expedition. I thank the Stoutheart for suggesting it, for the business likes me well."

"Thou wert ever prone to court danger, Glumm," said Erling with a laugh, as they hurried towards Haldorstede, "and methinks thou art going to be blessed with a full share of it just now, for this Harald Haarfager is not a man to be trifled with. Although thou and I could hold our own against some odds, we shall find the odds too much for us in the King's camp, should he set his face against us. However, the cause is a good one, and to say truth, I am not sorry that they had the goodness to pitch on thee and me to carry out the plan."

Thus conversing they arrived at Ulfstede, where Herfrida met them at the door, and was soon informed of their mission. She immediately went to an inner closet, where the best garments and arms were kept, and brought forth Erling's finest suit of armour, in order that he might appear with suitable dignity at court.

She made him change his ordinary shoes for a pair made of tanned leather, on which he bound a pair of silver spurs, which had been taken from a cavalier of southern lands in one of Haldor's viking cruises. She brought, and assisted him to put on, a new suit of mail, every ring of which had been brightly polished by the busy hands of Ingeborg, who was unusually fond of meddling with everything that pertained to the art of war; also a new sword-belt of yellow leather, ornamented with gold studs. On his head she placed a gilt helmet with his favourite crest, a pair of hawk's wings expanded upwards, and a curtain of leather covered with gilt-steel rings to defend the neck. Over his shoulders she flung a short scarlet cloak, which was fastened at the throat by a large silver brooch, similar to the circular brooches which are still to be found in the possession of the rich bonders of Norway. Then she surveyed her stalwart son from head to foot, and said that he would stand comparison with any king in the land, small or great.

At this Erling laughed, and asked for his sword.

"Which one, my son?"

"The short one, mother. I had indeed thought of taking my good old axe with me, but that would not look well in a man bent on a mission of peace. Would it, Glumm? And if I should have to fight, why, my short sword is not a light one, and by putting to a little more force I can make it bite deep enough. So now, Glumm, I am ready for the road. Farewell, mother."

The young men went out and hastened down the valley to Glummstede, near Horlingend.

Now it chanced that Hilda and her foster-sister Ada had resolved, about that time of the day, to walk up the dale together, and as there was only one road on that side of the river, of necessity they were met by their lovers; and it so fell out that the meeting took place in a picturesque part of the dale, where the road passed between two high precipitous cliffs.

The instant that Ada's eyes fell on Glumm her active brain conceived the idea of treating him to a disappointment, so she said hurriedly to her friend:

"Hilda, wilt thou manage to lead Glumm aside and keep talking to him for a short time, while I speak with Erling? I want to ask him something about that sword-belt which I am making for Glumm, and which I intend to send him as the gift of an enemy."

"I will do as ye desire," replied Hilda, with a feeling of disappointment; "but with what truth canst thou send it, Ada, as an enemy's gift?"

"Simple Hilda!" said the other, with a laugh, "am I not an enemy to his peace of mind? But hush! they will overhear us."

It chanced that Hilda was on the same side of the road with Erling, and Ada on that with Glumm, and both youths observed this fact with secret satisfaction as they approached and wished the maids "good day"; but just as they were about to shake hands Ada crossed in front of her companion, and taking Erling's outstretched hand said:

"Erling, I am glad to meet thee, because I have a knotty point which I wish thine aid to disentangle. I will turn and walk with thee a short way, because I know thy business is pressing. It is always so with men, is it not?"

"I know not," answered Erling, smiling at the girl's arch look, despite his surprise and chagrin at the unexpected turn affairs had taken, for he had noted the readiness with which Hilda had turned towards Glumm, and almost, as he imagined, led him aside purposely! "But it seems to me, Ada, that, however pressing a man's business may be, woman has the power to delay it."

"Nay, then, if thine is indeed so pressing just now," said Ada, with a toss of the head (which Glumm, who walked behind with Hilda, took particular note of), "I will not presume to —"

"Now, Ada," said Erling, with a light laugh, "thou knowest that it is merely waste of time to affect indignation. I know thee too well to be deceived. Come, what is it that ye would consult me about? not the forging of a battle-axe or spear-head, I warrant me."

"Nay, but a portion of armour scarce less important, though not so deadly. What say you to a sword-belt?"

"Well, I am somewhat skilled in such gear."

"I am ornamenting one for a friend of thine, Erling, but I will not tell his name unless I have thy promise not to mention to him anything about our conversation."

"I promise," said Erling, with an amused glance.

"It is for Glumm."

"For Glumm!" repeated Erling in surprise; "does Glumm then know —"

"Know what?" asked Ada, as Erling stopped abruptly.

"Does he know that thou art making this belt for him?"

"Know it? why, how could it be a secret if he knew it?"

"Ah, true, I — well?"

"Besides," continued Ada, "I am not *making* it; I said I was going to ornament it. Now it is with reference to that I would consult thee."

Here Ada became so deeply absorbed in the mysteries of ornamental armour that she constrained Erling at least to appear interested, although, poor man, his heart was behind him, and he had much difficulty in resisting the desire to turn round when he heard Hilda's voice — which, by the way, was heard pretty constantly, for Glumm was so uncommonly gruff and monosyllabic in his replies that she had most of the talking to herself.

This unpleasant state of things might have lasted a considerable time, had not the party reached the path which diverged to the left, and, crossing the river over a narrow bridge composed of two tall trees thrown across, led to Glumm-stede. Here Erling stopped suddenly, and wheeling round, said:

"I regret that we cannot go farther down the dale to-day, as Glumm and I must fare with all speed to the Springs to meet King Harald."

"I trust thine errand is one of peace?" said Hilda in a slightly anxious tone.

"To judge by their looks," said Ada, glancing expressively at Glumm, "I should say that their intentions were warlike!"

"Despite our looks," replied Erling, with a laugh, "our business with the King is of a peaceful nature, and as it is pressing, ye will excuse us if —"

"Oh! it *is* pressing, after all," cried Ada; "come, sister, let us not delay them."

So saying, she hurried away with her friend, and the two youths strode on to Glummstede in a very unenviable frame of mind.

Having refreshed themselves with several cuts of fresh salmon — drawn that morning from the foaming river — and with a deep horn of home-brewed ale, the young warriors mounted a couple of active horses, and rode up the mountain path that led in a zigzag direction over the fells to the valley of the Springs. They rode in silence at first — partly because the nature of the track compelled them to advance in single file, and partly because each was in the worst possible humour of which his nature was capable, while each felt indignant at the other, although neither could have said that his friend had been guilty of any definable sin.

It may here be mentioned in passing, that Glumm had clothed and armed himself much in the same fashion as his companion, the chief difference being that his helmet was of polished steel, and the centre of his shield was painted red, while that of Erling was white. His only offensive weapons were a dagger and the long two-handed sword which had been forged for him by his friend, which latter was slung across his back.

An hour and a half of steady climbing brought the youths to the level summit of the hills, where, after giving their steeds a few minutes to breathe, they set off at a sharp gallop. Here they rode side by side, but the rough nature of the ground rendered it necessary to ride with care, so that conversation, although possible, was not, in the circumstances, very desirable. The silence, therefore, was maintained all the way across the fells. When they came to descend on the other side they were again obliged to advance in single file, so that the silence remained unbroken until they reached the base of the mountains.

Here Erling's spirit revived a little, and he began to realise the absurdity of the conduct of himself and his friend.

"Why, Glumm," he exclaimed at last, "a dumb spirit must have got hold of us! What possesses thee, man?"

"Truly it takes two to make a conversation," said Glumm sulkily.

"That is as thou sayest, friend, yet I am not aware that I refused to talk with thee," retorted Erling.

"Nor I with thee," said Glumm sharply, "and thy tongue was glib enough when ye talked with Ada in Horlingdal."

A light flashed upon Erling as his friend spoke.

"Why, Glumm," he said lightly, "a pretty girl will make most men's tongues wag whether they will or no."

Glumm remembered his own obstinate silence while walking with Hilda, and deeming this a studied insult he became furious, reined up and said:

"Come, Erling, if ye wish to settle this dispute at once we need fear no interruption, and here is a piece of level sward."

"Nay, man, be not so hot," said Erling, with a smile that still more exasperated his companion; "besides, is it fair to challenge me to fight with this light weapon while thou bearest a sword so long and deadly?"

"That shall be no bar," cried the other, unslinging his two-handed sword; "thou canst use it thyself, and I will content me with thine."

"And pray, how shall we give account of our mission," said Erling, "if you and I cut each other's heads off before fulfilling it?"

"That would then concern us little," said Glumm.

"Nay, thou art more selfish than I thought thee, friend. For my part, I would not that *she* should think me so regardless of her welfare as to leave undelivered a message that may be the means of preventing the ruin of Horlingdal. My regard for Ada seems to sit more heavily on me than on thee."

At this Glumm became still more furious. He leaped off his horse, drew his sword, and flinging it down with the hilt towards Erling, cried in a voice of suppressed passion:

"No longer will I submit to be trifled with by man or woman. Choose thy weapon, Erling. This matter shall be settled now and here, and the one who wins her shall prove him worthy of her by riding forth from this plain alone. If thou art bent on equal combat we can fall to with staves cut from yonder tree, or, for the matter of that, we can make shift to settle it with our knives. What! has woman's love unmanned thee?"

At this Erling leaped out of the saddle, and drew his sword.

"Take up thy weapon, Glumm, and guard thee. But before we begin, perhaps it would be well to ask for whose hand it is that we fight."

"Have we not been talking just now of Ada the Dark-eyed?" said Glumm sternly, as he took up his sword and threw himself into a posture of defence, with the energetic action of a man thoroughly in earnest.

"Then is our combat uncalled for," said Erling, lowering his point, "for I desire not the hand of Ada, though I would fight even to the death for her blue-eyed sister, could I hope thereby to win her love."

"Art thou in earnest?" demanded Glumm in surprise.

"I never was more so in my life," replied Erling; "would that Hilda regarded me with but half the favour that Ada shows to thee!"

"There thou judgest wrongly," said Glumm, from whose brow the frown of anger was passing away like a thundercloud before the summer sun. "I don't pretend to understand a girl's thoughts, but I have wit enough to see what is very plainly revealed. When I walked with Hilda to-day I noticed that her eye followed thee unceasingly, and although she talked to me glibly enough, her thoughts were wandering, so that she uttered absolute nonsense at times — insomuch that I would have laughed had I not been jealous of what I deemed the mutual love of Ada and thee. No, Erling, thy suit will prosper, depend on't. It is I who have reason to despond, for Ada loves me not."

Erling, who heard all this with a certain degree of satisfaction, smiled, shook his head, and said:

"Nay, then, Glumm, thou too art mistaken. The dark-eyed Ada laughs at everyone, and besides, I have good reason to know that her interest in thee is so great that she consulted me to-day about — about — a—"

The promise of secrecy that he had made caused Erling to stammer and stop.

"About what?" asked Glumm.

"I may not tell thee, friend. She bound me over to secrecy, and I must hold by my promise; but this I may say, that thou hast fully greater cause for hope than I have."

"Then it is my opinion," said Glumm, "that we have nothing to do but shake hands and proceed on our journey."

Erling laughed heartily, sheathed his sword, and grasped his friend's hand, after which they remounted and rode forward; but they did not now ride in silence. Their tongues were effectually loosened, and for some time they discussed their respective prospects with all the warmth and enthusiasm of youthful confidants.

"But Ada perplexes me," suddenly exclaimed Glumm, in the midst of a brief pause; "I know not how to treat her."

"If thou wilt take my advice, Glumm, I will give it thee."

"What is that?" asked Glumm.

"There is nothing like fighting a woman with her own weapons."

"A pretty speech," said Glumm, "to come from the lips of a man who never regards the weapons of his foes, and can scarce be prevailed on to carry anything but a beloved battle-axe."

"The case is entirely the reverse when one fights with woman," replied Erling. "In war I confess that I like everything to be straightforward and downright, because when things come to the worst a man can either hew his way by main force through thick and thin, or die. Truly, I would that it were possible to act thus in matters of love also, but this being impossible — seeing that women will not have it so, and insist on dallying — the next best thing to be done is to act on their own principles. Fight them with their own weapons. If a woman is outspoken and straightforward, a man should be the same — and rejoice, moreover, that he has found a gem so precious. But if she *will* play fast and loose, let a man — if he does not give her up at once — do the same. Give Ada a little taste of indifference, Glumm, and thou wilt soon bring her down. Laugh at her as well as with her. Show not quite so much attention to her as has been thy wont; and be more attentive to the other girls in the dale —"

"To Hilda, for instance," said Glumm slyly.

"Aye, even so, an it please thee," rejoined Erling; "but rest assured thou wilt receive no encouragement in that quarter; for Hilda the Sunbeam is the very soul of innocence, truth, and straightforwardness."

"Not less so is Ada," said Glumm, firing up at the implied contrast.

Erling made a sharp rejoinder, to which Glumm made a fierce reply; and it is probable that these hot-blooded youths, having quarrelled because of a misunderstanding in regard to their mistresses, would have come to blows about their comparative excellence, had they not come suddenly upon a sight which, for the time, banished all other thoughts from their minds.

During the discussion they had been descending the valley which terminated in the plain where the recent battle of the Springs had been fought. Here, as they galloped across the field, which was still strewn with the bodies of the slain, they came upon the blackened ruins of a hut, around which an old hag was moving, actively engaged, apparently, in raking among the ashes with a forked stick for anything that she could draw forth.

Near to her a woman, who had not yet reached middle age, was seated on the burnt earth, with her hands tightly clasped, and her bloodshot eyes gazing with a stony stare at a blackened heap which lay on her lap. As the young men rode up they saw that part of the head and face of a child lay in the midst of the charred heap, with a few other portions of the little one that had been only partially consumed in the fire.

The Northmen did not require to be told the cause of what they saw. The story was too plainly written in everything around them to admit of uncertainty, had they even been ignorant of the recent fight and its consequences. These were two of the few survivors of that terrible night, who had ventured to creep forth from the mountains and search among the ashes for the remains of those whose smiles and voices had once made the sunshine of their lives. The terrible silence of these voices and the sight of these hideous remains had driven the grandmother of the household raving mad, and she continued to rake among the still smouldering embers of the old house, utterly regardless of the two warriors, and only complaining, in a querulous tone now and then, that her daughter should sit there like a stone and leave her unaided to do the work of trying to save at least some of the household from the flames. But the daughter neither heard nor cared for her. She had found what was left of her idol — her youngest child — once a ruddy, fearless boy, with curly flaxen hair, who had already begun to carve model longships and wooden swords, and to talk with a joyous smile and flashing eye of war! but now — the fair hair gone, and nothing left save a blackened skull and a small portion of his face, scarcely enough — yet to a mother far more than enough — to recognise him by.

Erling and Glumm dismounted and approached the young woman, but received no glance of recognition. To a remark made by Erling no reply was given. He therefore went close to her, and, bending down, laid his large hand on her head, and gently smoothed her flaxen hair, while he spoke soothingly to her. Still the stricken woman took no notice of him until a large hot tear, which the youth could not restrain, dropped upon her forehead, and coursed down her cheek. She then looked suddenly up in Erling's face and uttered a low wail of agony.

"Would ye slay her too?" shrieked the old woman at that moment, coming forward with the pole with which she had been raking in the ashes, as if she were going to attack them.

Glumm turned aside the point of the pole, and gently caught the old woman by the arm.

"Oh! spare her," she cried, falling on her knees and clasping her withered hands; "spare her, she is the last left — the last. I tried to save the others — but, but, they are gone — all gone. Will ye not spare *her*?"

"They won't harm us, mother," said the younger woman huskily. "They are friends. I *know* they are friends. Come, sit by me, mother."

The old woman, who appeared to have been subdued by exhaustion, crept on her hands and knees to her side, and laying her head on her daughter's breast, moaned piteously.

"We cannot stay to aid thee," said Erling kindly; "but that matters not because those will soon be here who will do their best for thee. Yet if thou canst travel a few leagues, I will give thee a token which will ensure a good reception in my father's house. Knowest thou Haldorstede in Horlingdal?"

"I know it well," answered the woman.

"Here is a ring," said Erling, "which thou wilt take to Herfrida, the wife of Haldor, and say that her son Erling sent thee, and would have thee and thy mother well cared for."

He took from his finger, as he spoke, a gold ring, and placed it in the woman's hand, but she shook her head sadly, and said in an absent tone: "I dare not go. Swart might come back and would miss me."

"Art thou the wife of Swart of the Springs?"

"Yes; and he told me not to quit the house till he came back. But that seems so long, long ago, and so many things have happened since, that —"

She paused and shuddered.

"Swart is dead," said Glumm.

On hearing this the woman uttered a wild shriek, and fell backward to the earth.

"Now a plague on thy gruff tongue," said Erling angrily, as he raised the woman's head on his knee. "Did you not see that the weight was already more than she could bear? Get thee to the spring for water, man, as quickly as may be."

Glumm, whose heart had already smitten him for his inconsiderate haste, made no reply, but ran to a neighbouring spring, and quickly returned with his helmet full of water. A little of this soon restored the poor woman, and also her mother.

"Now haste thee to Horlingdal," said Erling, giving the woman a share of the small supply of food with which he had supplied himself for the journey. "There may be company more numerous than pleasant at the Springs to-morrow, and a hearty welcome awaits thee at Haldorstede."

Saying this he remounted and rode away.

"I was told last night by Hilda," said Erling, "that, when we were out after the Danes, and just before the attack was made by the men of their cutter on Ulfstede, the hermit had been talking to the women in a wonderful way about war and the God whom he worships. He thinks that war is an evil thing; that to fight in self-defence — that is, in defence of home and country — is right, but that to go on viking cruise is wrong, and displeasing to God."

"The hermit is a fool," said Glumm bluntly.

"Nay, he is no fool," said Erling. "When I think of these poor women, I am led to wish that continued peace were possible."

"But it is, happily, *not* possible; therefore it is our business to look upon the bright side of war," said Glumm.

"That may be thy business, Glumm, but it is my business to look upon *both* sides of everything. What would it avail thee to pitch and paint and gild the outside of thy longship, if no attention were given to the timbering and planking of the inside?"

"That is a different thing," said Glumm.

"Yes, truly; yet not different in this, that it has two sides, both of which require to be looked at, if the ship is to work well. I would that I knew what the men of other lands think on this point, for the hermit says that there are nations in the south where men practise chiefly defensive warfare, and often spend years at a time without drawing the sword."

"Right glad am I," said Glumm, with a grim smile, "that my lot has not fallen among these."

"Do you know," continued Erling, "that I have more than once thought of going off on a cruise far and wide over the world to hear and see what men say and do? But something, I know not what, prevents me."

"Perchance Hilda could tell thee!" said Glumm.

Erling laughed, and said there was some truth in that; but checked himself suddenly, for at that moment a man in the garb of a thrall appeared.

"Ho! fellow," cried Glumm, "hast heard of King Harald Haarfager of late?"

"The King is in guest-quarters in Updal," answered the thrall, "in the house of Jarl Rongvold, my master."

"We must speed on," said Erling to Glumm, "if we would speak with the King before supper-time."

"If you would speak with the King at all," said the thrall, "the less you say to him the better, for he is in no mood to be troubled just now. He sets out for the Springs to-morrow morning."

Without making a reply the youths clapped spurs to their horses and galloped away.

CHAPTER XI.

Describes our Hero's Interview with Jarl Rongvold
and King Harald Haarfager.

Late in the evening, Erling and Glumm arrived in the neighbourhood of the house of Jarl Rongvold, where King Harald Haarfager was staying in guest-quarters with a numerous retinue.

In the days of which we write there were no royal palaces in Norway. The kings spent most of their time — when not engaged in war or out on viking cruises — in travelling about the country, with a band of "herd-men", or men-at-arms, in "guest-quarters". Wherever they went the inhabitants were bound by law to afford them house-room and good cheer at their own cost, and the kings usually made this tax upon their people as light as possible by staying only a few days at each place.

Rongvold, who entertained the King at this time, was one of those Jarls or Earls — rulers over districts under himself — of whom he had recently created many throughout the land, to supersede those small independent kings who refused to become subject to him. He was a stout warrior, an able courtier, and a very dear friend of the King.

Just before his arrival at Jarl Rongvold's house, King Harald had completed a considerable part of the programme which he had laid down in the great work of subduing the whole of Norway to himself. And wild bloody work it had been.

Hearing that several of the small kings had called a meeting in the uplands to discuss his doings, Harald went, with all the men he could gather, through the forests to the uplands, came to the place of meeting about midnight without being observed by the watchmen, set the house on fire, and burnt or slew four kings with all their followers. After that he subdued Hedemark, Ringerige, Gudbrandsdal, Hadeland, Raumarige, and the whole northern part of Vingulmark, and got possession of all the land as far south as the Glommen. It was at this time that he was taunted by the girl Gyda, and took the oath not to clip his hair until he had subdued the whole land — as formerly related. After his somewhat peculiar determination, he gathered together a great force, and went northwards up the Gudbrandsdal and over the Doverfielde. When he came to the inhabited land he ordered all the men to be killed, and everything wide around to be delivered to the flames. The people fled before him in all directions on hearing of his approach — some down the country to Orkadal, some to Gaulerdal, and some to the forests; but many begged for peace, and obtained it on condition of joining him and becoming his men. He met no decided opposition till he came to Orkadal, where a king named Gryting gave him battle. Harald won the victory. King Gryting was taken prisoner, and most of his men were killed. He took service himself, however, under the King, and thereafter all the people of Orkadal district swore fidelity to him.

Many other battles King Harald fought, and many other kings did he subdue — all of which, however, we will pass over at present, merely observing that wherever he conquered he laid down the law that all the udal property should belong to him, and that the bonders — the hitherto free landholders — both small and great, should pay him land dues for their possessions. It is due, however, to Harald Fairhair, to say that he never seems to have aimed at despotic power; for it is recorded of him that over every district he set an earl, or jarl, to judge *according to the law of the land and to justice*, and also to collect the land dues and the fines; and for this each earl received a third part of the dues and services and fines for the support of his table and other expenses. Every earl had under him four or more bersers, on each of whom was bestowed an estate of twenty merks yearly, for which he was bound to support twenty men-at-arms at his own expense — each earl being obliged to support sixty retainers. The King increased the land dues and burdens so much that his earls had greater power and income than the kings had before, and when this became known at Drontheim many of the great men of that district joined the King.

Wherever Harald went, submission or extinction were the alternatives; and as he carried things with a high hand, using fire and sword freely, it is not a matter of wonder that his conquests were rapid and complete. It has been said of Harald Fairhair by his contemporaries, handed down by the scalds, and recorded in the Icelandic Sagas, that he was of remarkably handsome appearance, great and strong, and very generous and affable to his men.

But to return.

It was late in the evening, as we have said, when Erling and Glumm reached the vicinity of Jarl Rongvold's dwelling. Before coming in sight of it they were met by two of the mounted guards that were posted regularly as sentries round the King's quarters. These challenged them at once, and, on being informed that they desired to have speech with the King on matters of urgency, conveyed them past the inner guard to the house.

The state of readiness for instant action in which the men were kept did not escape the observant eyes of the visitors. Besides an outlying mounted patrol, which they had managed to pass unobserved, and the sentries who conducted them, they found a strong guard round the range of farm buildings where the King and his men lay. These men were all well armed, and those of them who were not on immediate duty lay at their stations sound asleep, each man with his helmet on his head, his sword under it, his right hand grasping the hilt, and his shield serving the purpose of a blanket to cover him.

Although the young men observed all this they did not suffer their looks to betray idle curiosity, but rode on with stern countenances, looking, apparently, straight before them, until they reined up at the front door of the house.

In a few minutes a stout handsome man with white hair came out and saluted Erling in a friendly way. This was Jarl Rongvold, who was distantly related to him.

"I would I could say with truth that I am glad to see thee, cousin," he said, "but I fear me that thine errand to the King is not likely to end in pleasant intercourse, if all be true that is reported of the folk in Horlingdal."

"Thanks, kinsman, for the wish, if not for the welcome," replied the youth, somewhat stiffly, as he dismounted; "but it matters little to me whether our intercourse be pleasant or painful, so long as it is profitable. The men of Horlingdal send a message to Harald Haarfager; can my companion and I have speech with him?"

"I can manage that for thee, yet would I counsel delay, for the King is not in a sweet mood to-night, and it may go ill with thee."

"I care not whether the King's mood be sweet or sour," replied Erling sternly. "Whatever he may become in the future, Harald is not yet the all-powerful king he would wish to be. The men of Horlingdal have held a Thing, and Glumm and I have been deputed to see the King, convey to him their sentiments, and ask his intentions."

A grim smile played on the jarl's fine features for a moment, as he observed the blood mantling to the youth's forehead.

"No good will come to thee or thine, kinsman, by meeting the King with a proud look. Be advised, Erling," he continued in a more confidential tone; "it is easier to swim with the stream than against it — and wiser too, when it is impossible to turn it. Thou hast heard, no doubt, of Harald's doings in the north."

"I have heard," said Erling bitterly.

"Well, be he right or be he wrong, it were easier to make the Glommen run up the fells than to alter the King's determination; and it seems to me that it behoves every man who loves his country, and would spare further bloodshed, to submit to what is inevitable."

"Every lover of his country deems bloodshed better than slavery," said Erling, "because the death of a few is not so great an evil as the slavery of all."

"Aye, when there is hope that good may come of dying," rejoined the jarl, "but now there is no hope."

"That is yet to be proved," said the youth; and Glumm uttered one of those emphatic grunts with which men of few words are wont to signify their hearty assent to a proposition.

"Tut, kinsman," continued Rongvold, with a look of perplexity, "I don't like the idea of seeing so goodly a youth end his days before his right time. Let me assure thee that, if thou wilt join us and win over thy friends in Horlingdal, a splendid career awaits thee, for the King loves stout men, and will treat thee well; he is a good master."

"It grieves me that one whose blood flows in my veins should call any man master!" said Erling.

"Now a plague on thee, for a stupid hot-blood," cried the jarl; "if thou art so displeased with the word, I can tell thee that it need never be used, for, if ye will take service with the King, he will give thee the charge and the revenues of a goodly district, where thou shalt be master and a jarl too."

"I am a king!" said Erling, drawing himself proudly up. "Thinkest thou I would exchange an old title for a new one, which the giver has no right to create?"

Glumm uttered another powerfully emphatic grunt at this point.

"Besides," continued Erling, "I have no desire to become a scatt-gatherer."

The jarl flushed a little at this thrust, but mastering his indignation said, with a smile —

"Nay, then, if ye prefer a warrior's work there is plenty of that at the disposal of the King."

"I have no particular love for war," said Erling. Jarl Rongvold looked at his kinsman in undisguised amazement.

"Truly thou art well fitted for it, if not fond of it," he said curtly; "but as thou art bent on following thine own nose, thou art like to have more than enough of that which thou lovest not. — Come, I will bring thee to the King."

The jarl led the two young men into his dwelling, where nearly a hundred men-at-arms were carousing. The hall was a long, narrow, and high apartment, with a table running down each side, and one at either end. In the centre of each table was a raised seat, on which sat the chief guests, but, at the moment they entered, the highest of these seats was vacant, for the King had left the table. The fireplace of the hall was in the centre, and the smoke from it curled up among the rafters, which it blackened before escaping through a hole in the roof.

As all the revellers were armed, and many of them were moving about the hall, no notice was taken of the entrance of the strangers, except that one or two near whom they passed remarked that Jarl Rongvold owned some stout men-at-arms.

The King had retired to one of the sleeping-chambers off the great halt in which he sat at a small window, gazing dreamily upon the magnificent view of dale, fell, fiord, and sea, that lay stretched out before the house. The slanting rays of the sun shone through the window, and through the heavy masses of the King's golden hair, which fell in enormous volumes, like a lion's mane, on a pair of shoulders which were noted, even in that age of powerful men, for enormous breadth and strength. Like his men, King Harald was armed from head to foot, with the exception of his helmet, which lay, with his shield, on the low wolf-skin couch on which he had passed the previous night.

He did not move when the jarl and the young men entered, but on the former whispering in his ear he let his clenched fist fall on the window sill, and, turning, with a frown on his bold, handsome face, looked long and steadily at Erling. And well might he gaze, for he looked upon one who bore a singularly strong resemblance to himself. There was the same height and width and massive strength, the same bold, fearless look in the clear blue eyes, and the same firm lips; but Erling's hair fell in softer curls on his shoulders, and his brow was more intellectual. Being a younger man, his beard was shorter.

Advancing a step, after Jarl Rongvold had left the room, Erling stated the sentiments of the men of Horlingdal in simple, blunt language, and ended by telling the King that they had no wish to refuse due and lawful allegiance to him, but that they objected to having the old customs of the land illegally altered.

During the progress of his statement both Erling and Glumm observed that the King's face flushed more than once, and that his great blue eyes blazed with astonishment and suppressed wrath. After he had concluded, the King still gazed at him in ominous silence. Then he said, sternly:

"For what purpose camest thou hither if the men of Horlingdal hold such opinions?"

"We came to tell you, King Harald, what the men of Horlingdal think, and to ask what you intend to do."

There was something so cool in this speech that a sort of grin curled the King's moustache, and mingled with the wrath that was gathering on his countenance.

"I'll tell thee what I will do," he said, drawing his breath sharply, and hissing the words; "I will march into the dale, and burn and s —" He stopped abruptly, and then in a soft tone added, "But what will *they* do if I refuse to listen to them?"

"I know not what the men of Horlingdal will do," replied Erling; "but I will counsel them to defend their rights."

At this the King leaped up, and drew his sword half out of its scabbard, but again checked himself suddenly; for, as the Saga tells us, "it was his invariable rule, whenever anything raised his anger, to collect himself and let his passion run off, and then take the matter into consideration coolly."

"Go," he said, sitting down again at the window, "I will speak with thee on this subject to-morrow."

Erling, who during the little burst of passion had kept his blue eyes unflinchingly fixed on those of the King, bowed and retired, followed by Glumm, whose admiration of his friend's diplomatic powers would have been unbounded, had he only wound up with a challenge to the King, then and there, to single combat!

CHAPTER XII.

Describes a Terrific and Unequal Combat.

"Now, kinsman, let me endeavour to convince thee of thy folly," said Jarl Rongvold to Erling, on the morning that followed the evening in which the interview with the King had taken place, as they walked in front of the house together.

"It needs no great power of speech to convince me of that," said Erling. "The fact that I am still here, after what the King let out last night, convinces me, without your aid, that I am a fool."

"And pray what said he that has had such powerful influence on thine obtuse mind?"

"Truly he said little, but he expressed much. He gave way to an unreasonable burst of passion when I did but claim justice and assert our rights; and the man must be slow-witted indeed who could believe that subdued passion is changed opinion. However, I will wait for another interview until the sun is in the zenith — after that I leave, whatever be the consequences. So it were well, kinsman, that you should see and advise with your *master.*"

The jarl bit his lip, and was on the point of turning away without replying, when a remarkably stout and tall young man walked up and accosted them.

"This is my son Rolf," said the jarl, turning round hastily. — "Our kinsman, Erling the Bold. I go to attend the King. Make the most of each other, for ye are not likely to be long in company."

"Are you that Rolf who is styled Ganger?" enquired Erling with some interest.

"Aye," replied the other gruffly. "At least I am Rolf. Men choose to call me Ganger because I prefer to gang on my legs rather than gang on the legs of a horse. They say it is because no horse can carry me; but thou seest that that is a lie, for I am not much heavier than thyself."

"I should like to know thee better, kinsman," said Erling.

Rolf Ganger did not respond so heartily to this as Erling wished, and he felt much disappointed; for, being a man who did not often express his feelings, he felt all the more keenly anything like a rebuff.

"What is your business with the King?" asked Rolf, after a short pause.

"To defy him," said our hero, under the influence of a burst of mingled feelings.

Rolf Ganger looked at Erling in surprise.

"Thou dost not like the King, then?"

"I hate him!"

"So do I," said Rolf.

This interchange of sentiment seemed to break down the barriers of diffidence which had hitherto existed between the two, for from that moment their talk was earnest and confidential. Erling tried to get Rolf to desert the King's cause and join his opponents, but the latter shook his head, and said that they had no chance of success; and that it was of no use joining a hopeless cause, even although he had strong sympathy with it. While they were conversing, Jarl Rongvold came out and summoned Erling to the presence of the King.

This was the first and last interview that our hero had with that Rolf Ganger, whose name – although not much celebrated at that time – was destined to appear in the pages of history as that of the conqueror of Normandy, and the progenitor of line of English kings.

"I have sent for thee, Erling," said the King, in a voice so soft, yet so constrained, that Erling could not avoid seeing that it was forced, "to tell thee thou art at liberty to return to thy dalesmen with this message – King Harald respects the opinions of the men of Horlingdal, and he will hold a Thing at the Springs for the purpose of hearing their views more fully, stating his own, and consulting with them about the whole matter. – Art satisfied with that?" he asked, almost sternly.

"I will convey your message," said Erling.

"And the sooner the better," said the King. "By the way, there are two roads leading to the Springs, I am told; is it so?" he added.

"There are," said Erling; "one goes by the uplands over the fells, the other through the forest."

"Which would you recommend me to follow when I fare to the Springs?"

"The forest road is the best."

"It is that which thou wilt follow, I suppose?"

"It is," replied Erling.

"Well, get thee to horse, and make the most of thy time; my berserk here will guide thee past the guards."

As he spoke, a man who had stood behind the King motionless as a statue advanced towards the door. He was one of a peculiar class of men who formed part of the bodyguard of the King. On his head there was a plain steel helmet, but he wore no "serk", or shirt of mail (hence the name of berserk, or bare of serk), and he was, like the rest of his comrades, noted for being capable of working himself up into such a fury of madness while in action, that few people of ordinary powers could stand before his terrible onset. He was called Hake, the berserk of Hadeland, and was comparatively short in stature, but looked shorter than he really was, in consequence of the unnatural breadth and bulk of his chest and shoulders. Hake led Erling out to the door of the house, where they found Glumm waiting with two horses ready for the road.

"Thou art sharp this morning, Glumm."

"Better to be too sharp than too blunt," replied his friend. "It seemed to me that whatever should be the result of the talk with the King to-day, it were well to be ready for the road in good time. What is yonder big-shouldered fellow doing?"

"Hush, Glumm," said Erling, with a smile, "thou must be respectful if thou wouldst keep thy head on thy shoulders. That is Hake of Hadeland, King Harald's famous berserk. He is to conduct us past the guards. I only hope he may not have been commissioned to cut off our heads on the way. But I think that perchance you and I might manage him together, if our courage did not fail us!"

Glumm replied with that expression of contempt which is usually styled turning up one's nose, and Erling laughed as he mounted his horse and rode off at the heels of the berserk. He had good reason to look grave, however, as he found out a few moments later. Just as they were about to enter the forest, a voice was heard shouting behind, and Jarl Rongvold was seen running after them.

"Ho! stay, kinsman, go not away without bidding us farewell. A safe and speedy journey, lad, and give my good wishes to the old folk at Haldorstede. Say that I trust things may yet be happily arranged between the men of Horlingdal and the King."

As he spoke the jarl managed to move so that Erling's horse came between him and the berserk; then he said quickly, in a low but earnest whisper:

"The King means to play thee false, Erling. I cannot explain, but do thou be sure to take *the road by the fells*, and let not the berserk know. Thy life depends on it. I am ordered to send this berserk with a troop of nineteen men to waylay thee. They are to go *by the forest road.* — There, thou canst not doubt my friendship for thee, for now my life is in thy hands! Haste, thou hast no chance against such odds. Farewell, Glumm," he added aloud; "give my respects to Ulf, when next ye see him."

Jarl Rongvold waved his hand as he turned round and left his friends to pursue their way.

They soon reached the point where they had met the two guards on the previous day. After riding a little farther, so as to make sure of being beyond the outmost patrol, the berserk reined up.

"Here I leave you to guard yourselves," he said.

"Truly we are indebted to thee for thy guidance thus far," said Erling.

"If you should still chance to meet with any of the guards, they will let you pass, no doubt."

"No doubt," replied Erling, with a laugh, "and, should they object, we have that which will persuade them."

He touched the hilt of his sword, and nodded good-humouredly to the berserk, who did not appear to relish the jest at all.

"Your road lies through the forest, I believe?" said Hake, pausing and looking back as he was about to ride away.

"That depends on circumstances," said Erling. "If the sun troubles me, I may go by the forest, — if not, I may go by the fells. But I never can tell beforehand which way my fancy may lead, and I always follow it."

So saying he put spurs to his horse and galloped away.

The berserk did the same, but it was evident that he was ill at ease, for he grumbled very much, and complained a good deal of his ill luck. He did not, however, slacken his pace on that account, but rather increased it, until he reached Rongvoldstede, where he hastily summoned nineteen armed men, mounted a fresh horse, and, ordering them to follow, dashed back into the forest at full speed.

For some time he rode in silence by the side of a stout man who was his subordinate officer.

"Krake," he said at length, "I cannot make up my mind which road this Erling and his comrade are likely to have taken, so, as we must not miss our men, the King's commands being very positive, I intend to send thee by the mountain road with nine of the men, and go myself by the forest with the other nine. We will ride each at full speed, and will be sure to overtake them before they reach the split rock on the fells, or the double-stemmed pine in the forest. If thou shalt fall in with them, keep them in play till I come up, for I will hasten to join thee without delay after reaching the double pine. If I meet them I will give the attack at once, and thou wilt hasten to join me after passing the split rock. Now, away, for here our roads part."

In accordance with this plan the troop was divided, and each portion rode off at full speed.

Meanwhile Erling and Glumm pursued their way, chatting as they rode along, and pausing occasionally to breathe their horses.

"What ails thee, Erling?" said Glumm abruptly. "One would fancy that the fair Hilda was behind thee, so often hast thou looked back since the berserk left us."

"It is because the fair Hilda is before me that I look so often over my shoulder, for I suspect that there are those behind us who will one day cause her grief," replied Erling sadly; then, assuming a gay air, he added — "Come, friend Glumm, I wish to know thy mind in regard to a matter of some importance. How wouldst thou like to engage, single handed, with ten men?"

Glumm smiled grimly, as he was wont to do when amused by anything — which, to say truth, was not often.

"Truly," said he, "my answer to that must depend on thine answer to this — Am I supposed to have my back against a cliff, or to be surrounded by the ten?"

"With thy back guarded, of course."

"In that case I should not refuse the fight, but I would prefer to be more equally matched," said Glumm, "Two to one, now, is a common chance of war, as thou knowest full well. I myself have had four against me at one time — and when one is in good spirits this is not a serious difficulty, unless there chance to be a berserk amongst them; even in that case, by the use of a little activity of limb, one can separate them, and so kill them in detail. But ten are almost too many for one man, however bold, big, or skilful he may be."

"Then what — wouldst thou say to twenty against two?" asked Erling, giving a peculiar glance at his friend.

"That were better than ten to one, because two stout fellows back to back are not easily overcome, if the fight be fair with sword and axe, and arrows or spears be not allowed. Thou and I, Erling, might make a good stand together against twenty, for we can use our weapons, and are not small men. Nevertheless, I think that it would be our last fight, though I make no doubt we should thin their number somewhat. But why ask such questions?"

"Because I have taken a fancy to know to what extent I might count on thee in case of surprise."

"To what extent!" said Glumm, flushing, and looking his friend full in the face. "Hast known me so long to such small purpose, that ye should doubt my willingness to stand by thee to the death, if need be, against any odds?"

"Nay, be not so hasty, Glumm. I doubt not thy courage nor thy regard for me, but I had a fancy to know what amount of odds thou wouldst deem serious, for I may tell thee that our powers are likely to be put to the proof to-day. My kinsman, Jarl Rongvold, told me at parting that twenty men — and among them Hake the berserk — are to be sent after us, and are doubtless even now upon our track."

"Then why this easy pace?" said Glumm, in a tone of great surprise. "Surely there is no reason why we should abide the issue of such a combat when nothing is to be gained by it and much to be lost; for if we are killed, who will prepare the men of Horlingdal for the King's approach, and tell of his intentions?"

"That is wisely spoken, Glumm; nevertheless I feel disposed to meet King Harald's men."

"This spirit accords ill with the assertion that thou art not fond of war," returned Glumm, with a smile.

"I am not so sure of that," rejoined Erling, with a look of perplexity. "It is more the consequences of war — its evil effects on communities, on women and children — that I dislike, than the mere matter of fighting, which, although I cannot say I long for it, as some of our friends do, I can truly assert I take some pleasure in, when engaged in it. Besides, in this case I do not wish to meet these fellows for a mere piece of brag, but I think it might teach King Harald that he has to do with men who have heart and skill to use their weapons, and show him what he may expect if he tries to subdue this district. However, be that as it may, the question is, shall we hang back and accept this challenge — for such I regard it — or shall we push on?"

"Yonder is an answer to that question, which settles it for us," said Glumm quietly, pointing to a ridge on the right of the bridle path, which rose high above the tree tops. A troop of horsemen were seen to cross it and gallop down the slope, where they quickly disappeared in the forest.

"How many didst thou count?" asked Erling, with a look of surprise.

"Only ten," answered Glumm.

"Come," cried Erling cheerfully, as he drew his sword, "the odds are not so great as we had expected. I suppose that King Harald must have thought us poor-looking warriors, or perchance he has sent ten berserkers against us. Anyhow I am content. Only one thing do I regret, and that is, that, among the other foolish acts I have been guilty of at this time, I left my good battle-axe behind me. This is a level piece of sward. Shall we await them here?"

"Aye," was Glumm's laconic answer, as he felt the edge of his long two-handed sword, settled himself more firmly on his seat, and carefully looked to the fastenings of his armour.

Erling did the same, and both drew up their steeds with their backs towards an impenetrable thicket. In front lay a level stretch of ground, encumbered only here and there with one or two small bushes, beyond which they had a view far into the dark forest, where the armour of the approaching horsemen could be seen glancing among the tree stems.

"It is likely," muttered Erling, "that they will try to speak us fair at first. Most assassins do, to throw men off their guard. I counsel that our words be few and our action quick."

Glumm gave vent to a deep, short laugh, which sounded, however, marvellously like a growl, and again said —

"Aye."

Next moment the ten horsemen galloped towards them, and reined up at the distance of a few yards, while two of them advanced. One of these, who was no other than Krake the berserk, said in a loud, commanding voice —

"Yield thee, Erling, in the name of the King!"

"That for the King!" cried Erling, splitting the head of Krake's horse with the edge of his sword, and receiving Krake himself on the point of it as he fell forward, so that it went in at his breast and came out at his back. At the same time Glumm's horse sprang forward, his long sword whistled sharply as it flashed through the air, and, next moment, the head of the second man was rolling on the ground.

So sudden was the onset that the others had barely time to guard themselves when Glumm's heavy sword cleft the top of the shield and the helmet of one, tumbling him out of the saddle, while the point of Erling's lighter weapon pierced the throat of another. The remaining six turned aside, right and left, so as to divide their opponents, and then attacked them with great fury — for they were all brave and picked men. At first Erling and Glumm had enough to do to defend themselves, without attempting to attack, but at a critical moment the horse of one of Glumm's opponents stumbled, and his rider being exposed was instantly cut down. Glumm now uttered a shout, for he felt sure of victory, having only two to deal with. Erling's sword proved to be too short for such a combat, for his enemies were armed with long and heavy weapons, and one of them had a spear. He eluded their assaults, however, with amazing activity, and wounded one of them so badly that he was obliged to retire from the fray. Seeing this our hero made a sudden rush at one of the men who fought with a battle-axe, seized the axe by the handle, and with one sweep of his sword lopped off the man's arm.

Then did Erling also feel that victory was secure, for he now wielded an axe that was almost as good and heavy as his own, and only one man stood before him. Under the impulse of this feeling he uttered a shout which rang through the forest like the roar of a lion.

Now, well would it have been for both Erling and Glumm if they had restrained themselves on that occasion, for the shouts they uttered served to guide two bands of enemies who were in search of them.

It will be remembered that Hake the berserk had gone after our heroes by the forest road, but, not finding them so soon as he had anticipated, and feeling a sort of irresistible belief that they had after all gone by the fells, he altered his own plans in so far that he turned towards the road leading by the mountains, before he reached the pine with the double stem. Thus he just missed those whom he sought, and, after some time, came to the conclusion that he was a fool, and had made a great mistake in not holding to his original plan. By way of improving matters he divided his little band into two, and sending five of his men in one direction, rode off with the remaining four in another. Krake, on the contrary, had fulfilled his orders to the letter; had gone to the split rock, and then hastened to the double-stemmed pine, not far from which, as we have seen, he found the men of whom he was in search, and also met his death.

One of the bands of five men chanced to be within earshot when Erling shouted, and they immediately bore down in the direction, and cheered as they came in sight of the combatants. The three men who yet stood up to our friends wheeled about at once and galloped to meet them, only too glad to be reinforced at such a critical moment.

There was a little stream which trickled over the edge of a rock close to the spot where the combat had taken place. Erling and Glumm leaped off their horses as if by one impulse, and, running to this, drank deeply and hastily. As they ran back and vaulted into their saddles, they heard a faint cheer in the far distance.

"Ha!" exclaimed Erling, "Harald doubtless *did* send twenty men after all, for here come the rest of them. It is good fortune that a berserk is seldom a good leader — he should not have divided his force. These eight must go down, friend Glumm, before the others come up, else are our days numbered."

The expression of Glumm's blood-stained visage spoke volumes, but his tongue uttered never a word. Indeed, there was no time for further speech, for the eight men, who had conversed hurriedly together for a few seconds, were now approaching. The two friends did not await the attack, but, setting spurs to their horses, dashed straight at them. Two were overturned in the shock, and their horses rolled on them, so that they never rose again. On the right Erling hewed down one man, and on the left his friend cut down another. They reined up, turned round, and charged again, but the four who were left were too wise to withstand the shock; they swerved aside. In doing so the foot of one of their horses caught in a bramble. He stumbled, and the rider was thrown violently against a tree and stunned, so that he could not remount. This was fortunate, for Erling and Glumm were becoming exhausted, and the three men who still opposed them were comparatively fresh. One of these suddenly charged Glumm, and killed his horse. Glumm leaped up, and, drawing his knife, stabbed the horse of the other to the heart. As it fell he caught his rider by the right wrist, and with a sudden wrench dislocated his arm. Erling meanwhile disabled one of the others, and gave the third such a severe wound that he thought it best to seek safety in flight.

Erling now turned to Glumm, and asked if he thought it would be best to ride away from the men who were still to come up, or to remain and fight them also.

"If there be five more," said Glumm, leaning against a tree, and removing his helmet in order to wipe his brow, "then is our last battle fought, for, although I have that in me which could manage to slay one, I have not strength for two, much less three. Besides, my good steed is dead, and we have no time to catch one of the others."

"Now will I become a berserk," cried Erling, casting his gilt helmet on the ground and undoing the fastenings of his coat of mail. "Armour is good when a man is strong, but when he is worn out it is only an encumbrance. I counsel thee to follow my example."

"It is not a bad one," said Glumm, also throwing down his helmet and stripping off his armour. "Ha! there are more of them than we counted on — six."

As he spoke six horsemen were seen approaching through the distant glades of the forest.

The two friends ran to the fountain before mentioned, slaked their thirst, and hastily bathed their heads and faces; then, seizing their swords and shields, and leaving the rest of their armour on the sward, they ran to a rugged part of the ground, where horses could not act. Mounting to the highest point of a rocky mound, they awaited the approach of their foes.

Quickly they came forward, their faces blazing with wrath as they rode over the field of battle, and saw their slaughtered comrades. Hake the berserk rode in front, and, advancing as near as possible to the place where his enemies stood, said tauntingly:

"What, are ye so fearful of only six men, after having slain so many?"

"Small meat would we make of thee and thy men, so that the crows might pick it easily, if we were only half as fresh as ye are," said Erling; "but we chose to rest here awhile, so if ye would fight ye must come hither to us on foot."

"Nay, but methinks it would be well for both parties," returned the berserk, "that they should fight on level ground."

Erling and Glumm had thrown themselves on the rocks to get as much rest as possible before the inevitable combat that was still before them. They consulted for a few seconds, and then the former replied:

"We will gladly come down, if ye will meet us on foot."

"Agreed," cried the berserk, leaping off his horse, and leading it to a neighbouring tree, to which he fastened it. The others followed his example. Then our two heroes arose and stretched themselves.

"It has been a good fight," said Erling. "Men will talk of it in days to come, after we are far away in the world of spirits."

There was deep pathos in the tone of the young warrior as he spoke these words, and cast his eyes upwards to the blue vault as if he sought to penetrate that spirit world, on the threshold of which he believed himself to stand.

"If we had but one hour's rest, or one other man on our side; but —" He stopped suddenly, for the six men now stood in the middle of the little plain where Erling and Glumm had fought so long and so valiantly that day, and awaited their coming.

Hastily descending the mound, the two friends strode boldly towards their opponents, scorning to let them see by look or gesture that they were either fatigued or depressed. As they drew near, Erling singled out Hake, and Glumm went towards a tall, powerful man, who stood ready with a huge sword resting on his shoulder, as if eager to begin the combat. Glumm had arranged in his own mind that that man and he should die together. Beside him stood a warrior with a battle-axe, and a steel helmet on his head. Before Glumm could reach his intended victim the tall man's sword flashed in the air like a gleam of light, and the head with the steel helmet went spinning on the ground!

"That's the way that Kettle Flatnose pays off old scores," cried the Irish thrall, turning suddenly upon his late friends, and assailing one of them with such fury that he cut him down in a few seconds, and then ran to draw off one of the two who had attacked Erling. Glumm's amazement at this was, as may well be believed, excessive; but it was nothing to the intensity of his joy when he found suddenly that the fight was now equalised, and that there stood only one man to oppose him. His heart leaped up. New life gave spring to his muscles; and to these new feelings he gave vent in one loud shout, as he sprang upon his adversary and cleft him to the chin with one sweep of his sword!

Meanwhile Kettle Flatnose had killed his man; and he was about to come up behind Hake and sweep off his head, when he was seized by Glumm and dragged violently back.

"Would ye rob Erling of the honour of slaying this noted berserk?" he said sternly.

"Truly," replied Kettle, somewhat abashed, "I did not know that he was noted; and as for the honour of it, I do think that Erling seems to have got honour enough to-day (if all this be his work) to content him for some time to come; but as ye will," he added, putting the point of his sword on the ground, and resting his arms on the hilt.

Glumm also leaned on his sword; and standing thus, these two watched the fight.

Now, it may perhaps seem to some readers that as the other men had been disposed of so summarily, it was strange that Erling the Bold should be so long in dispatching this one; but for our hero's credit, we must point out several facts which may have perhaps been overlooked. In the first place, Kettle Flatnose was a thoroughly fresh man when he began the fight, and although he killed two men, it must be remembered that one of these was slain while off his guard. Then, Glumm did indeed slay his man promptly, but he was one of King Harald's ordinary men-at-arms; whereas Erling was opposed by one of the most celebrated of the King's warriors — Hake, the berserk of Hadeland — a man whose name and prowess were known far and wide, not only in Norway, but in Denmark, and all along the southern shores of the Baltic. It would have been strange indeed had such a man fallen easily before any human arm, much more strange had he succumbed at once to one that had been already much exhausted with fighting.

True to the brotherhood to which he belonged, the berserk attacked Erling with incredible fury. He roared more like a mad bull than a man as he made the onset; his eyes glared, his mouth foamed, and he bit his shield as he was driven back. Being fresh, he danced round Erling perpetually, springing in to cut and thrust, and leaping back to avoid the terrific blows which the latter fetched at him with his weighty axe. Once he made a cut at Erling's head, which the latter did not attempt to parry, intending to trust to his helmet to defend him, and forgetting for the moment that he had cast that useful piece of armour on the plain. Luckily the blow was not truly aimed. It shore a lock from Erling's head as he swung his axe against his opponent's shield, and battered him down on his knees; but the berserk leaped up with a yell, and again rushed at him. Hake happened just then to cast his eyes on the two men who were quietly looking on, and he so managed the fight for a few moments afterwards that he got near to them. Then turning towards them with a howl of demoniacal fury, he made a desperate cut at the unsuspecting Glumm, who was taken so thoroughly by surprise that he made no movement whatever to defend himself. Fortunately. Kettle Flatnose was on the alert, but he had only time to thrust his sword awkwardly between Glumm's head and the descending weapon. The act prevented a fatal gash, but it could not altogether arrest the force of the blow, which fell on the flat of his sword, and beat it down on Glumm's skull so violently that he was instantly stretched upon the green sward. Erling's axe fell on the helm of the berserk almost at the same time. Even in that moment of victory a feeling of respect for the courage and boldness of this man touched the heart of Erling, who, with the swiftness of thought, put in force his favourite practice — he turned the edge of the axe, and the broad side of it fell on the steel headpiece with tremendous force, causing the berserk of Hadeland to stretch himself on the green sward beside Glumm the Gruff; thus ending the famous battle of the "Berserkers and the Bold", in regard to which Thikskul the scald writes:

> "The Bold one and his doughty friend,
> Glumm the Gruff of Horlingsend,
> Faced, fought, and felled, and bravely slew,
> Full twenty men — a berserk crew
> Sent by King Harald them to slay —
> But much he rued it — lack-a-day!
>> The heroes cut and hacked them sore,
>> Hit, split, and slashed them back and fore —
>> And left them lying in their gore."

CHAPTER XIII.

Shows that Eloquence does not always flow when it is expected, and that Glumm begins a New Course of Action.

On examination it was found that Glumm's hurt was not severe. He had merely been stunned by the force of the blow, and there was a trifling wound in the scalp from which a little blood flowed. While Kettle held a helmet full of water, and Erling bathed the wound, the latter said:

"How comes it, Kettle, that ye discovered our straits, and appeared so fortunately?"

Kettle laughed and said: "The truth is, that accident brought me here. You know that I had all but wrought out my freedom by this time, but in consideration of my services in the battle at the Springs, Ulf set me free at once, and this morning I left him to seek service with King Harald Haarfager."

"That was thankless of thee," said Erling.

"So said Ulf," rejoined Kettle; "nevertheless, I came off, and was on my way over the fells to go to the King when I fell in with Hake the berserk — though I knew not that it was he — and joined him."

Erling frowned, and looked enquiringly at Kettle as he said:

"But what possessed thee, that thou shouldst quit so good a master for one so bad, and how comes it thou hast so readily turned against the King's men?"

"Little wonder that you are perplexed," said Kettle, "seeing that ye know not my motive. The truth is, that I had a plan in my head, which was to enter Harald's service, that I might act the spy on him, and so do my best for one who, all the time I have been in thraldom, has been as kind to me as if he had been my own father."

"Thou meanest Ulf?" said Erling.

"I do," replied Kettle with enthusiasm, "and I'd willingly die for him if need be. As ye know full well, it needs no wizard to tell that such men as Ulf and your father will not easily be made to bend their necks to the King's yoke; and for this I honour them, because they respect the law of the land more than they respect the King. Happy is the nation where such men abound; and in saying this I do no dishonour to the King, but the reverse."

Erling looked in surprise at Kettle, while he continued to bathe the face of his still unconscious friend, for his language and bearing were much altered from what they had been when he was in thraldom, and there was an air of quiet dignity about him, which seemed to favour the common report that he had been a man of note in his own land.

"Well," continued Kettle, "it is equally certain that Harald is not a man who will tamely submit to be thwarted in his plans, so I had made up my mind to take service with him, in order that I might be able to find out his intentions and observe his temper towards the men of Horlingdal, and thus be in a position to give them timely warning of any danger that threatened. On my way hither I met Hake, as I have said. On hearing that he belonged to King Harald, I told him that I had just got my freedom from Ulf, and wished to join the King. He seemed very glad, and said he thought I would make a good berserk; told me that he was out in search of some of the King's enemies, and proposed that I should assist him. Of course this suited me well; but it was only when we found you that I became aware who the King's enemies were, and resolved to act as ye have seen me do. I did not choose to tell Ulf my intention, lest my plan should miscarry; but, now that I find who the King counts his foes, and know how sharply he intends to treat them, it seems to me that I need go no farther."

"Truly thou needst not," said Erling, "for Harald is in the worst possible humour with us all, and did his best to stop me from going home to tell the fact."

"Then is my mission ended. I will return to Ulfstede," said Kettle, throwing the water out of his helmet, and replacing it on his head, as he rose and grasped his sword. "Meanwhile, I will cut off Hake's head, and take it back with me."

"Thou wilt do so at thy peril," said Erling; "Hake fell to my hand, and I will finish the work which I have begun. Do thou go catch three or four of the horses, for I see that Glumm is recovering."

"I will not interfere with your business," said Kettle, with a laugh, "only I thought you meant to leave his carcass lying there unheeded, and was unwilling to go off without his head as a trophy."

Kettle went to catch the horses — three of which he tied to trees to be ready for them, while he loaded the fourth with the most valuable of the arms and garments of the slain. Meanwhile Glumm groaned, and, sitting up, rubbed his head ruefully.

"I thought someone had sent me to Valhalla," he said, fetching a deep sigh.

"Not yet, friend Glumm, not yet. There is still work for thee to do on earth, and the sooner ye set about doing it the better, for methinks the King will wonder what has become of his berserkers, and will send out men in search of them ere long. Canst mount thy horse?"

"Mount him? aye," said Glumm, leaping up, but staggering when he had gained his legs, so that Erling had to support him for a few minutes. He put his hand to his forehead, and, observing blood on it, asked: "Is the wound deep?"

"Only a scratch," said Erling, "but the blow was heavy. If the sword of Kettle Flatnose had not caught it in time, it would have been thy death."

"Truly it has not been far from that as it is, for my head rings as if the brain were being battered with Thor's hammer! Come, let us mount."

As he spoke, Kettle brought forward the horses. Glumm mounted with difficulty, and they all rode away. But Erling had observed a slight motion of life in the body of Hake, and after they had gone a few yards he said: "Ride on slowly, Glumm, I will go back to get a ring from the finger of the berserk, which I forgot."

He turned, and rode quickly back to the place where the berserk's body lay, dismounted, and kneeled beside it. There was a large silver ring on the middle finger of Hake's right hand, which he took off and put on his own finger, replacing it with a gold one of his own. Then he ran to the spring, and, filling his helmet with water, came back and laved the man's temples therewith, at the same time pouring a little of it into his mouth. In a few minutes he began to show symptoms of revival, but before he had recovered sufficiently to recognise who his benefactor was, Erling had vaulted into the saddle and galloped away.

They arrived at Glummstede that evening about supper-time, but Glumm was eager to hear the discussion that was sure to take place when the news of the fight and of Harald's state of mind was told, so he rode past his own home, and accompanied his friend to Ulfstede. We cannot say for certain that he was uninfluenced by other motives, for Glumm, as the reader knows, was not a communicative man; he never spoke to anyone on the subject; we incline, however, to the belief that there were mingled ideas in his brain and mixed feelings in his heart as he rode to Ulfstede!

Great was the sensation in the hall when Erling, Glumm, and Kettle entered with the marks of the recent fight still visible upon them — especially on Glumm, whose scalp wound, being undressed, permitted a crimson stream to trickle down his face — a stream which, in his own careless way, he wiped off now and then with the sleeve of his coat, thereby making his aspect conspicuously bloody. Tremendous was the flutter in Ada's heart when she saw him in this plight, for well did she know that deeds of daring had been done before such marks could have been left upon her gruff lover.

The hall was crowded with armed men, for many bonders had assembled to await the issue of the decision at the Thing, and much anxiety as well as excitement prevailed. Ulf recognised his late thrall with a look of surprise, but each of them was made to quaff a brimming tankard of ale before being allowed to speak. To say truth, they were very willing to accept the draught, which, after the fatigues they had undergone, tasted like nectar.

Erling then stood up, and in the midst of breathless silence began to recount the incidents which had befallen him and his companion while in the execution of their mission.

"In the first place," he said, "it is right to let ye all know that the King's countenance towards us is as black as a thundercloud, and that we may expect to see the lightning flash out before long. But it is some comfort to add that Glumm and Kettle and I have slain, or rendered unfit to fight, twenty of Harald's men."

In the midst of the murmur of congratulation with which this announcement was received, Erling observed that Hilda, who had been standing near the door, went out. The result of this was, that the poor youth's spirit sank, and it was with the utmost difficulty he plucked up heart to relate the incidents of the fight, in which he said so little about himself that one might have imagined he had been a mere spectator. Passing from that subject as quickly as possible, he delivered his opinion as to the hopes and prospects before them, and, cutting his speech short, abruptly quitted the hall.

Any little feeling of disappointment that might have been felt at the lame way in which Erling had recounted his exploits was, however, amply compensated by Glumm, who, although usually a man of few words, had no lack of ideas or of power to express them when occasion required, in a terse, stern style of his own, which was very telling. He gave a faithful account of the fight, making mention of many incidents which his friend had omitted to touch on, and dwelling particularly on the deeds of Kettle. As to that flat-nosed individual himself, when called upon to speak, he addressed the assembly with a dignity of manner and a racy utterance of language which amazed those who had only known him as a thrall, and who now for the first time met him as a freed man. He moreover introduced into his speech a few touches of humour which convulsed his audience with laughter, and commented on the condition of affairs in a way that filled them with respect, so that from that hour he became one of the noted men of the dale.

Erling meanwhile hurried towards one of the cliffs overlooking the fiord. He was well acquainted with Hilda's favourite haunts, and soon found her, seated on a bank, with a very disconsolate look, which, however, vanished on his appearing.

"Wherefore didst thou hasten away just as I began to speak, Hilda?" he said, somewhat reproachfully, as he sat down beside her.

"Because I did not wish to hear details of the bloody work of which thou art so fond. Why wilt thou always be seeking to slay thy fellows?"

The girl spoke in tones so sad and desponding, that her lover looked upon her for some time in silent surprise.

"Truly, Hilda," he said, "the fight was none of my seeking."

"Did I not hear thee say," she replied, "that Kettle and Glumm and thou had slain twenty of the King's men, and that ye regarded this as a comforting thought?"

"Aye, surely; but these twenty men did first attack Glumm and me while alone, and we slew them in self-defence. Never had I returned to tell it, had not stout Kettle Flatnose come to our aid."

"Thank Heaven for that!" said Hilda, with a look of infinite relief. "How did it happen?"

"Come. I will tell thee all from first to last. And here is one who shall judge whether Glumm and I are to blame for slaying these men."

As he spoke, the hermit approached. The old man looked somewhat paler than usual, owing to the loss of blood caused by the wound he had received in his recent defence of Ulfstede. Erling rose and saluted him heartily, for, since the memorable prowess in the defence of Ulfstede, Christian had been high in favour among the people of the neighbourhood.

"Hilda and I were considering a matter of which we will make thee judge," said Erling, as they sat down on the bank together.

"I will do my best," said the hermit, with a smile, "if Hilda consents to trust my judgment."

"That she gladly does," said the maid.

"Well, then, I will detail the facts of the case," said Erling; "but first tell me what strange marks are those on the skin thou holdest in thy hand?"

"These are words," said the hermit, carefully spreading out a roll of parchment, on which a few lines were written.

Erling and Hilda regarded the strange characters with much interest. Indeed, the young man's look almost amounted to one of awe, for he had never seen the scroll before, although Hilda, to whom it had several times been shown and explained, had told him about it.

"These marks convey thoughts," said Christian, laying his forefinger on the characters.

"Can they convey intricate thoughts," asked Erling, "such as are difficult to express?"

"Aye; there is no thought which can quit the tongue of one man and enter the understanding of another which may not be expressed by these letters in different combinations."

"Dim ideas of this have been in my mind," said Erling, "since I went on viking cruise to the south, when first I heard of such a power being known to and used by many, but I believed it not. If this be as thou sayest, and these letters convey thy thoughts, then, though absent, thy thoughts might be known to me — if I did but understand the tracing of them."

"Most true," returned the hermit; "and more than that, there be some who, though dead, yet speak to their fellows, and will continue to do so as long as the records are preserved and the power to comprehend them be maintained."

"Mysterious power," said Erling; "I should like much to possess it."

"If thou wilt come to my poor abode on the cliff I will teach it thee. A few months, or less, will suffice. Even Hilda knows the names of the separate signs, and she has applied herself to it for little more than a few days."

Hilda's face became scarlet when Erling looked at her in surprise, but the unobservant hermit went on to descant upon the immense value of written language, until Hilda reminded him that he had consented to sit in judgment on a knotty point.

"True, I had forgotten. — Come now, Erling, let me hear it."

The youth at once began, and in a few minutes had so interested his hearers that they gazed in his face and hung upon his words with rapt attention, while he detailed the incidents of the combats with a degree of fluency and fervour that would have thrown the oratory of Glumm and Kettle quite into the shade had it been told in the hall.

While Erling was thus engaged, his friend Glumm, having finished the recital of his adventures for the twentieth time, and at the same time eaten a good supper, was advised by his companions to have the wound in his head looked to.

"What! hast thou not had it dressed yet?" asked Ulf; "why, that is very foolish. Knowest thou not that a neglected wound may compass thy death? Come hither, Ada; thy fingers are skilled in such offices. Take Glumm to an inner chamber, and see if thou canst put his head to rights."

"Methinks," cried Guttorm Stoutheart, with a laugh, "that she is more likely to put his heart wrong than his head right with these wicked black eyes of hers. Have a care, Glumm: they pierce deeper than the sword of the berserk."

Ada pretended not to hear this, but she appeared by no means displeased, as she led Glumm to an inner chamber, whither they were followed by Alric, whose pugnacious soul had been quite fascinated by the story of the recent fight, and who was never tired of putting questions as to minute points.

As Glumm sat down on a low stool to enable Ada to get at his head, she said (for she was very proud of her lover's prowess, and her heart chanced to be in a melting mood that night), "Thou hast done well to-day, it would seem?"

"It is well thou thinkest so," replied Glumm curtly, remembering Erling's advice. — "No, boy," he added, in reply to Alric, "I did not kill the one with the black helmet; it was Erling who gave him his deathblow."

"Did Hake the berserk look *dreadfully* fierce?" asked Alric.

"He made a few strange faces," replied Glumm.

"The wound is but slight," observed Ada, in a tone that indicated a little displeasure at the apparent indifference of her lover.

"It might have been worse," replied Glumm.

"Do tell me all about it again," entreated Alric.

"Not now," said Glumm; "I'll repeat it when Hilda is by; she has not heard it yet — methinks she would like to hear it."

"Hilda like to hear it!" cried the lad, with a shout of laughter; "why, she detests fighting almost as much as the hermit does, though, I must say, for a man who hates it, he can do it wonderfully well himself! But do tell me, Glumm, what was the cut that Erling gave when he brought down that second man, you know — the big one —"

"Which? the man whose head he chopped off, with half of the left shoulder?"

"No; that was the fourth. I mean the other one, with —"

"Oh, the one he split the nose of by accident before battering down with —"

"No, no," cried Alric, "I mean the one with the black beard."

"Ha!" exclaimed Glumm, "that wasn't the second man; his fall was much further on in the fight, just after Erling had got hold of the battle-axe. He whirled the axe round his head, brought it from over the left down on Blackbeard's right shoulder, and split him to the waist."

"Now, that is finished," said Ada sharply, as she put away the things that she had used in the dressing of the wound. "I hope that every foe thou hast to deal with in future may let thee off as well."

"I thank thee, Ada, both for the dressing and the good wish," said Glumm gravely, as he rose and walked into the hall, followed by his persevering and insatiable little friend.

Ada retired hastily to her own chamber, where she stood for a moment motionless, then twice stamped her little foot, after which she sat down on a stool, and, covering her face with both hands, burst into a passionate flood of tears.

CHAPTER XIV.

*In which Alric boasts a little, discovers Secrets, confesses a
little, and distinguishes himself greatly.*

Next day there was great bustle at Ulfstede, and along the shores of the
fiord, for the men of Horlingdal were busy launching their ships and making
preparations to go to the Springs to meet and hold council with King Harald
Haarfager.

It had been finally resolved, without a dissentient voice, that the whole district should go forth to meet him in arms, and thus ensure fair play at the delib-
erations of the Thing. Even Haldor no longer objected; but, on the contrary,
when he heard his son's account of his meeting with the King, and of the das-
tardly attempt that had been made to assassinate him and his friend, there shot
across his face a gleam of that wild ferocity which had procured him his title. It
passed quickly away, however, and gave place to a look of sad resignation, which
assured those who knew him that he regarded their chance of opposing the King
successfully to be very small indeed.

The fleet that left the fiord consisted of the longships of Ulf, Haldor,
Erling, Glumm, and Guttorm, besides an innumerable flotilla of smaller crafts
and boats. Many of the men were well armed, not only with first-rate weapons,
but with complete suits of excellent mail of the kinds peculiar to the period —
such as shirts of leather, with steel rings sewed thickly over them, and others covered with steel scales — while of the poorer bonders and the thralls some wore
portions of defensive armour, and some trusted to the thick hides of the wolf,
which were more serviceable against a sword-cut than many people might suppose. All had shields, however, and carried either swords, bills, spears, javelins,
axes, or bows and arrows, so that, numbering as they did, about a thousand men,
they composed a formidable host.

While these rowed away over the fiord to the Springs to make war or
peace — as the case might be — with King Harald, a disappointed spirit was left
behind in Horlingdal.

"I'm sure I cannot see why I should not be allowed to go too," said little
Alric, on returning to Haldorstede, after seeing the fleet set forth. "Of course I
cannot fight so well as Erling *yet*, but I can do *something* in that way; and can even
face up to a full-grown man when occasion serves, as that red-haired Dane knows
full well, methinks, if he has got any power of feeling in his neck!"

This was said to Herfrida, who was in the great hall spreading the board for
the midday meal, and surrounded by her maidens, some of whom were engaged
in spinning or carding wool, while others wove and sewed, or busied themselves
about household matters.

"Have patience, my son," said Herfrida. "Thou art not yet strong enough
to go forth to battle. Doubtless, in three or four years —"

"Three or four years!" exclaimed Alric, to whom such a space of time appeared an age. "Why, there will be no more fighting left to be done at the end of three or four years. Does not father say that if the King succeeds in his illegal plans all the independence of the small kings will be gone for ever, and – and – of course I am old enough to see that if the small kings are not allowed to do as they please, there will be no more occasion for war – nothing but a dull time of constant peace!"

Herfrida laughed lightly, while her warlike son strutted up and down the ancestral hall like a bantam cock, frowning and grunting indignantly, as he brooded over the dark prospects of peace that threatened his native land, and thought of his own incapacity, on account of youth, to make glorious hay while yet the sun of war was shining.

"Mother," he said, stopping suddenly, and crossing his arms, as he stood with his feet planted pretty wide apart, after the fashion of those who desire to be thought very resolute – "mother, I had a dream last night."

"Tell it me, my son," said Herfrida, sitting down on a low stool beside the lad.

Now, it must be known that in those days the Northmen believed in dreams and omens and warnings – indeed, they were altogether a very superstitious people, having perfect faith in giants, good and bad; elves, dark and bright; wraiths, and fetches, and guardian spirits – insomuch that there was scarcely one among the grown-up people who had not seen some of these fabulous creatures, or who had not seen some other people who had either seen them themselves or had seen individuals who *said* they had seen them! There were also many "clear-sighted" or "fore-sighted" old men and women, who not only saw goblins and supernatural appearances occasionally, and, as it were, accidentally, like ordinary folk, but who also had the gift – so it is said – of seeing such things when they pleased – enjoyed, as it were, an unenviable privilege in that way. It was therefore with unusual interest that Herfrida asked about her son's dream.

"It must have been mara[10], I think," he said, "for though I never had it before, it seemed to me very like what Guttorm Stoutheart says he always has after eating too hearty a meal."

"Relate it, my son."

"Well, you must know," said Alric, with much gravity and importance, for he observed that the girls about the room were working softly that they might hear him, "I dreamed that I was out on the fells, and there I met a dreadful wolf, as big as a horse, with two heads and three tails, or three heads and two tails, I mind not which, but it gave me little time to notice it, for, before I was aware, it dashed at me, and I turned to run, but my feet seemed to cleave to the earth, and my legs felt heavy as lead, so that I could scarce drag myself along, yet, strange to say, the wolf did not overtake me, although I heard it coming nearer and nearer every moment, and I tried to shout, but my voice would not come out."

10   nightmare

"What hadst thou to supper last night?" asked Herfrida.

"Let me think," replied the boy meditatively; "I had four cuts of salmon, three rolls of bread and butter, half a wild-duck, two small bits of salt-fish, some eggs, a little milk, and a horn of ale."

"It must have been mara," said she, thoughtfully; "but go on with thy dream."

"Well, just as I came to the brink of the river, I looked back and saw the wolf close at my heels, so I dropped suddenly, and the wolf tumbled right over me into the water, but next moment it came up in the shape of another monster with a fish's tail, which made straight at me. Then it all at once came into my head that my guardian spirit was behind me, and I turned quickly round but did not see it."

"Art thou quite sure of that, my son?"

Herfrida asked this in a tone of great anxiety, for to see one's own guardian spirit was thought unlucky, and a sign that the person seeing it was "fey", or death-doomed.

"I'm quite sure that I did not," replied Alric, to the manifest relief of his mother; "but I saw a long pole on the ground, which I seized, and attacked the beast therewith, and a most notable fight we had. I only wish that it had been true, and that thou hadst been there to see it. Mara fled away at once, for I felt no more fear, but laid about me in a way that minded me of Erling. Indeed, I don't think he could have done it better himself. Oh! how I do wish, sometimes, that my dreams would come true! However, I killed the monster at last, and hurled him into the river, after which I felt tossed about in a strange way, and then my senses left me, and then I awoke."

"What thinkest thou of the dream?" said Herfrida to a wrinkled old crone who sat on a low stool beside the fire.

The witch-like old creature roused herself a little and said:

"Good luck is in store for the boy."

"Thanks for that, granny," said Alric; "canst say what sort o' good luck it is?"

"No; my knowledge goes no further. It may be good luck in great things, it may be only in small matters; perhaps soon, perhaps a long time hence: I know not."

Having ventured this very safe and indefinite prophecy, the old woman let her chin drop on her bosom, and recommenced the rocking to and fro which had been interrupted by the question; while Alric laughed, and, taking up a three-pronged spear, said that as he had been disappointed in going to see the fun at the Springs, he would console himself by going and sticking salmon at the foss[11].

"Wilt thou not wait for midday meal?" said Herfrida.

11   waterfall

"No, mother; this roll will suffice till night."

"And then thou wilt come home ravening, and have mara again."

"Be it so. I'd run the risk of that for the sake of the chance of another glorious battle such as I had last night!"

Saying this the reckless youth sallied forth with the spear or leister on his shoulder, and took the narrow bridle path leading up the glen.

It was one of those calm bright days of early autumn in which men *feel* that they draw in fresh life and vigour at each inhalation. With the fragrant odours that arose from innumerable wild flowers, including that sweetest of plants, the lily of the valley, was mingled the pleasant smell of the pines, which clothed the knolls, or hung here and there like eyebrows on the cliffs. The river was swollen considerably by recent heat, which had caused the great glaciers on the mountain tops to melt more rapidly than usual, and its rushing sound was mingled with the deeper roar of the foss, or waterfall, which leaped over a cliff thirty feet high about two miles up the valley. Hundreds of rills of all sizes fell and zigzagged down the mountains on either side, some of them appearing like threads of silver on the precipices, and all, river and rills, being as cold as the perpetual ice-fields above which gave them birth. Birds twittered in the bushes, adding sweetness to the wild music, and bright greens and purples, lit up by gleams of sunshine, threw a charm of softness over the somewhat rugged scene.

The Norse boy's nature was sensitive, and peculiarly susceptible of outward influences. As he walked briskly along, casting his eager gaze now at the river which foamed below him, and anon at the distant mountain ridges capped with perennial snows, he forgot his late disappointment, or, which is the same thing, drowned it in present enjoyment. Giving vent to his delight, much as boys did a thousand years later, by violent whistling or in uproarious bursts of song, he descended to the river's edge, with the intention of darting his salmon spear, when his eye caught sight of a woman's skirt fluttering on one of the cliffs above. He knew that Hilda and Ada had gone up the valley together on a visit to a kinswoman, for Herfrida had spoken of expecting them back to midday meal; guessing, therefore, that it must be them, he drew back out of sight, and clambered hastily up the bank, intending to give them a surprise. He hid himself in the bushes at a jutting point which they had to pass, and from which there was a magnificent view of the valley, the fiord, and the distant sea.

He heard the voices of the two girls in animated conversation as they drew near, and distinguished the name of Glumm more than once, but, not being a gossip by nature, he thought nothing of this, and was intent only on pouncing out on them when they should reach a certain stone in the path. Truth constrains us to admit that our young friend, like many young folk of the present day, was a practical joker — yet it must also be said that he was not a very bad one, and, to his honour be it recorded, he never practised jokes on old people!

It chanced, however, that the two friends stopped short just before reaching the stone, so that Alric had to exercise patience while the girls contemplated the view — at least while Hilda did so, for on Ada's face there was a frown, and her eyes were cast on the ground.

"How lovely Horlingdal looks on such a day!" observed Hilda.

"I have no eyes for beautiful things to-night," said Ada pettishly; "I cannot get over it — such cool, thankless indifference when I took the trouble to dress his — his — stupid head, and then, not satisfied with telling the whole story over to thee, who cares no more for it than if it were the slaying of half a dozen sheep, he must needs go and pay frequent visits to Ingeborg and to Halgerda of the Foss — and — and — But I know it is all out of spite, and that he does not care a bodkin for either of them, yet I cannot bear it, and I *won't* bear it, so he had better look to himself. And yet I would not for the best mantle in the dale that he knew I had two thoughts about the matter."

"But why play fast and loose with him?" said Hilda, with a laugh at her companion's vehemence.

"Because I like it and I choose to do so."

"But perchance he does not like it, and does not choose to be treated so."

"I care not for that."

"Truly thy looks and tone belie thee," said Hilda, smiling. "But in all seriousness, Ada, let me advise thee again to be more considerate with Glumm, for I sometimes think that the men who are most worth having are the most easily turned aside."

"Hast thou found it so with Erling?" demanded Ada half-angrily.

Hilda blushed scarlet at this and said:

"I never thought of Erling in this light; at least I never — he never — that is —"

Fortunately at this point Alric, in his retreat among the bushes, also blushed scarlet, for it only then flashed upon him that he had been acting the mean part of an eavesdropper, and had been listening to converse which he should not have heard. Instead, therefore, of carrying out his original intention, he scrambled into the path with as much noise as possible, and coughed, as he came awkwardly forward.

"Why, the wicked boy has been listening," cried Ada, laying her hand upon the lad's shoulder, and looking sternly into his face.

"I have," said Alric bluntly.

"And art thou not ashamed?"

"I am," he replied, with a degree of candour in his self-condemnation which caused Ada and Hilda to burst into a hearty fit of laughter.

"But," said Ada, becoming grave again, "thou hast heard too much for thy good."

"I know it," he replied, "and I'm sorry, Ada, but cannot help it now. This will I say, however: I had no wish or intention to hear when I hid myself. My desire was only to startle thee and Hilda, and before I thought what thou wert talking of the thing was out, and now I have got it I cannot unget it."

"True, but thou canst keep it," said Ada.

"I can, and ye may rest assured no word or look of mine shall betray thee. I'll even try to conceal it from myself, and think it was a dream, unless, indeed, I see a good chance of helping thee in this affair!"

Alric laughed as he said this, and the girls joined him, after which they all went on towards Haldorstede together.

On reaching the place where Alric had intended to fish, Ada suggested that he should go and try his fortune, so he ran down to the river, and the girls followed him to the bank.

The spot selected was a rapid which terminated in a small and comparatively quiet but deep pool. We say comparatively, because in the state of the river at that time even in the quietest places there was considerable commotion. Just below the pool the river opened out into a broad shallow, over which it passed in noisy foam, but with little depth, except in the centre. Below this, again, it narrowed, and formed another deep pool.

Alric ran into the water till he was about knee-deep, and then plunged his spear. Nothing resulted from the first plunge, but the effect of the second was more tremendous than had ever before happened to the young sportsman, for the pole of the trident received a twist so violent that it would infallibly have been torn from the boy's grasp had he not held on with the tenacity of a vice, and allowed himself to be dragged bodily into the pool. As we have said, the pool was deep, but that was nothing to Alric, who could swim like a duck. The Norse maidens who watched him knew this, and although slightly alarmed, felt on the whole more inclined to laugh than to tremble as his head emerged and sank again several times, while the fish which he had struck dragged him about the pool. After a few seconds of violent and wild exertion it rushed down the pool into the rapid, and then it was that the girls perceived that Alric had struck and was clinging to one of the largest-sized salmon that ever appeared in Horlingdal river.

Fortunate it was for the boy that the fish took the rapid, for it had almost choked him in the deep pool; but now he scrambled on his feet, and began to do battle gallantly — endeavouring to thrust the fish downwards and pin it to the stones whenever it passed over a shallow part, on which occasions its back and silver sides became visible, and its great tail — wide spreading, like a modern lady's fan — flashed in the air as it beat the water in terror or fury. Alric's spirit was ablaze with excitement, for the fish was too strong for him, so that every time it wriggled itself he was made to shake and stagger in a most ridiculously helpless manner, and when it tried to bolt he was pulled flat down on his face and had to follow it — sometimes on his knees, sometimes at full length, for, over and over again, when he was about to rise, or had half-risen, there was another pull, and down he went again, quite flat, while the roaring torrent went right over him.

But no limpet ever stuck to rock with greater tenacity than did Alric to the handle of that trident; and it is but just to add, for the information of those who know it not, that the difficulty of retaining one's foothold on the pebbly bed of a river when knee-deep in a foaming rapid is very great indeed, even when one has nothing more to do than attend to the balancing of one's own body — much greater, of course, in circumstances such as we describe.

At last the salmon made a rush, and was swept over a shallow part of the rapid, close under the bank on which the girls stood. Here Alric succeeded in thrusting it against a large stone. For the first time he managed to stand up erect, and, although holding the fish with all his might, looked up, and breathed, or rather gasped, freely:

"Hoch! hah! *what* a fish! sk-ho!"

"Oh, I wish we could help thee!" exclaimed the girls, with flashing eyes and outstretched hands, as if they could hardly restrain themselves from leaping into the water, which was indeed the case!

"N-no! ye can't! 's not poss'ble — hah! my! oh there 'e goes again — s-t-swash!"

Down he went, flat, as he spoke, and water stopped his utterance, while the fish wriggled into the centre of the channel, and carried him into the deep pool below!

Here the scene was not quite so exciting, because the battle was not so fierce. The salmon had it all his own way in the deep water, and dragged his attached friend hither and thither as he pleased. On the other hand, Alric ceased to contend, and merely held on with his right hand, while with his left he kept his head above water. The pool circled about in large oily wavelets flecked with foam, so that there was a great contrast in all this to the tremendous turmoil of the raging rapid. But the comparative calm did not last long. The huge fish made a frantic, and apparently a last, effort to get free. It rushed down to the foot of the pool, and passed over the edge into the next rapid.

The girls shrieked when they saw this, for, unlike the former, this one was a deep rush of the river, between narrower banks, where its course was obstructed by large rocks. Against these the stream beat furiously. Alric knew the spot well, and was aware of the extreme danger of his position. He therefore made a violent effort to drag the fish towards a point where there was a slight break or eddy among a number of boulders, intending to let him go, if necessary, rather than lose his life. He succeeded, however, in getting upon one of the rocks quite close to the bank, and then endeavoured to lift the fish out of the water. In this also he was successful; made a splendid heave, and flung it with all his force towards the bank, on which it alighted, trident and all, at the feet of Hilda. But in letting go his hold of the handle Alric lost his balance, flung his arms above his head in a vain endeavour to recover himself, and, with a loud shout, fell back into the roaring torrent and was swept away.

A few moments sufficed to carry him into the pool below, to the edge of which the girls rushed, and found that he was floating round and round in a state of insensibility, every moment passing near to the vortex of the rapid that flowed out of it. Hilda at once rushed in waist-deep and caught him by the collar. She would have been swept away along with him, but Ada also sprang forward and grasped Hilda by the mantle. She could not, however, drag her back; neither could Hilda in any way help herself. Thus they stood for a few moments swaying to and fro in the current, and, doubtless, one or more of them would have soon been carried down had not efficient aid been at hand.

High up on the cliff over the scene where this incident occurred, Christian the hermit was seated on a log before his door. He sat gazing dreamily out upon the landscape when Alric began to fish, but, seeing the danger to which the lad exposed himself, after he had speared the fish, and fearing that there might be need of his aid, he quickly descended to the scene of action. He did not arrive a moment too soon, for the whole event occurred very rapidly. Running to the rescue he caught Ada round the waist with both hands, and drew her gently back; she was soon out of danger, after which there was no great difficulty in dragging the others safely to land.

At once the hermit stripped off the boy's coat, loosened the kerchief that was round his throat, and sought, by every means in his power, to restore him to consciousness. His efforts were successful. The boy soon began to breathe, and in a short time stood up, swaying himself to and fro, and blinking.

The first thing he said was:

"Where is the salmon?"

"The salmon? Oh, I forgot all about it," said Ada.

"Never mind it, dear Alric," said Hilda.

"Never mind it?" he cried, starting into sudden animation; "what! have ye left it behind?"

Saying this he burst away from his friends, and ran up the bank of the river until he came to where the fish was lying, still impaled on the barbed prongs of the trident. The run so far restored him that he had sufficient strength to shoulder the fish, although it afterwards turned out to be a salmon of thirty-five pounds weight, and he quickly rejoined his friends, who returned with him to Haldorstede, where, you may be quite sure, he gave a graphic account of the adventure to willing and admiring ears.

"So, granny," he said, at the conclusion of the narrative, to the old crone who was still seated by the fire, "thy prophecy has come true sooner than ye expected, and it has come doubly true, for though the good luck in store for me was a matter of small general importance, no one can deny that it is a great fish!"

CHAPTER XV.

Treats of Ancient Diplomacy among the Norsemen, and shows how our Hero turns the Tables on a would-be Assassin.

When King Harald heard the news of the defeat of Hake and the slaughter of his men by Erling and Glumm, great was his wrath at first, and Jarl Rongvold had much ado to appease him and prevent him from going at once to Horlingdal to ravage it with fire and sword. But when he had cooled a little, and heard the details of the fight from Hake himself, his anger against the young warriors changed into admiration of their dauntless courage.

Harald Fairhair was a kingly man in spirit as well as in appearance, and was above encouraging a mean or vengeful mood. He was indeed fierce and violent in his rage, and often did things which, when read of in the calm of a comparatively peaceful time, make one shudder; but it must not be forgotten that the age in which he lived was a cruel and bloody one, and, in Norway, without one touch of the gentle religion of Christ to soften its asperities. He could never have retained his power and rule over the stern warriors of his day had he not possessed much of their own callous indifference to the horrors and cruelties of war.

"Thou hadst tougher work than thou countedst on, it would seem," he said to Hake; then, turning to Jarl Rongvold, with a laugh, "Methinks I would fain have this Erling the Bold and his friend Glumm the Gruff among my men-at-arms."

"I fear, sire, that they will not be easily induced to enter thy service, for they are both Sea-kings, and independent spirits."

"Such men have submitted to us before now," said the King, with a peculiar glance.

"Most true," returned the jarl, flushing; "but all men have not the same belief in your wisdom."

"That may be, yet methinks I could tame this Sea-king — this Erling. Perchance costly gifts might win him, or it may be that rough blows would suit him better. What thinkest thou, Hake? thou hast had some experience in that way."

"If you mean, sire, that you have a mind to receive rough blows at his hand, I will guarantee him both able and willing to gratify you. I know not the weight of Thor's hammer, but I am bound to say that it occurred to my mind when Erling's axe came down on my steel headpiece, and set a host of stars dancing in my brain."

"I believe thee," said the King, smiling grimly, "and thy visage speaks for itself."

This was indeed the case. The berserk's countenance was very pale. He still suffered from the crashing blow with which he had been felled, and his heart rankled under his defeat, for he was not aware that the blow, heavy though it was, had been delivered in mercy, or that if his enemy had not turned aside the edge of his axe it would have cleft him to the chin. Perchance, if he *had* known this it would not have improved the state of his feelings; for Hake possessed no nobility of spirit.

"It may be," continued Harald, "that thou shalt have another opportunity of measuring swords with this Sea-king. Meanwhile, Jarl Rongvold, go thou with Rolf, and bring round the Dragon and the other longships to the fiord, for I mistrust the men of this district, and will fare to the Springs by sea."

In accordance with these instructions the jarl brought the King's fleet round without delay. On the following morning they embarked, and set sail for the appointed place of meeting.

Here the fleet under Haldor and Ulf had already cast anchor. The ships lay close to the rocks, near the mouth of the river into which Erling had thrust his cutter just before the battle with the Danes; and a fine sight it was to behold these, with their painted shields and gilded masts and figure-heads, lying in the still water, crowded with armed warriors, while Harald's longship, the Dragon, and all his other vessels, came by twos and threes into the fiord, the oars tossing foam on the blue waters, and the gaily coloured sails swelling out before a gentle breeze.

The King laid his ship alongside of a point of rocks on the south side of the bay. Then, when all the fleet had assembled, both parties landed, and the Thing was summoned by sound of horn. It was held on the level ground where the recent battle had been fought. There were still strewn about many evidences of the ferocity of that fight; and when the King looked upon the host of stout and well-armed men who had assembled, not only from Horlingdal, but from the whole of the surrounding district, he felt that, however much he might wish to force obedience on his subjects, "discretion" was at that time "the better part of valour."

When the Thing was assembled the King stood up to speak, and there was probably not a man upon the ground who did not in his heart acknowledge that the tall, stout warrior, with the thick mass of golden locks, and the large masculine features, was, as far as physique went, a worthy wearer of the crown of Norway. It may be added that physique went a very long way indeed in those days; yet it is due to the Northmen to say that, at the same time, intellect was held in higher repute among them than among any of the feudally governed nations of Europe. One evidence of this was, that at the Things the best speaker, no matter what his rank, had a better chance of swaying the people than the King himself; while, in other countries, might to a large extent was right, and no one dared to open his mouth against him who chanced to be in power.

But King Harald Haarfager's power lay not merely in his personal appearance and indomitable will. He was also a good speaker, and, like all good speakers in a wrong cause, was an able sophist. But he had men to deal with who were accustomed to think and reason closely, as must ever be more or less the case with a self-governed people. There were acute men there, men who had the laws of the land "by heart", in the most literal sense of those words, — for there were no books to consult and no precedents to cite in those days; and his hearers weighed with jealous care each word he said.

The King began by complimenting the men of the district for their spirit, and their resolution to defend the laws of the realm; and he enlarged a little on these laws and on the wisdom of his own father, Halfdan the Black, and the men of his time, who had made and modified many of them. Then he went on to say that with time the circumstances of nations altered, and that, with these alterations, there arose a necessity for the alteration and modification of old laws as well as for the making of new ones. He deprecated the idea that he wished, as had been said of him, to trample the laws under his feet, and rule the country according to his own will and pleasure. Nothing was further from his intention or his desire. His wish was to amend the laws, especially those of them that touched on the relative position of King and people.

Up to this point the people heard him with respectful attention, and hundreds of those who were more addicted to fighting than to reasoning, especially among the younger men, began to think that after all, Harald entertained exceedingly just opinions, and appeared to possess a spirit of candour and fair play which did not seem to justify the outcry that had been raised against him. Even these, however, remembered that it was not very long since a small king of one of the northern glens had been summoned by Harold to submit to his views of government, and, on his declining to do so, had been burnt, with all his family and followers, in his own house, contrary to law! They therefore knitted their brows and waited to hear more.

The King then began to explain his ideas with regard to the royal authority over the chief men of the districts, some of which are already known to the reader. At this point the assembly listened with deep, earnest attention. Some of the men sat with hands clasped on their knees, and with stern downcast brows. Some gazed up at the clouds with the peculiar expression of men who listen and weigh arguments. Others leaned on their swords or shields, and, with compressed lips and suspicious gaze, looked the King full in the face, while a few regarded him with a sneer; but the expression on the faces of the greater part denoted manliness of feeling and honesty of purpose.

After Harald had stated his views, and assured them that his great aim was to consolidate the kingdom and to prevent the evils that flowed from the almost unlimited independence of the petty kings, he asked the assembly to aid him in carrying out his wishes, and to set an example of fidelity and obedience, which would restrain others from showing that unseemly opposition to him which had only resulted in severe and merited punishment.

He then sat down amid a murmur of mingled applause and disapprobation.

After a few minutes of animated converse among themselves, there arose an old man with a bald head, a flowing beard, and sightless eyes. He was the "lagman" or district judge, and law-expounder of Horlingdal. Deep silence ensued, and he said, in a decided though somewhat tremulous tone —

"King Harald, I am a very old man now, and can remember the time when your noble sire, Halfdan the Black, ruled in Norway. I have fought by his side, and lost my eyes in his service — in a fight in which our opponents gave us the tooth-ache.[12] I have also heard him speak those words of wisdom to which you have referred, and have seen him bow to the laws which were made *not* by himself, but by him in conjunction with the Thing legally assembled for the purpose."

There was a loud murmur of applause at this point.

"And now that we have heard the King's opinions," continued the old man, turning to the people, "and know that his intentions are good, although the manner in which he has set about carrying them into effect is undoubtedly wrong, my counsel is that we nevertheless submit to him in this matter, for we know that a great number of the small kings have already submitted, and it were better to have a beneficial change — even when not carried out exactly according to law — than to plunge this country into prolonged and useless warfare, in which much blood will assuredly be spilt, and nothing of any value gained."

The lagman sat down, but only a few of those present indicated their approval of his sentiments.

Immediately Haldor the Fierce stood up, and men could see that his spirit was stirred within him, for a dark frown lowered on a brow which was at most times fair and unruffled like the summer sky. There was deep silence in the assembly before he began to speak, and the King, despite the suppressed anger which rankled in his breast, could not choose but look upon his commanding figure with respect, also with surprise, for he recognised the strong resemblance between him and Erling, though he knew not their relationship.

"I agree not," said Haldor, "with what has just been said by our respected lagman. A change, even for the better, ought *never* to be accepted if not made according to law, No one can say that any change will certainly be for the better until it is tried; and should this one, perchance, turn out for the worse, then shall we have neither advantage nor law on our side. For my part I had rather see my country plunged into warfare — which no one, unless he is gifted with the foreknowledge of the gods, can say will be either prolonged or useless — than see her laws trampled under foot; for well do I know that, if the King be permitted to make himself an outlaw, blood will be kept boiling perpetually from one end of the land to the other, and it were better, methinks, that that blood should spill than boil. My counsel is, that the King be advised to call a Thing in the regular way, so that the changes he would make shall be fully considered, and either be made law or rejected; for, if he attempts to enforce his plans on us as he has done on other small kings, we will assuredly resist him as long as there is a man left in the district to wield a battle-axe."

There was a great shout and clash of arms when this was said, and the King's face became crimson with rage, for he saw clearly that the feeling of the majority was against him.

12   Norse expression signifying 'the worst of it'.

At this point Jarl Rongvold stood up and spoke in the bland tones of a man who wishes to throw oil on troubled waters.

He said that it was his earnest entreaty to the bonders and house-holding men, both great and small, then and there assembled, that they should calmly consider the proposals of the King, and not allow themselves to be carried away by unsound reasoning, although it might seem very plausible, for he was certain that the King's desire was the good of the country; and although circumstances had rendered it necessary that some of the rebellious should be punished, no one could say that the King was not willing and ready to do all that he did in a fair, open, and straightforward manner.

At this Erling was unable to restrain himself. He sprang up, and, with a passionate flow of words that burst forth like a mountain torrent, exclaimed —

"Thinkest thou, Jarl Rongvold, that our brains are so addled that we cannot distinguish between black and white? Is thy memory so short, is thy slavery to the King so complete, that thou must say evil is good and good evil? Hast thou and has the King so soon forgotten that two strangers came to the court with a message from one of the legal assemblies of this land, — that, trusting to the honour of the King, they came without following, and with only such arms as were needful for personal defence, — and that the honour to which they trusted was not proof against the temptation to send a noted berserk and nineteen men to waylay and slay them? Is all this clean gone from your memory, Jarl and King? or is your wit so small that ye should think we will believe in soft words about fair play when such foul deeds are so recent that the graves are yet wet with the blood of those whom Glumm and I were compelled to slay in self-defence?"

At this the King started up, and his face became white and red by turns, as he said —

"Ye shall, both of you, rue this day, Erling and Glumm!"

Erling made no reply, but Glumm started up and was in so great a passion that he could hardly speak; nevertheless he made shift to splutter out —

"Threats, King Harald, are like water spilt on a shield which can only rust if left there; I wipe them off and fling them away!"

He could add no more, but with a contemptuous motion of the hand he struck his fist violently against his shirt of mail, and the bonders laughed while they applauded him.

Then stood up a man in the troop of the Springdal men, who was of great stature and grim countenance, clad in a leather cloak, with an axe on his shoulder and a great steel hat upon his head. He looked sternly, and said —

"When rights are not respected then the crows flap their wings and caw, for they know that ere long they shall glut themselves with human blood."

He sat down, and immediately after Ulf of Romsdal stood up. Ulf had fully as much fire as Erling or Glumm, but he possessed greater power of self-restraint, and, as he spoke with deliberation, his words had all the more weight. He said —

"King Harald, when in the exercise of our udal rights we bonders elected thee to be our King at the Thing held in Drontheim, we stated and traced thy descent from Odin through the Vingling dynasty, proved thy udal right to the crown, and truly thought that we had placed it on the head of one who would walk in the footsteps of his father, and respect that authority and power in virtue of which he held his own high position. But we now find that thou hast constituted thyself a law higher than the law which made thee what thou art, and thou now wouldst have us, of our own free will, bend our necks so low that thou mayest with the more ease set thy foot on them and keep us down. We have served thee in all good faith up to the present time; we have readily met thy demands for men, ships, arms, and money, by calling together our assemblies and voting these supplies; and now thou wouldst rob us of this our old right, and tax us without our consent, so that thou mayest raise men for thyself, and have it all thine own way. This must not, shall not, be. Even now, we bonders will unanimously hold by the law if it be passed in the proper assembly and receives our yea, and we will follow thee and serve thee as our King as long as there is a living man amongst us. But thou, King, must use moderation towards us, and only require of us such things as it is lawful or possible for us to obey thee in. If, however, thou wilt take up this matter with a high hand, and wilt try thy power and strength against us, we have resolved among ourselves to part with thee, and to take to ourselves some other chief who will respect those laws by which alone society can be held together. Now, King Harald, thou must choose one or other of these conditions before the Thing is ended."

The loud applause which followed this speech showed that the bonders heartily sympathised with it, and indeed several of them rose and said that it expressed their will exactly, and they would stand or fall by what had been spoken.

When silence had been restored, Jarl Rongvold, who had whispered in the King's ear some earnest words, stood forth and said:

"It is King Harald's will to give way to you in this matter for he does not wish to separate himself from your friendship."

This brought the Thing to a close. Thereafter the two parties returned to their ships, intending to feast and pass the night in them.

The King was very affable, and invited Haldor and some of the others whose language had been comparatively moderate to feast with him, but they declined the honour, and retired to their own ships.

In the evening, while the sounds of revelry were heard everywhere, a boat approached Erling's ship. It was rowed by a single man, who, when it touched her side, leaped on board and went aft to where Erling was seated with Guttorm Stoutheart.

"King Harald would speak with thee," said the man, who was no other than Hake the berserk.

"Methinks his intentions can scarce be friendly," said Erling, with a grim smile, "when he sends so trusty a messenger."

"It may be so," replied Hake coolly, "but that is nothing to me. My business is to deliver the message and offer to conduct thee to him."

"And pray, what surety have I that thou wilt not upset me in the fiord?" asked Erling, laughing.

"The surety that if I upset thee we shall be on equal terms in the water," replied Hake gruffly.

"Nay, that depends on which of us can swim best," returned Erling; "and, truly, if thou canst fight as well in the water as on the land, we should have a rare struggle, Hake."

"Am I to say to the King that thou art afraid of him?" asked the berserk, with a look of scorn.

"Yea, truly, if it is thy desire to tell him a lie," retorted Erling. "But get thee into the boat, fellow; I will follow anon."

Hake turned on his heel and returned to the boat, while Erling took Guttorm aside.

"Now, art thou fey?"[13] said Guttorm. "What has made thee so tired of life that thou shouldest put thy neck under his heel thus readily?"

"Fear not, my friend," said Erling; "now that I have seen King Harald a second time, I think him a better man than at first I did. Ambition will no doubt lead him to do many things that are contrary to his nature; but I do not think he will violate the laws of hospitality after what has passed. However, I may be wrong; so I would ask thee, Guttorm, to go aboard of your ship, which lies nearest to that of the King, and, should ye see anything like a struggle, or hear a shout do thou haste to the rescue. I will have my men also in readiness."

While the stout-hearted old Sea-king, in compliance with this request, got into a small boat and rowed to his own vessel, Erling gave particular directions to his chief house-carle to keep a sharp lookout and be ready to act at a moment's notice. Then he went into Hake's boat, and was rowed alongside the Dragon, where the King received him with much condescension, and took him aft to the cabin under the high poop. Here he offered him a horn of ale, which, however, Erling declined, and then began to use his utmost powers of persuasion to induce him to enter his service. At first he tried to influence him by flattery, and commended him for his bold and straightforward conduct at the Thing, which, he said, showed to all men that he merited well his distinctive title; but, on finding that our hero was not to be won by flattery, he quickly and adroitly changed his ground, began to talk of the future prospects of Norway, and the necessity for improved legislation. In this he was so successful that he secured the interest, and to some extent the sympathy, of the young warrior, who entered eagerly and somewhat more respectfully into the discussion.

"But, sire," he said, at the close of one of the King's remarks, "if these are your sentiments, why did you not state them more fully to-day at the Thing, and why should you not even now call a meeting of the Stor Thing, and have the matter properly discussed by all in the land who have a right to speak?"

13   Death-doomed.

"Hadst thou had any experience of kingcraft, Erling, thou hadst not asked the question. If I were now to do as thou dost suggest, the numerous small kings who have already been put down by force would band against me, and bring such a following of opponents to the Thing that fair discussion would be out of the question."

Erling thought in his own mind, "One false step always necessitates another; you should have called a meeting of the Thing before putting down anyone;" however, he did not give utterance to the thought, but said —

"I think you are mistaken, sire; there may be many who, out of revenge, might oppose you, but certain am I that those who would vote for that which is for the wellbeing of the land would form a vast majority. Besides, it is the only course left open to you."

At this the King flushed with a feeling of anger, and, drawing himself up, touched the hilt of his sword without uttering a word.

"When I said the only course," remarked Erling, "I meant the only lawful course. Sorry should I be to see you, King Harald, draw the sword in a bad cause; but if you do, be assured that thousands of good blades will gleam in opposition."

At this the King's eyes flashed, and, turning suddenly upon Erling, he shook back the masses of his yellow hair with lion-like ferocity, exclaiming —

"Dost thou dare to speak thus to me in mine own ship, Erling?"

"It is because I am in your ship that I dare. Were I in my own, the laws of hospitality had shut my mouth."

"Knowest thou not," said the King, waxing still more angry at the rebuke conveyed in this speech, and laying his hand on his sword, "that I have power to shut thy mouth now and for ever?"

"It may be so, and it may be not so," replied Erling, stepping back, and laying his hand on the hilt of his own weapon.

At this the King laughed sarcastically. "And if," said he, "thou hadst the power and skill to overcome my feeble arm, hast thou the folly to think that ye could clear the Dragon of all her men?"

Erling replied: "The remembrance, King Harald, of the way in which I treated some of thy men in the woods not long ago, inclines me to believe that I could give them some trouble to slay me, and the thought of that transaction induced me, before I came hither, to make such arrangements that at all events my fall should not go unavenged."

For a moment or two the King's countenance lowered ferociously on the youth, and he ground his teeth together as if unable to restrain his passion; but suddenly he uttered a short laugh, and said —

"Truly thou shouldst have been styled prudent as well as bold. But go, I will take counsel with others, and perhaps thou shalt hear again of this matter."

Our hero retired immediately, but he observed in passing that Hake was summoned to attend the King, and that another man stepped into the boat to row him to his own ship.

"Is all well?" growled the rich voice of old Guttorm as he passed the vessel of that worthy.

Erling told the rower to stop, and, glancing up, beheld the stern yet good-humoured visage of his bluff friend looking over the rows of bright shields that hung on the bulwarks.

"All is well," replied Erling.

"It is well for the King that it is so," rejoined Guttorm, "for my hand was itching to give him a taste of our northern metal. Assuredly, if a mouse had but squeaked on board the Dragon, I had deemed it sufficient ground on which to have founded an immediate onslaught. But get thee to bed, Erling, and let me advise thee to sleep with thy windward eye open."

"Trust me," said Erling, with a laugh, as he pushed off; "I will not sleep with both eyes shut to-night!"

Getting on board his own ship, Erling said to his foot-boy —

"I will not sleep in my bed to-night, for I suspect there may be treachery abroad. Thou shalt keep watch, therefore, in case anything may happen in the night; and if thou shalt see me strive with anyone, do not alarm the men. Meanwhile go thou and fetch me a billet of wood, and let it be a large one."

The boy quickly brought from the hold one of the largest billets of wood he could find, and gave it to his master, who laid it in his own bed, which was under a small tent spread over the aft part of the vessel, close to the poop. Having covered it up carefully, he sent the boy forward, and went himself to lie down elsewhere.

At midnight a boat was rowed stealthily alongside. It was guided by one man, and moved so silently that the lightest sleeper on board could not have been awakened by it. The man stepped on board; lifted up the cloth of the tent over the bulwarks; looked cautiously all round him, and then went up and struck in Erling's bed with a great axe, so that it stuck fast in the billet of wood. Next instant the man felt his neck in a grip like that of an iron vice, and his face was thrust upon the ground and held there, while a heavy knee pressed into the small of his back, so that he was utterly unable to rise.

Erling's foot-boy saw the whole of this, and heard what followed, for the curtain of the tent was raised; but he moved neither hand nor foot, though he held a spear ready for instant action if required.

"It ill becomes thee, Hake," said Erling, "to seek my life a second time, after making such poor work of it the first. What! wilt thou not lie quiet?"

While he was speaking the berserk struggled with the fury of a madman to free himself, but Erling's grip (perhaps his own wisdom also!) prevented him from shouting, and Erling's knee prevented the struggles from making much noise. Finding, however, that he would not be quiet, our hero tightened the pressure of his left hand until the tongue and eyes of the berserk began to protrude, and his face to get black, while with his right hand he drew his knife, and ran the point of it about a quarter of an inch into the fleshy part of Hake's back. The effect was instantaneous! Hake could face danger and death bravely, and could hurl defiance at his foe with the best, when on his legs; but when he felt the point of the cold steel, and knew that the smallest impulse would cause it to find a warm bed in his heart, his fury vanished. Brave and bold though he was, and a berserk to boot, he sank quietly down, and lay perfectly still!

Erling at once relaxed the pressure of his fingers, and allowed Hake to breathe, but he let the point of the knife remain, that it might refresh his memory, while he read him a lesson:

"Now, Hake, let me tell thee that thou richly deservest to lose thy life, for twice hast thou sought to take mine in an unfair way, and once have I spared thine. However, thou art but a tool after all, so I will spare it again — and I do it the more readily that I wish thee to convey a message to thy master, King Harald, who, I doubt not, has sent thee on this foul errand."

Erling here signalled to his foot-boy, whom he directed to bind Hake's arms securely behind his back. This having been done, Erling suffered him to rise and stand before him.

"See now," he said, taking a silver ring from his finger, "knowest thou this ring, Hake? Ah, I see by thy look that thou dost. Well, I will return it to thee and claim mine own."

He turned the berserk round, took off the gold ring which he had placed on his finger on the day of the fight and put the silver one in its place.

"By these tokens," said he, "thou mayest know who it was that cared for thee in the wood after the fight, and restored thy consciousness, instead of cutting off thy head, as he might easily have done. I know not why I did it, Hake, save that the fancy seized me, for thou art an undeserving dog. But now we will take thee back to thy master, and as our message can be conveyed without the use of speech, we will bind up thy mouth."

So saying, Erling gagged the berserk (who looked dreadfully sulky) with a strip of sailcloth. Then he made him sit down, and tied his legs together with a piece of rope, after which he lifted him in his arms to the side of the ship and laid him down.

"Go fetch me a stout carle," he said to the foot-boy, who went forward and immediately returned with a strapping man-at-arms.

The man looked surprised, but asked no questions, as Erling directed him in a low tone to assist in lifting the prisoner into the boat as quietly as possible. Then they placed the lump of wood with the axe sticking in it beside him. This accomplished, they rowed silently to the side of the Dragon, where a sentinel demanded what they wanted.

"We bring a prisoner to King Harald," answered Erling. "We have him here tied hand and foot."

"Who is he?" asked the sentinel; for there was not so much light as is usual at midnight of that time of the year, owing to a mist on the sea.

"Thou shalt see when he is aboard."

"Hoist him up, then," said the man, Erling and his carle raised Hake over the bulwarks, and let him drop heavily on the deck. Then Erling seized the lump of wood and hurled it on board with considerable force, so that, hitting the sentinel on the head, it bounded onwards to the after part of the ship, and struck against the tent under which Harald lay. The King sprang out, sword in hand, but Erling had pushed off, and was already enveloped in the mist. As they rowed away they heard a great clamour on board the Dragon, but it was quickly hushed by a stern voice. which Erling knew to be that of the King.

No pursuit was attempted. Erling got back to his own ship, and, setting a watch, lay down to rest.

In the morning no notice was taken of what had occurred during the night. The King evidently pretended that he knew nothing about the matter. He again met with the chief men of the district, and made them many promises and many complimentary speeches, but in his heart he resolved that the day should come when every one of them should either bow before his will or lose his life. The bonders, on the other hand, listened with due respect to all the King said, but it need scarcely be added that their lips did not express all their thoughts; for while the sanguine and more trustful among them felt some degree of hope and confidence, there were others who could not think of the future except with the most gloomy forebodings.

In this mood the two parties separated. The King sailed with his warships out among the skerries, intending to proceed north to Drontheim, while Haldor the Fierce, with his friends and men, went back to Horlingdal.

CHAPTER XVI.

Relates to such Elementary Matters as the A B C, and touches on Love-making in the Olden Time.

After the occurrence of the events just narrated, King Harald's attention was diverted from the people of Horlingdal and the neighbouring districts by the doings of certain small kings, against whom it became necessary that he should launch his whole force. These were King Hunthiof, who ruled over the district of Möre, and his son Solve Klofe; also King Nokve, who ruled over Romsdal, and was the brother of Solve's mother. These men were great warriors. Hearing that King Harald was sailing north, they resolved to give him battle.

For this purpose they raised a large force, and went out among the skerries to intercept him.

We do not intend here to go into the details of the fight that followed, or its consequences. It is sufficient for the proper development of our tale to say that they met at an island in North Möre named Solskiel, where a pitched battle was fought, and gained by Harald. The two kings were slain, but Solve Klofe escaped, and afterwards proved a great thorn in Harald's side, plundering in North Möre, killing many of the King's men, pillaging some places, burning others, and generally making great ravage wherever he went; so that, what with keeping him and similar turbulent characters in check, and establishing law and order in the districts of the two kings whom he had slain, King Harald had his hands fully occupied during the remainder of that summer, and was glad to go north to spend the winter peacefully in Drontheim.

The families and neighbours, therefore, of those with whom our tale has chiefly to do had rest during that winter. How some of them availed themselves of this period of repose may be gathered from a few incidents which we shall now relate.

In the first place, Erling the Bold spent a large proportion of his time in learning the alphabet! Now this may sound very strange in the ears of many people in modern times, but their surprise will be somewhat abated when we tell them that the art of writing was utterly unknown (though probably not unheard of) in Norway at the end of the ninth century, and long after that; so that Erling, although a gentleman of the period, and a Sea-king to boot, had not up to the time we write of, learned his A B C!

It is just possible that antiquaries, recalling to mind the fact that the art of writing was not introduced among the Norse colonists of Iceland until the eleventh century, may be somewhat surprised to learn that our hero acquired the art at all! But the fact is, that there always have been, in all countries, men who were what is popularly termed "born before their time" — men who were in advance, intellectually, of their age — men who, overleaping the barriers of prejudice, managed to see deeper into things in general than their fellows, and to become more or less famous.

Now our hero, Erling the Bold, was one of those who could see beyond his time, and who became almost prophetically wise; that is to say, he was fond of tracing causes onwards to their probable effects, to the amusement of the humorous, the amazement of the stupid, and the horrification of the few who, even in those days of turmoil, trembled at the idea of "change"! Everything, therefore, that came under his observation claimed and obtained his earnest attention, and was treated with a species of inductive philosophy that would have charmed the heart of Lord Bacon, had he lived in those times. Of course this new wonder of committing thoughts to parchment, which the hermit had revealed to him, was deeply interesting to Erling, who began to study it forthwith. And we beg leave to tell antiquaries that we have nothing to do with the fact that no record is left of his studies — no scrap of his writing to be found. We are not responsible for the stupidity or want of sympathy in his generation! Doubtless, in all ages there have been many such instances of glorious opportunities neglected by the world — neglected, too, with such contempt, that not even a record of their having occurred has been made. Perchance some such opportunities are before ourselves just now, in regard to our neglect of which the next generation may possibly have to hold up its hands and turn up its eyes in amazement! But be this as it may, the fact remains that although no record is handed down of any knowledge of letters at this period in Norway, Erling the Bold *did* nevertheless become acquainted with them to some extent.

Erling began his alphabet after he had passed the mature age of twenty years, and his teacher was the fair Hilda. It will be remembered that in one of their meetings the hermit had informed Erling of his having already taught the meaning of the strange characters which covered his parchments to the Norse maiden, and that she had proved herself an apt scholar. Erling said nothing at the time, except that he had a strong desire to become better acquainted with the writing in question, but he settled it then and there in his heart that Hilda, and not the hermit, should be his teacher. Accordingly, when the fishings and fightings of the summer were over, the young warrior laid by his sword, lines, and trident, and, seating himself at Hilda's feet, went diligently to work.

The schoolroom was the hermit's hut on the cliff which overlooked the fiord. It was selected of necessity, because the old man guarded his parchments with tender solicitude, and would by no means allow them to go out of his dwelling, except when carried forth by his own hand. On the first occasion of the meeting of the young couple for study, Christian sat down beside them, and was about to expound matters, when Erling interposed with a laugh.

"No, no, Christian, thou must permit Hilda to teach me, because she is an old friend of mine, who all her life has ever been more willing to learn than to teach. Therefore am I curious to know how she will change her character."

"Be it so, my son," said the hermit, with a smile, folding his hands on his knee, and preparing to listen, and if need be to correct.

"Be assured, Erling," said Hilda, "that I know very little."

"Enough for me, no doubt," returned the youth.

"For a day or two, perhaps," said the too-literal Hilda; "but after that Christian will have —"

"After that," interrupted Erling, "it will be time enough to consider that subject."

Hilda laughed, and asked if he were ready to begin. To which Erling replied that he was, and, sitting down opposite to his teacher, bent over the parchment, which for greater convenience she had spread out upon her knee.

"Well," began Hilda, with a slight feeling of that pardonable self-importance which is natural to those who instruct others older than themselves, "that is the first letter."

"Which?" asked Erling, gazing up in her face.

"That one there, with the long tail to it. Dost thou see it?"

"Yes," replied the youth.

"How canst thou say so, Erling," remonstrated Hilda, "when thou art looking all the time straight in my face!"

"But I *do* see it," returned he, a little confused; "I am looking at it *now*."

"Well," said she, "that is —"

"Thou art looking at it upside down, my son," said the hermit, who had been observing them with an amused expression of countenance.

"Oh, so he is; I never thought of that," cried Hilda, laughing; "thou must sit beside me, Erling, so that we may see it in the same way."

"This one, now, with the curve *that* way," she went on, "dost thou see it?"

"See it!" thought Erling, "of course I see it: the prettiest little hand in all the dale!" But he only said —

"How can I see it, Hilda, when the point of thy finger covers it?"

"Oh! well," drawing the finger down a little, "thou seest it now?"

"Yes."

"Well, that is — why! where is Christian?" she exclaimed, looking up suddenly in great surprise, and pointing to the stool on which the hermit certainly had been sitting a few minutes before, but which was now vacant.

"He must have gone out while we were busy with the — the parchment," said Erling, also much surprised.

"He went like a mouse, then," said Hilda, "for I heard him not."

"Nor I," added her companion.

"Very strange," said she.

Now there was nothing particularly strange in the matter. The fact was that the old man had just exercised a little of Erling's philosophy in the way of projecting a cause to its result. As we have elsewhere hinted, the hermit was not one of those ascetics who, in ignorance of the truth, banished themselves out of the world. His banishment had not been self-imposed. He had fled before the fierce persecutors. They managed to slay the old man's wife, however, before they made him take to flight and seek that refuge and freedom of conscience among the Pagan Northmen which were denied him in Christian Europe. In the first ten minutes after the A B C class began he perceived how things stood with the young people, and, wisely judging that the causes which were operating in their hearts would proceed to their issue more pleasantly in his absence, he quietly got up and went out to cut firewood.

After this the hermit invariably found it necessary to go out and cut firewood when Erling and Hilda arrived at the school, which they did regularly three times a week.

This, of course, was considered a very natural and proper state of things by the two young people, for they were both considerate by nature, and would have been sorry indeed to have interrupted the old man in his regular work.

But Erling soon began to feel that it was absolutely essential for one of them to be in advance of the other in regard to knowledge, if the work of teaching was to go on; for, while both remained equally ignorant, the fiction could not be kept up with even the semblance of propriety. To obviate this difficulty he paid solitary nocturnal visits to the hut, on which occasions he applied himself so zealously to the study of the strange characters that he not only became as expert as his teacher, but left her far behind, and triumphantly rebutted the charge of stupidity which she had made against him.

At the same time our hero entered a new and captivating region of mental and spiritual activity when the hermit laid before him the portions of Holy Scripture which he had copied out before leaving southern lands, and expounded to him the grand, the glorious truths that God had revealed to man through Jesus Christ our Lord. And profoundly deep, and startling even to himself, were the workings of the young Norseman's active mind while he sat there, night after night, in the lone hut on the cliff, poring over the sacred rolls, or holding earnest converse with the old man about things past, present, and future.

CHAPTER XVII.

In which Glumm takes to hunting on the Mountains for Consolation, and finds it unexpectedly, while Alric proves himself a Hero.

"I go to the fells to-day," said Glumm to Alric one morning, as the latter opened the door of Glummstede and entered the hall.

"I go also," said Alric, leaning a stout spear which he carried against the wall, and sitting down on a stool beside the fire to watch Glumm as he equipped himself for the chase.

"Art ready, then? for the day is late," said Glumm.

"All busked," replied the boy. — "I say, Glumm, is that a new spear thou hast got?"

"Aye; I took it from a Swedish viking the last fight I had off the coast. We had a tough job of it, and left one or two stout men behind to glut the birds of Odin, but we brought away much booty. This was part of it," he added, buckling on a long hunting-knife, which was stuck in a richly ornamented sheath, "and that silver tankard too, besides the red mantle that my mother wears, and a few other things — but my comrades got the most of it."

"I wish I had been there, Glumm," said Alric.

"If Hilda were here, lad, she would say it is wrong to wish to fight."

"Hilda has strange thoughts," observed the boy.

"So has Erling," remarked his companion.

"And so has Ada," said Alric, with a sly glance.

Glumm looked up quickly. "What knowest *thou* about Ada?" said he.

The sly look vanished before Glumm had time to observe it, and an expression of extreme innocence took its place as the lad replied —

"I know as much about her as is usual with one who has known a girl, and been often with her, since the day he was born."

"True," muttered Glumm, stooping to fasten the thongs that laced the untanned shoes on his feet. "Ada has strange thoughts also, as thou sayest. Come now, take thy spear, and let us be gone."

"Where shall we go to-day?" asked Alric.

"To the wolf's glen."

"To the wolf's glen? that is far."

"Is it too far for thee, lad?"

"Nay, twice the distance were not too far for me," returned the boy proudly; "but the day advances, and there is danger without honour in walking on the fells after dark."

"The more need for haste," said Glumm, opening the door and going out.

Alric followed, and for some time these two walked in silence, as the path was very steep, and so narrow for a considerable distance, that they could not walk abreast.

Snow lay pretty thickly on the mountains, particularly in sheltered places, but in exposed parts it had been blown off, and the hunters could advance easily. In about ten minutes after setting out they lost sight of Glummstede. As they advanced higher and deeper into the mountains, the fiord and the sea, with its innumerable skerries, was lost to view, but it was not until they had toiled upwards and onwards for nearly two hours that they reached those dark recesses of the fells to which the bears and wolves were wont to retreat after committing depredations on the farms in the valleys far below.

There was something in the rugged grandeur of the scenery here, in the whiteness of the snow, the blackness of the rocks which peeped out from its voluminous wreaths, the lightness of the atmosphere, and, above all, the impressive silence, which possessed an indescribable charm for the romantic mind of Alric, and which induced even the stern matter-of-fact Glumm to tread with slower steps, and to look around him with a feeling almost akin to awe. No living thing was to be seen, either among the stupendous crags which still towered above, or in the depths which they had left below; but there were several footprints of wolves, all of which Glumm declared, after careful examination, to be old.

"See here, lad," he said, turning up one of these footprints with the butt of his spear; "observe the hardish ball of snow just under the print; that shows that the track is somewhat old. If it had been quite fresh there would have been no such ball."

"Thou must think my memory of the shortest, Glumm, for I have been told that every time I have been out with thee."

"True, but thou art so stupid," said Glumm, laying his spear lightly across the boy's shoulders, "that I have thought fit to impress it on thee by repetition, having an interest in thine education, although thou dost not deserve it."

"I deserve it, mayhap, more than ye think."

"How so, boy?"

"Why, because I have for a long time past taken an uncommon interest in thy welfare."

Glumm laughed, and said he did not know that there was any occasion to concern himself about his welfare.

"Oh yes, there is!" cried Alric, "for, when a man goes moping about the country as if he were fey, or as if he had dreamed of seeing his own guardian spirit, his friends cannot help being concerned about him."

"Why, what is running in the lad's head?" said Glumm, looking with a perplexed expression at his young companion.

"Nothing runs in my head, save ordinary thoughts. If there be any unusual running at all, it must be in thine own."

"Speak, thou little fox," said Glumm, suddenly grasping Alric by the nape of the neck and giving him a shake.

"Nay then, if that is thy plan," said the boy, "give it a fair trial. Shake away, and see what comes of it. Thou mayest shake out blood, bones, flesh, and life too, and carry home my skin as a trophy, but be assured that thou shalt not shake a word off my tongue!"

"Boldly spoken," said Glumm, laughing, as he released the lad; "but I think thy tone would change if I were to take thee at thy word."

"That it would not. Thou art not the first man whom I have defied, aye, and drawn blood from, as that red-haired Dane —"

Alric stopped suddenly. He had reached that age when the tendency to boast begins, at least in manly boys, to be checked by increasing good sense and good taste. Yet it is no disparagement of Alric's character to say that he found it uncommonly difficult to refrain, when occasion served, from making reference to his first warlike exploit, even although frequent rebukes and increasing wisdom told him that boasting was only fit for the lips of cowards.

"Why do ye stop?" asked Glumm, who quite understood the boy's feelings, and admired his exercise of self-control.

"Be — because I have said enough."

"Good is it," observed the other, "when man or boy knows that he has said enough, and has the power to stop when he knows it. But come, Alric, thou hast not said enough to me yet on the matter that — that —"

"What matter?" asked Alric, with a sly look.

"Why, the matter of my welfare, to be sure."

"Ah, true. Well, methinks, Glumm, that I could give thee a little medicine for thy mind, but I won't, unless ye promise to keep thy spear off my back."

"I promise," said Glumm, whose curiosity was aroused.

"It is a sad thing when a man looks sweet and a maid looks sour, but there is a worse thing; that is when the maid *feels* sour. Thou lovest Ada —"

"Hold!" cried Glumm, turning fiercely on his companion, "and let not thy pert tongue dare to speak of such things, else will I show thee that there are other things besides spears to lay across thy shoulders."

"Now art thou truly Glumm the Gruff," cried Alric, laughing, as he leaped to the other side of a mass of fallen rock; "but if thy humour changes not, I will show thee that I am not named Lightfoot for nothing. Come, don't fume and fret there like a bear with a headache, but let me speak, and I warrant me thou wilt be reasonably glad."

"Go on, then, thou incorrigible."

"Very well; but none of thy hard names, friend Glumm, else will I set my big brother Erling at thee. There now, don't give way again. What a storm-cloud thou art! Will the knowledge that Ada loves thee as truly as thou lovest her calm thee down?"

"I see thou hast discovered my secret," said Glumm, looking at his little friend with a somewhat confused expression, "though how the knowledge came to thee is past my understanding. Yet as thou art so clever a warlock I would fain know what ye mean about 'Ada's love for me'. Hadst thou said her hatred, I could have believed thee without explanation."

"Let us go on, then," said Alric, "for there is nothing to be gained and only time to be lost by thus talking across a stone."

The path which they followed was broad at that part, and not quite so rugged, so that Alric could walk alongside of his stout friend as he related to him the incident that was the means of enlightening him as to Ada's feelings towards her lover. It was plain from the expression on the Norseman's face that his soul was rejoiced at the discovery, and he strode forward at such a pace that the boy was fain to call a halt.

"Thinkest thou that my legs are as long as thine?" he said, stopping and panting.

Glumm laughed; and the laugh was loud and strong. He would have laughed at anything just then, for the humour was upon him, and he felt it difficult to repress a shout at the end of it!

"Come on, Alric, I will go slower. But art thou sure of all this? Hast not mistaken the words?"

"Mistaken the words!" cried the boy; "why, I tell thee they were as plain to my ears and my senses as what thou hast said this moment."

"Good," said Glumm; "and now the question comes up, how must I behave to her? But thou canst not aid me herein, for in such matters thou hast had no experience."

"Out upon thee for a stupid monster!" said the boy; "have I not just proved that my experience is very deep? I have not, indeed, got the length thou hast — of wandering about like a poor ghost or a half-witted fellow, but I have seen enough of such matters to know what common sense says."

"And, pray, what does common sense say?"

"Why, it says, Act towards the maid like a sane man, and, above all, a true man. Don't go about the land gnashing thy teeth until everyone laughs at thee. Don't go staring at her in grim silence as if she were a wraith; and, more particularly, don't pretend to be fond of other girls, for thou didst make a pitiful mess of that attempt. In short, be Glumm without being Gruff, and don't try to be anybody else. Be kind and straightforward to her, worship her, or, as Kettle Flatnose said the other day, 'kiss the ground she walks on', if thou art so inclined, but don't worry her life out. Show that thou art fond of her, and willing to bide *her* time. Go on viking cruise, for the proverb says that an 'absent body makes a longing spirit', and bring her back shiploads of kirtles and mantles and armlets, and gold and silver ornaments — that's what common sense says, Glumm, and a great deal more besides, but I fear much that it is all wasted on thee."

"Heyday!" exclaimed Glumm, "what wisdom do I hear? Assuredly we must call thee Alric hinn Frode hereafter. One would think thou must have been born before thine own grandfather."

"Truly that is not so difficult to fancy," retorted Alric. "Even now I feel like a great-grandfather while I listen to thee. There wants but a smooth round face and a lisping tongue to make thine appearance suitable to thy wisdom! But what is this that we have here?"

The boy pointed to a track of some animal in the snow a few yards to one side of the path.

"A wolf track," said Glumm, turning aside.

"A notably huge one," remarked the boy.

"And quite fresh," said the man.

"Which is proved," rejoined Alric in a slow, solemn voice, "by the fact that there is no ball of snow beneath the —"

"Hold thy pert tongue," said Glumm in a hoarse whisper, "the brute must be close to us. Do thou keep in the lower end of this gorge — see, yonder, where it is narrow. I will go round to the upper end; perchance the wolf is there. If so, we stand a good chance of killing him, for the sides of the chasm are like two walls all the way up. But," added Glumm, hesitating a moment, and looking fixedly at the small but sturdy frame of his companion, whose heightened colour and flashing eyes betokened a roused spirit, "I doubt thy — that is — I have no fear of the spirit, if the body were a little bigger."

"Take thine own big body off, Glumm," said Alric, "and leave me to guard the pass."

Glumm grinned as he turned and strode away.

The spot which the hunters had reached merits particular notice. It was one of those wild deep rents or fissures which are usually found near the summits of almost inaccessible mountains. It was not, however, at the top of the highest range in that neighbourhood, being merely on the summit of a ridge which was indeed very high — perhaps five or six thousand feet — but still far below the serried and shattered peaks which towered in all directions round Horlingdal, shutting it out from all communication with the rest of the world except through the fiord and the pass leading over to the Springs.

On the place where Alric parted from his friend the rocks of the gorge or defile rose almost perpendicularly on both sides, and as he advanced he found that the space between became narrower, until, at the spot where he was to take his stand, there was an opening of scarcely six feet in width. Beyond this the chasm widened a little, until, at its higher end, it was nearly twenty yards broad; but, owing to the widening nature of the defile, the one opening could not be seen from the other, although they were little more than four hundred yards apart.

The track of the wolf led directly through the pass into the gorge. As the lad took his stand he observed with much satisfaction that it was that of an unusually large animal. This feeling was tempered, however, with some anxiety lest it should have escaped at the other opening. It was also mixed with a touch of agitation; for although Alric had seen his friend and Erling kill wolves and bears too, he had never before been left to face the foe by himself, and to sustain the brunt of the charge in his own proper person. Beyond an occasional flutter of the heart, however, there was nothing to indicate, even to himself, that he was not as firm as the rock on which he stood.

Now, let it not be supposed that we are here portraying a hero of romance in whom is united the enthusiasm of the boy with the calm courage of the man. We crave attention, more particularly that of boys, to the following observations:

In the highly safe and civilised times in which we live, many thousands of us never have a chance, from personal experience, of forming a just estimate of the powers of an average man or boy, and we are too apt to ascribe that to heroism which is simply due to knowledge. A man *knows* that he can do a certain thing that seems extremely dangerous, therefore he does it boldly, not because he is superlatively bold by any means, but because he knows there is no risk — at least none to him. The proverb that "Familiarity breeds contempt" applies as truly to danger as to anything else; and well is it for the world that the majority of human beings are prone to familiarise themselves with danger in spite of those well-meaning but weak ones who have been born with a tendency to say perpetually, "Take care," "Don't run such risk", &c. "Whatever thy hand findeth to do, do it with thy might;" and man has echoed the sentiment in the proverb, "Whatever is worth doing is worth doing well". Do you climb? — then do it well — do it in such circumstances that your spirit will get used to seeing profound depths below you without your heart melting into hot water and your nerves quaking. Do you leap? — then do it well — do it so that you may be able to turn it to some good account in the day of trial; do it so that you may know *how* to leap off a runaway carriage, for instance, without being killed. Learn to jump off high cliffs into deep water, so that, should the opportunity ever offer, you may be able to plunge off the high bulwarks of a vessel to save a sister, or mother, or child, with as little thought about yourself as if you were jumping off a sofa. Observe, we do not advocate recklessness. To leap off a cliff so high that you will be sure to be killed is not leaping "well"; but neither is it well to content yourself with a jump of three or four feet as your utmost attainment, because that is far short of many a leap which may have to be taken in this world to save even your own life, not to mention the lives of others. But enough of this disquisition, which, the reader will observe, has been entered upon chiefly in order to prove that we do not ascribe heroic courage to Alric when we say that, having been familiar with danger from his birth, he prepared to face a wolf of unknown size and ferocity with considerable coolness, if not indifference to danger.

Glumm meanwhile reached the other end of the ravine, and there, to his intense disappointment, found the track of the wolf leading away towards the open mountains beyond. Just where it left the ravine, however, the animal had run about so much that the track was crossed and recrossed in confusion. Glumm therefore had difficulty at first in following it up, but when he did so, great was his joy to find that it doubled back and re-entered the defile. Pressing quickly forward, he came to a broken part, near the centre, where, among a heap of grey, weather-worn rocks he perceived two sharp-pointed objects, like a pair of erect ears! To make certain, he hurled a stone towards the place. The objects instantly disappeared!

Immediately afterwards, a long grey back and a bushy tail were visible as the wolf glided among the rocks, making for the side of the precipice, with the intention, doubtless, of rushing past this bold intruder.

Glumm observed the movement, and promptly went in the same direction. The wolf noticed this, and paused abruptly — remaining still, as if uncertain what to do. The hunter at once put to flight his uncertainty by gliding swiftly towards him. Seeing this, the wolf abandoned the attempt at concealment and bounded into the centre of the ravine, where, with his bristles erect, his back slightly arched, and all his glittering teeth and blood-red gums exposed, he stood for a moment or two the very picture of intensified fury. The hunter advanced with his spear levelled, steadily, but not hastily, because there was sufficient space on either hand to render the meeting of the animal in its rush a matter of extreme difficulty, while at every step he took, the precipices on either side drew closer together. The brute had evidently a strong objection to turn back, and preferred to run the risk of passing its foe, for it suddenly sprang to one side and ran up the cliff as far as possible, like a cat, while it made for the upper end of the ravine.

The Norseman, whose powerful frame was by this time strung to intensity of action, leaped to the same side with the agility of a panther, and got in before it. The wolf did not stop, but with a ferocious growl it swerved aside, and bounded to the other side of the ravine. Again the hunter leaped across, and stood in its way. He bent forward to resist the animal's weight and impetus, but the baffled wolf was cowed by his resolute front. It turned tail, and fled, followed by Glumm with a wild halloo!

When the first growl was heard by Alric, it strung him up to the right pitch instantly, and the next one caused the blood to rush to his face, for he heard the halloo which Glumm uttered as he followed in pursuit. The distance was short. Another moment and the boy saw the infuriated animal springing towards him, with Glumm rushing madly after it. Alric was already in the centre of the pass with the spear levelled, and his body bent in anticipation of the shock. The wolf saw him, but did not check its pace — with a furious Norseman bounding behind there was no room for hesitation. It lowered its head, increased its speed, and ran at the opening like a thunderbolt. When within three yards of the boy it swerved, and, leaping up, pawed the cliff on the left while in the air. Alric had foreseen this — his only doubt had been as to which side the brute would incline to. He sprang at the same moment, and met it full in the face as it came down. The point of his spear entered the wolf's chest, and penetrated deep into its body. A terrific yell followed. The spear handle broke in the middle, and the boy fell on his face, while the wolf went right over him, yelling and biting the spear, as, carried on by its impetus, it rolled head over heels for several yards among the rocks.

Alric jumped up unhurt, and, for want of a better weapon, seized a mass of stone, which he raised above his head, and hurled at the wolf, hitting it fairly on the skull. At the same moment Glumm ran up, intending to transfix the brute with his spear.

"Hold thy hand, Glumm," gasped the boy.

Glumm checked himself.

"In truth it needs no more," he said, bringing the butt of his weapon to the ground, and leaning on it, while he looked on at the last struggles of the dying wolf. "Fairly done, lad," he added, with a nod of approval, "this will make a man of thee."

The boy did not speak, but stood with his chest still heaving, his breath coming fast, and the expression of triumph on his countenance showing that for him a new era had opened up — that the days of boasting had ended, and those of manly action had fairly and auspiciously begun.

CHAPTER XVIII.

*Shows what some of the Men of Old could do in Cold Blood,
and treats of Heathen Festivities at Harald's Court, mingled
with Plot and Counter Plot.*

Winter — with its frost and snow, its long nights and its short days, its feasts in the great halls, and its tales round the roaring wood fires — at length began to pass away, and genial spring advanced to gladden the land of Norway. The white drapery melted in the valleys, leaving brilliant greens and all the varied hues of rugged rocks to fill the eyes with harmonious colour. High on the mighty fells the great glaciers — unchanging, almost, as the "everlasting hills" — gleamed in the sunlight against the azure sky, and sent floods of water down into the brimming rivers. The scalds ceased, to some extent, those wild legendary songs and tales with which they had beguiled the winter nights, and joined the Norsemen in their operations on the farms and on the fiords. Men began to grow weary of smoked rafters and frequent festivities, and to long for the free, fresh air of heaven. Some went off to drive the cattle to the "saeters" or mountain pastures, others set out for the fisheries, and not a few sailed forth on viking cruises over the then almost unknown sea. Our friends of Horlingdal bestirred themselves, like others, in these varied avocations, and King Harald Fairhair, uprising from his winter lair in Drontheim like a giant refreshed, assembled his men, and prepared to carry out his political plans with a strong hand. But resolute men cannot always drive events before them as fast as they would wish. Summer was well advanced before the King was ready to take action.

There was a man of the Drontheim district named Hauskuld, who was noted for ferocity and wickedness. He was also very strong and courageous, so that King Harald made him one of his berserks.

One morning the King sent for this man, and said to him —

"Hauskuld, I have a business for thee to do, which requires the heart of a brave fellow. There is a man near Horlingdal who has not only refused to submit to my will, but has gathered a band of seventy men or more about him, and threatens to raise the country against me. It does not suit me to go forth to punish this dog just now, for my preparations are not yet complete. Nevertheless it is important that he should be crushed, as he dwells in the heart of a disaffected district. It is therefore my purpose to send thee with a small body of picked men to do thy worst by him."

"That suits me well," said Hauskuld; "what is his name?"

"Atli," answered the King.

"He is my foster-brother!" said Hauskuld, with a peculiar and unpleasant smile.

The King looked a little perplexed.

"Thou wilt not have much heart to the business if that be so," he said.

"When you command, sire, it is my duty to obey," replied Hauskuld.

"Nay, but I can find other stout men for this thing. There is Hake of Hadeland. Go, send him hither. I will not put this on thy shoulders."

"Sire, you are considerate," said Hauskuld, "but this foster-brother of mine I count an enemy, for reasons that I need not tell. Besides, he is said to be a warlock, and for my part I firmly believe that he is in league with Nikke, so that it would be a service to the gods to rid the world of him. If you will permit me, I will gladly go on this errand, and as this Atli is a stout man, it would be well to take Hake and a few of the berserkers along with me."

"Do as thou wilt," replied the King, with a wave of his hand, as he turned away; "only, what thou doest, see thou do it well and quickly."

The berserk shouldered his battle-axe and left the hall. As he walked away the King stood in the doorway looking after him with a mingled expression of admiration and dislike.

"A stalwart knave," he muttered to himself, while a grim smile played on his large handsome features; "a good fighting brute, no doubt, but, with such a spirit, a bad servant, I fear."

"There are many such in your army," said a deep, stern voice behind him.

The King turned quickly round, with a look of anger, and fixed a searching glance on the huge form of Rolf Ganger, who stood leaning on the hilt of his sword with a quiet, almost contemptuous smile on his face.

"It is well known that birds of a feather are fond of flying in company," said the King, with a flushed countenance; "no doubt thou speakest from personal knowledge and experience."

It was now Rolf's turn to flush, but the King did him injustice, having no ground for such a speech, further than a knowledge that there existed between them mutual antipathy which neither was particularly careful to conceal.

"Have I done aught to merit such words?" demanded Rolf sternly.

Harald was on the point of making an angry rejoinder, but, placing a powerful restraint upon himself, he said —

"It may be that thine actions are loyal, but, Rolf, thy words are neither wise nor true. It is not wise to attempt to shake my confidence in my followers, and it is not true that many of them are untrustworthy. But, if thou wouldst prove thyself a real friend, go, get thy longships ready with all speed, for we fare south a few days hence, and there will be work for the weapons of stout men ere long."

"I go to prepare myself for the fight, King Harald," returned Rolf, "but I have no occasion to give thee further proof of friendship. The world is wide enough for us both. My ocean steeds are on the fiord. Henceforth I will fight for my own hand."

For one moment the King felt an almost irresistible impulse to draw his sword and hew down the bold Rolf, but with characteristic self-restraint he crushed down his wrath at the time and made no reply, good or bad, as the other turned on his heel and left him. When he had gone some distance the King muttered between his set teeth —

"Another good fighting brute and bad servant! Let him go! Better an open foe than an unwilling friend."

That night Hauskuld and Hake set sail southward with a small body of picked men; and Rolf Ganger, with a large body of devoted followers, left Harald's camp and travelled eastward. In the course of several days Hauskuld and his men arrived at the small fiord near the head of which stood the dwelling of Atli.

This Atli was an unusually intelligent man, a man of great influence in his district, and one who, like Erling the Bold, was determined to resist the tyranny of Harald Fairhair. A large force had been gathered by him towards the end of winter, and at the time of Hauskuld's visit he was living in his own house with about seventy chosen men. Unfortunately for these, the peaceful winter had induced them to relax a little in vigilance. Knowing from the report of spies that the King was still feasting in the Drontheim district, they felt quite safe, and for some time past had neglected to set the usual night watch, which, in time of war, was deemed indispensable. Thus it happened that when Hauskuld and his men came upon them in the dead of a dark night, they found everything quiet, and went up to the door of the house unchallenged. On trying the latch they found it fast, but from the sounds within they knew that a great many men were sleeping there. Hauskuld and Hake had approached the house alone. They now returned to their companions, who were concealed in the deep shades of the neighbouring woods.

"What dost thou advise?" asked Hake of his brother berserk.

"That we burn them all in their nest," replied Hauskuld.

"What! foster-brother too?" said the other.

"Aye, wherefore not? He is a warlock. So are most of the men with him. Burning is their due."

"There is wood enough here for that purpose," said Hake, with a grim smile.

Hauskuld immediately directed the greater part of his force to gather dry wood, and silently pile it all round the house, while he and Hake with a few men stood in front of the doors and windows to guard them. The work was accomplished in a much shorter time than might have been expected, for those who performed it were strong and active, and well accustomed to such deeds. In less than an hour the whole of Atli's house was surrounded by a thick pile of dry inflammable brushwood. When it was all laid the men completely surrounded the house, and stood with arrows fitted to the strings, and swords loosened in the sheaths. Then Hauskuld and several others applied lights to the brushwood at various points. For a few seconds there was an ominous crackling, accompanied by little flashes of flame, then a dense smoke rose up all round. Presently the rushing fire burst through the black pall with a mighty roar, and lit up the steading with the strength of the sun at noonday, while flame and smoke curled in curious conflict together over the devoted dwelling, and myriads of sparks were vomited up into the dark sky. At the same instant doors and windows were burst open with a crash, and a terrible cry arose as men, half clad and partly armed, leaped out and rushed through the circle of fire, with the flame kindling on their hair and garments.

Not less relentless than the fire was the circling foe outside. Whizzing arrows pierced the scorched breasts of some, and many fell dead. Others rushed madly on sword or spear point, and were thrust violently back into the fire, or fell fighting desperately for their lives. Some of the attacking party were killed, and a few wounded, but not one of the assailed succeeded in bursting through the line. Atli and all his followers perished there!

It is dreadful to think that such diabolical deeds were ever done; but still more dreadful is it to know that the spirit which dictated such atrocities still haunts the breast of fallen men, for the annals of modern warfare tell us all too plainly that unregenerate man is as capable of such deeds now as were the Norsemen in days of old.

Having fulfilled his mission, Hauskuld left the place as quickly as possible, and hastened back to Drontheim; not, however, without learning on the way that preparations were being secretly made all over that district to resist the King, and that, in particular, Solve Klofe was in the fiord at Horlingdal, with several ships of war, doing his best to fan the flame of discontent, which was already burning there briskly enough of its own accord!

On returning again to King Harald's quarters, Hauskuld found that energetic monarch engaged in celebrating one of the heathen feasts, and deemed it prudent for some hours to avoid his master, knowing that when heated with deep potations he was not in the best condition to receive or act upon exasperating news. He therefore went into the great hall, where the King and his guests were assembled, and quietly took his place at the lower end of one of the long tables near the door.

As is usual with men of inferior and debased minds, the berserk misunderstood and misjudged his master. He had counted on escaping notice, but the King's eye fell on him the instant he entered the hall, and he was at once summoned before him, and bidden tell his tale. While he related the details of the dreadful massacre Hauskuld felt quite at ease, little dreaming that the King's fingers twitched with a desire to cut him down where he stood; but when he came to speak of the widespread disaffection of the people in the south, he stammered a little, and glanced uneasily at the flushed countenance of the King, fearing that the news would exasperate him beyond endurance. Great, therefore, was his surprise when Harald affected to treat the matter lightly, made some jesting allusion to the potent efficacy of the sword in bringing obstinate people to reason, and ordered one of the waiting-girls to fetch the berserk a foaming tankard of ale.

"There, drink, Hauskuld, my bold berserk! drink down to a deeper peg, man. After such warm work as thou hast had, that will serve to cool thy fiery spirit. Drink to the gods, and pray that thou mayest never come to die, like an old woman, in thy bed — drink, I say, drink deep!"

The King laughed jovially, almost fiercely, in his wild humour, as he made this allusion to the well-known objection that the Norse warriors of old had to dying peacefully in bed; but for the life of him he could not resist the temptation, as he turned on his seat, to touch with his elbow the huge silver tankard which the berserk raised to his lips! The instantaneous result was that a cataract of beer flowed down Hauskuld's face and beard, while the rafters rang with a shout of laughter from the Sea-kings and court-men who sat in the immediate neighbourhood of the King's high seat. Of course Harald blamed himself for his clumsiness, but he too laughed so heartily that the masses of his fair hair shook all over his shoulders, while he ordered another tankard to be filled for his "brave berserk". That brave individual, however, protested that he had had quite enough, and immediately retired with a very bad grace to drink his beer in comfort out of a horn cup among kindred spirits.

Immediately after he was gone the King sent for Hake, for whom he also ordered a silver tankard of ale; but to him the King spoke earnestly, and in a low whispering voice, while his courtiers, perceiving that he wished his converse with the berserk to be private, quaffed their liquor and talked noisily.

The young woman who filled Hake's tankard at the King's bidding was no other than Gunhild, the unfortunate widow of Swart of the Springs. For some time after the death of her husband she had dwelt at Haldorstede, and had experienced much kindness at the hands of the family; but having taken a longing to visit her relatives, who belonged to the Drontheim district, she was sent thither, and had become a member of Harald's household, through the influence of King Hakon of Drontheim, the father of Ada of Horlingdal.

Hakon had from necessity, and much against his inclination, become one of Harald Fairhair's jarls. During the feast of which we write, he sat on the King's left hand.

After filling Hake's tankard Gunhild retired, but remained within earshot.

"Hake," said the King, leaning over the arm of his high seat, "it is now time that we were moving south; and the news thou hast brought decides me to complete my arrangements without delay. It seems that Ulf of Romsdal and that fellow Erling the Bold, with his fierce father, are making great preparations for war?"

"Truly they are," said Hake. "I saw as much with my own eyes."

"But may this not be for the purpose of going on viking cruise?"

"Had that been so, mine ears would have guided me, and we had brought a different report, but when men talk loudly and ill of the King, and knit their brows, and wish for a south wind, it needs not the wisdom of a warlock to fathom their meaning. Moreover," he continued earnestly, "I have heard that news has come from the southland that the people of Hordaland and Rogaland, Agder and Thelemark, are gathering, and bringing together ships, men, and arms — what can all this mean if it be not resistance to the King?"

"Right," said Harald thoughtfully. "Now, Hake, I will tell thee what to do, and see thou waste not time about it. Most of my ships are ready for sea. A few days more will suffice to complete them for a cruise, and then will I sail forth to teach these proud men humility. Meanwhile do thou get ready the ships under thy charge, and send Hauskuld in a swift boat with a few chosen men south to Horlingdal fiord. There let him watch the proceedings of the people — particularly of that fellow Erling and his kin — and when he has seen enough let him sail north to give me warning of their movements. They shall be saved the trouble of coming here to meet me, for I will fare south and slay them all, root and branch. Let thy tongue be quiet and thy motions swift, and caution Hauskuld also to be discreet. Another draught of ale, Hake, and then — to thy duty."

These last words the King spoke aloud, and while the berserk was drinking he turned to converse with Hakon of Drontheim, but finding that that chief had left the board, he turned to one of the courtiers, and began to converse on the news recently brought from the south.

Gunhild meanwhile slipped out of the hall, and found King Hakon hasting to his house.

"Ye heard what the King threatened?" she said, plucking him by the sleeve.

"I did, and will — but why dost thou speak to me on this subject?" asked Hakon warily.

"Because I know your daughter Ada is among the doomed and ye would not see her perish. My heart is in the house of Haldor the Fierce. Great kindness have I received there, therefore would I go and warn them of what is coming. I have friends here, and can get a swift cutter to bear me south. Shall I tell them to expect aid from you?"

Hakon was glad to hear this, and told her to inform Haldor that he would soon be in the fiord with his longship, that he would aid the people of Horlingdal in resisting Harald, and that it was probable Rolf Ganger would also join them.

Bearing these tidings Gunhild left Drontheim secretly, and in a swift boat with a stout crew set off for the south a considerable time before Hauskuld sailed, although that worthy did his best to carry out his master's commands without delay. King Hakon also pushed forward his preparations, and that so briskly that he too was enabled to start before the berserk.

Meanwhile King Harald gave himself up entirely to festivity — laughed and talked with his courtiers, and seemed so light of heart that the greater part of his followers thought him to be a careless, hearty man, on whom the weighty matters of the kingdom sat very lightly. But Jarl Rongvold knew that this free-and-easy spirit was affected, and that the King's mind was much troubled by the state of things in several parts of the kingdom. He also knew, however, that Harald had an iron will, which nothing could bend from its purpose, and he felt convinced that the course which his sovereign pursued would end either in his total overthrow or in the absolute subjection of Norway.

It happened that at this time one of the festivals of sacrifice was being celebrated by the people of the Drontheim country. It was an old custom that, when there was sacrifice, all the bonders should come to the spot where the heathen temple stood, and bring with them all that they required while the festival of the sacrifice lasted. The men were expected to bring ale with them, and all kinds of cattle as well as horses, which were to be slaughtered, boiled, and eaten.

In order to conciliate the people, the King on this occasion issued a proclamation that he meant to pay all the expenses of the festival. This had the double effect of attracting to the locality a vast concourse of people, and of putting them all in great good humour, so that they were quite ready to listen to, and fall in with, the plans of the King, whatever these might be. Of course there were many freeborn noble-spirited udallers who could not thus be tickled into the selling of their birthright; but Harald's tremendous energy and power, coupled with his rigorous treatment of all who resisted him, had the effect of reducing many of these to sullen silence, while some made a virtue of necessity, and accepted the fate which they thought it impossible to evade.

On the evening of the day of which we write, the fire was kindled in the middle of the floor of the temple, and over it hung the kettles. Full goblets were handed across the fire, and the King blessed the full goblets and all the meat of the sacrifice. Then, first, Odin's goblet was emptied for victory and power to the King; thereafter Niord's and Freya's goblets for peace and a good season. After that there was much feasting; and when the ale began to mount to the brains of the revellers, many of them stood up, and raising aloft the "braga goblet" — that over which vows were wont to be made — began, in more or less bombastic strains, to boast of what they meant to do in the future. Having exhausted all other sentiments, the guests then emptied the "remembrance goblet" to the memory of departed friends.

Soon the desire for song and story began to be felt, and there was a loud call for the scald. Whereupon, clearing his throat and glancing round on the audience with a deprecatory air — just as amateur scalds of the present day are wont to do — Thiodolph hinn Frode of Huina stood up to sing. His voice was mellow, and his music wild. The subject chosen showed that he understood how to humour both King and people, and if the song was short it was much to the point.

Song of the Scald.

Of cup and platter need has none,
The guest who seeks the generous one —
Harald the bounteous — who can trace
His lineage from the giant race;
For Harald's hand is liberal, free.
The guardian of the temple he.
He loves the gods, his open hand
Scatters his sword's gains o'er the land.

The scald sat down with the prompt energy of a man who believes he has said a good thing, and expects that it will be well received. He was not disappointed, for the rafters rang with the wild huzzas of the revellers as they leaped to their feet and shouted "Victory to the King!"

This was just what the King wanted, and he carefully fanned the flame which the scald had so judiciously kindled. The result was that when he afterwards called for men to go forth with him to do battle with the turbulent spirits of Horlingdal, hundreds of those who would otherwise have been malcontent, or lukewarm followers, busked themselves eagerly for the fight, and flocked to his standard. His longships were crowded with picked men, and war vessels of all sizes — from little boats to dragons with thirty banks of rowers — augmented his fleet. At length he sailed from Drontheim with perhaps the strongest armament that had ever swept over the northern sea.

CHAPTER XIX.

*Tells something of the Doings of Solve Klofe and Others,
and treats of a few of the Marvellous Adventures
of Guttorm Stoutheart.*

The scene is changed. It is night; yet how different from night in most other inhabited parts of the earth! The midnight sun is just sinking beneath the horizon, close to the spot whence, in about twenty minutes, he will rise, to repeat his prolonged course of nearly four-and-twenty hours through the northern sky. But if the darkness of night is absent, its deep quietude is there. The mighty cliffs that rise like giant walls to heaven, casting broad, heavy shadows over the sea, send forth no echoes, for the innumerable birds that dwell among them are silently perched like snowflakes on every crag, or nestled in every crevice, buried in repose. The sea resembles glass, and glides with but a faint sigh upon the shore. All is impressively still on mountain and fiord. Everything in nature is asleep, excepting the wakeful eye of day, the hum of distant rills, the boom of inland cataracts, and the ripple on the shore. These sounds, however, do but render the universal silence more profound by suggesting the presence of those stupendous forces which lie latent everywhere.

A white mist floats over the sea like a curtain of gauze, investing insignificant objects with grandeur, and clothing caverns, cliffs, and mountain gorges with unusual sublimity.

Only one object suggestive of man is visible through the haze. It is a ship — of the old, old-fashioned build — with high stem and stern, and monstrous figurehead. Its forefoot rests upon the strip of gravel in yonder bay at the foot of the cliff, whose summit is lost in the clouds. The hull reposes on its own reflected image, and the taper mast is repeated in a wavy but distinct line below. It is the "longship"; the "war vessel"; the "sea horse" of Solve Klofe, the son of King Hunthiof of Möre, whom Harald Fairhair slew.

Solve had, as we have before said, spent the winter in taking his revenge by herrying the coast in his longship, and doing all in his power to damage the King's men, as well as those who were friendly to his cause. Among other things he had, early in spring, persuaded Haldor the Fierce to let him have the use of one of his warships, with a few of his best men, to accompany him on a viking cruise. Erling had resisted his pressing invitation to bear him company, because of important business, the nature of which he did not think it necessary to disclose. His friend Glumm the Gruff also declined from similar reasons. At all events, he was similarly pre-engaged and taciturn. Thorer the Thick, however, and Kettle Flatnose, and young Alric — the latter by special and importunate request — were allowed to accompany him on this expedition.

We do not intend to give the details of this foray, although it was unusually stirring and prolific of adventure. Suffice it to say, that they had several hard fights both with Swedish and Danish vikings, in all of which Alric distinguished himself for reckless daring, and would certainly have been carried home dead upon his own shield had not Kettle Flatnose watched over him with the solicitude of a father, and warded off many a blow that was aimed at his pugnacious head. We fear it must be added that Alric was not sufficiently impressed with his friend's services in this way. The truth is that he entertained the firm belief that nobody could kill him, and that he could kill anybody — which was all very well as far as it went, but would not have carried him scathless through the cruise, had not the stout Irishman been at his back.

Immense and valuable booty was gained at this time, for one of the vessels which they captured had been cruising in southern lands, and was returning with a large quantity of gold and silver ornaments when Solve Klofe attacked it. A misfortune befell them, however. On their way home a storm drove Thorer's vessel on the rocks in a fog, and it became a total wreck. The crew were all saved, however, and much of the lading, by Solve, who stowed the goods in his own ship, and brought home the men. They were within a day's sail of Horlingdal, when they put ashore to take a few hours' repose.

Three hours after midnight Solve Klofe, whose breathing up to that time had resembled that of an infant, gave vent to a prolonged bass snore, and opened his eyes. This was followed by the shutting of his mouth, and with one of those satisfactory stretchings of the body with which a sound sleeper is wont in the morning to dismiss repose and recall his energies. Having lain still a few moments to enjoy the result, Solve sat up, and stretching forth his hand, drew aside the curtain of the tent under which he slept, and looked out. The sight that gladdened his eyes was beautiful beyond description, for the sun was up in all his northern glory, and shone on the silver sea with dazzling light, while he scattered away the mists of morning. But the best sight of all to the bold viking was the splendid warship which, with painted sides and shields, and gilded masts and prow, glowed and glittered like a beautiful gem in a setting of the brightest azure blue.

Turning his eyes inside his tent again, Solve gazed with the expressionless aspect of a still drowsy man upon the countenance of Kettle, whose flat nose and open mouth gave vent to tones resembling those of a bassoon. Beside him, and nestling close to him, lay the youthful Alric, with his curly head resting on Kettle's broad bosom; for the lad, albeit manly enough when awake, had sufficient of the child still about him to induce a tendency on his part, when asleep, to make use of any willing friend as a pillow. Thorer the Thick was also there, with his head on his arm, his body sprawling indescribably, his shield above him like a literal coverlet, and his right hand on his sword-hilt.

"Ho!" exclaimed Solve, in a tone that marvellously resembled the tones of modern men in similar circumstances.

Kettle and Thorer, however, sprang up to a sitting posture with very primitive alacrity, for in those days a man's life often depended on his being and keeping very wide-awake.

Poor Alric was tumbled somewhat unceremoniously to one side, but that failed to awaken him, for he was not yet sufficiently trained to sleep in the midst of alarms, and felt very naturally inclined to growl and bite when shaken or told to "get up!"

In a few minutes, however, his lethargy was overcome; the men were aroused; the tents were struck; the longship was pushed off, and, under the influence of thirty pair of oars, it crept like a monstrous insect away over the sea.

Those who had not to work at the oars sat at first quietly on the thwarts, or leaned over the gunwale gazing into the deep, or up at the sky, enjoying the warm air and their own fancies. But after a time talkative spirits began to loose their tongues, and ere long a murmur of quiet conversation pervaded the ship.

"I wonder what news we shall hear at the stede when we arrive?" said Thorer to Kettle, who with several others sat on the poop beside Solve.

"I hope it won't be bad news," answered Kettle. "Harald is not the man to sleep through the summer when there is work to be done. If it wasn't that I expect to give him the tooth-ache before I go, surely I should have been in Ireland long ago."

"Whom didst thou serve under, Kettle, before we brought thee to Norway?" asked Alric.

"Under the King of Dublin," replied Kettle.

"Was he a great king?"

"A great king? Aye, never was there a greater; and a great king he is yet, if he's alive, though I have my own fears on that point, for he was taking badly to ale when I left."

There was something pathetic yet humorous in the tone and expression with which Kettle said this which caused Alric to laugh. The Irishman started, and for an instant his huge countenance blazed with a look of wrath which was quite majestic, and overawed the boy, bold though he was. But it passed away in a moment, and was replaced by a sorrowful look as Kettle shook his head and said —

"Ah! boy, your laugh reminded me of the laugh of the villain Haabrok who took the old king's throne at the time I was carried off, bound hand and foot. Lucky was it for him that my hands were not free then. — Well, well, this sounds like bragging," he added with a smile, "which is only fit for boys and cowards."

Alric winced a little at this, for he was quite aware of his own tendency to boast, and for a moment he felt a strong inclination to stand up for "boys", and assert, that although boasting was common enough with cowardly boys, it was not so with all boys; but on consideration he thought it best to hold his tongue, on that point, at least until he should have freed himself of the evil of boasting. To change the subject he said —

"Was the old king fond of thee, Kettle?"

"Aye, as fond of me as of his own son."

"Was he like my father?" pursued the boy.

"No; there are not many men like thy father, lad; but he was a stout and brave old man, and a great warrior in his day. Now I think of it, he was very like Guttorm Stoutheart."

"Then he was a handsome man," said Solve Klofe with emphasis.

"He was," continued Kettle, "but not quite so desperate. Old Guttorm is the most reckless man I ever did see. Did I ever tell ye of the adventure I had with him when we went on viking cruise south to Valland?"

"No," said Solve; "let us hear about it; but stay till I change the oarsmen."

He went forward and gave the order to relieve the men who had rowed from the land, and when the fresh men were on the benches he returned and bade Kettle go on.

"'Tis a fine country," said the Irishman, glancing round him with a glowing eye, and speaking in a low tone, as if to himself — "one to be proud of."

And in truth there was ground for his remark, for the mists had by that time entirely cleared away, leaving unveiled a sea so calm and bright that the innumerable islets off the coast appeared as if floating in air.

"That is true," said Thorer. "I sometimes wonder, Kettle, at thy longing to return to Ireland. I am in the same case with thyself — was taken from my home in Jemteland, laboured as a thrall, wrought out my freedom, and remained in Haldor's service, but have never wished to return home."

"Didst thou leave a wife and children behind thee?" asked Kettle.

"Nay; I was carried away while very young."

"Is thy father alive, or thy mother?"

"No, they are both dead."

"Then I wonder not that ye have no desire to return home. My father and mother are both alive — at least I have good reason to believe so — my wife and children are waiting for me. Canst wonder, man, that I long to behold once more the green hills of Ireland?"

"Nay, if that be so, I wonder not," replied Thorer.

"Come, Kettle, thou forgettest that we wait for the story about old Guttorm Stoutheart," said Solve Klofe, arranging the corner of a sail so as to protect his back from the sun.

"'Tis an old story now in Horlingdal," said Kettle; "but as thou hast not been in this quarter for a long time, no doubt it is new to thee. Thorer there knows it well; but I find that it bears telling more than once. Well, it was, as I have said, two years past that Guttorm went south to Valland on viking cruise. He called at Horlingdal in passing, and got some of the dalesmen. Among others, I was allowed to go. He and I got on very well together, and we were fortunate in getting much booty. One day we came to a part of the coast where we saw a strong castle of stone on the top of a hill a short way inland. We also saw plenty of cattle on a plain near the sea, so Guttorm ordered his longship to be steered for the shore, and we began to drive some of the cattle down to the beach, intending to slaughter them there, as our provisions were getting low. On seeing this, a party of men came out from the castle and bade us begone. We told them to be easy in their minds, for we only wanted a little food. We even went so far as to ask it of them civilly, but the men were such surly fellows that they refused to listen to reason, and attacked us at once. Of course we drove them back into their castle, but in doing so we lost one or two of our best men. This angered old Guttorm, who is not a quarrelsome man, as ye know. He would have gone away peaceably enough if he had been let alone to help himself to a few beasts; but his blood was set up by that time, so he ordered all the men on shore, and we pitched our tents and besieged the castle. Being made of stone, there was no chance of setting it on fire, and as the walls were uncommonly high, it was not possible to take it by assault. Well, we sat down before it, and for two days tried everything we could think of to take it, but failed, for there were plenty of men in it, and they defended the walls stoutly. Besides this, to say the truth, we had already lost a number of good men on the cruise and could ill afford to lose more.

"On the third day some of our chief men advised Guttorm to give it up, but that made him so furious that no one dared speak to him about it for another two days. At the end of that time his nephew plucked up heart, and going to him, said —

"'Uncle, do you see the little birds that fly back and forward over the castle walls so freely, and build their nests in the thatch of the housetops?'

"'I do, nephew,' says Guttorm. 'What then?'

"'My advice is,' says the nephew, 'that you should order the men to make each a pair of wings like those the birds have, and then we shall all fly over the walls, for it seems to me that there is no other way of getting into the castle.'

"'Thou art a droll knave,' replies Guttorm, for he was ever fond of a joke; 'but thou art wise also, therefore I advise thee to make a pattern pair of wings for the men; and when they are ready — '

"Here Guttorm stopped short, and fell to thinking; and he thought so long that his nephew asked him at last if he had any further commands for him.

"'Yes, boy, I have. There is more in this matter of the wings than thou dreamest of. Go quickly and order the men to make snares, and catch as many of these little birds as they can before sunset. Let them be careful not to hurt the birds, and send Kettle Flatnose and my house-carle hither without delay.'

"When I came to the old man I found him walking to and fro briskly, with an expression of eagerness in his eye.

"'Kettle,' he said smartly, 'go and prepare two hundred pieces of cord, each about one foot long, and to the end of each piece tie a small chip of wood as long as the first joint of thy thumb, and about the size of a goose quill. Smear these pieces of wood over with pitch, and have the whole in my tent within three hours.'

"As I walked away to obey this order, wondering what it could all be about, I heard him tell his chief house-carle to have all the men armed and ready for action a little after sunset, as quietly as possible.

"Before the three hours were out, I returned to the tent with the two hundred pieces of cord prepared according to orders, and found old Guttorm sitting with a great sack before him, and a look of perplexity on his face that almost made me laugh. He was half-inclined to laugh too, for the sack moved about in a strange way, as if it were alive!

"'Kettle,' said he, when I came forward, 'I need thy help here. I have got some three hundred little birds in that sack, and I don't know how to keep them in order, for they are fluttering about and killing themselves right and left, so that I shall soon have none left alive for my purpose. My thought is to tie one of these cords to a leg of each bird, set the bit of stick on fire and let it go, so that when it flies to its nest in the thatch it will set the houses in the castle on fire. Now, what is thy advice?'

"'Call as many of the men into the tent as it will hold, and let each catch a bird, and keep it till the cords are made fast; says I.'

"This was done at once, but we had more trouble than we expected, for when the mouth of the sack was opened, out flew a dozen of the birds before we could close it! The curtain of the tent was down, however, so, after a good deal of hunting, we caught them again. When the cords were tied to these the men were sent out of the tent, each with a little bird in his hand, and with orders to go to his particular post and remain there till further orders. Then another batch of men came in, and they were supplied with birds and cords like the others; but ye have no notion what trouble we had. I have seen a hundred viking prisoners caught and held fast with half the difficulty and less noise! Moreover, while some of the men squeezed the birds to death in their fear lest they should escape, others let theirs go in their anxiety not to hurt them, and the little things flew back to their nests with the cords and bits of chip trailing after them. At last, however, all was ready. The men were kept in hiding till after dark; then the little chips were set on fire all at the same time, and the birds were let go. It was like a shower of stars descending on the castle, for each bird made straight for its own nest; but just as we were expecting to behold the success of our plan, up jumped a line of men on the castle walls, and by shouting and swinging their arms scared the birds away. We guessed at once that the little birds which had escaped too soon with the strings tied to their legs had been noticed, and the trick suspected, for the men in the castle were well prepared. A few of the birds flew over their heads, and managed to reach the roofs, which caught fire at once; but wherever this happened, a dozen men ran at the place and beat the fire out. The thing was wisely contrived, but it was cleverly met and repelled, so we had only our trouble and the disappointment for our pains.

"After this," continued Kettle, "old Guttorm became like a wolf. He snarled at everyone who came near him for some time, but his passion never lasted long. He soon fell upon another plan.

"There was a small river which ran at the foot of the mound on which the castle stood, and there were mudbanks on the side next to it, One night we were all ordered to go to the mudbanks as quiet as mice, with shovels and picks in our hands, and dig a tunnel under the castle. We did so, and the first night advanced a long way, but we had to stop a good while before day to let the dirt wash away and the water get clear again, so that they might not suspect what we were about. The next night we got under the castle wall, and on the fifth night had got well under the great hall, for we could hear the men singing and shouting as they sat at meat above us. We had then to work very carefully for fear of making a noise, and when we thought it ready for the assault we took our swords and shields with us, and Guttorm led the way. His chief house-carle was appointed to drive through the floor, while Guttorm and I stood ready to egg him on and back him up.

"We heard the men above singing and feasting as usual, when suddenly there was a great silence, for one of the big stones over our heads was loosened, and they had evidently felt or seen it. Now was the time come; so, while the house-carle shovelled off the earth, some of us got our fingers in about the edge of the stone, and pulled with all our force. Suddenly down it came and a man along with it. We knocked him on the head at once, and gave a loud huzza as the house-carle sprang up through the hole, caught a shower of blows on his shield, and began to lay about him fiercely. Guttorm was very mad at the carle for going up before him, but the carle was light and the old man was heavy, so he could not help it. I was about to follow, when a man cut at my head with a great axe as I looked up through the hole. I caught the blow on my shield, and thrust my sword up into his leg, which made him give back; but just at that moment the earth gave way under our feet, and a great mass of stones and rubbish fell down on us, driving us all back into the passage through which we had come, except the house-carle, who had been caught by the enemy and dragged up into the hall. As soon as we could get on our feet we tried to make for the hole again, but it was so filled with earth and stones that we could not get forward a step. Knowing, therefore, that it was useless to stay longer there, we ran back to the entrance of the tunnel, but here we found a body of men who had been sent out of the castle to cut off our retreat. We made short work of these. Disappointment and anger had made every man of us equal to two, so we hewed our way right through them, and got back to the camp with the loss of only two men besides the house-carle.

"Next morning when it was daylight, the enemy brought the poor prisoner to the top of the castle wall, where they lopped off his head, and, having cut his body into four pieces, they cast them down to us with shouts of contempt.

"After this Guttorm Stoutheart appeared to lose all his fire and spirit. He sent for his chief men, and said that he was going to die, and that it was his wish to be left to do so undisturbed. Then he went into his tent, and no one was allowed after that to go near him except his nephew.

"A week later we were told that Guttorm was dying, and that he wanted to be buried inside the castle; for we had discovered that the people were what they called Christians, and that they had consecrated ground there.

"When this was made known to the priests in the castle they were much pleased, and agreed to bury our chief in their ground, if we would bring his body to a spot near the front gateway, and there leave it and retire to a safe distance from the walls. There was some objection to this at first, hit it was finally agreed to — only a request was made that two of the next of kin to Guttorm might be allowed to accompany the body to the burial-place, as it would be considered a lasting disgrace to the family if it were buried by strange hands when friends were near. This request was granted on the understanding that the two relations were to go into the castle unarmed.

"On the day of the funeral I was summoned to Guttorm's tent to help to put him into his coffin, which had been made for him after the pattern of the coffins used in that part of the country. When I entered I found the nephew standing by the side of the coffin, and the old Sea-king himself sitting on the foot of it.

"'Thou art not quite dead yet?' says I, looking hard in his face.

"'Not yet,' says he, 'and I don't expect to be for some time.'

"'Are we to put you into the coffin?' I asked.

"'Yes,' says he, 'and see that my good axe lies ready to my hand. Put thy sword on my left side, nephew, that thou mayst catch it readily. They bury me in consecrated ground to-day, Kettle; and thou, being one of my nearest of kin, must attend me to the grave! Thou must go unarmed too, but that matters little, for thy sword can be placed on the top of my coffin, along with thy shield, to do duty as the weapons of the dead. When to use them I leave to thy well-known discretion. Dost understand?'

"'Your speech is not difficult for the understanding to take in,' says I.

"'Ha! especially the understanding of an Irishman,' says he, with a smile. 'Well, help me to get into this box, and see that thou dost not run it carelessly against gate-posts; for it is not made to be roughly handled!'

"With that old Guttorm lay back in the coffin, and we packed in the nephew's sword and shield with him, and his own axe and shield at his right side. Then we fastened down the lid, and two men were called to assist us in carrying it to the appointed place.

"As we walked slowly forward I saw that our men were drawn up in a line at some distance from the castle wall, with their heads hanging down, as if they were in deep grief, — and so they were, for only a *few* were aware of what was going to be done; yet all were armed, and ready for instant action. The appointed spot being reached, we put the coffin on the ground, and ordered the two men, who were armed, to retire.

"'But don't go far away, lads,' says I; 'for we have work for ye to do.'

"They went back only fifty ells or so, and then turned to look on.

"At the same time the gate of the castle opened, and twelve priests came out dressed in long black robes, and carrying a cross before them. One of them, who understood the Norse language, said, as they came forward —

"'What meaneth the sword and shield?'

"I told him that it was our custom to bury a warrior's arms along with him. He seemed inclined to object to this at first, but thinking better of it, he ordered four of his men to take up the coffin, which they did, shoulder high, and marched back to the castle, closely followed by the two chief mourners.

"No sooner had we entered the gateway, which was crowded with warriors, than I stumbled against the coffin, and drove it heavily against one of the posts, and, pretending to stretch out my hands to support it, I seized my sword and shield. At the same moment the lid of the coffin flew into the air, the sides burst out, and old Guttorm dropped to the ground, embracing two of the priests so fervently in his descent that they fell on the top of him. I had only time to observe that the nephew caught up his sword and shield as they fell among the wreck, when a shower of blows from all directions called for the most rapid action of eye and limb. Before Guttorm could regain his feet and utter his war-cry, I had lopped off two heads, and the nephew's sword was whirling round him like lightning flashes, but of course I could not see what he did. The defenders fought bravely, and in the first rush we were almost borne back; but in another moment the two men who had helped us to carry the coffin were alongside of us; and now, having a front of five stout men, we began to feel confident of success. This was turned into certainty when we heard, a minute later, a great rushing sound behind us, and knew that our men were coming on. Old Guttorm swung his battle-axe as if it had been a toy, and, uttering a tremendous roar, cut his way right into the middle of the castle. We all closed in behind him; the foe wavered — they gave way — at last they turned and fled; for remembering, no doubt, how they had treated the poor house-carle, they knew they had no right to expect mercy. In a quarter of an hour the place was cleared, and the castle was ours."

"And what didst thou do with it?" asked Alric, in much excitement.

"Do with it? Of course we feasted in it till we were tired; then we put as much of its valuables into our ships as they could carry, after which we set the place on fire and returned to Norway."

"'Twas well done, and a lucky venture," observed Solve Klofe.

Alric appeared to meditate for a few minutes, and then said with a smile —

"If Christian the hermit were here he would say it was ill done, and an unlucky venture for the men of the castle."

"The hermit is a fool," said Solve.

"That he is not," cried the boy, reddening. "A braver and better man never drew bow. But he has queer thoughts in his head."

"That may be so. It matters naught to me," retorted Solve, rising and going forward to the high prow of the ship, whence he looked out upon the island-studded sea. — "Come, lads, change hands again, and pull with a will. Methinks a breeze will fill our sails after we pass yonder point, and if so, we shall sleep to-night in Horlingdal."

CHAPTER XX.

In which the Sky again becomes Overcast — The War-token is sent out — Alric gets a Surprise, and a Berserk catches a Tartar.

Erling the Bold was very fond of salmon-fishing, and it was his wont, when the weather suited, and nothing of greater importance claimed his attention, to sally forth with a three-pronged spear to fish in the Horlingdal river, which swarmed with salmon in the summer season of the year.

One evening he left Haldorstede with his fishing-spear on his shoulder, and went up to the river, accompanied by one of the house-carles. They both wore shirts of mail, and carried shield and sword, for these were not times in which men could venture to go about unarmed. On reaching a place where the stream ran shallow among rocks, our hero waded in, and at the first dart of his spear struck a fish of about fifteen pounds weight, which he cast, like a bar of burnished silver, on the grassy bank.

"That will be our supper to-night," observed the carle, as he disengaged the spear.

Erling made no reply, but in a few minutes he pulled out another fish, and said, as he threw it down —

"That will do for a friend, should one chance to turn in to us to-night."

After that he tried again, but struck no more, although he changed his ground frequently; so he cast his eyes upwards as if to judge of the time of evening, and appeared to doubt whether or not he should persevere any longer.

"Try the foss," suggested the house-carle; "you seldom fail to get one there."

"Well, I will try it. Do thou leave the fish under that bush, and follow me. It needs three big fish to make a good feast for my father's household."

"Besides," said the carle, "there is luck in an odd number, as Kettle Flatnose is fond of telling us."

They were about to ascend the bank to the track which led to the waterfall, about half a mile farther up the river, when their attention was arrested by a shout; looking down the stream in the direction whence it came, they saw a figure approaching them at full speed.

"That must be my brother Alric," said Erling, on hearing the shout repeated.

"It looks like him," said the carle.

All doubt on the point was quickly set at rest by the lad, who ran at a pace which soon brought him near. Waving his cap above his head he shouted —

"News! news! good news!"

"Out with thy news, then," said Erling, as Alric stood before him, panting violently, "though I dare say the best news thou hast to give is that thou hast come back to us safe and well."

"Hah! let me get wind! nay, I have better news than that," exclaimed Alric; "Harald is coming — King Harald Haarfager — with a monstrous fleet of longships, cutters, dragons, and little boats, and a mighty host of men, to lay waste Horlingdal with fire and sword, and burn us all alive, perhaps eat us too, who knows!"

"Truly if this be good news," said Erling, with a laugh, "I hope I may never hear bad news. But where got ye such news, Alric?"

"From the widow Gunhild, to be sure, who is true to us as steel, and comes all the way from Drontheim, out of love to thee, Erling, to tell it. But, I say, *don't* you think this good news? I always thought you would give your best battle-axe to have a chance of fighting Harald!"

"Aye, truly, for a chance of fighting Harald, but not for that chance coupled with the other chance of seeing Horlingdal laid waste with fire and sword, to say nothing of being eaten alive, which, I suppose, is thine own addition to the news, boy. But come, if this be so, we do not well to waste time chattering here. Fetch the two fish, carle. To-night we must be content with what luck lies in an even number in spite of the opinion of Kettle Flatnose. — Come, Alric, thou canst tell me more of this as we hasten home."

"But I have more good news than that to tell," said the lad, as they hurried towards Haldorstede. "Solve Klofe with his men have come back with us — indeed, I may rather say that we have come back with Solve, for our own ship has been wrecked and lost, but Kettle and I and Thorer and all the men were saved by Solve, with nearly everything belonging to us, and all the booty. It is not more than an hour since we sailed into the fiord, loaded to the shield-circle with, oh! *such* splendid things — gold, silver, cups, tankards, gems, shawls — and — and I know not what all, besides captives. It was just after we landed that a small boat came round the ness from the north with the widow Gunhild in it, and she jumped ashore, and told what she had seen and heard at Drontheim, and that we may expect Ada's father, King Hakon, in his longship, to our aid; perhaps he may be coming into the fiord even now while we are talking. And — and, she said also that Rolf Ganger had left the King in a huff, and perhaps we might look for help from him too. So methinks I bring good news, don't I?"

"Good, aye, and stirring news, my boy," cried Erling striding onward at such a pace that the carle with the fish was left behind, and Alric was compelled to adopt an undignified trot in order to keep up with his huge brother. "From this I see," continued Erling in a tone of deep seriousness, "that the long-looked — for time is at last approaching. This battle that must surely come will decide the fate of freemen. King Harald Haarfager must now be crushed, or Norway shall be enslaved. Alric, my boy, thou hast been styled Lightfoot. If ever thou didst strive to merit that title, strive this night as ye have never striven before, for there is urgent need that every friendly blade in the land should assemble in the dale without delay. I will send thee forth with the split arrow as soon as I have seen and spoken with my father. — Ha! I see him coming. Go into the house, lad, and sup well and quickly, for no sleep shall visit thine eyelids this night."

Alric's breast swelled with gratification at being spoken to thus earnestly and made of such importance by his brother, whom he admired and loved with an intensity of feeling that no words can convey. Looking up in his face with sparkling eyes, he gave him a little nod. Erling replied with another little nod and a sedate smile, and the boy, turning away, dashed into the house, at which they had now arrived.

"Hast heard the news, Erling?" asked Haldor, as his son drew near.

"Aye, Alric has told it me."

"What thinkest thou?"

"That the game is about to be played out."

Haldor looked full in Erling's face, and his own noble countenance glowed with an expression of majesty which cannot be described, and which arose from the deep conviction that one of the most momentous eras in his life had arrived — a period in which his own fate and that of all he held most dear would in all probability be sealed. Death or victory, he felt assured, were now the alternatives; and when he reflected on the great power of the King, and the stern necessity there was for the exertion of not only the utmost bravery, but the most consummate skill, his whole being glowed with suppressed emotion, while his bearing betokened the presence, and bore the dignified stamp, of a settled purpose to do his best, and meet his fate, for weal or woe, manfully.

"Come," said he, putting his arm within that of his stout son, "let us turn into the wood awhile. I would converse with thee on this matter."

"Alric is ready to start with the token," said Erling.

"I know it, my son. Let him sup first; the women will care well for him, for they will guess the work that lies before him. The people of Ulfstede are with us to-night, and Glumm is here; but Glumm is not of much use as a counsellor just now, poor fellow. It were kind to let him be, until it is time to rouse him up to fight!"

A quiet smile played on Haldor's lips as he thus alluded to the impossibility of getting Glumm to think of anything but love or fighting at that time.

While the father and son strolled in the wood conversing earnestly, a noisy animated scene was presented in the great hall of Haldorstede; for in it were assembled, besides the ordinary household, the family from Ulfstede, a sprinkling of the neighbours, Gunhild and her men, Guttorm Stoutheart, and Solve Klofe, with Kettle Flatnose, Thorer the Thick, and the chief men who had arrived from the recent viking cruise; all of whom were talking together in the utmost excitement, while the fair Herfrida and her daughters and maids prepared a sumptuous meal.

In those days, and at such an establishment as that of Haldor the Fierce, it was not possible for friends to appear inopportunely. A dozen might have "dropped in" to breakfast, dinner, or supper, without costing Dame Herfrida an anxious thought as to whether the cold joint of yesterday "would do", or something more must be procured, for she knew that the larder was always well stocked. When, therefore, a miniature army of hungry warriors made a sudden descent upon her, she was quite prepared for them — received them with the matronly dignity and captivating smile for which she was celebrated, and at once gave directions to her commissariat department to produce and prepare meat and drink suitable to the occasion.

The evening which had thus grown so unexpectedly big with present facts and future portents had begun in a very small way — in a way somewhat equivalent to the modern "small tea party". Ulf of Romsdal, feeling a disposition "to make a night of it", had propounded to Dame Astrid the idea of "going up to Haldorstede for the evening". His wife, being amiably disposed, agreed. Hilda and Ada were equally willing, and Glumm, who by a mere chance happened to be there at the time, could not choose but accompany them!

The family at Haldorstede were delighted to see their friends. Dame Herfrida carried off Dame Astrid to her apartment to divest her of her hat and mantle. Ingeborg bore off Ada, and the younger girls of the household made away with Hilda, leaving Ulf to talk the politics of the day with Haldor, while Glumm pretended to listen to them, but listened, in reality, for Ada's returning footsteps. In a short time the fair ones re-entered the hall, and there they had supper, or, more properly, an interlude supper — a sort of supperlet, so to speak, composed of cold salmon, scones, milk, and ale, which was intended, no doubt, to give them an appetite for the true supper that should follow ere long. Over this supperlet they were all very talkative and merry, with the exception, poor fellow, of Glumm, who sat sometimes glancing at, and always thinking of, Ada, and pendulating, as usual, between the condition of being miserably happy or happily miserable.

No mortal, save Glumm himself, could have told or conceived what a life Ada led him. She took him up by the neck, figuratively speaking, and shook him again and again as a terrier shakes a rat, and dropped him! But here the simile ceases, for whereas the rat usually crawls away, if it can, and evidently does not want more, Glumm always wanted more, and never crawled away. On the contrary, he crawled humbly back to the feet of his tormentor, and by looks, if not words, craved to be shaken again!

It was while Glumm was drinking this cup of mingled bliss and torment, and the others were enjoying their supperlet, that Solve Klofe and his men, and Kettle Flatnose, Thorer the Thick, and the house-carles, burst clamorously into the hall, with old Guttorm Stoutheart, who had met them on the beach. Scarcely had they got over the excitement of this first invasion when the widow Gunhild and her niece arrived to set the household ablaze with her alarming news. The moment that Haldor heard it he dispatched Alric in search of Erling, who, as we have seen, immediately returned home.

Shortly afterwards he and Haldor entered the hall.

"Ho! my men," cried the latter, "to arms, to arms! Busk ye for the fight, and briskly too, for when Harald Haarfager lifts his hand he is not slow to strike. Where is Alric?"

"Here I am, father."

"Hast fed well, boy?"

"Aye, famously," answered Alric, wiping his mouth and tightening his belt.

"Take the war-token, my son, and see that thou speed it well. Let it not fail for want of a messenger. If need be, go all the round thyself, and rest not as long as wind and limb hold out. Thy fighting days have begun early," he added in a softer tone, as he passed his large hand gently over the fair head of the boy, "perchance they will end early. But, whatever betide, Alric, quit thee like a man — as thou art truly in heart if not in limb."

Such words from one who was not at any time lavish of praise might, a short time before, have caused the boy to hold up his head proudly, but the last year of his life had been fraught with many lessons. He listened with a heaving breast and beating heart indeed, but with his head bent modestly down, while on his flushed countenance there was a bright expression, and on his lips a glad smile which spoke volumes. His father felt assured, as he looked at him, that he would never bring discredit on his name.

"Ye know the course," said Haldor; "away!"

In another minute Alric was running at full speed up the glen with the war-token in his hand. His path was rugged, his race was wild, and its results were striking. He merely shouted as he passed the windows of the cottages low down in the dale, knowing that the men there would be roused by others near at hand; but farther on, where the cottages were more scattered, he opened the door of each and showed the token, uttering a word or two of explanation during the brief moment he stayed to swallow a mouthful of water or to tighten his belt.

At first his course lay along the banks of the river, every rock and shrub of which he knew. Farther on he left the stream on the right, and struck into the mountains just as the sun went down.

High up on the fells a little cottage stood perched on a cliff. It was one of the "saeters" or mountain dairies where the cattle were pastured in summer long ago — just as they are at the present day. Alric ran up the steep face of the hill, doubled swiftly round the corner of the enclosure, burst open the door, and, springing in, held up the token, while he wiped the streaming perspiration from his face.

A man and his wife, with three stout sons and a comely daughter, were seated on a low bench eating their supper of thickened milk.

"The war-token!" exclaimed the men, springing up, and, without a moment's delay, taking down and girding on the armour which hung round the walls.

"King Harald is on his way to the dale," said Alric; "we assemble at Ulfstede."

"Shall I bear on the token?" asked the youngest of the men.

"Aye; but go thou with it up the Wolf's Den Valley. I myself will bear it round by the Eagle Crag and the coast."

"That is a long way," said the man, taking his shield down from a peg in the wall.

Alric replied not, for he had already darted away, and was again speeding along the mountain side.

Night had begun to close in, for the season had not yet advanced to the period of endless daylight. Far away in an offshoot vale, a bright ruddy light gleamed through the surrounding darkness. Alric's eye was fixed on it. His untiring foot sped towards it. The roar of a mighty cataract grew louder on his ear every moment. He had to slacken his pace a little, and pick his steps as he went on, for the path was rugged and dangerous.

"I wonder if Old Hans of the Foss is at home?" was the thought that passed through his mind as he approached the door.

Old Hans himself answered the thought by opening the door at that moment. He was a short, thick-set, and very powerful man, of apparently sixty years of age, but his eye was as bright and his step as light as that of many a man of twenty.

"The war-token," he said, almost gaily, stepping back into the cottage as Alric leaped in. "What is doing, son of Haldor?"

"King Harald will be upon us sooner than we wish. Ulfstede is the meeting-place. Can thy son speed on the token in the next valley?"

The old warrior shook his head sadly, and pointed to a low bed, where a young man lay with the wasted features and bright eyes that told of a deadly disease in its advanced stage.

An exclamation of regret and sympathy escaped from Alric. "I cannot go," he said; "my course lies to the left, by the Stor foss. Hast no one to send?"

"I will go, father," said a smart girl of fifteen, who had been seated behind her mother, near the couch of the sick man.

"Thou, bairn?"

"Yes, why not? It is only a league to Hawksdal, where young Eric will gladly relieve me."

"True," said the old warrior, with a smile, as he began to don his armour. "Go; I need not tell thee to make haste!"

Alric waited to hear no more, but darted away as the little maid tripped off in another direction.

Thus hour by hour the night passed by and Alric ran steadily on his course, rousing up all the fighting men in his passage through the district. As he advanced, messengers with war-tokens were multiplied, and, ere the morning's sun had glinted on the mountain peaks or lighted up the white fields of the Justedal glacier, the whole country was in arms, and men were crowding to the rendezvous.

Daylight had just commenced to illumine the eastern sky, when Alric, having completed his round, found himself once more on the cliffs above the sea. But he was still six or eight miles from Ulfstede, and the path to it along the top of the cliffs was an extremely rugged one. Earnestly then did the poor boy wish that he had remembered to put a piece of bread in his wallet before leaving home, but in his haste he had forgotten to do so, and now he found himself weary, foot-sore, and faint from exertion, excitement, and hunger, far from any human habitation. As there was no remedy for this, he made up his mind to take a short rest on the grass, and then set off for home as fast as possible.

With this end in view he selected a soft spot, on a cliff overlooking the sea, and lay down with a sigh of satisfaction. Almost instantly he fell into a deep slumber, in which he lay, perfectly motionless, for some hours. How long that slumber would have lasted it is impossible to say, for it was prematurely and unpleasantly interrupted.

In his cat-like creepings about the coast, Hauskuld the berserk, having obtained all the information that he thought would be of use to his royal master, landed for the last time to reconnoitre the position of Ulfstede, and see as much as he could of the doings of the people before turning his prow again to the north. The spot where he ran his boat ashore was at the foot of a steep cliff, up which he and a comrade ascended with some difficulty.

At the top, to his surprise, he found a lad lying on the grass sound asleep. After contemplating him for a few minutes, and whispering a few words to his comrade, who indulged in a broad grin, Hauskuld drew his sword and pricked Alric on the shoulder with it. An electric shock could not have been more effective. The poor boy sprang up with a loud cry, and for a few seconds gazed at the berserks in bewilderment. Then it flashed upon his awakening faculties that he was standing before enemies, so he suddenly turned round and fled, but Hauskuld sprang after him, and, before he had got three yards away, had caught him by the nape of the neck with a grip that made him gasp.

"Ho, ho! my young fox, so ye thought to leave the hounds in the lurch? Come, cease thy kicking, else will I give thee an inch of steel to quiet thee. Tell me thy name, and what thou art about here, and I will consider whether to make use of thee or hurl thee over the cliffs."

By this time Alric had fully recovered his senses and his self-possession. He stood boldly up before the berserk and replied —

"My name is Alric — son of Haldor the Fierce, out of whose way I advise thee to keep carefully, if thou art not tired of life. I have just been round with the war-token rousing the country."

"A most proper occupation for an eaglet such as thou," said Hauskuld; "that is to say, if the cause be a good one."

"The cause is one of the best," said Alric.

"Prithee, what may it be?"

"Self-defence against a tyrant."

Hauskuld glanced at his comrade, and smiled sarcastically as he asked —

"And who may this tyrant be?"

"Harald Haarfager, tyrant King of Norway," replied the lad stoutly.

"I thought so," said Hauskuld, with a grim twist of his features. "Well, young eaglet, thou art worthy to be made mincemeat of to feed the crows, but it may be that the tyrant would like to dispose of thee himself. Say now, whether will ye walk down that cliff quietly in front of me, or be dragged down?"

"I would rather walk, if I *must* go."

"Well, thou *must* go, therefore — walk, and see thou do it as briskly as may be, else will I apply the spur, which thou hast felt once already this morning. Lead the way, comrade; I will bring up the rear to prevent the colt from bolting."

As he knew that resistance would be useless, the boy promptly and silently descended the cliff with his captors, and entered the boat, which was immediately pushed off and rowed along-shore.

"Now listen to me, Alric, son of Haldor," said Hauskuld, seating himself beside his captive: "King Harald is not the tyrant you take him for; he is a good king, and anxious to do the best he can for Norway. Some mistaken men, like your father, compel him to take strong measures when he would fain take mild. If you will take me to a spot where I may safely view the valley of Horlingdal, and tell me all you know about their preparations for resistance, I will take you back to Drontheim, and speak well of you to the King, who will not only reward you with his favour, but make good terms, I doubt not, with your father."

The wily berserk had changed his tone to that of one who addresses a superior in rank while he thus tempted the boy; but he little guessed the spirit of his captive.

"What!" he exclaimed scornfully; "wouldst thou have me turn traitor to my own father?"

"Nay, I would have you turn wise for the sake of your father and yourself. Think well of what I say, and all I ask of you is to guide me to a good point of observation. There is a cave, they say, near Ulfstede, with its mouth to the sea, and a secret entrance from the land. No doubt I could find it myself with a little trouble, but it would save time if you were to point it out."

"Never!" exclaimed Alric sternly.

"Truly thou art a chip of the old tree," said Hauskuld, taking Alric's ear between his finger and thumb; "but there are means to take which have been known to bend stouter hearts than thine. Say, wilt thou show me the cave?"

He pinched the ear with gradually increasing force as he spoke, but Alric neither spoke nor winced, although the blood which rushed to his face showed that he felt the pain keenly.

"Well, well," said the berserk, relaxing his grip, "this is a torture only fit for very small boys after all. Hand me the pincers, Arne."

One of the men drew in his oar, and from a locker pulled out a pair of large pincers, which he handed to his chief, who at once applied them to the fleshy part at the back of Alric's arm, between the elbow and the shoulder.

"When thou art willing to do as I bid thee, I will cease to pinch," said Hauskuld.

Poor Alric had turned pale at the sight of the pincers, for he knew well the use they would be put to; but he set his teeth tightly together, and determined to endure it. As the pain increased the blood rushed again to his face, but an extra squeeze of the instrument of torture sent it rushing back with a deadly chill to his heart. In spite of himself, a sharp cry burst from his lips. Turning suddenly round, he clenched his right hand, and hit his tormentor on the mouth with such force that his head was knocked violently against the steering oar, and two or three of his front teeth were driven out.

"Thou dog's whelp!" shouted Hauskuld, as soon as he could speak. "I'll —"

He could say no more; but, grasping the boy by the hair of the head, he seized his sword, and would certainly have slain him on the spot, had not the man named Arne interposed.

"The King will not thank thee for his slaying," said he, laying his hand on

Hauskuld's arm.

The latter made no reply except to utter a curse, then, dropping his sword, he struck Alric a blow on the forehead with his fist, which knocked him insensible into the bottom of the boat.

"Yonder is the mouth of the cave," exclaimed one of the men.

"It may be the one we look for," muttered Hauskuld. "Pull into it."

So saying, he steered the boat into the cavern, and its keel soon grated on the gravelly beach inside. The sound aroused Alric, who at first could not see, owing to the gloom of the place, and the effects of the blow; but he was brought suddenly to a state of mental activity and anxiety when he recognised the sides of the well-known cave. Rising quickly but cautiously, he listened, and knew by the sounds that the boatmen, of whom there were eight, were searching for an outlet towards the land. He therefore slipped over the side of the boat, and hastened towards the darkest side of the cave, but Hauskuld caught sight of him.

"Ha! is the little dog trying to get away?" he shouted, running after him.

The lad formed his plan instantly. "Come on, Hauskuld," he shouted, with a wild laugh; "I will show thee the outlet, and get out before thee too."

He then ran to the inner part of the cave that was farthest from the secret opening, shouting as he ran, and making as much noise as possible. The berserk and his men followed. The instant he reached the extremity of the place Alric became as silent as a mouse, kicked off his shoes, and ran nimbly round by the intricate turnings of the inner wall, until he came to the foot of the dark natural staircase, which has been referred to at the beginning of our tale. Up this he bounded, and reached the open air above, while his pursuers were still knocking their shins and heads on the rocks at the wrong end of the cave below.

Without a moment's pause the exulting boy dashed away towards Ulfstede. He had not run two hundred yards, however, when he observed three men standing on the top of the little mound to which the people of Ulfstede were wont to mount when they wished to obtain an uninterrupted view of the valley and the fiord. They hailed him at that moment, so he turned aside, and found, on drawing near, that they were his brother Erling, Glumm the Gruff, and Kettle Flat-nose.

"Why, Alric!" exclaimed Erling in surprise, on seeing the boy's swelled and bloody face, "what ails thee?"

"Quick, come with me, all of ye! There is work for your swords at hand. Lend me thy sword, Erling. It is the short one, and the axe will be enough for thee."

The excited lad did not wait for permission, but snatched the sword from his brother's side, and without further explanation, ran back towards the cliffs, followed closely by the astonished men. He made straight for the hole that led to the cave, and was about to leap into it when Hauskuld stepped out and almost received him in his arms. Before the berserk could plant his feet firmly on the turf, Alric heaved up his brother's sword and brought it down on Hauskuld's head with right good will. His arm, however, had not yet received power to cleave through a steel helmet, but the blow was sufficient to give it such a dint that its wearer tumbled back into the hole, and went rattling down the steep descent heels over head into the cave. The boy leaped down after him, but Hauskuld, although taken by surprise and partially stunned, had vigour enough left to jump up and run down to the boat. His men, on hearing the noise of his fall, had also rushed to the boat, and pushed off. The berserk sprang into the water, and swam after them, just as his pursuers reached the cave. Seeing this, his men being safe beyond pursuit, lay on their oars and waited for him. But Hauskuld's career had been run out. Either the fall had stunned him, or he was seized with a fit, for he suddenly raised himself in the water, and, uttering a cry that echoed fearfully in the roof of the cavern, he sank to the bottom. Still his men waited a minute or two, but seeing that he did not rise again, they pulled away.

"It is unlucky that they should have escaped thus," said Alric, "for they go to tell King Harald what they have seen."

"Friends," said Erling, "I have a plan in my head to cheat the King. I shall send Thorer round with my Swan to this cave, and here let it lie, well armed and provisioned, during the battle that we shall have to fight with Harald ere long. If ill luck should be ours, those of us who survive will thus have a chance of escaping with the women."

"What need is there of that?" said Glumm; "we are sure to give him the tooth-ache!"

"We are sure of nothing in this world," replied Erling, "save that the sun will rise and set and the seasons will come and go. I shall do as I have said, chiefly for the sake of the women, whom I should not like to see fall into the hands of King Harald; and I counsel thee to do the same with thy small ship the Crane. It can well be spared, for we are like to have a goodly force of men and ships, if I mistake not the spirit that is abroad."

"Well, I will do it," said Glumm.

"And Alric will not object, I dare say, to stand sentinel over the ships in the cave with two or three men till they are wanted," said Erling.

"That will not I," cried Alric, who was delighted to be employed in any service rather than be left at home, for his father, deeming him still too young, had strictly forbidden him to embark in the fleet.

"Well then, the sooner this is set about the better," said Erling, "for there is no counting on the movements of the King."

"Humph!" ejaculated Glumm.

"Ill luck to the tyrant!" said Kettle Flatnose, as they turned and left the cave.

CHAPTER XXI.

Glumm gains a Great Private Victory — The Dalesmen assemble to fight for Freedom — The Foe appears, and the Signal of Battle is sounded.

Again we return to the mound near Ulfstede, the top of which was now bathed in the rays of the morning sun — for the day had only begun, the events narrated at the end of the last chapter having occurred within a period of less than three hours.

Here stood the fair Hilda and the volatile Ada, the former leaning on the arm of the latter, and both gazing intently and in silence on the heart-stirring scene before them. Once again Horlingdal with its fiord was the scene of an assembly of armed men, but this time the concourse was grander, because much greater, than on a previous occasion. Men had learned by recent events that momentous changes were taking place in the land. The news of the King's acts had been carried far and wide. Everyone felt that a decisive blow was about to be struck somewhere, and although many hundreds had little or no opinion of their own as to what was best for the interests of the kingdom, they knew that a side must be taken, and were quite willing to take that which appeared to be the right, or which seemed most likely to win, while a large proportion of them were intelligently and resolutely opposed to the King's designs. Thus, when the war-token was sent round, it was answered promptly. Those who dwelt nearest to the place of rendezvous were soon assembled in great numbers, and, from the elevated point on which the girls stood, their glittering masses could be seen on the shore, while they launched their longships and loaded them with stones — the ammunition of those days — or passed briskly to and fro with arms and provisions; while all up the valley, as far as the eye could see, even to the faint blue distance, in the haze of which the glaciers and clouds and mountain tops seemed to commingle, troops of armed men could be seen pouring down from gorge and glen, through wood and furze and fen. On the fiord, too, the same activity and concentration prevailed, though not quite to the same extent. Constantly there swept round the promontories to the north and south, boat after boat, and ship after ship, until the bay close below Ulfstede was crowded with war-craft of every size — their gay sails, and in some cases gilded masts and figureheads, glancing in the sunshine, and their shield-circled gunwales reflected clearly in the sea.

"What a grand sight!" exclaimed Ada with enthusiasm, as she listened to the deep-toned hum of the busy multitude below.

"Would God I had never seen it!" said her companion.

"Out upon thee, Hilda! I scarce deem thee fit to be a free Norse maiden. Such a scene would stir the heart of stone."

"It *does* stir my heart strangely, sister," replied Hilda, "I scarcely can explain how. I feel exultation when I see the might of our district, and the bold bearing of our brave and brisk men; but my heart sinks again when I think of what is to come — the blood of men flowing like water, death sweeping them down like grain before the sickle; and for what? Ada, these go not forth to defend us from our enemies, they go to war with brothers and kindred — with Norsemen."

Ada beat her foot impatiently on the sod, and frowned a little as she said —

"I know it well enough, but it is a grand sight for all that, and it does no good to peep into the future as thou art doing continually."

"I do not peep," replied Hilda; "the future stares me full in the face."

"Well, let it stare, sister mine," said Ada, with a laugh, as she cleared her brow, "and stare past *its* face at what lies before thee at present, which is beautiful enough, thou must allow."

At that moment there seemed to be increasing bustle and energy on the part of the warriors on the shore, and the murmur of their voices grew louder.

"What can that mean, I wonder?" said Ada.

"Fresh news arrived, perhaps," replied her friend. "The Christians' God grant that this war may be averted!"

"Amen, if it be His will," said a deep voice behind the girls, who turned and found the hermit standing at their side. "But, Hilda," he continued, "God does not always answer our prayers in the way we expect — sometimes because we pray for the wrong thing, and sometimes because we pray that the right thing may come to us in the wrong way. I like best to end my petitions with the words of my dear Saviour Jesus Christ — 'Thy will be done'. Just now it would seem as if war were ordained to go on, for a scout has just come in to say that King Harald with his fleet is on the other side of yonder point, and I am sent to fetch thee down to a place of safety without delay."

"Who sent thee?" demanded Ada.

"Thy foster-father."

"Methinks we are safe enough here," she said, with a gesture of impatience.

"Aye, if we win the day, but not if we lose it," said the old man.

"Come," said Hilda, "we must obey our father."

"I have no intention of disobeying him," retorted the other, tossing her head.

Just then Alric ran up with a look of anxiety on his swelled and blood-stained face.

"Come, girls, ye are in the way here. Haste — ah! here comes Erling — and Glumm too."

The two young men ran up the hill as he spoke.

"Come with us quickly," cried Erling; "we do not wish the King's people to see anyone on this mound. Let me lead thee down, Hilda."

He took her by the hand and led her away. Glumm went forward to Ada, whose old spirit was evidently still alive, for she glanced at the hermit, and appeared as if inclined to put herself under his protection, but there was something in Glumm's expression that arrested her. His gruffness had forsaken him, and he came forward with an unembarrassed and dignified bearing. "Ada," he said, in a gentle but deliberate voice, while he gazed into her face so earnestly that she was fain to drop her eyes, "thou must decide my fate *now*. To-day it is likely I shall fight my last battle in my fatherland. Death will be abroad on the fiord, more than willing to be courted by all who choose to woo him. Say, dear maid, am I to be thy protector or not?"

Ada hesitated, and clasped her hands tightly together, while the tell-tale blood rushed to her cheeks. Glumm, ever stupid on these matters, said no other word, but turned on his heel and strode quickly away.

"Stay!" she said.

She did not say this loudly, but Glumm heard it, turned round, and strode back again. Ada silently placed her hand in his — it trembled as she did so — and Glumm led her down the hill.

The girls were escorted by their lovers only as far as Ulfstede. With all the other women of the place, and the old people, they were put under the care of the hermit, who conveyed them safely to Haldorstede, there to await the issue of the day.

Meanwhile, Haldor, Erling, Glumm, Hakon of Drontheim, Ulf, Guttorm Stoutheart, and all the other Sea-kings, not only of Horlingdal, but of the surrounding valleys, with a host of smaller bonders, unfreemen, and thralls, went down to the shores of the bay and prepared for battle.

It is needless to say that all were armed to the teeth — with coats of mail and shirts of wolf-skin; swords and battle-axes, bows and arrows, halberds and spears, "morning stars" and bills, scythes, javelins, iron-shod poles — and many other weapons.

The principal ships of the fleet were of course those belonging to Haldor, Ulf, and the wealthier men of the district. Some of these were very large — having thirty benches of rowers, and being capable of carrying above a hundred and fifty men. All of them were more or less decorated, and a stately brilliant spectacle they presented, with their quaint towering figureheads, their high poops, shield-hung sides, and numerous oars. Many proud thoughts doubtless filled the hearts of these Sea-kings as they looked at their ships and men, and silently wended their way down to the strand. In the case of Haldor and Erling, however, if not of others, such thoughts were tempered with the feeling that momentous issues hung on the fate of the day.

Well was it for all concerned that the men who led them that day were so full of forethought and energy, for scarcely had they completed their preparations and embarked their forces when the ships of Harald Fairhair swept round the northern promontory.

If the fleet of the small kings of Horlingdal and the south was imposing, that of the King of Norway was still more so. Besides, being stronger in numbers, and many of the warships being larger — his own huge vessel, the Dragon, led the van, appearing like a gorgeous and gigantic sea-monster.

The King was very proud of this longship. It had recently been built by him, and was one of the largest that had ever been seen in Norway. The exact dimensions of it are not now known, but we know that it had thirty-two banks for rowers, from which we may infer that it must have been of nearly the same size with the Long Serpent, a war vessel of thirty-four banks, which was built about the end of the tenth century, and some of the dimensions of which are given in the Saga of Olaf Tryggvesson. The length of her keel that rested on the grass, we are told, was about 111 feet, which is not far short of the length of the keel of one of our forty-two gun frigates. As these warships were long in proportion to their breadth, like our modern steamers, this speaks to a size approaching 400 tons burden. As we have said, the Dragon was a gorgeous vessel. It had a high poop and forecastle, a low waist, or middle part, and a splendidly gilt and painted stern, figurehead, and tail. The sides, which were, as usual, hung round with the red and white painted shields of the crew, were pierced for sixty-four oars, that is, thirty-two on each side, being two oars to each bank or bench, and as there were three men to each oar, this gave a total crew of 192 men; but in truth the vessel contained, including steersmen and supernumeraries, above 200 men. Under the feet of the rowers, in the waist, were chests of arms, piles of stones to be used as missiles, provisions, clothing, goods, and stores, all of which were protected by a deck of movable hatches. On this deck the crew slept at nights, sheltered by an awning or sail, when it was not convenient for them to land and sleep on the beach in their tents, with which all the vessels of the Norsemen were usually supplied. There was but one great mast, forty feet high, and one enormous square sail to this ship. The mast was tipped with gilding, and the sail was of alternate strips of red, white, and blue cloth. Each space between the banks served as the berth of six or eight men, and was divided into half berths — starboard and larboard — for the men who worked the corresponding oars. On the richly ornamented poop stood the King himself, surrounded by his bodyguard and chief men of the Court, including Jarl Rongvold and Thiodolph the scald. From the stem to the mid-hold was the forecastle, on which were stationed the King's berserkers, under Hake of Hadeland. All the men of Hake's band were splendid fellows; for King Harald, having a choice of men from the best of every district, took into his house troop only such as were remarkable for strength, courage, and dexterity in the use of their weapons.

It must not be supposed that the rest of Harald's fleet was composed of small vessels. On the contrary, some of them were not far short of his own in point of size. Many of his jarls were wealthy men, and had joined him, some with ten or twenty, and others with thirty, or even forty, ships of various sizes. Many of them had from twenty to thirty banks for rowers, with crews of 100 or 150 men. There were also great numbers of cutters with ten or fifteen banks, and from thirty to fifty men in each, besides a swarm of lesser craft, about the size of our ordinary herring boats.

There were many men of note in this fleet, such as King Sigurd of Royer and Simun's sons; Onund and Andreas; Nicolas Skialdvarsson; Eindrid, a son of Mörnef, who was the most gallant and popular man in the Drontheim country, and many others; the whole composing a formidable force of seven or eight thousand warriors.

With Haldor the Fierce, on the other hand, there was a goodly force of men and ships; for the whole south country had been aroused, and they came pouring into the fiord continuously. Nevertheless they did not number nearly so large a force as that under King Harald. Besides those who have been already named, there were Eric, king of Hordaland; Sulke, king of Rogaland, and his brother Jarl Sote; Kiotve the Rich, king of Agder, and his son Thor Haklang; also the brothers Roald Ryg, and Hadd the Hard, of Thelemark, besides many others. But their whole number did not exceed four thousand men; and the worst of it all was that among these there were a great many of the smaller men, and a few of the chiefs whose hearts were not very enthusiastic in the cause, and who had no very strong objection to take service under Harald Fairhair. These, however, held their peace, because the greater men among them, and the chief leaders, such as Haldor and Ulf, were very stern and decided in their determination to resist the King.

Now, when the report was brought that Harald's fleet had doubled the distant cape beyond Hafurdsfiord, the people crowded to the top of the cliffs behind Ulfstede to watch it; and when it was clearly seen that it was so much larger than their own, there were a few who began to say that it would be wiser to refrain from resistance; but Haldor called a Thing together on the spot by sound of horn, and a great many short pithy speeches were made on both sides of the question. Those who were for war were by far the most able men, and so full of fire that they infused much of their own spirit into those who heard them. Erling in particular was very energetic in his denunciation of the illegality of Harald's proceedings; and even Glumm plucked up heart to leap to his feet and declare, with a face blazing with wrath, that he would rather be drowned in the fiord like a dog, or quit his native land for ever, than remain at home to be the slave of any man!

Glumm was not, as the reader is aware, famed for eloquence; nevertheless the abruptness of his fiery spirit, the quick rush of his few sputtered words, and the clatter of his arms, as he struck his fist violently against his shield, drew from the multitude a loud burst of applause. He had in him a good deal of that element which we moderns call "go". Whatever he did was effectively done.

The last who spoke was Solve Klofe. That redoubtable warrior ascended the hill just as Glumm had finished his remarks. He immediately stood forward, and raised his hand with an impassioned gesture. "Glumm is right," he cried. "It is now clear that we have but one course to take; and that is to rise all as one man against King Harald, for although outnumbered, we still have strength enough to fight for our ancient rights. Fate must decide the victory. If we cannot conquer, at all events we can die. As to becoming his servants, that is no condition for *us*! My father thought it better to fall in battle than to go willingly into King Harald's service, or refuse to abide the chance of weapons like the Numedal kings."

"That is well spoken," cried Haldor, after the shout with which this was received had subsided. "The Thing is at an end, and now we shall make ready, for it can be but a short time until we meet. Let the people take their weapons, and every man be at his post, so that all may be ready when the war-horn sounds the signal to cast off from the land.[14] Then let us throw off at once, and together, so that none go on before the rest of the ships, and none lag behind when we row out of the fiord. When we meet, and the battle begins, let people be on the alert to bring all our ships in close order, and ready to bind them together. Let us spare ourselves in the beginning, and take care of our weapons, that we do not cast them into the sea, or shoot them away in the air to no purpose. But when the fight becomes hot, and the ships are bound together, *then* let each man show what spirit is in him, and how well he can fight for country, law, and freedom!"

A loud ringing cheer was the answer to this speech, and then the whole concourse hurried down the hill and embarked; the vessels were quickly arranged in order according to their size; the war-horn sounded; thousands of oars dipped at the same moment, the blue waters of the fiord were torn into milky foam, and slowly, steadily, and in good order the fleet of the Sea-kings left the strand, doubled the cape to the north of Horlingfiord, and advanced in battle array to meet the foe.

14   Signals by call of trumpet were well understood in those times. We read, in the ancient Sagas, of the trumpet-call to arm, to advance, to attack, to retreat, to land, and also to attend a Court Thing, a House Thing, a General Thing. These instruments were made of metal, and there were regular trumpeters.

CHAPTER XXII.

Describes a Great Sea Fight and its Consequences.

Harald Fairhair stood on the poop of the great Dragon, and held the steering oar. When he saw the fleet of the Sea-kings approaching, he called Jarl Rongvold to him and said —

"Methinks, jarl, that I now see the end of this war with the small kings. It is easy to perceive that the utmost force they are able to raise is here. Now, I intend to beat them to-day, and break their strength for ever. But when the battle is over, many of them will seek to escape. I would prevent that as much as may be."

The King paused, as if engaged in deep thought.

"How do you propose to do it, sire?"

"By means of a boom," said the King. "Go thou, summon hither the trustiest man in the fleet for such a purpose, let him detach as many men and ships as he deems needful, and go into yonder small fiord where there is a pine wood on the hillside. There let him make a long and strong boom of timber, while we are engaged in the fight. I will drive as many of the ships as I can into Horlingfiord, and when that is done let him come out and stretch the boom right across, so that none of them shall escape. And, harkee, see that the man thou choosest for this duty is an able man, and does it well, else shall his head be lopped off."

After issuing this command the King resigned the helm, and ordered his banner to be set up, which was done immediately. At the same time his opponents shook out their banners, and both fleets were put in order of battle.

As both were arrayed much in the same way, it will be sufficient to describe the arrangements made by Haldor the Fierce, who had been elected commander-in-chief of the small kings' fleet.

When Haldor saw the King's banner displayed, he unfurled his own in the centre of the fleet, and arranged his force for attack right against it. Alongside of him on the right was Ulf of Romsdal with thirty ships, and on his left was old Guttorm Stoutheart with twenty-five ships. These composed the centre of the line. Kettle Flatnose commanded the men on the forecastle in Ulf's longship, and Thorer the Thick was over those in Haldor's vessel.

The right wing was commanded by Solve Klofe, under whom were Eric of Hordaland with fifteen ships; Sulke of Rogaland and his brother Sote with thirty ships, as well as Kiotve of Agder, and some others with many ships — all of large size.

The left wing was led by King Hakon of Drontheim, under whom were Roald Ryg and Hadd the Hard, and Thor Haklang, with a good many ships. Solve Klofe laid his ships against King Harald's left wing, which was under Eindrid, son of Mörnef, and Hakon laid his against King Sigurd of Royer, who led Harald's right wing. All the chiefs on either side laid their ships according as they were bold or well equipped. When all was ready, they bound the ships together by the stems, and advanced towards each other at the sound of the war-trumpet. But as the fleets were so large, many of the smaller vessels remained loose, and, as it were, went about skirmishing independently. These were laid forward in the fight, according to the courage of their commanders, which was very unequal.

Among these roving warriors were our heroes Erling and Glumm, each in one of his own small cutters, with about forty men.

As soon as the war-blast sounded the men rode forward to the attack, and soon narrowed the small space that lay between the hostile fleets. Then Haldor and the other commanders went down to the sides of their ships, where the men stood so thick that their shields touched all round, and encouraged them to fight well for the freedom of old Norway — to which they replied with loud huzzas. Immediately after the air was darkened with a cloud of arrows, and the fight began.

There were scalds in both fleets at that fight, these afterwards wrote a poem descriptive of it, part of which we now quote:

> "With falcon eye and courage bright,
> Haldor the Fierce prepared for fight;
> 'Hand up the arms to one and all!'
> He cries. 'My men, we'll win or fall!
> Sooner than fly, heaped on each other,
> Each man will fall across his brother!'
> Thus spake, and through his vessels' throng
> His mighty warship moved along.
> He ran her gaily to the front,
> To meet the coming battle's brunt —
> Then gave the word the ships to bind
> And shake his banner to the wind.
> Our oars were stowed, our lances high
> Swung to and fro athwart the sky.
> Haldor the Fierce went through the ranks,
> Drawn up beside the rowers' banks,
> Where rows of shields seemed to enclose
> The ship's deck from the boarding foes,
> Encouraging his chosen crew,
> He tells his brave lads to stand true,
> And rows against — while arrows sing —
> The Dragon of the tyrant King.
> With glowing hearts and loud huzzas,
> His men lay on in freedom's cause.
> The sea-steeds foam; they plunge and rock:
> The warriors meet in battle shock;
> The ring-linked coats of strongest mail
> Could not withstand the iron hail.
> The fire of battle raged around;
> Odin's steel shirts flew all unbound.

The pelting shower of stone and steel,
Caused many a Norseman stout to reel,
The red blood poured like summer rain;
The foam was scarlet on the main;
But, all unmoved like oak in wood,
Silent and grim fierce Haldor stood,
Until his axe could reach the foe —
Then — swift he thundered blow on blow.
And ever, as his axe came down,
It cleft or crushed another crown.

Elsewhere the chiefs on either side
Fought gallantly above the tide.
King Hakon pressed King Sigurd sore,
And Ulf made Hake the berserk roar,
And Kettle Flatnose dared to spring
On board the ship of Norway's King.
Old Guttorm Stoutheart's mighty shout
Above the din was heard throughout,
And Solve Klofe, 'gainst Mörnef's son,
Slew right and left till day was done.
While, all around the loose ships rowed —
Where'er they went the red stream flowed.
Chief among these was Erling bold
And Glumm the Gruff, of whom 'tis told
They rushed in thickest of the fray, —
Whatever part the line gave way, —
And twice, and thrice, retrieved the day.
But heart, and strength, and courage true,
Could not avail where one fought two.
King Harald, foremost in the fight,
With flashing sword, resistless might,
Pushed on and slew, and dyed with red
The bright steel cap on many a head.
Against the hero's shield in vain,
The arrow-storm sends forth its rain.
The javelins and spear-thrusts fail
To pierce his coat of ringèd mail.
The King stands on the blood-stained deck;
Trampling on many a foeman's neck;
And high above the dinning stound
Of helm and axe, and ringing sound
Of blade, and shield, and raven's cry
Is heard the shout of — 'Victory!'"

In this poem the scald gives only an outline of the great fight. Let us follow more closely the action of those in whom we are peculiarly interested.

For more than two hours the battle raged with unabated fury — victory inclining to neither side; but as the day advanced, the energy with which Solve Klofe pushed the right wing began to tell, and the King's men gave way a little at that part. Harald, however, was on the alert. He sent some of his loose ships to reinforce them, and so regained his position. A short time after that, some of Solve's ships were boarded, but at that moment Erling and Glumm chanced to pass in their cutters — for they kept always close together — and they gave such a shout, while they turned and pulled to the rescue, that the men, who were wavering, took heart again and drove the foe overboard. Just then the ship on the right of Solve Klofe's vessel was also boarded by the enemy. Seeing this, Erling called to Glumm that there was need of succour there, and they rowed swiftly to the spot.

"Art thou hard pressed, Solve?" asked Erling, as he ranged up to the stern of his friend's ship.

Solve was so furious that he could not answer, but pointed to the ship next his, and sprang on the edge of his own, intending to leap into that of the enemy, and get to the forefront. At the same time Eindrid, son of Mörnef, stood up on the high foredeck of his ship with a large stone in his hand. He was a very powerful man, and hurled the stone with such force against Solve's shield that it battered him down, and he fell back into his own ship much stunned. Seeing this, Erling bade two of his men follow him, leaped into Solve's ship, and thence into the one where the fight was sharpest. Glumm followed him closely with his long two-handed sword, and these two fought so dreadfully that Eindrid's men were driven back into their own ship again. Then Erling ran to the place where the high stern was wedged between two of the enemy's ships, and sprang on the forecastle of Eindrid's ship.

"Thou art a bold man!" said Eindrid, turning on him.

"That may be as thou sayest," replied Erling, at the same time catching a thrust on his shield, which he returned with such interest with his axe that Eindrid's head was nearly severed from his body. At the same moment Glumm cut down a famous berserk who ran at him, and in a few minutes they had cleared the deck of the ship, and taken possession of it. But this was scarcely accomplished when a cry arose that the left wing under King Hakon was giving way.

At once Erling and Glumm ran back to their cutters, and made towards that part of the line, followed by several of the loose ships. Here they found that King Hakon was very hard pressed by Sigurd of Royer, so they pushed in among the ships, and soon Erling's well-known war-cry was heard, and his tall form was seen sweeping men down before him with his great axe, like a mower cutting grass. Glumm, however, did not keep close to him this time, but made direct for Hakon's ship, for he remembered that he was Ada's father, and thought he might do him some service.

As he was coming near he saw Swankie, a famous berserk, fighting furiously on board Hakon's ship, and roaring, as was the wont of berserkers sometimes, like a wild bull. Hakon's men had formed a shield-circle round their chief, and were defending him bravely; but the berserk was an uncommonly stout man, very brisk and active, and exceedingly furious, as well as dexterous with his weapons. He slew so many men that the shield-circle was broken, and he made at Hakon just as Glumm leaped into the ship at the stern. King Hakon was a stout man and brave, but he was getting old, and not so active as he used to be. Nevertheless he met Swankie like a man, and dealt him a blow on his helmet which made him stagger. The berserk uttered a fearful roar, and struck at Hakon so fiercely that he split the upper part of his shield and cut open his helmet. Hakon fell, but before he could repeat the blow Glumm was upon him.

"What! is it thou, Swankie?" he cried. "Dog, methought I had killed thee long ago!"

"That is yet to be done," cried the berserk, leaping upon Glumm with a sweeping blow of his sword. Glumm stooped quickly, and the blow passed over his head; then he fetched a sudden cut at Swankie, and split him down from the neck to the waist, saying, "It is done now, methinks," as he drew out his sword. Glumm did not go forward, but let his men drive back the foe, while he turned and kneeled beside Hakon.

"Has the dog hurt thee badly?" he asked, raising the old warrior's head on his knee, and speaking in a voice of almost womanly tenderness.

Hakon made an effort to speak, but for some time was unable to do so, and Glumm held his shield over him to keep off the stones and arrows which fell thickly around them. After a few moments Hakon wiped away the blood which flowed from a deep wound in his forehead, and looked up wildly in Glumm's face. He tried again to speak, and Glumm, misunderstanding the few words he muttered, said: "Thou art already avenged, King Hakon; Swankie the berserk is dead."

The dying man made another effort to speak, and was successful.

"That concerns me little, Glumm. Thou lovest Ada, I know. This ring — take it to her, say her father's last thoughts were of her. Be a good husband, Glumm. The brooch — see."

"Which?" asked Glumm, looking at several silver brooches with which the old warrior's armour was fastened — "this one on thy breast?"

"Aye, take it — it was — her mother's."

The warrior's spirit seemed to be relieved when he had said this. He sank down into a state resembling sleep. Once or twice afterwards he opened his eyes and gazed up into the bright sky with a doubtful yet earnest and enquiring gaze. Gradually the breathing became fainter, until it ceased altogether, and Glumm saw that the old man was dead.

Fastening the brooch on his own broad chest, and putting the ring on his finger, Glumm rose, seized his sword, and rushed again into the thick of the fight with tenfold more fury than he had yet displayed, and ere long the danger that threatened the left wing was for the time averted.

Meanwhile in the centre there was an equally uncertain and obstinate conflict — for the chiefs on either side were mighty men of valour. Wherever Old Guttorm's voice was heard, there victory inclined. Haldor, on the other hand, did not shout, but he laid about him with such wild ferocity that many men quailed at the very sight of him, and wherever he went he was victorious. It was some time before he managed to get alongside of King Harald Fairhair's ship, but when he did so the fight became sharp in the extreme.

All the men in King Harald's ship, except the berserks, were clad in coats of ring mail, and wore foreign helmets, and most of them had white shields. Besides, as has been said, each man was celebrated for personal strength and daring, so that none of those who were opposed to them could make head against them. The arrows and spears fell harmless from their shields, casques, and coats of mail, and it was only now and then — as when a shaft happened to enter a man's eye — that any fell. When Haldor's forecastle men attacked the berserkers on the high fore deck of the Dragon, the fighting was terrible, for the berserkers all roared aloud and fought with the wild fury of madmen, and so fierce was their onslaught that Haldor's men were forced at first to give back. But Thorer the Thick guarded himself warily, and being well armed escaped injury for a time. When he saw the berserkers beginning to flag, he leaped forward like a lion, and hewed them down right and left, so that his men drove the enemy back into the Dragon. Some of them slipped on the gun-wales, and so did some of Haldor's men, all of whom fell into the sea, and a few of them were drowned, while others were killed, but one or two escaped by swimming.

Ulf's ship was also pretty close to the Dragon, and he wished greatly to board it, but was so hard beset by the ship of Nicolas Skialdvarsson that he could not do so for a long time. Here Kettle Flatnose did prodigies of valour. He stood on the high fore-deck with his favourite weapon, the hook, and therewith pulled a great number of men off the enemy's deck into the sea. At last he got a footing on their gunwale, dropped his hook, drew his sword, and soon cleared his way aft. Ulf leaped after him, drove the men into the waist, and then the most of them were slain, and lay in heaps one upon another. After that it was not difficult to clear the poop. Skialdvarsson defended it well, but he could not stand before Ulf, who finally cut off his head, and so the ship was won.

This vessel lay alongside that of King Harald; and although the King was fully engaged with Haldor at the time, he observed the conquest of Skialdvarsson by Ulf, and also perceived that Ulf's men were crowding the side of the vessel, and throwing grappling-irons into his own ship with a view to board it; for there was a space between the ships a little too wide for men to leap. Springing to the side, the King cut the grappling-irons with a sweep of his sword.

"That was well tried," he said.

"It shall be tried again," cried Ulf, heaving another iron, which nearly struck the King, but Harald's sword flashed through the air, and again the iron was cut.

At that moment Kettle Flatnose stepped back a few paces, and with a mighty rush leaped right over the space in all his war gear, and alighted on the Dragon's deck within a yard of the King. It was a tremendous leap, and so nearly beyond the compass of Kettle's powers that he was scarcely able to retain his foothold, but stood for a moment on the edge of the vessel with shield and sword upheaved, as he staggered to regain his balance. Thus exposed, he might have easily been slain; but the King, instead of using his sword, stepped forward, and with his left hand pushed the Irishman overboard. The cheer which greeted his daring leap had scarcely ceased to ring when he fell heavily into the sea.

"A goodly man, and a bold attempt," said the King, with a smile, as he turned to Jarl Rongvold. "'Twould have been a pity to slay him outright. If he can swim he may yet live to fight another battle."

"True, sire," replied the jarl, who was looking over the side at the place where Kettle fell; "but methinks he has struck his head on an oar, and will never succeed in swimming towards a friendly hand."

This indeed seemed to be true; for Kettle lay with his arm over an oar, and his head hanging down in the water, like a dead man. Yet there was life in him, for his fingers moved. Ulf had witnessed all this, and was on the point of attempting to leap across to Harald's ship when Kettle fell. He paused, and, seeing that his comrade was apparently being drowned, at once dropped sword and shield, and sprang into the sea after him.

At that moment a number of the King's boldest and best armed men observed that the two ships had drawn a little nearer to each other. In a moment they leaped across the intervening space, took their opponents by surprise, and quickly regained the ship.

While this had been going on at the poop, the fight on the forecastle had raged with extreme fury, for Haldor the Fierce had gained a footing on the Dragon's deck, and was engaged in mortal combat with Hake the berserk, whom he was slowly but surely driving back. His son Erling the Bold, who observed what was going on, had run his cutter along the stern of his father's ship, and was hastening to his aid, when King Harald became aware that his men were giving way, and rushed to their support. He went forward raging with anger, and as he ran he picked up a huge stone, which he hurled before him. Haldor was at the moment in the act of fetching a deadly cut at Hake, whom he had disarmed. The stone struck him full in the chest, and he fell backward just as Erling reached his side.

A great cheer arose at this time on the right; for there the wing of the Southland men was broken, and everywhere King Harald's men were victorious.

"Hold thou them in check, Glumm," cried Erling to his friend, as he quickly raised his father in his arms and bore him away to his cutter.

Glumm, who had followed his friend like his shadow, sprang forward and engaged Hake, who had recovered his sword, and who found this new enemy little, if at all, less formidable than the other.

Erling placed his father carefully in the cutter.

"Here, Thorer," he said, "do thou guard my father, and hold thyself and the carles in readiness to push off. The day is lost, I see. I go to slay the King, and will return presently."

He leaped away as he spoke, and regained the foredeck of the Dragon, where Glumm and his men were still engaged with the berserkers, just as the King came to the front. The instant he saw Erling he leaped upon him with a fierce shout, and shook back his shaggy flaxen locks as a lion might shake his mane. Erling was not a whit behind him in anxiety to meet. He sprang upon him with a crashing blow of his great pole-axe, which rang loudly on the King's shield, but did him no hurt. They were a well-matched pair. Harald was fully as stout, though not quite so tall as his opponent, whose fine silky hair was almost as bushy as that of the King, though neither so long nor so tangled.

Men drew back and stood aside when they heard the shock and shout of their onset, and suspended the fight around them, while they gazed on in silent awe. For a time it seemed doubtful which was the better man; for the King's blade whirled incessantly around his head like flashing light, and rang on Erling's shield, which was ever upraised to meet it. At the same time the axe of our hero, if not so swift in its gyrations, was more tremendous in its action; more than once the King was seen to stagger beneath its thundering blows, and once he was beaten down on one knee. How long this might have lasted it is impossible to tell; but, seeing that the King was likely to get the worst of it, one of his men crept round by the outside of the ship, and coming suddenly up behind Erling, put out his hand and caught him by the leg, causing him to stagger backwards, so that he fell overboard. In falling our hero caught the man by the throat, and both fell into the sea together.

It was seen that Erling dived with his foe and dragged him down as if to force him to perish along with him, and everyone looked for a few moments at the water, expecting to see them rise. Glumm gazed among the rest; and he had leaped down into Haldor's ship to be ready to lend a hand. But Erling did not rise again. Seeing this, Glumm sprang up with sudden fury and dashed at the enemy, but by this time they had recovered from their surprise, and now poured into the ship in such overwhelming numbers that the men were driven back and slain, or they leaped overboard and trusted to escape by swimming.

Meanwhile Erling the Bold having choked off his antagonist, dived under his father's ship and came up at the stern of his own cutter, into which he speedily clambered by means of a rope which hung over the side. He found that his father was seated on the poop with his head resting on the gunwale, recovering consciousness slowly, and Thorer was engaged in the difficult task of preventing the men from leaving the vessel to succour their comrades.

"Keep back, men," cried Erling in a voice which none dared to disobey. "Stay where ye are and get out the oars. — Come, Thorer, follow me with a stout man, and keep them back while I rescue Glumm."

He jumped into Haldor's ship, and ran to the fore part of the poop, where Glumm was fighting against overwhelming odds, with the blind desperation of a man who has resolved to sell his life as dearly as he can. Thorer and a tall stout man followed him, and instantly assailed King Harald's men with such fury that they gave back a little. At the same moment Erling seized Glumm by the neck; almost strangled him; dragged him violently to the stern, and half sprang, half tumbled with him into the cutter, where, despite his frantic struggles to rise, he held him down.

"Now, my brisk lads," shouted Erling, who was gasping by this time, "come back and jump in! Push off an ell or so. Steady!"

Thorer and the other man heard the shout, and, turning at once, ran to the stern and leaped into the cutter, which was instantly thrust off, so that one or two of their opponents who ventured to jump after them were left floundering in the sea.

By this time King Harald's victory was complete. Both wings had been beaten for some time, and now the centre had given way — only one or two of the more desperate leaders were still keeping up the fight.

As Erling rowed towards the shore he could see that all the loose vessels of the fleet were flying up the fiord, pursued by a few of the loose vessels of the enemy. But the greater part of both fleets being tied together, could take no part in the chase until they were cut asunder.

"The day is lost, father," said Erling, as he stood by the steering oar.

"I know it, my son," replied Haldor, who was now able to sit up and look about him; "Norway is henceforth enthralled."

He said this in a tone of such deep sadness that Erling forbore to continue the subject.

"They are cutting asunder the fleet," observed Glumm, who had recovered self-possession, and stood looking back at the scene of the recent conflict; "surely some of them are trying to escape."

As he spoke, one of the large vessels shot out from among the others, and rowed rapidly away. There was desperate fighting on board of it for a few minutes, and then a number of men were pushed or thrown overboard, and a loud cheer of victory arose.

"Well done, Solve Klofe!" cried Erling with enthusiasm. "That is his shout. I should know it among a thousand. He at least is bent on being free!"

Several of Harald's ships, which had been also cut loose, immediately gave chase, but Solve's men pulled so well that they soon left them behind, and hoisting their sail to a light breeze which was blowing just off the mouth of the fiord, soon doubled the point and bore away to the south.

"Is that someone swimming in the water?" asked Erling, pointing as he spoke to an object which moved forward among the debris of oars, portions of clothing, and wreck, which was floating about everywhere.

One of the men at the bow oar stood up, and after a short glance, said that he thought it was a man.

"Look out on the starboard bow. Mind your oars and be ready, someone, to lean over the waist and catch hold of him."

As he spoke, the cutter ranged up to the object, which appeared to be the dishevelled and blood-bespattered head of a man. He suddenly gave vent to a wild shout — "Come on, thou tyrant! Down with ye, dog — huzza!" At the last shout a pair of arms were swung wildly in the air, and the next moment the man's voice was stifled in the water as he sank, while another head appeared beside him.

"That is the voice of Kettle Flatnose, or his wraith," exclaimed Erling; "pull gently, lads; hold water."

"Why, Ulf, is it thou?"

"Truly," exclaimed Ulf, grasping the extended hand of Glumm, "I don't feel quite sure! Haul gently, Glumm. I've got Kettle here. Another hand or two. Now then, heave together!"

Several stout men leaned over the side, and, acting in accordance with these instructions, hauled Ulf and Kettle out of the sea; the former in a state of great exhaustion, the latter almost dead, for his last dip had well-nigh choked him.

"It has been a long swim," said Ulf, sitting down and leaning languidly against the bulwarks, while Glumm and Haldor proceeded to chafe the Irishman into a state of consciousness. "Once or twice I sank under him, for he was very wild when he came to himself, after I got hold of him, and struggled to be up and fight the King; but I held him fast. Yet methought once or twice," added Ulf, with a smile, "that I had at last got into Valhalla."

A horn of ale refreshed Ulf, and another of the same was shortly after given to Kettle, by which his wandering faculties were soon restored.

By this time they were drawing near the bay at Ulfstede, and Erling urged on the rowers, for they could see that Harald's ships were now cast loose, and giving chase to those that endeavoured to escape, while several of the largest, including the Dragon, made direct for the land.

"Our whole effort now," said Haldor, "must be to rescue the women."

"That will not be easy," observed Ulf gloomily.

"But it is not impossible," said Erling with decision. "We shall have time to get into the woods, and so round to the cave. By the way, does anyone know aught of Hakon of Drontheim?"

"He is dead," said Glumm.

"Dead!"

At that moment Haldor started up with a wild exclamation, and pointed towards the spot on which his own dwelling stood, where, above the trees, there arose a cloud of dense black smoke. The truth was soon all too plain, for, on rounding the point which had hitherto concealed the bay from their view, several of the enemy's largest ships were seen with their bows on the shore. It was evident that part of the left wing of the enemy, which was first victorious, had, unobserved by them, made for the shore, and landed a large force of men, who had hastened to Ulfstede, and, finding it deserted, had pushed on to Haldorstede, which they had set on fire.

"Now indeed would death be welcome!" cried Haldor, stamping fiercely on the deck, while every feature of his face blazed with wrath.

We need scarcely say that the hearts of all had sunk within them, but Erling said — "Death would be unwelcome yet, father. The men, no doubt, are killed, but be sure they will not hurt the women while King Harald is on his way to the stede. We may yet die in defending them, if we cannot save them."

"True, my son," said Haldor, clasping his hands, and looking upwards with a solemnity of expression that was in strong contrast with his recent burst of passion; "we may perchance save them, as thou sayest; but woe is me for poor Alric!"

"Alric is safe, I am certain," said Erling energetically, as he turned a meaning glance on Glumm.

"How knowest thou that?" asked Haldor.

Erling hesitated to reply, not wishing to raise hopes that after all might prove to be fallacious.

Before the question could be repeated the cutter's keel grated on the sand of a small bay which was close to the large one, and concealed from it by a small rocky islet. Here they all jumped ashore – all except Kettle Flatnose, who, on attempting to rise, found himself so weak that he fell down again, and nearly fainted.

"This is bad," said Erling. "But come, we have no time to waste. Give me the chief command of our men, father; I have a plan in my head."

"Do as thou wilt," said Haldor, with a strange mixture of despair, resignation, and ferocity in his tone.

"Come then, form up, men, and follow me!"

So saying, Erling lifted Kettle in his arms, and hurried away with him as if he had been no heavier than a little boy! He led the way to the secret entrance to the cave, where, true as steel to his trust, little Alric was found with a few men guarding the two warships of Erling and Glumm.

CHAPTER XXIII.

The End of an Old Sea-King.

Haldor the Fierce said nothing when he heard Alric's blithe voice in the cavern, but he caught him up in his arms, and gave him a hug that almost made him cry out.

"Why, father, what ails thee?" asked the boy in surprise, when Haldor set him free.

"Never mind, lad," interposed Erling, "but lend a hand to keep Kettle in order. He is a little wild just now, and as I intend to leave him in thy charge we must restrain him a bit. Hand me that rope."

The boy obeyed in silence, but with much wonder depicted on his face while Erling lashed Kettle's hands together, and, lifting him in a half-unconscious state into his ship, bound him in as comfortable a position as he could to one of the rowers' banks.

"Now, Alric, come aside with me, quick! I have only time for a few words. It is enough to tell thee that the day is lost. I go with our father and the men to save our mother and the other women, or to die. Thou wilt stay here with a few men to guard the ships, and be ready to cast off at a moment's notice. If we return not before night, do thou creep out and try to ascertain what has become of us, and if ye have reason to think we are killed, cut Kettle's bonds and let him do what he will, poor fellow. At present his head has got a knock that renders him a dangerous comrade, so he must remain tied. Of course, if the cave is attacked thou wilt set him free at once. There is a little boat at the stern of my Swan. Escape if thou canst. But be watchful. We may return in a few hours. If so, all shall yet be well. Dost understand me, boy?"

"I do, but methinks ill luck awaits us."

Erling made no reply, but, kissing Alric's forehead, he returned to his men, of whom there were about sixty, and led them out of the cave, leaving six with his little brother to guard the ships.

While our hero is thus hastening to the rescue, let us turn aside for a little to follow the course of Guttorm Stoutheart. That brave old Sea-king had escaped scathless throughout the whole of the disastrous day until near the end, when he received his death-wound from a javelin which pierced his thigh, and cut some important blood vessel, to stanch which defied the skill of his attendants. He immediately ordered his ship to be cut loose, and his was among the first to escape round the southern point of the fiord, just before the battle ended.

At first the men pulled as if their lives depended on it. So great was their haste that they did not take time to throw their dead comrades overboard, but left them lying in a ghastly heap on the lower deck. When, however, they got round the next point, and found that no pursuit was made, they slackened speed and began to heave out the dead, when Guttorm, who reclined near the helm, steering the vessel, ordered them to desist.

"My men," said he, in a voice which had already lost much of its deep richness of tone, "we will land on the next point. My days are run out. I go to Odin's halls, and I am glad, for it becomes not an old warrior to die in his bed, which I had begun to fear was going to be my fate; besides, now that Norway is to be no longer a free land, it is time that the small kings should be going home. Ye will carry me to the top of yonder headland cliff, and leave me where I can see the setting sun, and the fords and fells of my native land. Would that my bones might have been burned, as those of my fathers were! but this may not be. Ye can lay beside me the comrades who have gone before, and then push off and leave me with the dead."

There was a low murmur among the men as they again dipped their oars, but not a word was spoken in reply. Just as they reached the point a vessel came in sight behind them under sail.

"Too late!" muttered Guttorm bitterly, as he looked back; "we are pursued, and must hold on."

"Not so," answered one of his chief men; "that is Solve Klofe's ship."

"Is that so?" cried Guttorm, while the colour mounted to his pale cheek, and the fire shone in his old eyes; "then have I better luck than I had looked for. Quick, get to land! The breeze that brings Solve down will reach us soon. Get out your arms, and go hail Solve as he passes. Ye shall sail with him to-night. I will hie me out upon the sea."

He spoke somewhat like his former self for a moment, but soon his voice sank, for the life-blood was draining fast away.

Ere many minutes had passed, the breeze freshened into a squall of considerable force. It came off the land, and swept down the fiord, lashing its waters into seething waves. Solve answered the hail of Guttorm's men, and landed.

"What news?" he asked: "there is but short space for converse."

The men told him that old Guttorm was dying in his ship. He walked up the plank that lay from the shore to the gunwale, and found the old warrior lying on the poop beside the helm, wrapped in his mantle, and giving directions to his men, who were piling brushwood on the deck.

"This is an ill sight," said Solve, with much feeling, as he knelt beside the dying chief, who received him with a smile, and held out his hand.

"Ha! Solve, I am glad thou art here. My last battle has been fought, and it has been a good one, though we did get the tooth-ache. If it had only been a victory, I had recked little of this wound."

"Can nothing be done for thee?" asked Solve. "Perchance I may be able to stop the bleeding."

Guttorm shook his head, and pointed to the blood which had already flowed from him, and lay in a deep pool in the sides of the ship.

"No, no, Solve, my fighting days are over, and, as I have said, the last fight has been a good one! Ye see what I am about, and understand how to carry out my will. Go, relieve me of the trouble, and see that it is done well. I would rest now."

Solve pressed the hand of his friend in silence, and then went forward to assist actively in the preparations already referred to. The men heaped up the funeral pile round the mast, fastened the stern ropes to the shore, plied the dead upon the deck, and, when all was ready, hoisted sail. The squall had increased so that the mast bent, and the ship strained at her stern ropes like an impatient charger. Then the men went on shore, and Solve, turning to Guttorm, bent over him, and spoke a few words in a low, earnest tone, but the old man's strength was almost gone. He could only utter the single word "Farewell", and wave his hand as if he wished to be left alone. Solve rose at once, and, applying a light to the pile, leaped ashore. Next moment the cables were cut; the brushwood crackled with a fierce noise as the fire leaped up and the "ocean steed" bounded away over the dark blue sea. Guttorm was still seated by the helm, his face pale as death, but with a placid smile on his mouth, and a strange, almost unearthly, fire in his eyes.

The longship rushed over the waves with the foam dashing on her bows, a long white track in her wake, and a dense black cloud curling overhead. Suddenly the cloud was rent by a fork of flame, which was as suddenly quenched, but again it burst upwards, and at last triumphed; shooting up into the sky with a mighty roar, while below there glowed a fierce fiery furnace, against which was strongly depicted the form of the grand old Sea-king, still sitting motionless at the helm. Swiftly the blazing craft dashed over the waves, getting more and more enveloped in smoke and flame. Ere long it could be seen in the far distance, a rushing ball of fire. Gradually it receded, becoming less and less, until at last it vanished, like a setting star, into the unknown waste of the great western sea.

CHAPTER XXIV.

Hopes and Fears — The Burning of Haldorstede, and Escape of the Family.

Meanwhile the family at Haldorstede had made a narrow escape, and some members of it were still in great peril. When Hilda and Ada were sent thither, with the females of Ulfstede, under the charge of Christian the hermit, as already related, they found Dame Herfrida and her maidens busily engaged in making preparations for a great feast.

"I prithee," said Dame Astrid, in some surprise, "who are to be thy guests to-night?"

"Who should be," replied Herfrida, with a smile, "but the stout fellows who back my husband in the fight to-day! Among them thine own goodman, Dame Astrid, and his house-carles; for if no one is left at Ulfstede there can be no supper there for them; and as the poor lads are likely to be well worn out, we must have something wherewith to cheer them."

"But what if ill luck betide us?" suggested Astrid.

"Ill luck never betides us," replied Herfrida, with an expression of bland assurance on her handsome face. "Besides, if it does, we shall be none the worse for having done our part."

"*Some* people are always forecasting evil," muttered Ingeborg, with a sour look, as she kneaded viciously a lump of dough which was destined to form cakes.

"And some other people are always forecasting good," retorted Ada, with a smile, "so that things are pretty well balanced after all. Come now, Ingeborg, don't be cross, but leave the dough, and let us go to thy room, for I want to have a little gossip with thee alone."

Ingeborg was fond of Ada, and particularly fond of a little gossip, either public or private. She condescended, therefore, to smile, as it were under protest, and, rubbing the dough from her fingers, accompanied her friend to her chamber, while the others broke into several groups, and chatted more or less energetically as they worked, or idled about the house.

"Is there any fear of our men losing the day?" asked Hilda of the hermit, who stood looking out of a window which commanded a view of the fiord, where the ships of the opposing fleets could be seen engaged in the battle, that had just begun.

Poor Hilda asked the question with a look of perplexity in her face; for hitherto she had been so much accustomed to success attending the expeditions of her warlike father and friends, that she had never given much thought to the idea of defeat and its consequences.

"It is not easy to answer that question," replied the hermit; "for the success or failure of thy father's host depends on many things with which I am not acquainted. If the forces on both sides are about equal in numbers, the chances are in his favour; for he is a mighty man of valour, as well as his son, and also thy father. Besides, there are many of his men who are not far behind them in strength and courage; but they may be greatly outnumbered. If so, defeat is possible. I would say it is probable, did I not know that the Ruler of events can, if He will, give victory to the weak and disaster to the strong. Thy father deems his cause a righteous one — perhaps it is so."

"Well, then," said Hilda, "will not God, who, you say, is just and good, give victory to the righteous cause?"

"He may be pleased to do so; but He does not always do so. For His own good and wise ends He sometimes permits the righteous to suffer defeat, and wrongdoers to gain the victory. This only do I know for certain, that good shall come out of all things to His people, whether these things be grievous or joyful; for it is written, 'All things work together for good to them that love God, to them that are the called according to His purpose'. This is my consolation when I am surrounded by darkness which I cannot understand, and which seems all against me. That things often pass my understanding does not surprise me; for it is written, 'His ways are wonderful — past finding out'."

"Past finding out indeed!" said Hilda thoughtfully. "Would that I had faith like thine, Christian; for it seems to enable thee to trust and rejoice in darkness as well as in sunshine."

"Thou mayst have it, daughter," answered the hermit earnestly, "if thou wilt condescend to ask it in the name of Jesus; for it is written, 'Faith is the gift of God'; and again it is written, 'Whatsoever ye shall ask the Father in my name, He will give it you'. One of our chief sins consists in our desire to produce, by means of our own will, that faith which God tells us we cannot attain to by striving after, but which He is willing to bestow as a free gift on those who ask."

The conversation was interrupted here by the old house-carle Finn the One-eyed, who said in passing that he was going down to the cliffs to see and hear what was doing, and would return ere long to report progress. For an hour after that, the people at Haldorstede continued to watch the fight with intense interest; but although they could see the motion of the ships on the fiord, and could hear the shout of war, as it came floating down on the breeze like a faint murmur, the distance was too great to permit of their distinguishing the individual combatants, or observing the progress of the fight. That it was likely to go ill with their friends, however, was soon made known by Finn, who returned in hot haste to warn them to prepare for flight.

"Be sure," said Dame Herfrida, "that there is no need to flee until Haldor or Erling come to tell us to get ready."

"That may be so," said Finn; "but if Haldor and Erling should chance to be slain, ill will it be for you if ye are not ready to fly."

"Now it seems to me," said Dame Astrid, who was of an anxious temperament, "that thou art too confident, Herfrida. It would be wise at all events to get ready."

"Does anyone know where Alric is?" asked Ingeborg.

As everyone professed ignorance on this point, his mother said that she had no doubt he was safe enough; for he was a bold little man, and quite able to take care of himself.

"If he has had his own way," observed Ivor the Old, who came in at that moment, "he is in the fleet for he is a true chip of the old tree; but we are not like to see him again, methinks, for I have seen the fleet giving back on the right wing, and hasted hither to tell ye."

This report had the effect of shaking Herfrida's confidence to the extent of inducing her to give up her preparations for the feast, and assist the others in making arrangements for a hasty flight with such household valuables as could be easily carried about the person. Some time after they had begun this work, a young man, who was a cripple, and therefore a non-combatant, hobbled into the hall, and announced the fact that Haldor's fleet was routed everywhere, and fleeing. He had seen it from the cliff behind the stede, and indeed it could partly be seen from the hall window.

"Now," cried Finn the One-eyed bitterly, "all is lost, and I must carry out Erling's last instructions. He told me, if the fight went against us, and the King's men gained the day, I was to lead ye down by the forest path to the cave behind Ulfstede, where there is a ship big enough to carry the whole household. If alive, he and his friends are to meet us there. Come, we must make haste; some of the ships are already on the beach, and if they be the King's men we shall soon see them here."

Everyone was now so thoroughly convinced of their desperate case that without reply each went to complete arrangements as fast as possible.

"Wilt thou go with us?" said Finn to the hermit, when all were assembled in front of the house at the edge of the forest.

"I will, since God seems to order it so," said the hermit; "but first I go to my hut for the rolls of the Book. As ye have to pass the bottom of the cliff on which my dwelling is perched, I will easily overtake you."

"Let us go with him," said Hilda to Ada. "There is a roll in the hut which Erling and I have been trying to copy; Christian may not be able to find it, as I hid it carefully away — and," she continued, blushing slightly, "I should not like to lose it."

"You had better go with *us*," said Finn gravely.

"We will do what seems best to ourselves," replied Ada; "go on, Christian, we follow."

The hermit advised the girls to go with Finn, but as they were self-willed he was fain to conduct them up the steep and narrow path that led to his hut upon the cliff, while Finn put himself at the head of a sad band of women, children, and aged retainers, who could advance but slowly along the rugged and intricate path which he thought it necessary to take through the forest.

Not twenty minutes after they had left Haldorstede the first band of King Harald's men came rushing up the banks of the river, enraged at having found Ulfstede deserted, and thirsting for plunder. They ran tumultuously into the house, sword in hand, and a yell of disappointment followed when they discovered that the inmates had fled. There is no doubt that they would have rushed out again and searched the woods, had not the feast which Herfrida had been preparing proved too attractive. The cold salmon and huge tankards of ale proved irresistible to the tired and thirsty warriors, who forthwith put the goblets to their bearded lips and quaffed the generous fluid so deeply that in a short time many of them were reeling, and one, who seemed to be more full of mischief than his fellows, set the house on fire by way of a joke.

It was the smoke which arose after the perpetration of this wanton act that had attracted the attention of Haldor and his friends, when they were making for the shore after the battle.

Of course the hermit and the two girls heard the shouts of the marauders, and knew that it was now too late to escape along with the baud under Finn, for the only practicable path by which they could join them passed in full view of Haldorstede, and it was so hemmed in by a precipice that there was no other way of getting into the wood — at least without the certainty of being seen. Their retreat up the river was also cut off, for the hermit, in selecting the spot for his dwelling, had chosen a path which ascended along the rugged face of a precipice, so that, with a precipice above and another below, it was not possible to get to the bank of the river without returning on their track. There was no alternative, therefore, but to ascend to the hut, and there wait patiently until the shades of night should favour their escape.

Finn pushed on as fast as was possible with a band in which there were so many almost helpless ones. He carried one of the youngest children in his arms, and Ivor the Old brought up the rear with a very old woman leaning on his arm. They were a long time in descending the valley, for the route Finn had chosen was circuitous, and the first part of it was extremely trying to the cripples, running as it did over a somewhat high spur of the mountain which extended down from the main ridge to the river. Gradually, however, they drew near to the coast, and Finn was in the act of encouraging them with the assurance that they had now only a short way to go, when the hearts of all sank within them at the sight of a band of armed men who suddenly made their appearance in their path.

The wail of despair which burst from some of them at sight of these, was, however, changed into an exclamation of joy when four of the band ran hastily towards them, and were recognised to be Haldor, Erling, Ulf, and Glumm!

"Now thanks be to the gods," said Haldor, stooping to print a kiss on his wife's lips. "But — but — where are Hilda and Ada?"

Erling and Glumm, glancing quickly round the group with looks of intense disappointment and alarm, had already put this question to Finn, who explained the cause of their absence.

"Now this is the worst luck of all," cried Glumm, grinding his teeth together in passion, and looking at Finn with a dark scowl.

Erling did not speak for a few minutes, but his heaving chest and dilated nostrils told of the storm that raged within him.

"Art thou sure they went to the hermit's hut?" asked Ulf in a stern voice.

"Quite sure," replied Finn. "I cautioned them not to go, but —"

"Enough," cried Erling. "Father, wilt thou go back to the cave with the women, and a few of the men to guard them?"

"I will, my son, and then will I rejoin thee."

"That do an it please thee. It matters little. Death must come sooner or later to all. — Come, men, we will now teach this tyrant that though he may conquer our bodies he cannot subdue our spirits. Up! and if we fail to rescue the girls, everlasting disgrace be to him who leaves this vale alive!"

Haldor had already selected a small detachment of men, and turned back with the women and others, while Erling and his men went on as fast as they could run. A short time sufficed to bring them to the edge of the wood near Haldorstede. The old place was now a smoking ruin, with swarms of men around it, most of whom were busily engaged in trying to put out the fire, and save as much as possible from its fury. The man who had kindled it had already paid dearly for his jest with his life. His body was seen swinging to the limb of a neighbouring tree. Harald Fairhair himself, having just arrived, was directing operations.

There were by that time one or two thousand of the King's men on the ground, while others were arriving every moment in troops — all bloodstained, and covered with marks of the recent conflict — and Erling saw at once he had no chance whatever of accomplishing his aim by an open attack with only fifty men. He therefore led his force silently by a path that he well knew to an adjacent cliff, over the edge of which they could see all that went on below, while they were themselves well concealed. Here the three leaders held a consultation.

"What dost thou advise, Ulf?" asked Erling.

"*My* advice," interposed Glumm fiercely, "is that we should make a sudden assault without delay, kill the King, and then sell our lives dearly."

"And thus," observed Ulf, with something like a sneer, "leave the girls without protectors, and without a chance of deliverance. No," he continued, turning to our hero, "my advice is to wait here as patiently as we can until we ascertain where the girls are. Few, perhaps none, of our men are known to Harald's men; one of them we can send down to mingle with the enemy as a spy. Whatever we do must be done cautiously, for the sake of the girls."

"That is good advice," said a voice behind them, which was that of the hermit, who had crept towards them on his hands and knees.

"Why, Christian, whence comest thou?" said Ulf.

"From my own hut," replied the hermit, raising himself, "where I have just left Hilda and Ada safe and well. We had deemed ourselves prisoners there till night should set us free; but necessity sharpens the wit even of an old man, and I have discovered a path through the woods, which, although difficult, may be traversed without much chance of our being seen, if done carefully. I have just passed along it in safety, and was on the point of returning to the hut when I came upon you here."

"Lead us to them at once," cried Glumm, starting up.

"Nay," said the hermit, laying his hand on the youth's arm, "restrain thine ardour. It would be easier to bring the girls hither, than to lead a band of armed men by that path without their being discovered. If ye will take the advice of one who was a warrior in his youth, there is some hope that, God permitting, we may all escape. Ye know the Crow Cliff? Well, the small boat is lying there. It is well known that men dare not swim down the rapid, unless they are acquainted with the run of the water and the formation of the rock. Thy men know it well, the King's men know it not. With a boat the maidens may descend in safety. The men can leap into the river and escape before the enemy could come at them by the hill road."

"Excellently planned," exclaimed Erling in an eager tone; "but, hermit, how dost thou propose to fetch the maidens hither?"

"By going and conducting them. There is much risk, no doubt, but their case is desperate, for their retreat is certain to be discovered."

"Away then," said Ulf, "minutes are precious. We will await thee here, and, at the worst, if they should be captured, we can but die in attempting their rescue."

Without uttering another word the hermit rose, re-entered the underwood, sank down on his hands and knees, and disappeared with a cat-like quietness that had been worthy of one of the red warriors of America.

CHAPTER XXV.

In which is Described a Desperate Attempt at Rescue,
a Bold Leap for Freedom, and a Triumphant Escape.

The Crow Cliff, to which Christian had referred, was a high precipitous rock that jutted out into the river just below Haldorstede. It was the termination of the high ridge on the face of which Erling had posted his men, and could be easily reached from the spot where they lay concealed, as well as from the stede itself, but there was no possibility of passing down the river in that direction by land, owing to the precipitous nature of the ground. The ordinary path down the valley, which elsewhere followed the curvatures of the river, made at this point a wide detour into the woods, went in a zigzag form up the steep ascent of the ridge, descended similarly on the other side, and did not rejoin the river for nearly half a mile below. The waters were so pent up by the Crow Cliff that they rushed along its base in a furious rapid, which, a hundred yards down, descended in a perpendicular fall of about fifteen feet in depth. The descent of this rapid by a boat was quite possible, for there was a little bay at the lower end of Crow Cliff, just above the foss, into which it could be steered by a dexterous rower; but this mode of descent was attended with the imminent risk of being swept over the fall and dashed to pieces, so that none except the daring young spirits of the glen ever attempted it, while all the rest were content to cross the ridge by the longer and more laborious, but safe, path which we have just described. To descend this rapid by swimming was one of the feats which the youths of the place delighted to venture, and often had Erling and Glumm dared it together, while not a few of their companions had lost their lives in the attempt.

A few words from Erling gave the men to understand what was expected of them. It was arranged that while he, Ulf, Glumm, and the hermit should put the girls into the little boat and guide them down the rapid, the men were to leap into the water and swim down. All were to land in the little bay, and then make for the cave on the coast in a body, and fight their way thither, if need be; but it was believed there would be no occasion for that, because before the plan was carried out most of the King's men would probably be assembled above the Crow Cliff at the stede. A few who could not swim were sent off at once by the track to warn Haldor. All these well-laid plans, however, were suddenly frustrated, for, while Erling was still consulting with Ulf and Glumm as to details, and peeping through the underwood, they beheld a sight which caused their hearts almost to stand still.

From the elevated spot where they lay they could see the hermit advancing rapidly towards them in a crouching attitude, closely followed by the maidens, while at the same time there advanced from the stede a large band of men under a chief, who was evidently commissioned to execute some order of the King. Erling and his friends could clearly see these two parties unwittingly approaching each other, at right angles, each making for a point where the two paths crossed, and where they were certain to meet. They could see their friends quietly but swiftly gliding towards the very fate they sought to avoid, and experienced all the agony of being unable to give a shout of warning, or to prevent the foe from capturing them; for, even if there had been time to rush upon them before the meeting, which there was not, Erling by so doing would have been obliged to place the whole of Harald's host between him and the boat at Crow Cliff. This consideration, however, would not have deterred him, but another idea had flashed upon his mind. What that was shall be seen presently.

Before the two parties met, the ears of the hermit, albeit somewhat dulled by age, became aware of the tramp of armed men, and at once he drew the girls hastily aside into the bushes; but the bushes at that part happened to be not very thick, and part of Ada's dress, which was a gay one with a good deal of scarlet about it, caught the attention of a sharp-eyed warrior. The man uttered a shout and sprang towards them; several others joined in the pursuit, a loud scream from one of the girls was heard, and next moment the fugitives were captured!

"Up and at them!" cried Glumm, endeavouring to rise, but he found himself pinned to the earth by Erling's powerful arms.

"Stay, Glumm, be quiet, I beseech thee," entreated Erling, as his comrade struggled violently but fruitlessly to escape from his powerful embrace. — "Do listen, Ulf; ye will spoil all by inconsiderate haste. I have a plan: listen — these men are not devils, but Norsemen, and will not hurt the girls; they will take them before the King. Hear me, and they shall yet be rescued!"

While the power of Erling's muscles restrained Glumm, the deep-toned impassioned earnestness of his voice held back Ulf, who had leaped up and drawn his sword; but it was with evident reluctance that he paused and listened.

"Now hear me," cried Erling; "I and Glumm will go down and mingle with Harald's men. Our faces are doubtless not known to any of them; besides, we are so bespattered with the blood and dust of battle that even friends might fail to recognise us. We will go boldly about among the men, and keep near to the girls until a fitting opportunity offers, when we will seize them and bear them off. This will not be so difficult as ye may think."

"Difficult!" cried Glumm, grinding his teeth; "I think nothing difficult except sitting still!"

"Because," continued Erling, "the King's men will be taken by surprise, and we shall be through the most of them before they are aware that there is need to draw their blades. But (and on this everything will depend) thou must be ready, Ulf, with all the men, to rush, in the twinkling of an eye, to our aid, the moment my shout is heard, for, if this be not done, we cannot fail to be overpowered by numbers. If thou dost but keep them well in play while we make for the boat, and then follow and leap into the river, we shall all escape."

"Come along, then," cried Glumm, in desperate impatience.

"Does the plan like thee, Ulf?" asked Erling.

"Not much," he replied, shaking his head, "but it is the only chance left, so get thee gone. I will not fail thee in the moment of need — away! See, the girls are already being led before the King."

Erling and Glumm instantly pulled their helmets well down on their brows, wrapped their mantles round them so as to conceal their figures as much as possible, then entered the wood and disappeared.

Meanwhile, on the open space in front of Haldor's ruined dwelling, King Harald Haarfager stood surrounded by his court men. He was still bespattered with the blood and dust of battle, and furiously angry at the escape of Haldor and the burning of the stede. His gilt helmet restrained the exuberance of his shaggy locks, and he stood on the top of a slight elevation or mound, from the base of which his men extended in a dense ring in front of him, eager to ascertain who it was that had been so unexpectedly captured. Erling and Glumm mingled with the crowd unnoticed, for so many of the men assembled there had been collected from various districts, that, to each, strange faces were the rule instead of the exception.

When the girls were led into the ring there was a murmur of admiration, and many complimentary remarks were made about them. The old hermit was dragged in after them, and excited a little attention for a few moments. He had experienced rough handling from his captors. His grey hair was dishevelled and his face bloodstained, for, although he had offered no resistance, some of the men who seized him were so much out of humour in consequence of the burning of the stede and the escape of its inmates, that they were glad to vent their anger on anyone.

"Good-looking girls, both of them," remarked the King to Jarl Rongvold, as they were being led forward. — "Who are ye?" he added, addressing them.

Ada looked round on the circle of men with a frightened glance, and cast down her eyes, but did not reply, while Hilda raised her eyes timidly to the King's face, but lacked courage to speak.

"Come," said the King sternly, "let us have no false modesty. Ye are before Norway's King, therefore speak, and to the point. Who art thou?"

He addressed himself to Hilda, who replied —

"I am Hilda, daughter of Ulf of Romsdal."

"And thou?" he added, turning to her companion.

"My name is Ada. My father is Hakon of Drontheim."

"Ha!" exclaimed the King, with a bitter smile. "Is it so? Thy father has met his desert, then, for he now lies at the bottom of the fiord."

Ada turned deadly pale, but made no reply.

"Know ye where Haldor the Fierce is, and his insolent son Erling?" asked the King.

Hilda flushed at this, and answered with some spirit that she did not know, and that if she did she would not tell.

"Of course not," said the King; "I might have guessed as much, and do but waste my time with ye. — Stand aside — bring forward yonder fellow."

The hermit was immediately led forward.

"Who art thou?" asked the King.

"An old wanderer on the face of the earth," replied Christian.

"That is easily seen," answered the King; "but not too old, it would seem, to do a little mischief when the chance falls in thy way."

"Methinks, sire," whispered Jarl Rongvold, "that this fellow is one of those strange madmen who have taken up with that new religion, which I do not profess to understand."

"Sayest thou so?" exclaimed Harald, "then will I test him. — Ho! fetch me a piece of horse flesh."

A piece of horse flesh was brought without delay, for some that had been sacrificed in the Drontheim temple had been packed up and carried off among other provisions when the expedition set forth.

"Here, old man, eat thou a portion of that," said Harald, holding the flesh towards him.

"I may not eat what has been sacrificed to idols," said the hermit.

"Ho! ho! then thou art not a worshipper of Odin? Say, dog, what art thou?"

"I am a follower of the Lord Jesus Christ. He is my Saviour. To Him I live, and for Him I can die."

"Can He save you from *me*?" demanded Harald.

"He can," answered the hermit earnestly, "and will save you too, King Harald, from your sins, and all who now hear me, if they will but turn to Him."

"Now will I test him," said the King. "Stand forth, Hake of Hadeland, and hew me the old man's head from his body."

"Spare him! O spare him!" cried Hilda, throwing herself suddenly between Hake and his victim, who stood with the resigned air of a man who had made up his mind to die. "He has twice saved *my* life, and has never done you evil in thought or deed."

"Stand aside, my pretty maid. Nay, then, if thou wilt not, I must grant thy request; but it is upon one condition: that this Saviour shall either come himself or send a champion to deliver the old man. — Come," he added, turning fiercely to the hermit, "pray that thy God shall send thee a champion now, for if He does not, as I live thou shalt die."

"I may not pray at thy bidding," said the hermit calmly; "besides, it needs not that I should, because I have already prayed — before dawn this morning — that He would grant me His blessing in the form that seemed best to Himself."

"And hast thou got it?"

"I have — in that I possess a quiet spirit, and do not fear to die, now that His time has come."

"'Tis something this, I admit," returned the King; "yet methinks 'tis but a poor blessing, after all, with death as the end of it."

"Death is not the end of it," said the hermit, with a kindling eye, "for after death is everlasting joy and glory with the Lord. Besides, King Harald, which were better, think you: to die with a willing spirit and bright hope, or to live full of restless ambition, disappointment, and rage, even although victorious and King of Norway?"

The King's countenance grew livid with anger as he turned to the berserk and said, in a voice of suppressed passion — "Go forward, Hake, and slay him!"

"Now — the time has come," whispered Erling to Glumm.

"Get as near to Ada as thou canst; for the rest, may Christian's God be with us!"

As he spoke he sprang into the circle, sword in hand, and stood suddenly between the astonished Hake and the hermit.

There was a loud murmur of amazement at this unexpected apparition, and not a few of the spectators were awestricken, supposing that this was actually a champion sent from the spirit world.

"Harald," cried Erling, for the berserk had shrunk back dismayed, "I do now accept the challenge, and come here to champion the old man."

At the sound of his voice the King's face lighted up with intelligence.

"Ha!" he exclaimed suddenly; "has the old man's God sent Erling the Bold?"

"Truly I think he has," replied Erling; "at all events it was not for this purpose that I came hither to-day. But now that I have come, and of mine own free will put myself in thy power, I claim the right to do battle for my old friend with thy stoutest man — so set him forth, King Harald."

"What sayest thou, Hake?" said the King, turning to his berserk with a smile; "art willing to join issue with the Bold one? — bold enough, truly, and insolent as well."

Hake, who had recovered his self-possession the instant he recognised Erling's voice, and who was by no means wanting in courage, suddenly uttered one of his terrible roars, and rushed upon Erling like a thunderbolt.

Our hero was too well accustomed to the ways of his class to be caught off his guard. Although Hake rained blows upon him so fast that it was almost impossible for the spectators to follow the motions of his flashing sword, Erling received them all on his shield, or parried them with his short sword — which, as being more manageable in a *mêlée*, he had selected for his present enterprise. The instant, however, that the berserk's furious onset began to slacken, Erling fetched him such a tremendous cut on the sword that the weapon was broken close off at the hilt. Disdaining to slay an unarmed foe, he leaped upon the berserk, and struck him a blow with the hilt of his sword, which drove the casque down upon his head and stretched him flat upon the sward.

Without waiting an instant Erling flung down his shield and walked to the place where Hilda stood, took her by the hand, and whispered, "Courage! come with me and thou shalt be saved." At the same moment Glumm stepped to Ada's side, and took her right hand in his left. No sword was drawn, for Glumm had not drawn his, and no one present had the faintest idea of what the young men intended to attempt. Indeed, they were all so amazed at the sudden termination of the fight, that the men of the inner part of the ring actually stood aside to let them pass, before the King had time to shout:

"Seize them!"

In other circumstances, at Harald's word a thousand swords would have been drawn, and the doom of Erling and his friends at once been sealed; but the natural ferocity of the tyrant's followers had been spellbound, and for the time paralysed by the calm bearing of old Christian and the prowess of his champion, whose opportune appearance had all the effect of a supernatural interposition, as it might well be deemed: and it will be readily believed that our hero and Glumm did not fail to use the advantage thus offered. Leading those whom they had come to rescue, and closely followed by the hermit, they passed completely through the circle of men. But at the repetition, in a voice of thunder, of the royal mandate, some hundreds of the King's men surrounded them, and, notwithstanding their wondrous strength and skill, they were being gradually overpowered by numbers, when suddenly a tremendous shout was heard, and next moment Ulf with his fifty men in battle array rushed out of the forest.

King Harald endeavoured hastily to draw up his men in something like order. Hearing the cry in rear, the men in front of Erling and Glumm fell aside, so that they quickly cut down those who still stood in their way, and ran towards their friends, who opened their ranks to let them pass — then reclosed, and fell upon the King's men with incredible fury. Although outnumbered by at least twenty to one, the disparity did not at first tell against them, owing to the confusion in the enemy's ranks, and the confined space of ground on which they fought. They were thus enabled to act with great vigour, and, being animated by the spirit of desperate men, they actually for some time kept driving back the King's forces.

But the continual assault of fresh foes began to tell, and several of Ulf's men had already fallen, when Erling's voice was heard ringing high above the din of battle. Instantly every man turned on his heel and fled towards the river madly pursued by the whole of the King's host.

By this time Erling and Glumm had got the girls into the boat, and steered them safely down the rapid into the little bay, where they waited for their companions as patiently as they could.

Meanwhile Ulf's men reached the foot of the Crow Cliff and one by one sprang into the boiling rapid. Ulf was among the first there, but he stayed to see them all pass. Before the last could do so their enemies were upon them, but Ulf kept them at bay for a few moments; and when the last of his men took the water he retreated fighting, and leaped backwards into the flood. One or two of the King's men followed, but they failed to catch him, were carried down stream, and, being ignorant of the dangers of the place, were swept over the foss and killed. Most of the host, however, turned suddenly, and set off at full speed to cross the ridge and pursue their enemies, by the path to which we have already referred. Before they had crossed it, Erling and his men were far on their way down the valley; and when the pursuers reached the coast there was no sign of the fugitives anywhere.

On reaching the cave Erling found that his father had got everything in readiness to start; so, assembling the people together without delay, he divided them into two bands, one of which he sent into the Swan, the other into Glumm's vessel, the Crane.

Haldor also went in the Swan, along with Ulf of Romsdal, Thorer the Thick, Kettle Flatnose, Alric, and the hermit, besides Dames Herfrida and

Astrid, and the widow Gunhild, Ingeborg, and all Haldor's younger children. With Glumm there were also several women besides Ada. Ivor the Old and Finn the One-eyed also went with him; but most of the old and crippled hangers-on of both families, as well as Glumm's mother, were taken by Erling into the Swan, as the accommodation there was better than on board the Crane.

"Now, Glumm," said Erling, when all were on board, "we must say farewell to Norway. Keep close in my wake. If they give chase we will do our best to escape, but if that may not be, we will fight and fall together." The friends shook hands; then, each getting into his ship, the stern ropes were cast off, the oars were dipped, and they shot out upon the blue fiord, which the sinking sun had left in a solemn subdued light, although his beams still glowed brightly on the snow-clad mountain peaks.

They had proceeded some distance down the fiord before their pursuers observed them. Then a mighty shout told that they were discovered; and the grinding of the heavy ships' keels was distinctly heard upon the shore, as they were pushed off into deep water. Immediately after, the splash of hundreds of oars warned them to make haste.

"Pull, my lads, — pull with heart," cried Erling; "and let these slaves see how freemen can make their ocean steeds leap across the sea! Pull! I see a breeze just off the mouth of the fiord. If we reach that, we may laugh at the tyrant King."

"What may yonder line on the water be?" said Haldor, with an anxious look, as he pointed towards the mouth of the fiord.

Erling caught his breath, and the blood rushed to his temples as he gazed for a moment in silence.

"'Tis a boom," cried Kettle, who had recovered by this time, and who now leaped towards the fore deck with terrible energy.

"All is lost!" exclaimed Ulf, in a tone of bitterness which words cannot express.

"Are ye sure it is a boom?" cried Erling quickly. Everyone looked with intense earnestness at the black line that stretched completely across the mouth of the fiord, and each gave it as his opinion that it was a boom. There could not indeed be any doubt on the point. King Harald's berserk, although somewhat tardy, had fulfilled his orders but too well; and now a succession of huge logs, or tree trunks, joined together by thick iron chains, completely barred their progress seaward.

"Surely we can burst through," suggested Kettle, returning to the poop, his huge frame quivering with contending emotions.

"Impossible," said Haldor; "I have tried it before, and failed. Of course we must make the attempt, but I have no hope except in this," he added, touching his sword, "and not much in that either, *now*."

"But I have tried it before, and did not fail, and I'll try it again," cried Erling heartily. "Come aft, men, quick, all of ye; every man except the rowers. Women, children, and cripples, get ye into the waist. The stoutest men to the oars — jump!"

These orders were obeyed at once. All the best men in the ship seized the oars, Erling himself, Kettle, and Haldor setting the example, while Thorer took the helm, and, hailing Glumm, bade him do as they did.

The effect of this was that the stern of the Swan was so weighed down with the weight of people on the poop, that her bows and a third of her keel were raised high out of the water, while the men, straining with every fibre of their muscles at the oars, sent her careering forward with trebled speed, and the foam rolled in milky billows in her wake.

"When I give the word 'Forward'," cried Erling, "leap like lightning, all of ye, to the fore deck."

The pursuers, elated by this time with the certainty of success, pulled also with unwonted energy.

When the Swan came within about twenty yards of the boom, which floated almost on a level with the water, Thorer gave the word —

"One stroke for freedom!"

"Ho! ho!" shouted Erling and Haldor, straining until their oars cracked again. The foam hissed from the blades, and the Swan rushed as if she had been suddenly endued with true vitality.

Next moment she stuck fast — with the boom amidships beneath her!

"Forward!" shouted Erling.

All the unengaged men sprang instantly to the forecastle, and their weight sank it slowly down, but it seemed inclined for a moment to remain balanced on the boom. Hereupon the men at the oars jumped up and also ran forward. The bow dipped at once, the good ship slid over with a plunge, and glided out upon the sea!

A great shout or yell told that this had been noticed by their foes, who still rowed madly after them; but heedless of this, Erling backed water and waited for Glumm, who had made similar preparations, and was now close on the boom. His vessel went fairly on, and stuck halfway, as the other had done; but when she was balanced and about to turn over, there was a terrible rending sound in the hull, then a crash, and the Crane broke in two, throwing half of her crew into the sea on the inner side of the boom, and the other half outside.

Well was it for them all then that the Swan had waited! She was at once backed towards the scene of disaster, and as many as possible were picked up. Among the rescued was Glumm, with Ada in his arms. But many were drowned, and a few stuck to the boom, refusing to let go, or to make any attempt to reach the Swan.

Erling knew, however, that these were sure to be picked up by the King's ships, so he once more ordered the rowers to give way, and the vessel sprang forth on her voyage some time before the pursuers reached the boom. When these did so, most of them attempted to leap it as the fugitives had done — for none of the Norsemen there lacked spirit. Some, however, failed to get on to it at all, others got on a short way and stuck fast, while two or three ships broke their backs, as Glumm's had done, and threw their crews into the water — but not one got over.

The men then leaped on the boom, and the sound of axes was heard as they laboured to cut it through, or to dash away its iron fastenings. It was, however, a thoroughly well-executed piece of work, and for a long time resisted their utmost efforts. When at length it did give way, and the King's ships passed through, the Swan was beyond pursuit — far away on the horizon, with all sail set, and running before a stiff breeze, while the shades of evening were closing in around her!

That night there was silence in the Norsemen's little ship as she ploughed her adventurous course over the northern sea, for the thoughts of all were very sad at being thus rudely driven from their native land to seek a home where best they might in the wide world. Yet in the hearts of some of them there was also much happiness.

Hilda's sanguine mind pictured many sweet and peaceful abodes, far from the haunts of warlike men. Alric was happy, because he was beginning, as he fondly hoped, a life of wild adventure. So was Kettle Flatnose, for he was now sailing westward, and he knew that Ireland was somewhere in that direction. But Glumm the Gruff was perhaps the happiest of all on board, for, besides the delight of having at last got possession of his bride, he enjoyed, for the first time in his life, the pleasure of comforting a woman in distress!

Ada's wild spirit was — we dare not say eradicated, but — thoroughly subdued at last. When she thought of her father she laid her head on Glumm's broad chest and wept bitterly.

Thus did those Sea-kings sail away from and forsake the land of Norway. On their voyage westward they fell in with many ships from other quarters containing countrymen, Sea-kings and vikings like themselves, who had also left their native land to seek new homes in Shetland, Orkney, and the other isles north of Scotland, rather than submit to the yoke of Harald Haarfager.

They joined company with these, and all sailed westward together.

Among them was a man named Frode, who was celebrated for daring and wisdom, especially for his knowledge of the stars, and his power of navigating the unknown ocean of the west. To this man was assigned the direction of the fleet, and all submitted to his guidance; but the Sea-kings invariably assembled together in council when it was intended to decide, what they should do or to what part of the world they should steer.

"My advice is," said Kettle Flatnose, the first time they assembled thus in council, "that we steer first to Ireland, where I can promise ye all a hearty welcome, for it is well known that the Irish are a hospitable people, and my father is a great man there."

"I fall in with that," said Glumm, glancing at Ada, whose eyes had now become his guiding stars!

"The advice is good," said Erling, "for, wherever we may finally come to an anchor, we will be none the worse of getting some provisions on the way."

As Haldor, Ulf, Frode, and all the rest were of one mind on this point, the ships were steered to Ireland; and when they reached that country they put ashore in a small bay not far from Dublin, where was a log hut. To this Kettle went up with Erling and Glumm, and asked the man of the house how things were going on in Ireland.

"As ill as can be in this district," said the man; "there is nothing but vengeance in the hearts of the people."

"That is a bad state," said Kettle, with a look of anxiety; "what may be the cause of discontent? Is the old King hard on ye?"

"Thou must have been long away to ask that. The old King is dead," said the man.

At this Kettle uttered a great and bitter cry; but, restraining himself, asked eagerly if the old Queen were alive. The man replied that she was. Then Kettle asked how the King met his death.

With a dark frown the man replied that Haabrok the Black had murdered him and seized the throne. On hearing this Kettle became pale, but was very calm, and listened attentively while the man went on to say that Haabrok was such a tyrant that the whole district was ready to start up as one man and dethrone him, if they had only someone who was fit to lead them.

"That they shall not long want for," said Kettle.

After some more earnest conversation he turned away, and went down to the shore.

"Now, Erling and Glumm," said he, "we must do a little fighting before I can offer ye the hospitality I spoke of. Will ye aid me in a venture I have in my mind?"

"That will we," they replied heartily.

Kettle thereupon explained his views, and said that he had learned from the man that his wife was still alive and well, but in the hands of the king of the district, who was a regicide and a tyrant. It was then arranged that the Swan should be rowed quietly up towards the town, and the men landed in the night at a spot where they could be ready to answer the summons of Kettle, Erling, Glumm, and Ulf, who were to go up unattended to the King's house in Dublin, with no other arms than their short swords.

On drawing near, these four found the hall of the King's house brilliantly lighted, for great festivities were going on there. No one interfered with them, because none guessed that so small a party would dare to go up half-armed for any other than peaceful purposes. They therefore went through the streets unmolested, and easily passed the guards, because Kettle plied them with a good deal of that which has since come to be known by the name of "blarney."

When they got into the hall, Kettle went straight up to the high seat or throne on which Haabrok the Black was seated.

"Ye are presumptuous knaves," said the tyrant, eyeing the strangers sternly; "is it thus that ye have been taught to approach the King? What is your errand?"

"For the matter of that, thou well-named villain," said Kettle, "our errand will but add to our presumption, for we have come to slay thee."

With that Kettle whipped out his sword and cut off Haabrok's head, so that it went rolling over the floor, while the body fell back and spouted blood all over the horrified court men!

Instantly every man drew his sword; but Erling, Ulf, and Glumm leaped on the low platform of the throne, and presented such a bold front, that the bravest men there hesitated to attack them. At the same moment Kettle raised his sword and shouted, "If there be yet a true man in this hall who loves his country and reveres the memory of the good old King whom this dead dog slew, let him come hither. It is the voice of the King's son that calls!"

"Sure, 'tis Kettle; I'd know his red head anywhere!" exclaimed a shrivelled old woman near the throne.

"Aye, nurse, it is Kettle himself — come back again," he said, glancing towards the old woman with a kindly smile.

A ringing cheer burst from the crowd and filled the hall; again and again it rose, as nearly all the men present rushed round the throne and waved their swords frantically over their heads, or strove to shake hands with the son of their old King. In the midst of the tumult a wild shriek was heard; and the crowd, opening up, allowed a beautiful dark-eyed woman to rush towards Kettle, with a stalwart boy of about five years of age clinging to her skirts.

We need scarcely pause to say who these were, nor who the handsome matron was who afterwards went and clung round Kettle's neck, and heaped fervent blessings on the head of her long-lost son. It is sufficient to say that the feast of that night was not interrupted; that, on the contrary, it was prolonged into the morning, and extended into every loyal home in the city; and that Kettle Flatnose entertained his Norse friends right royally for several days, after which he sent them away laden with gifts and benedictions. They did not quit Ireland, however, until they had seen him happily and securely seated on the throne of Dublin.

*   *   *

Sailing northward, the fleet touched at the Orkney and Shetland Islands, where they found that a number of the expatriated Sea-kings had comfortably settled themselves. Here some of Haldor's people would fain have remained, but Frode, who was a man of enterprise, resolved to penetrate farther into the great unknown sea, to lands which rumour said did certainly exist there. Accordingly they left Shetland, and went on until they came to the Faroe Islands. Here they thought of settling, but on landing they found that a few of the Sea-kings had taken up their abode there before them.

"Now," said Frode, "it is my great desire to break new ground. Shall we go and search farther to the west for that new island which has been lately discovered by Ingoll?"

To this Haldor and Ulf said they were agreed. Hilda plucked Erling by the sleeve, and whispered in his ear, after which he said that he too was agreed. Glumm glanced at Ada, who, with a little blush and smile, nodded. A nod was as good as a word to Glumm, so he also said he was agreed, and as no one else made objection, the ships' prows were again turned towards the setting sun.

North-westward they sailed over the world of waters, until they came one fine morning in sight of land. As they drew near they saw that it was very beautiful, consisting partly of snow-capped mountains, with green fertile valleys here and there, and streams flowing through them. They ran the vessels into a bay and landed, and the country looked so peaceful, and withal so desirable, that it was at once resolved they should make this place their abode. Accordingly, while most of the men set themselves to work to land the goods, put up the tents, and make the women and children comfortable, a select band, well armed, prepared to go on an expedition into the country, to ascertain whether or not it was inhabited. Before these set out, however, Christian the hermit stood up on a rising ground, and, raising his eyes and hands to heaven, prayed for God's blessing on their enterprise.

Thereafter plots of land were marked out, houses were built, "Things" were held, a regular government was established, and the island — for such it proved to be — was regularly taken possession of.

The exploring party found that this was indeed the island which they were in search of. It had been discovered about the middle of the ninth century, and a settlement had been made on it by Ingoll in the year 874; but the band of immigrants under Frode and Haldor was by far the most important that had landed on it up to that time.

In this manner, and under these circumstances, was Iceland colonised by expatriated Norsemen about the beginning of the tenth century!

*   *   *

Good reader, our tale is told. Gladly would we follow, step by step, the subsequent career of Erling and Glumm, for the lives of such men, from first to last, are always fraught with interest and instruction; but this may not be. We have brought them, with the other chief actors in this little tale, to a happy point in their adventurous career, and there we feel that we ought to leave them in peace. Yet we would fain touch on one or two prominent points in their subsequent history before bidding them a final farewell.

Let it be recorded, then, that many years after the date of the closing scene of our tale, there might have been seen in Iceland, at the head of a small bay, two pretty cottages, from the doors of which there was a magnificent view of as sweet a valley as ever filled the eye or gladdened the heart of man, with a distant glimpse of the great ocean beyond. On the sward before these cottages was assembled a large party of young men and maidens, the latter of whom were conspicuous for the sparkle of their blue eyes and the silky gloss of their fair hair, while the former were notable because of the great size and handsome proportions of their figures; some, however, of the men and maidens were dark and ruddy. The youths were engaged in putting the stone and throwing the hammer; the maidens looked on with interest — as maidens were wont to do on manly pastimes in days of old, and as they are not unwilling to do occasionally, even in modern times. Around these romped a host of children of all ages, sizes, and shades.

These were the descendants of Erling the Bold and Glumm the Gruff. The two families had, as it were, fused into one grand compound, which was quite natural, for their natures were diverse yet sympathetic; besides, Glumm was dark, Erling fair; and it is well known that black and white always go hand in hand, producing that sweet-toned grey, which Nature would seem to cherish with a love quite as powerful as the abhorrence with which she is supposed to regard a vacuum.

Beside each other, leaning against a tree, and admiring the prowess of the young men, stood Erling and Glumm, old, it is true, and past the time when men delight to exercise their muscles, but straight and stalwart, and still noble specimens of manhood. The most interesting group, however, was to be seen seated on a rustic bench near the door. There, sometimes conversing gravely with a silver-haired old man at his side, or stooping with a quiet smile to caress the head of a child that had rushed from its playmates for a little to be fondled by the "old one" — sat Haldor the Fierce, with Christian the hermit on one side, and Ulf of Romsdal on the other. Their heads were pure white, and their frames somewhat bent, but health still mantled on the sunburnt cheeks, and sparkled in the eyes of the old Norse Sea-kings.

Within the house might have been seen two exceedingly handsome matrons — such as one may see in Norway at the present time — who called each other Hilda and Ada, and who vied with a younger Hilda and Ada in their attentions upon two frail but cheery old women whom they called "Granny Heff" and "Granny Ast". How very unlike — and yet how like — were these to the Herfrida and Astrid of former days!

Between the old dames there sat on a low stool a man of gigantic proportions, who had scarcely reached middle age, and who was still overflowing with the fun and fire of youth. He employed himself in alternately fondling and "chaffing" the two old women, and he was such an exact counterpart of what Erling the Bold was at the age of thirty, that his own mother was constantly getting confused, and had to be reminded that he was *Alric*, and not Erling!

Alric's wife, a daughter of Glumm, was with the young people on the lawn, and his six riotous children were among the chief tormentors of old Haldor.

Ingeborg was there too, sharp as ever, but not quite so sour. She was not a spinster. There were few spinsters in those days! She had married a man of the neighbouring valley, whom she loved to distraction, and whom she led the life of a dog! But it was her nature to be cross-grained. She could not help it, and the poor man appeared to grow fonder of her the more she worried him!

As for Ivor the Old and Finn the One-eyed, they, with most of their contemporaries, had long been gathered to their fathers, and their bones reposed on the grassy slopes of Laxriverdale.

As for the other personages of our tale, we have only space to remark that King Harald Haarfager succeeded in his wish to obtain the undivided sovereignty of Norway, but he failed to perpetuate the change; for the kingdom was, after his death, redivided amongst his sons. The last heard of Hake the berserk was, that he had been seen in the midst of a great battle to have both his legs cut off at one sweep, and that he died fighting on his stumps! Jarl Rongvold was burnt by King Harald's sons, but his stout son, Rolf Ganger, left his native land, and conquered Normandy, whence his celebrated descendant, William the Conqueror, came across the Channel and conquered England.

Yes, there is perhaps more of Norse blood in your veins than you wot of, reader, whether you be English or Scotch; for those sturdy sea rovers invaded our lands from north, south, east, and west many a time in days gone by, and held it in possession for centuries at a time, leaving a lasting and beneficial impress on our customs and characters. We have good reason to regard their memory with respect and gratitude, despite their faults and sins, for much of what is good and true in our laws and social customs, much manly and vigorous in the British Constitution, of our intense love of freedom and fairplay, are pith, pluck, enterprise, and sense of justice that dwelt in the breasts of the rugged old Sea-kings of Norway!

THE END

www.ingramcontent.com/pod-product-compliance
Lightning Source LLC
Chambersburg PA
CBHW031430250626
47155CB00004B/1692